C000157110

INSPIRED BY REAL EVENTS

BURNING
SECRET

R J Lloyd

Copyright © 2022 R J Lloyd

The moral right of the author has been asserted.

Apart from any fair dealing for the purposes of research or private study,
or criticism or review, as permitted under the Copyright, Designs and Patents
Act 1988, this publication may only be reproduced, stored or transmitted, in
any form or by any means, with the prior permission in writing of the
publishers, or in the case of reprographic reproduction in accordance with
the terms of licences issued by the Copyright Licensing Agency. Enquiries
concerning reproduction outside those terms should be sent to the publishers.

This is a work of fiction. Names, characters, businesses, places, events
and incidents are either the products of the author's imagination
or used in a fictitious manner. Any resemblance to actual persons,
living or dead, or actual events is purely coincidental.

Matador
Unit E2 Airfield Business Park,
Harrison Road, Market Harborough,
Leicestershire. LE16 7UL
Tel: 0116 2792299
Email: books@troubador.co.uk
Web: www.troubador.co.uk/matador
Twitter: @matadorbooks

ISBN 978 1803131 498

British Library Cataloguing in Publication Data.
A catalogue record for this book is available from the British Library.

Printed and bound by CPI Group (UK) Ltd, Croydon, CR0 4YY
Typeset in 11pt Minion Pro by Troubador Publishing Ltd, Leicester, UK

Matador is an imprint of Troubador Publishing Ltd

In memory of
Kimberly Elizabeth Mason Gibbs and Susan Sperry,
my American cousins who enthusiastically
helped tell this story.

"The biggest tragedy of life is the utter impossibility to change what you have done"

John Galsworthy
English Novelist
1867–1933

"Life, Liberty and the pursuit of Happiness"

Thomas Jefferson
Third President of the United States
1743–1826

ONE

As he ascended the stone steps leading from the subterranean cells, the same thought returned. *It doesn't matter how hard you try; there's always someone ready to take it from you. All you can do is fight until life wears you out, and all that's left is home.*

This was not how it was supposed to end.

* * *

Like the word of the Almighty, the command thundered down, echoing off the high-domed ceiling which dominated proceedings.

'The defendant will stand. State your name, age and business.'

The court's commotion died away. A man in his late thirties, of above-average height and stocky build, shuffled to his feet. He hadn't shaved in several days, and his heavy, dark moustache was unkempt. He looked drawn and tired,

1

yet his hazel-green eyes were alert and intelligent. Stepping forward, he took hold of the wide brass railing surrounding the dock, revealing the size and strength of his hands. He cleared his throat. 'Enoch Thomas Price. Born Bristol 1844. Manufacturer of corset stays and...' His voice faded, weakening to a dry whisper.

'Is it Mr Rosenthal who represents you in your case of bankruptcy?' asked the court clerk, one hand cupped behind an ear in exaggerated theatrical condescension. 'Well, sir, speak up.'

Price nodded. His lips parted to form words, but none came. The judge impatiently waved him to be seated.

In black gown and stockings, the prosecutor, with the appearance of a crow in search of carrion, pointed an accusatory finger. 'You, sir, are nothing more than a scoundrel. A common cheat, conducting your nefarious business in broad daylight, and you do so as proud as any peacock. Am I wrong, sir? No, sir, I am not.'

Price, shaken by the condemnation, looked to the floor. His public humiliation was not yet complete, and the loss of his liberty seemed assured.

'By your simple omission of denial, sir, you have disclosed your guilt loud and clear,' the prosecutor charged on. 'All here see you for what you are and know you by your dishonest trade. You have the audacity, indeed the bare-faced temerity, to rely upon the good Mr Rosenthal,' pausing briefly to respectfully recognise the barrister sitting opposite, 'an acclaimed and honourable member of our profession, to keep you from well-deserved incarceration at London's Coldbath Prison. Am I not correct? Answer, sir. Come, let us hear you speak.'

Before Price could reply, the tall, elegant figure of Mr Rosenthal rose effortlessly and, with a commanding presence, brought a stillness upon the court. With dramatic effect, practised over many years, he addressed the judge. 'My Lord, most distinguished and learned eminence.' He waited a moment to allow graceful acknowledgement of the compliment. 'Contrary to my learned friend's rhetoric, my client is of the highest repute. A respectable gentleman of this city. An honest businessman from a long-established family. A family with a revered tradition of fair dealing. He finds himself fallen on hard times, not through any fault of his own. No, indeed not. The debt, which misfortune has thrust upon him, will be met in full. Indeed, it is to be repaid with the utmost alacrity.'

The plaintiff, Richard Dyson, the owner of warehousing on the London docks, leapt from his seat. Encouraged by a crescendo of jeers and catcalls from the clamour of those in the public gallery, he pushed his way malevolently towards Price. 'It's bloody nonsense! It's bollocks!' he sneered. 'He's a dishonest shit. He ain't got no means. He ain't even got a pot to piss in.'

'Only cos you've filched it!' shouted a raucous heckler from the gallery, provoking howls of laughter from the assembled onlookers, many of whom were regulars at the court's daily spectacle. The court usher moved to block Dyson's way, raising a stout wooden staff, ready to repel further progress.

Judge William Hazlitt, bewigged and cloaked in scarlet, looked on impassively from his elevated position. A single knock of his gavel was enough to halt Dyson in his tracks. The court fell silent in bated anticipation.

'Mr Dyson,' the judge spoke courteously with quiet authority, 'this court will not be addressed in such an indecorous manner.' Then, he added with intent, 'Not without risk to your liberty.'

The point struck home. Dyson resumed his seat.

With order restored, Judge Hazlitt continued. 'Mr Dyson, outrage at your financial deficiency is commendable. However, the court would be obliged if you allow the esteemed Mr Rosenthal continue his elocution without further interruption.'

* * *

An hour later, Price escaped the dark, rancid claustrophobia of the crowded court and stepped briskly into the weak, late afternoon sunlight, which had penetrated low along one side of Portugal Street. Wrapping his rough, woollen overcoat tight against the bitter cold, he turned to shake Rosenthal by the hand, thanking him heartily for securing a further adjournment and reprieve from prison.

Taking Enoch's outstretched hand, Rosenthal pulled him near to avoid being overheard. His mellifluous tones now turned venomous as he hissed a cautionary note. 'My dear, dear friend, I may have delayed your lodgings at the debtors' prison, but I've shortened your stay by not one day.' Releasing his grip, Rosenthal continued as if cheerfully taking leave of a favourite cousin on a summer lawn. 'May I wish you and your dear wife a prosperous New Year.' Then, lowering his voice, 'Should my services be again required, ensure my fees are settled in good time.'

'Will I be assured of justice?' enquired Enoch.

'You will receive the law, sir. Justice must wait a higher authority.' Tipping his silk top hat, Rosenthal bade his client farewell.

Glad of his freedom, Enoch made his way towards Covent Garden. By the time he reached King Street, the milky afternoon sky had darkened to deep indigo, and by the flickering gaslights, specks of frost sparkled on the damp cobblestones. The gutters were strewn with litter from the flower market and the putrid detritus discarded by itinerant costermongers, the last of whom were loading their barrows. The streets were now quiet, with few passers-by.

Occasionally, a carriage rattled past, taking its gentleman owner towards the theatres on Drury Lane. Too soon for a performance, but early enough for a plausibly denied assignation.

Enoch glanced movement in bundles of old rags and broken crates in dark corners – rats taking their first opportunity to venture from the sewers or, more likely, poor souls who, having pawned their bed for a glass of gin, were now seeking shelter against the cold night air.

On reaching Rose Street, he stepped into a narrow alleyway and through the portal of The Lamb and Flag. The hostelry was, as always, convivial, warm and inviting. The yellow glow of the gas mantles cast deep shadows across the wood panelling and crowded booths filled with laughter and whispered conspiracies. A good log fire spat and crackled, and the comforting aromas of tobacco and strong drink filled the air. For the first time that day, Enoch relaxed and took his ease on a familiar bench near the bar.

The landlord's ten-year-old daughter approached. 'Mr Price! If you ain't a sight for sore eyes.' Her gentle Irish lilt was discernible beneath the local cockney dialect. 'Can I bring you a drink to lessen your woes?'

'A small glass of ale will suffice, if you please, Biddy.'

'And I'll wager a slice of pie?'

'That would be grand. Thank you.'

On her return, Enoch had shed his heavy coat and was filling a clay pipe with his favourite dark shag. 'Is Michael at home?' he asked.

'I'll fetch our da directly – he'll be more than pleased to see you.' Then, adding to underscore the sentiment, 'We're always pleased to see you, Mr Price.'

* * *

Enoch saw his friend approach from a back room. Although on the lean side, it was plain that his muscular frame was no stranger to heavy labour. His blue eyes and fiery red hair shone, reflecting his confidence and joy of life. His powerful arms, resembling knotted ship's cable, enveloped Enoch, grasping and shaking him with evident pleasure.

'Where in the name of the Holy Mother have you been? We thought you dead or consigned to the rack at Coldbath.' Michael laughed at his own jest, little realising how close he'd come to the truth. 'It's good to see you, so it is.' And, in affectionate play, Michael boxed and jabbed, punching Enoch half-hearted about the body. They were hard blows, nonetheless, enough to floor most men, but Enoch rode them well. The two men took a vacant booth, where Michael continued enthusiastically, 'Are you here for the fight?' Before Enoch could reply, Michael slapped the table and was off again. 'Then, by Jesus, you've picked a grand night.

Your English champion, Foster-Smith, is here. He's not fighting, of course. You wouldn't find a gentleman brawling in a bucket of blood like this.' Then, lowering his voice to a whisper, he beckoned Enoch come closer. 'He's brought one of his young lads to go against my Conor.' Stretching further across the table, Michael came so close, Enoch felt his friend's breath as his whisper became little more than a murmur. 'There's a pretty penny to be turned here tonight.'

'It's no accident I'm here,' said Enoch. 'You tipped me the wink at the cockfight, promising a good start to the year.'

'So I did!' exclaimed Michael with the sudden joy of remembering. 'At the George, on Borough High Street? But that was a while ago. What's been keeping you?'

'To tell the truth, I've had a spot of bother.'

'How bad?'

'Enough for a stretch of hard labour at Coldbath.'

'Jesus Christ, what in God's name have you done?'

'The business pulled me down. Only this morning, I was in front of Hazlitt on charges of bankruptcy. It was only Rosenthal's weasel words that saved me from being banged up this very night. I truly believed I was a goner, but he's got me a reprieve on a pledge to clear my slate.'

'The better the lawyer, the kinder the law. It's true enough,' remarked Michael. 'But how did you come by this sorry state?'

'Dyson lured me on, but I've only myself to blame. I got cocky and dropped my guard. He saw his opening and caught me good and proper with tales of easy pickings. I don't mind admitting, it was greed that got the better of me.'

'I've never heard of you being taken in; it's usually you who's spinning a yarn.'

'Only goes to show – the prospect of something for nothing makes fools of us all.'

'How did he hook you?'

'Pride and vanity. All puffed up with my own success and ripe for the picking,' said Enoch, taking a swig from his tankard. 'As you know, I've not long opened a small shop on Great Prescot Street, and it was doing well, attracting fine ladies of fashion. If truth be told, it was the shop that took his notice. Anyway, Dyson, who's been warehousing my silks and brocade for the past many years, and, to be fair, he's always been straight with me, invites me for a drink at the Cock Tavern. Says he can do me a favour.

'It's here he introduces me to a banker by the name of Bawtree. He looked the part and said he was well connected in the city with offices on Lombard Street. I tells him I've been at business for the past ten or more years and was, at last, making a go of it. Bawtree says he can see I'm a man of good sense, a man to be trusted, and promises to invest, saying he can double the business within the year. Said he could get me a stand at the Crystal Palace. Said he would vouch for me and get my name known in high places.'

'So, he knew your bait, then,' said Michael. 'You always fancied your name being known. Like when fighting as Puncher Price, and proud of it, so you was.'

'For fuck sake, Michael, we was kids and full of it.'

'Well, cocksure and pride comes before a fall.'

Enoch ignored Michael's barbs and looked pensive as he studied his fingernails. He took a bite of pie. Michael waited patiently for him to finish eating. Eventually, Enoch spoke.

'Like a fool, I took the money and signed his contract, witnessed and sealed all proper by a lawyer. At first, things went well; even Charlie Harrod placed orders for his shop on the Brompton Road. That's when it dawned on me. Bawtree was a front, a sprat to catch a mackerel, and Dyson wasn't doing me no favours neither. It turns out Toff had put them up to it, to draw me on. It was Gabriel Toff's money I'd taken, and it wasn't no investment; it was a loan.'

'Holy Mother of God! You're in debt to Toff?'

'For a tidy penny, too. And it wasn't long before he upped the interest and with it the repayments. When I missed a week, he took finished garments twice the value of what I owed. Said it was to teach me to pay up on time. Worse still, after I made good on the arrears, I owed more than when I'd started.'

'For Christ's sake, Enoch, Toff's a dangerous fucker. Why didn't you come to me?'

'Well, maybe I should have, but I didn't know 'til it was too late. But what grieves me most is that his men broke in and stole every bolt of silk and lace I had. It finished me off.'

'How long since you took his money?'

'A year, come March.'

'Can he be reasoned with?'

'Too late for that. The lawyers have already picked me clean.'

'So, where's the money gone?'

'New machines, new workshop, six new stitchers, advertising and what Toff likes to call his percentage – a commission on every sale.'

Michael rubbed hard at the stubble on his chin. 'You had a bloody good business – how come it went belly-up so quick?'

'The debt was too much to keep pace with; the more I paid, the more I owed.'

'The bastard's stolen your business.'

'The very purpose of his loan. And he's done it all legal and I've paid handsomely for the privilege of being fleeced. The law's on his side, and it's me who's in the wrong. I've lost everything.'

'So, what's to be done?' demanded Michael, cracking his knuckles.

'Nothing, sharking's his stock-in-trade. While he's in the shadows, hiding behind a cloak of respectability, hobnobbing with the great and the good and protected by clever lawyers, his thugs are out cutting honest men from their livelihoods. I've even heard it said he's taken daughters in lieu and put um to work on the streets.'

'Christ! He's a nasty piece of work. It's about time he got dropped off the side of a mud barge at high tide.'

'No, Michael, don't you get involved. I don't want worse trouble than I've already got.'

'There must be something to be done?'

'Well, not all is lost. As soon as I knew his game, I slowed things down a tad, paying just enough to keep his roughs off my back while skimming a little for myself, keeping something back for a rainy day.'

'Enough to keep you from Coldbath?'

'No. Nowhere near it. But enough for a disappearing act.'

'And there'll be plenty more to swell your coffers here tonight.'

'Which I'm grateful for, but there's something I need you to do. I can't take Eliza and my girls with me – they'll only slow me down, and it won't be safe if the bailiffs or Toff's men come after me.'

Michael glanced around to see who was close by. Then, lowering his voice, he asked, 'Does Eliza know you're leaving?'

'Not yet, I've things to straighten first.'

'Leaving your girls won't be easy. You may have lost your business, but listen to me, Enoch, don't go losing your little treasures, too. Think hard on it – I couldn't leave without my Biddy. Being banged up for a stretch was hard enough. You need to be sure before you leave them behind. I tell you this as a friend – don't cut your nose to spite your face.'

'It won't be for long. I'll send for them as soon as I'm settled.'

'As long as you know what you're doing. Eliza's a kind woman who's stuck by you all these years, and many of them years were lean and not easy on her gentle nature.'

'I know it, but we'll be together again well before Christmas Day. In the meantime, my mother will provide lodgings. She's comfortable these days, having not long married a clergyman, and is living in a rectory at Bristol, with housekeepers, skivvies and all. Even so, I'd be obliged if you'd keep an eye. Make sure they're safe.'

'It's done – don't give it another thought. Now, let's speak no more of the matter and enjoy this evening's sport. After all, it's why you're here.'

A commotion drew their attention. A group of rakish young gentlemen, extravagantly dressed in velvets and silk waistcoats, escorted by attentive ladies of dubious repute, were making their presence known.

'Here they come now. My gentlemen have arrived,' said Michael, nodding towards the entrance. 'They're slumming from the gilded drawing rooms of Belgravia and have brought purses heavy with gold to squander on a wager.'

'By the look of their floozies, they're fresh from the pox houses of Regent Street,' said Enoch, scoffing. 'And if my eyes don't deceive me, one of them's a pretty backdoor molly boy.'

Michael ignored his friend's disapproving tone, but as he did so, his expression darkened and temperament turned mean; all revelry was suspended. This was the Michael not to be crossed, unpredictable and dangerous. Enoch knew the signs well, having more than once witnessed shocking brutality dispensed to those failing to recognise the sudden shift. Enoch responded warily, listening respectfully as a boy instructed at his father's side.

'Listen to me, and you listen damn close.' Michael jabbed his finger. 'My Conor is the older and bigger boy. He's not lost in six fights and is well favoured to win. The other boy is good but no match.' His tone was conspiratorial. 'Wager on our Conor to lose.' He waited to allow the implication of his words to settle. 'There's no gambling here tonight.' His ice-blue eyes were fixed and staring. 'Conor will do what's right by me.'

Enoch nodded to show he had heard and understood what was afoot.

Michael continued with the same menace. 'There's plenty here flush with sovereigns, but choose your mark with care. They're not fools. They'll be armed and not think twice to drop you dead.'

Enoch weighed Michael's words.

Michael continued, 'You'll need your wits about you. Things ain't so easy these days, not like when you stood in for me. Keep an eye out for the Yard's detectives; they're cunning bastards and nastier than most.' He stopped for a long moment, deep in thought, running through the risks and consequences. Satisfied he had covered his points, he said, 'Don't worry. Your guile and charm will see you safely to your bed.' But both men knew the dangers of the artifice. They sat silently, looking at each other for several seconds.

Enoch spoke first. 'And you?'

'I'm good. My wager's placed with a royal duke, and he's on the hook. To boot, I've a share of the purse with Foster-Smith.' His countenance warmed, and with the flame of humanity rekindled, a broad, confident smile returned. The affable Michael was back. 'Don't worry yourself on my account. I've had a penny palm read by the old gipsy woman. She says we're both to live long and wealthy lives.' He laughed aloud at his own banter as he eased himself free of the booth. The gathering clamour jostled around him as he grasped Enoch tightly by the hand and, before the crowd could sweep him up, he shook it hard. Over the din, Enoch heard him shout back, 'Be lucky!'

TWO

Dawn revealed London's skyline of steeples and majestic rooftops. A dusting of snow had fallen silently during the early hours.

Enoch stirred himself. Stretching, he tried to rid his bones of the stiffness that had set in overnight. He had spent the last few hours unobserved in a dark alcove secluded in the corner of the inn. He hadn't slept but felt rested all the same.

The bar, empty of its conviviality and devoid of its usual inhabitants, echoed every sound, and as the building cooled, its ancient timbers creaked and twisted eerily. The room was airless and fetid with the sour odours of stale ale, cheap tobacco and spent adrenalin. Detritus from the night's event was randomly scattered: broken bottles, food-smeared plates, a discarded top hat, a muddy right boot perched precariously on a chair. For reasons that may never be known, a torn lady's undergarment hung from a hook on the wall, and a bull terrier, bitten and bloodied from baiting, lay dead near the locked side door.

A small grey mouse in search of morsels scuttled from one hiding place to another. Two vagrants, who had secreted themselves about the premises before the tavern was bolted shut, searched the tables, swilling back stale dregs from half-empty tankards while keeping a sharp eye for lost coins and other flotsam dropped by careless owners. Having had their fill, they settled near the dying embers of the log fire to sleep off their pickings.

Whiling away the hours before first light, Enoch reflected on the evening's prizefight. It had been a rare spectacle. Crowds had gathered early and thronged the dimly lit alley where the fighters would punish each other until exhausted. The thrill and excitement of the promised aggression infected the commotion, whipping up a bellowing force of roaring hysteria.

It began on the stroke of midnight to a tumultuous cry, which could be heard as far as Charing Cross. Each fighter, half-naked and glistening with sweat and oil, began slowly, testing each other, eager to avoid the embarrassment of a schoolboy error and the humiliation of an early knockdown. They chasséd around each other, mimicking the elaborate courtship of exotic birds. But once the first stinging, bare-knuckle jabs found their mark, the battle was joined in earnest. Spectators, inflamed by the smell of blood and the pitiless violence, bayed like a pack of hounds.

Conor tore into his opponent, clawing, butting and splattering blood with callous savagery. The younger lad retaliated with equal brutality, viciously hitting low and repeatedly battering Conor's ribs with such force the crack of a bone was heard above the howling mob. Wounded and gasping for wind, Conor slowed and stepped away.

A man in the garb of a market porter, in danger of losing more than he could afford on the defeat of his favoured boy, broke free from the crowd and crashed headlong between the contestants. A gang of roughs, slashing and stabbing with blades, quickly extinguished the foolhardy intervention, a desperate attempt to give his champion time to recover, but the purpose was served, provoking an outbreak of angry scuffles and a free-for-all amongst opposing supporters.

During the melee, Conor's midriff was tightly bound and, regaining his composure, combat resumed. The younger boy, sensing he had weakened his adversary, launched a remorseless, pounding onslaught. Conor withstood the withering assault, replying with crashing hammer blows about the boy's head, opening a gash across an already swollen and lacerated cheekbone.

In desperation, his opponent thrust and gouged a thumb into Conor's eye and, in the torturous grapple, bit and ripped half Conor's ear from his head. Spitting it out, he again lunged forwards, butting his head with destructive force into Conor's nose, splitting it asunder and spraying blood and snot over those in proximity.

Enoch had watched as Conor faltered and, deliberately lowering his guard, opened his defence. This was the cue. Conor was beaten to his knees where, without pity, the boy kicked and stamped him to the ground with feral cruelty.

The alley reeked of the sordid stench of sweat, gore and vomit. This was the attraction and entertainment enjoyed by street urchin, navvy and aristocrat alike. It was what they'd come to witness. Conor took a bloody beating, but he was a good lad and had done his work well, in the end, going down convincingly. Enoch consoled himself with the thought that Conor was young and would soon heal, returning a few months later when, with malice, he would take his revenge.

* * *

Enoch's own work had not been easy, but with care and persistence, the night had finished profitably. The night's bounty weighed heavy in the poacher's pocket deep within his belted coat, and, now that the catch was safely landed, relief flooded his veins. He pushed himself up from his pew, knowing that he must stir before tiredness rocked him to sweet dreams of success.

The inn was coming back to life. There was movement from the floor above. Furniture shifted; a dog barked; and there were muffled voices still shrouded in sleep. Enoch slipped from the shadows of his hiding place and, deftly sidestepping the stupefied vagrants, relieved himself in the grate. He moved to the side door, released the fastening and stepped out into the fresh morning air. Across town, St Clement Danes chimed 7am. Donning his brown Derby bowler, he thrust his hands deep into his coat pockets and, turning into Long Acre, made towards home at Bethnal Green.

The inky morning sky brightened with every step. Flurries of snow fell softly in the breeze, melting as it pitched on the damp flagstone paths. With first light, it was safe to navigate through the narrow, deserted streets without fear of being robbed or set upon by cutthroats stalking the night in search of unsuspecting travellers. With dawn piercing their cloak of darkness, these nocturnal predators slunk invisibly back to the safety of their rookeries.

It would take a couple of hours to reach home. Journey by omnibus would be quicker, and he could afford a hansom, but there was no hurry. The still, cool air would clear his mind and afford the chance to weigh his situation and time enough to rehearse what he was to tell his dear wife, Eliza.

Deciding to walk, his route took him along the Strand, past Smithfield Market to Shoreditch and then onto Bethnal Green Road and from there to Harold Street, where his bed awaited.

He stopped at an all-night tuppenny coffee stand on Waterloo Bridge. A cab driver had drawn his carriage alongside and a boatman, taking refuge from the freezing river mist, sat smoking a clay pipe. The three men shared the pleasure of warmth radiating from the welcoming coke brazier.

Once past the meat market, Enoch crossed old Bunhill burial fields to arrive at a cabinetmaker on Curtain Road. A dray stacked heavily with furniture was tethered outside. A cross sweeper, a half-starved waif from the nearby workhouse, rested his slender frame on a twig broom, envious of the heavy draft horse, its head buried deep in a sack of oats.

Turning sharp into New Inn Yard, Enoch entered a small office with space enough for no more than two chairs and a narrow desk. It was musty and smelled like the foxed pages of old books. The room was piled high with cardboard boxes and leather-bound ledgers, all of which had seen better days and seen them many years before.

Looking through a batch of well-thumbed accounts was a man with the appearance of an ancient Hebrew prophet. He slowly raised his eyes over half-moon spectacles.

'Well, well, well! If it ain't young master Enoch.' Each word was draped in thick East European Slavonic, redolent of the place where, as a boy, he had once called home. But that was long ago, before the time when he and his kin had been hounded and chased away. 'Did your ears burn?' he asked. 'I was praying for you at Hanukkah, and now, like a bad penny, you are coming back.'

It sounded sarcastic, but Enoch could hear the avuncular wit, and, in the old man's watery eyes, shiny like two black beads, he saw kindness. 'What trouble do you bring me, my boy?' The old Jew spoke as if he had been expecting him, waiting the return of a prodigal son, and already knew the purpose of his visit.

Enoch answered respectfully, 'Shalom, and a happy New Year, Isaiah. It's good to see you looking so well.'

Isaiah interrupted him. 'Enoch, before I must listen to your stories of suffering and injustice, we should eat. Maybe you like to share a little salt beef and bagels and some hot tea? I know you like hot tea.'

After sharing Isaiah's frugal breakfast, Enoch felt able to make his enquiry. 'Isaiah.' He had never ventured the informality of calling him Isay, as the family did. 'I've a chance to sell some second-hand furniture.' He hesitated a fraction to see if Isaiah would respond. He did not. The old Jew sat motionless, looking into him as if he could see the words before they were spoken. Enoch continued, 'I was wondering if you have an interest in buying? Or at least making an offer?'

'You're a good boy, Enoch. I tell everyone. You always think of Isay first,' Isaiah began as if explaining elementary logic to a class of infants. 'I make new furniture. I sell new furniture. Customers come to me for new furniture. Why do I need old furniture?' He gestured with open arms to show the simplicity of his deduction.

Enoch acknowledged his reasoning and accepted the verdict with a weary sigh. Isaiah again took up the thread. 'Don't despair, my boy. There's always hope. Bradbrook is a dealer of all things useful; his emporium is near you on Green Street. Tell him Isay sent you.'

Enoch gratefully thanked the old man and was about to leave when Isaiah said, 'He takes lodgers, too and can be trusted.' Then, with a slow, resigned shake of his head, he smiled kindly and said, 'Blessings to your good wife. Only God knows the heavy burden she carries.'

* * *

London was where the riches of empire bloated the coffers of the fortunate few, and a crust was as scarce as diamonds for the unfortunate many. Every wickedness and corruption born of poverty found a crib in the overcrowded tenements, squalid alleyways and disease-ridden slums of Whitechapel, Spitalfields and Bethnal Green, and Bethnal Green was the worst. Here, paupers and homeless immigrants struggled to keep a breath in their bodies. Where felons, bullies and prostitutes vied for victims on which to leech. Where the displaced Jews – the tailors, shirtmakers and exhausted collar and corset-stitchers – lived cheek by jowl with every hue of immigrant, all competing to turn a farthing, and where a few hours' sleep huddled in a hard, mean corner was the only punctuation between drudgery and hunger, and Harold Street was its low ebb, a place where the constabulary were reluctant to venture. Enoch and his wife

Eliza, with their three daughters – Bertha, Florence and Beatrice – lived at number twenty, their home for the past thirteen years.

* * *

Eliza was born in 1849 in the sleepy hamlet of Mayfield in Sussex. Her mother died from tuberculosis the day before Eliza's sixteenth birthday. The following week, her father, a bricklayer by trade, fell while repairing a chimney. Crippled and unable to work, he was compelled by poverty to disperse his children to the care of others. The four youngest went into domestic service while Eliza travelled to London in search of paid employment.

It was at the Spitalfields' workshop of Edwin Izod, a tailor-turned-corset-maker, that Eliza and Enoch met, he stripping baleen whalebone, cutting and shaping stays for the silk and linen bodices stitched by Eliza.

On her nineteenth birthday, at St Pancras New Church, each pledged their everlasting vows of marriage in the sight of God. They took lodgings at 20 Harold Street, a narrow two-up two-down terraced house that, with its single outside privy, sheltered three families: fourteen souls in all. Their room was at the back on the upper floor, opposite a Mr and Mrs Davis, an infirm, elderly couple who spent their time cooped up and alone.

Bertha, the first of their three daughters, arrived in the spring of 1869. Florence and Beatrice followed in quick succession. The family shared the meagre comforts of their room to eat, sleep and wash, huddling for warmth around the hearth where cooking was done on the iron grate.

Propelled by the necessity to clothe and feed a growing family, Enoch left Izod's sweatshop and, working from the overcrowded lodgings, began his own corsetry business: the grandly named London & Paris Corset Company. Its pretentious title reflected his considerable ambitions and the contemporary fashion for Parisian haute couture, although neither he nor Eliza had ever visited France, nor indeed had they ventured beyond the shores of England.

For the first few years, the business struggled to produce barely enough to pay the rent and provide a meal each day. But, determined not to slip back into the clutches of Izod, Enoch battled through the many hardships, gradually building his reputation, and as he did, his sales grew. So much so that when Mr and Mrs Davis passed away, he took on the rent for their adjoining room. And when, the following year, both ground-floor rooms became vacant, he took on the rent for these too, converting one into a workshop. He and Eliza now enjoyed the run of the house to themselves, the only dwelling in the street occupied by a single family. Enoch enjoyed the prestige it brought, which was enhanced further when he employed two of the neighbours' children at a shilling a week.

With his increasing status, he had considered moving to a respectable, middle-class district but decided against it, preferring the loyalty and protection of his close network of trusted friends and neighbours.

* * *

It was shortly after 11am when Enoch finally arrived home. He was met in the narrow, cobbled street by his neighbour,

Hannah Agombar, who, draped in a moth-eaten shawl and surrounded by a gaggle of unruly children, called out in a theatrical voice as if to attract a crowd to a fairground spectacle, 'I say! My dear Mr Price! If you ain't up and about early on the Lord's Day. I hope you ain't been up to no good. Back from repenting your sins, no doubt? Or did your money run dry at the gin palace?'

Enoch took it all in good humour. She meant no harm. It was the way of the East End, taunting and mischief-making for the simple amusement of it.

He replied as if in all seriousness, 'You know me, Mrs Agombar, a good Methodist from the city of the Reverend Wesley. Now, when was the last time you saw me succumb to the demon drink? Or perhaps it's a case of the pot calling the kettle black, what do you say, Mrs Agombar?'

Ignoring his retort, she continued in her shrill voice, reminding Enoch of a market fishmonger spieling for trade, 'And how's your dutiful wife, Mr Price? Is she well? We ain't none of us seen her for a day or two.'

'She is well, Mrs Agombar, and I thank you for your kind enquiry,' he called back, trying to keep a civil tongue while eager to escape her taunts.

Stepping over his threshold, he was relieved to be back to the sanctuary of his own home.

* * *

Eliza hadn't slept and looked careworn. 'Thank the good Lord you're home. I thought they'd carted you to Coldbath, and none of us would ever see you again, and...' She was exhausted and gently wept.

23

'My dearest wife, don't worry yourself; some tea will settle us both.' Enoch took her in his arms. Her hot tears wet his cheeks, and he could feel her sobs as she struggled to stifle the forces intent on breaking her heart.

His three daughters jumped excitedly to catch his hands. Giggling and screaming, they dragged him to sit with them in his favourite armchair by the open coal fire. Through their shrieks of laughter, he called to Eliza, who was busy in the next room making tea.

'Yesterday was my lucky day,' he called, stopping to listen for her reply. None came. 'Rosenthal did me proud.' Again, listening. Again, no response. 'I've been celebrating with Michael.' Eliza disapproved of him associating with Michael. She thought him a bad influence and felt uneasy whenever in his company. 'And luck favoured me a second time with a wager on his son.' He paused again, waiting her reply. Perhaps she couldn't hear over the whistle of the kettle.

Bringing him tea, they sat close together, quietly watching the flames flicker over the warm embers in the grate. Neither spoke. The girls had exhausted their excitement and were now sitting quietly at his feet. Eliza was relieved to have him home, and the gentle touch of his strong hands calmed her troubled mind.

Enoch slept soundly in his chair. Eliza, covering him with a blanket, bade the girls not to disturb their father. It was dark when he awoke, and snow was again lightly drifting through the air. Retrieving the proceeds of his night's work, he set about counting his tally. Soon, small, gold towers in neat, serried rows, like soldiers on parade, appeared across the table. Finally, unfolding a wad of white fivers, he flattened the paper money with the heel of his hand as if kneading dough. Eliza watched in silence as he scribbled calculations.

'Is it enough to keep you from prison?' she asked.

'Yes, my love. Enough to avoid prison.'

Illuminated only by the glow of the fire, Enoch slowly recounted the events of the previous day, revealing each scene with vivid description and drama, as any raconteur might enthral his audience.

Although concerned by the turn of events, Enoch could see Eliza was fascinated with the way he had charted safe passage through perilous waters. Gilding and embellishing his tale with amusing anecdotes, he made light of the dangers. It was blarney and all part of his endearing gift of the gab, which she loved him for.

When he had finished, she kissed him gently and said with a long sigh, 'My dearest husband, for all the worries you bring, I forgive you still. What is ever to become of us?'

THREE

The house slumbered, still dark and icy from the bitter night air. Enoch had risen early and was warming his hands around a mug of hot tea when a heavy pounding on the front door shook the house.

'All right, all right, I'm coming!' he shouted, ready to remonstrate with the early morning culprit. 'Who in the Lord's name is disturbing the peace at this hour?'

The urgency and force of the banging jolted him to his senses. Had the constabulary come to take him? No. Gaol was a month away. This was more immediate.

Easing the door open, a freezing blast burst through. Peering out, Enoch could just make out two figures knee-deep in drifts of swirling snow. Familiarity told him they were his neighbours, Hannah and her sister-in-law Rosina Agombar. Both women were frantically imploring him, their half-sentences muffled by the thick air. The only discernible word was "help!".

Pulling them, stumbling and half falling into the house, they beseeched him. 'It's Esther!'

Struggling to understand, Enoch shouted for quiet, more in frustration than annoyance. A momentary silence descended. 'What's happened? Where's Esther?'

The reply was immediate. 'Fire! The house is on fire!'

'Jesus Christ!'

Pulling on his boots and grabbing his overcoat, he fled into the whiteness.

Nothing struck greater fear into London's tenement dwellers than fire. And, in this wind, it would be unstoppable, racing across the city and sweeping down to the river before nightfall.

A group of women, huddling together, watched as smoke billowed from the upstairs window of the Agombars' house. Colour had deserted the scene, only the empty shades of a charcoal sketch remained, but by the time Enoch had crossed the street, hues of yellows and reds had returned as flames licked upwards.

'Where's your menfolk?' he shouted. 'Where's Esther?'

A young woman, whom Enoch recognised as Rosina's sister, stepped closer to make herself heard above the howling wind. 'The baby's upstairs.' She pointed to where flames now leapt towards the roof. Then, as if remembering the question, she added, 'The men are at their looms, trapped overnight by the storm.'

Without another thought, Enoch dashed into the house and up the narrow stairway. Searing heat scorched his face; the choking smoke was dry and bitter in his mouth. Doors blistered and popped. A roof beam cracked and shifted, sending showers of burning embers cascading down.

From the street below, urgent voices called him back. Crouching low, he crept forwards into the smoke-filled room – the mattress smouldered and the laths in the ceiling had caught.

Coughing and barely able to draw breath, he searched the room. In the far corner, he glanced a bundle the shape and dimensions of a baby.

Falling heavily to the floor with arms outstretched, his fingertips scrabbled blindly across the scuffed wooden floorboards until feeling the rough edge of a swaddling blanket. Now cradling the bundle against his chest, his only thought was preservation. He couldn't stay a moment longer.

Crashing headlong down the stairs, bouncing awkwardly against the walls, twisting and turning to protect the precious cargo, he hit the hallway hard. Racked by searing pain, he lost the strength to lift himself and collapsed senseless before reaching safety.

Fresh air rushed to fill his lungs as he retched and vomited. Laying exhausted, he stared wide-eyed at the white sky above, snowflakes pitching cold on his face. At last, he was alone and, in the blessed silence, drifted peacefully towards sleep.

* * *

'So, you're back in the land of the living, are you not, Mr Price?'

Enoch opened his eyes. Whiteness still surrounded him, but the air was now warm and smelled of carbolic. The unfamiliar, lyrical birdsong came again.

'You're quite a hero, so you are.' The nightingale came into view. 'Good morning to you, sir. I'm Nurse Ryan. How are you feeling? A wee bit better, I hope.'

'Where am I?' he mouthed, struggling to anchor his

thoughts as images flooded his returning consciousness. His head ached, and his throat was painfully swollen.

'At Saint Thomas's,' she said, turning to leave.

Hoarse and barely audible, he beckoned her back. 'What happened?' He tried lifting himself but was paralysed by a flash of pain shooting through his body. Bandaging and a heavy wooden frame holding his left arm restrained him immobile.

'Don't you go moving!' she said, returning to his bedside. 'You're badly burned and need rest. Now just lay still.' And then, as if gossiping to a neighbour on her home streets of Dublin, she added, 'Well, you've caused quite a stir fetching that wee baby, so you have.'

'How did I get here?'

'An Irish gentleman brought you. Well, if you can call him a gentleman. Not that you'd know by appearances, indeed you would not.' Her blue eyes flashed, and, making a great play of straightening the spotless starched white apron adorning her full-length, deep-blue uniform, she cocked her head sideways to emphasise her low opinion. 'Anyways, it's not my place to say.'

'Does the baby live?'

'She does, and a grand wee thing she is, too. The people hereabouts are calling you a saviour.'

He lay back, exhausted by the effort, closed his eyes and rested his head into the deep pillows.

* * *

Disturbed by muffled voices from the corridor outside, Enoch glanced around. His was the only bed in the small side room. The sky had cleared, and shafts of bright sunlight streamed through the long sash window.

First to come through the door was the indomitable figure of the hospital matron, her stern face drawn tight, thin lips and sharp features framing an unmistakable bearing of authority. Following close behind was the hospital's senior physician, William MacCormac, an impressively tall gentleman in a black morning coat, grey pinstriped trousers and a burgundy paisley waistcoat decorated with a heavy gold fob chain. His long, grey hair and distinguished beard complemented his assured confidence, founded on unrivalled intellect and position.

As if by magic, the diminutive Nurse Ryan appeared from behind the two imposing figures and, with practised dexterity, began removing the bandages and grease lint dressings from his arm. When she had completed her task, Dr MacCormac spoke without any hint of his Irish origins.

'Good afternoon, Price, and how are you feeling?' His deep baritone resonated off the bare walls. 'Thank you, Matron, you can both leave us now,' he said, leaving no room for compromise. Once alone, the doctor gently lifted Enoch's arm and, examining it with close attention, said, 'You've certainly been through the wars.'

Enoch did not reply, staring for the first time at the swollen, raw, weeping wound that ached a deep, numbing pain now that the dressing was removed.

Dr MacCormac spoke with a studious tone. 'You've a grievous laceration aggravated by serious burns, which luckily haven't penetrated deeper into the lower tissues, so an amputation won't be necessary, at least, not for now. The surrounding skin is too damaged to suture, but, given time, the wound will heal well enough.' Then, more cheerily, he said, 'A pleasant reminder of a gallant escapade. Don't you agree, Price?'

Enoch replied with deference. 'Thank you, Doctor. I'm much obliged.'

'You'll live and likely as not keep the use of your arm. I've seen worse, and most mend without detriment.'

'Begging your pardon, Doctor, but how long before I can go home?'

'A week or so yet. I must see that the wound has closed and any risk of infection has passed.' After taking a moment for thought, he added, 'I believe we share a mutual acquaintance in Mr Michael O'Carroll.'

* * *

By the following morning, Enoch's appetite was fully restored. After two days without food, he made up for it with two large helpings of scrambled eggs and bacon, freshly baked bread with jam and hot tea. Nurse Ryan also delivered an edition of the previous day's *Globe* newspaper, conspicuously opened at the page describing the rescue of one-year-old Esther Agombar, which the headline sensationalised as an "inferno of death".

Nurse Ryan was finishing her morning chores when Dr MacCormac arrived, accompanied by Michael. The two men were in good spirits and made themselves comfortable at the bedside.

Listening as the two men spoke, Enoch learned that Michael had first met Dr MacCormac on the outskirts of Paris at the Battle of Sedan during the Franco-Prussian war in the summer of 1870. Having left home in search of work and adventure, Michael found himself as a stretcher-bearer at the French Army field hospital where Dr MacCormac, a volunteer surgeon with the Anglo-American Ambulance, plied his trade on the wounded and mangled bodies of young French soldiers.

The doctor was an accomplished amateur boxer, whereas Michael simply enjoyed a scrap, like any mongrel terrier, and to help relieve periods of boredom, as is common in times of war, both men enjoyed sparring in the makeshift ring of the tented hospital. The bond between these two men was firm and enduring, but Enoch guessed it wasn't boxing that had bound their friendship but the shared privations of the horrors following the French defeat, perhaps each owing the other his life.

* * *

Eliza and their three daughters arrived later that afternoon. They were overjoyed to see Enoch and eager to tell him their news, describing how Mr Agombar and his uncles had struggled home to fight the fire using buckets of snow passed hand to hand along lines of neighbours. How Michael had assembled a gang of toughs to collect Enoch and carry him by stretcher to the hospital, and how Rosenthal had sent word saying Enoch's court appearance was adjourned until 18 April, the day after Easter Sunday.

Once their excited chatter was exhausted, the three girls played happily, watching streams of traffic crossing Westminster Bridge.

Eliza leaned closer. 'Enoch, you've given us quite a shock, risking life and limb like that. Did you not think of us? How was we supposed to manage with you in the cemetery and us begging on the street? Whatever possessed you to do it?'

How was he to answer? That she or the children hadn't crossed his mind. Should he have turned his neighbour away? Is that what she was saying? No. He had done the right thing.

'Can we afford the doctor? And the hospital ain't cheap neither,' she continued.

'Don't worry, my love; I'm cared for by charity arranged by Michael.'

He closed his eyes as he felt her gently take up his hand in hers and tenderly kiss his lips. She was warm and fragrant, and he thought of their first kiss so many years before. He wanted to take her in his arms and hold her close, where she would be safe. He sighed deeply, wishing to be free of bankruptcy and the shadow of prison. He wished he could undo what was done.

'Enoch, promise me you'll never do such a thing again. Promise you'll always think of us first; we need you at home where you belong.'

'I promise you, my love... I promise... my dearest wife, I won't ever...' His voice broke off as sleep came and took him from her.

* * *

Enoch was discharged on the last day of January, not a moment too soon, and Eliza and the children were pleased to have him back, fussing over him like a wounded soldier home from the front. He had barely sat himself down when the Agombars came calling, bringing in gratitude a fruit cake and half a side of bacon.

After supper, Enoch joyfully entertained his daughters, telling them stories of enchantment, fairy princesses and the good deeds of gallant knights until each fell blissfully asleep.

In the quietness of their own company, Eliza held him close for comfort, but her tired eyes betrayed the fears that plagued her.

'Enoch, our dear girls have missed their father. It's been hard on us all these past weeks, what with you in hospital and all, but the prospect of gaol… well, I swear I'll not survive you being banged away, not even for a month. I'll go mad, and, as God is my witness, they'll be carting me to the loony bin.'

He could feel her trembling like a frightened sparrow. Taking her hands, he softly intertwined their fingers and, looking into her sorrowful eyes, said, 'My dearest wife, I've a plan that sees us gone from here. Things will be better; I swear it. We'll put these troubles behind us.'

'Are we to leave London?'

'If I'm to escape confinement, then I must be away from here; that much is certain.'

'Husband, as much as I love you, I can't go on the run, not like a gipsy woman on the road, dragging our children from place to place, constantly on the lookout for Toff and those following on behind. I need the peace and security of a home to raise our girls, and they need their father, and by no mistake, he needs them, too.' She paused, clearing her throat and straightening her posture to convey the seriousness of her concerns. 'We can go north. I've heard there's plenty of work. We can start again. I've an aunt in Manchester. We need only a room to call home, where we can be together, like when we first came here. As long as we're together, we'll have a home, a place where we can be happy.'

'Yes, my dearest, you are right. We'll start again, and together we'll find happiness. Trust me; I'll do what's right – I promise.'

FOUR

A fortnight before Easter, Enoch arrived home earlier than usual. He looked pleased with himself, and Eliza knew her wait was over.

Enoch took her in his arms. 'My dearest wife, we're to be free of this place and have a bright future ahead of us.'

'Don't tell me it's to be Ireland, or worse, travelling the road like tinkers.'

'Canada, my love. We're to—'

'Canada! Canada is to be our future? A wilderness. Our daughters raised as savages.'

'It's nothing like that, my dear. The city of Saint John is modern, with many grand houses and a seaport where we can prosper cutting and trading whalebone and stitching fine corsetry and fur garments too. I have friends there who—'

'I feared the worst and believed it was Ireland you'd take us, but Canada and the other side of the world! Is this any better than the torments of Coldbath?'

'My dearest wife, I understand your concerns; it's natural for a woman to worry and come on so, but I'll establish myself with comfortable lodgings and sound employment before sending for you. In the meantime, you'll stay with my mother in Bristol. She has agreed to provide comfortable accommodation at the rectory and a daily maid to help with chores.'

'You're leaving us behind? You're travelling alone?'

'I must be gone before my summons.'

'We're to be apart on Easter Day, the day of our Lord's resurrection and promise of new beginnings.'

'To evade Toff and the bailiffs, I must travel alone. The moment they discover I've absconded, they'll raise the alarm and be on the lookout for a family travelling together. Once I arrive at Saint John, I'll find work and lodgings and send—'

'Enoch, please stop. After all these years. After everything we've been through, sharing life's troubles as husband and wife, our vows binding us until death, and...' Struggling to understand what sin had condemned her, she pleaded, 'What have I done to deserve this cruel parting? Please, Enoch, don't desert me – I beg you. If it's to be Canada, then we will travel together.'

'My love, we'll be apart for a few weeks only, perhaps a month or two. We'll be together again well before Christmas Day – I swear it.'

'For the love of God, Enoch, think about what you are doing. If only for the sake of your blessed children. This will break all our hearts.'

* * *

Enoch arranged for Eliza and the children to leave early on the morning before Good Friday. He had chosen the date carefully. There would be crowds as businesses hurriedly prepared to close for the holy day. If the authorities got wind of him fleeing, they would be in no position to act before the Monday, the day of his trial, by which time his absence would be plain to all.

Eliza would travel by the 8.30am train from Paddington to Bristol Temple Meads, where Enoch's mother, Bethia, and stepfather, James Harris, minister at the Totterdown Baptist Chapel, would meet them.

* * *

Eliza waited in the parlour with the children, who were excited at the prospect of travelling by train. Enoch hugged each daughter, promising to join them soon. He held Eliza close and kissed her lovingly. 'My dear beloved wife, we'll be together before Christmas Day. I swear it.'

Gently touching his lips with her trembling forefinger, she said, 'Enough promises, Enoch. Take care and write when you arrive.'

No sooner had Eliza left the house than Enoch made his way to Bradbrook's on Green Street, returning soon after in the company of two labourers on a haulage dray drawn by a piebald nag. Thirty minutes later, every stick of furniture was loaded and secured under canvas and heading back to Bradbrook's saleroom. But before Enoch could take his leave, he noticed Hannah Agombar approaching. The street was uncommonly empty; even the usual gaggle of children were absent. Questions and sarcastic repartee were not what he needed; his only thought was of the urgency to be on his way. 'You've no worries, Mr Price,' she said. 'If anyone comes looking, any strangers poking their noses about, we'll tell um you're down Sussex way. Is that what we're to say?'

'Thank you, Hannah. Yes, Sussex with relatives.'

'Then good luck to you,' she said, stepping back into her doorway.

* * *

Making his way towards Bradbrook's, where he was to take lodgings for two nights, Enoch stopped off at Jacob Feintuch, the tailor.

Jacob greeted him amiably, 'Enoch, my dear friend, I've been expecting you. Everything is as you requested and ready for collection.'

'Did it fit in the travelling case?'

'Just as you requested. Two suits with waistcoats of the finest worsted. I've packed everything you listed: shirts, neckties, a new pair of laced ankle boots and a silk top hat in the opera style.'

'And the new brown Derby?'

'Of course, I nearly forgot. The memory at my age is not so good. You're going to wear it now, I believe?'

'Thank you, Jacob; as always, you're a class act.'

'I wish you luck, Mr Price, and may God watch over your good wife.'

* * *

Enoch took the Saturday morning train from Euston to Liverpool Lime Street, arriving late in the afternoon. The journey was uneventful. He spoke to no one and remained anonymous amongst the crowds that jostled the platforms and carriages.

He found accommodation at the Argyle Hotel on Paradise Street, a small boarding house offering the cheapest rooms in the least desirable district near the docks. He paid a little extra for the luxury of a clean sheet and a jug of hot water to be brought each morning. The room was spartan but dry and reasonably warm.

That night he slept little, disturbed by the rowdy, drunken sailors brawling in the street below and their frequent visits up and down the stairs to the prostitutes occupying the adjoining rooms. But this was as he wanted, a place where none knew his name, and none cared to know it, and where neither police nor bailiffs would venture after dark.

Monday, 18 April 1881 dawned with heavy grey clouds covering the port city in a fine mist, drenching everything it touched. He rose early and took breakfast at a pie and sausage shop on Dale Street. Steam from the tea urn and the smell of burnt fat and frying onions filled the stale air, and a mix of grime and condensation obscured the windows.

The place was busy with men. Some sat alone, despondent and lost in their thoughts. Others stood leaning against the back wall, unkempt and gazing aimlessly into the middle distance, dragged from their fitful slumber by the chill dawn light to face their lonely reality, briefly replaced the night before by strong drink and the warmth of paid for affections.

Observing their demeanour, he mirrored their vacant stare, their constant sniffling and hunched posture. No one noticed him sitting at the corner table.

As he sipped his hot tea, his imagination turned to the scene playing out at the London courts. Rosenthal would be explaining his client's absence in erudite terms, while Judge Hazlitt, impassive as always, was signing a warrant for his arrest and committal to prison.

Finishing his breakfast, Enoch walked out into the grey drizzle and turned towards Cowen & Company on Chapel Street, ticket agents for transatlantic passage. Broad granite steps led from the street to their grand offices, where lofty ceilings and high gothic, arched windows allowed light to flood in and reflect generously off the polished oak flooring, giving a sense of reassuring long-established trust and respectability. The furnishings were equally well appointed, with large, mahogany desks and deeply padded leather chairs. Framed pictures of steamships and posters advertising worldwide travel aboard glamorous ships of the Cunard, P&O and White Star Line adorned the walls.

Evading discovery was Enoch's primary consideration, and he had thought carefully about his port of entry. Canada was the most inconspicuous disembarkation. An Englishman stepping ashore in a British dominion would be unremarkable and go unnoticed and unrecorded. As a French-speaking city, Montreal had an additional complication for pursuing bailiffs and a hindrance to London's telegraphic enquiries. He had considered a passage to New York, with its advantage of a bustling port with hundreds of immigrants of every nationality arriving daily, but its new, stricter regulations and screening questions provided too many opportunities to arouse suspicion.

A young man in a well-tailored, dark, woollen business suit with a high collar and bow tie approached. His black hair, neatly cut short, glistened with oil and smelt lightly perfumed. He greeted Enoch with a weak, damp handshake. 'Good morning, sir.' He spoke with an almost indiscernible Liverpudlian accent. 'How may we be of assistance?'

Enoch noticed that he was the only customer and guessed it was still too early for most of their usual clientele. 'I'm seeking a passage to Montreal,' he said with certainty.

'Do you have any preferences for a particular line or ship, sir?'

'The soonest and fastest would suit my purpose,' replied Enoch. 'My business is with the importation of timber.' His reply was confidently matter-of-fact yet conveyed the need for urgency.

'Of course, sir. The Allan Line operates weekly crossings. Were you considering first class, intermediate or…' here the clerk briefly paused, 'or were you thinking of something a little less—'

'Intermediate will be adequate for my needs.'

'An excellent choice, sir. Our intermediate class is the most popular and is very comfortable and the most reasonably priced for the discerning traveller. If you'd like to take a seat, I'll check the sailing times and prices.'

A few minutes later, the young man returned with a handful of pamphlets extolling the virtues of speed and comfort to a country of untold riches and opportunity.

'Excuse me, sir, but may I ask the type of lumber you import? Is it pine or cedar? Or those majestic redwoods we hear so much about?'

Enoch was taken aback by the enquiry and hesitated. He hadn't expected to be questioned on the merits of the timber trade, about which he knew nothing.

The clerk continued, 'I only ask, sir, because my uncle has a timber yard on the wharf with all manner of trees arriving from Canada.' He quickly added, 'Not that I've ever visited his establishment, you understand.'

Enoch was regretting ever mentioning timber and wondered why he had thought it necessary. He had expected the purchase of a ticket to take no longer than a few minutes. He was now in danger of getting out of his depth and leaving a memorable impression with the clerk who, in his chosen profession, must be on the watch for foreigners, undesirables and those absconding justice. Enoch replied abruptly, verging on rudeness, 'Any timber I can sell; it matters not.' The young man registered the rebuff and returned to the business at hand.

'I've the schedule for the SS *Polynesian*, one of Allan Line's finest vessels. It sails from Liverpool to Quebec this coming Thursday.' He read the fine print to confirm the accuracy of his information. 'Cowen & Company can make all necessary arrangements for your onwards travel by train to Montreal with the convenience of our through-ticket.'

Enoch nodded his agreement. This was better than expected. The onwards train journey from Quebec would further complicate any pursuit. In his mind's eye, he was already planning to discard the onwards ticket to Montreal and instead buy a ticket to the city of Saint John, doubly ensuring his trail went cold.

The young man, confident of a sale, persisted. 'If sir were considering emigration, then we can provide speedy travel and comfortable accommodation at little or no cost, all subsidised by the Canadian government.'

The salesman drew breath, waiting for a response, but none came. Not put off by Enoch's silence, the salesman continued. 'Let's say, British Columbia, a wonderful province full of opportunity for the enterprising—'

Enoch interrupted. 'No. I only need to visit Montreal for a few weeks to conclude my business and—'

'In which case, sir, our return ticket will afford the greatest economy. May I suggest that—'

'No. No, thank you. A one-way ticket will suffice.'

Enoch felt himself becoming entangled in a web from which he couldn't extricate himself without leaving an indelible impression. He wanted only to pay for his ticket and get back to the street where he was anonymous. Although the clerk persevered with his well-practised patter, Enoch was no longer listening; his mind had turned to how he was to spend the remaining days before departure. His hearing abruptly returned when the young man's words broke in, 'Just a moment, sir, while I prepare your ticket.'

A few minutes later, the young man returned with a ticket for a shared intermediate cabin in the name of Mr Thomas Price.

Enoch marvelled at the piece of card which held the surprising power to grant him a new start in life, free from the shackles of prison and the burden of debt. Leaning across the table, Enoch stretched to collect his prized possession, but before his fingertips could reach, the clerk deftly slid the ticket to one side. 'I just need your signature before the cashier issues your receipt. We like to have everything properly documented and recorded. I'm sure you understand, sir.'

Pleased to be again stepping out onto Chapel Street, Enoch felt the ticket in his pocket – three days until departure.

* * *

The wet drizzle had turned to a heavy shower, running in rivulets across the cobblestones and along the gutters. Opposite the offices of Cowen & Company – on the corner of Covent Garden, a narrow street which bore no resemblance to the original London market – was The Pig and Whistle. The bar's soft-yellow gaslights sparkled through its rain-drenched windows, and, after watching a gaggle of customers hurry inside, Enoch briskly crossed the street into what he imagined was a welcoming and convivial pub.

But the bar was nothing as he had hoped. The awkward tranquillity of the place gave it the atmosphere of a railway waiting room full of strangers impatient to be on their way. A handful of customers cradled small glasses of dark beer; their belongings, packed in trunks and boxes strapped with canvas ties, were perched at their side. Apart from the occasional murmur, most were absorbed by the anxieties of what their futures might hold.

After buying a large glass of whisky, Enoch found a corner seat furthest from the door. It was a rare treat to be drinking spirits, let alone at 11am, but he considered a modest celebration was called for. Comfortably settled, he lit a clay pipe filled with his favourite dark shag and, collecting a well-thumbed copy of the previous day's *Liverpool Daily Post*, which had lain abandoned on an adjoining table, he began to read.

The headlines were dominated by reports of rioting in Jerusalem, the expulsion of Jews from Russia and accounts of soldiers returning from the war in South Africa. But the story which captured Enoch's imagination was of a Wild West shootout on the streets of Dodge City. Bat Masterson, the notorious gunslinger and lawman, had single-handedly cornered and shot dead three escaped outlaws.

Enoch took his time reading the paper from the first page to last and, for the first time, realised how little he knew of world affairs. Besides the Bible, which his mother had drilled into him, he couldn't ever recall reading anything from cover to cover.

Reading and the art of the deceitful dodge were the only valuable things his mother had taught him. After his father died, everything in life involved cunning and slight. Any casual misdirection was justified if it meant an extra rasher of bacon or a half bucket of coal for warmth. She would stoop to almost any depth to keep a roof over their heads and their stomachs half full. Even her second marriage to James Harris, the Baptist preacher, had involved a forged birth certificate showing her age to be twelve years younger.

At age nine, less than a year after his father had passed, she had put him to work at the Bristol tannery, where, except for church on Sundays, he never laboured fewer than fourteen hours a day. And now that he thought about it, earning a shilling and making ends meet seemed to have consumed his every waking hour ever since. But he now had three idle days and decided to use them educating himself.

* * *

Outside, the sky had cleared and the granite paving flags dried in the warm spring sun. Finishing his drink and leaving the pub, Enoch found a pavement vendor spieling the latest news. The man was wrapped in several woollen scarves and draped in an old overcoat several sizes too large. His thick tweed cap was pulled well down. From common courtesy, Enoch bought a newspaper before asking directions to the nearest public reading rooms. Pointing towards the Picton Rooms on William Brown Street, the seller said, 'That way, matey, near Lime Street.' Then, looking away, he again began his pitch.

Enoch soon found the newly built library, a gift to the city by one of its wealthy philanthropists. From the outside, the drum-shaped building, with its Corinthian columns, was impressive, but once inside, Enoch was astounded at the sheer splendour and opulence of the domed glass roof, the gold leaf, its exuberant wood carvings, exquisite marble floors and elaborate décor. Before him stood a cliff face of books towering to the heavens.

For a modest donation, he acquired a reader's card, allowing him free rein of what the librarian proudly described as "this palace of knowledge and learning". Enoch spent the afternoon moving from one shelf to another, exploring beautifully bound and illustrated books on every subject. Exhausted and exhilarated by his discovery, he wondered how it was that, only a few hundred yards from the library's portals, people were living in filth and squalor, while bound paper and card were extravagantly cared for in baronial surroundings.

* * *

Making his way back towards his lodgings, he replayed his experiences of buying the ticket at Cowen's and became increasingly annoyed with himself. It had been a clumsy mistake saying he was a timber merchant. What had made him think of such a tale? Why had he felt the need to explain his journey? He had almost given himself away and admonished himself for his lack of thought. He had to get his story straight: who he was, what he was doing, and why. Without a plausible story, he would soon be discovered.

The following day, he again took breakfast at the pie and sausage shop, where he leisurely read the newspaper before making his way across town to the Picton Rooms. With several thousand books to choose from, he restricted himself to the handful of recommendations given to him by the helpful librarian. By reading only one or two chapters from each, he was able to quickly discard some, while in others, he indulged himself by reading on. The afternoon was spent with back copies of *Harper's Magazine*, a monthly American publication filled with short stories and authoritative articles on politics, society and topical matters.

He became aware that reading gave him immense pleasure, allowing him to escape to many worlds far removed from his own experiences, and so decided to take a book to accompany him on his journey.

The previous day, he had seen a bookshop on Victoria Street. It was a double-fronted shop with the latest publications displayed in its large bay windows. He hoped to find James Fenimore Cooper's *Last of the Mohicans*. But, mainly because of their much-reduced price, he bought two well-worn, second-hand editions instead: Wilkie Collins' *The Law and the Lady* and Victor Hugo's *The Hunchback of Notre Dame*.

FIVE

On the day of departure, Enoch paid his landlady and, carrying his valise, headed down Paradise Street towards Pier Head and the waiting SS *Polynesian*. As he crossed James Street, two constables turned the corner and began to briskly approach. Walking side by side, they blocked the entire width of the pavement. His heart quickened. How had they found him? Had the landlady been a copper's nark? The narrow, cobbled street provided no means of escape. His knees weakened as he slowed his progress. A pace or two before the officers reached him, each stepped aside and passed without a second glance. Enoch stopped to gather his nerves and, not daring to look behind, fixed his stare ahead. At the end of the road, he could just make out an overhead hoarding: Allan Shipping Line – Embarkation.

Crossing through the wide dock gates, he entered the enormous embarkation hall, where a deafening clamour of several hundred passengers waited excitedly. Women tearfully hugging and kissing their menfolk farewell, mothers giving final instructions to sons and daughters, and stoic grandparents fussing over small children, all promising to write soon and praying for a safe and speedy journey. At the far end, a man in naval uniform with a white peaked cap bellowed through a loudhailer, 'Intermediate passengers this end, first-class the far end, steerage, please wait.'

The crowd, drifting in different directions, soon organised itself into small groups and lines. With surprising speed, Enoch found himself being called forward by a clerk behind a heavy oak lectern.

'Good morning, sir. Thank you for sailing with Allan Line. May I see your ticket?' The clerk made a cursory inspection. 'I need a few details for the Canadian authorities.' Moving his forefinger across a double-paged ledger, his eyes scanned the manifest. 'Yes, here you are, sir. Mr Thomas Price. Born Bristol. Aged thirty-nine. And what's your occupation?'

'Tanner.'

The clerk wrote "labourer".

'What luggage are you taking aboard?'

'Just this case.' Enoch was about to add, "I'm only visiting for a few weeks" but stopped himself. After his mistake at Cowen's, he had decided to say no more than was necessary. His gift of the gab had served him well, but now he must learn to bite his tongue.

'Thank you, sir. Cabin twenty-four on the mid-deck.'

The clerk unhooked a heavy rope barrier, allowing Enoch to pass onto the quayside, where the SS *Polynesian* rested majestically with her two rigged sailing masts and single smokestack. She was much larger than Enoch had imagined. Her steel hull, gleaming black, was decorated with a freshly painted broad red band running its length.

A porter approached. 'Can I help with your luggage, sir?'

'No. No thank you,' replied Enoch, staring up at the ship in awe.

'Right you are, sir. Just make your way to the aft gangway.' He pointed towards the ship's stern.

Enoch was the first to arrive to the cabin, which was hot and airless with a residual smell of oil and coal tar. It was twice the size of a train compartment but decorated in much the same livery. The walls were painted in a rich, chocolate-brown with cream detailing, varnished teak panelling, dark-blue moquette seating, with two opaque glass lampshades that diffused light from small oil lamps hinged on brass gimballed fittings.

Through a narrow side door was a toilet and washbasin. Natural light entered through a small porthole, no larger than the width of a man's hand. Hundreds of large iron rivets – binding the ship's bulkheads to its outer steel plates – ran in endless stitching across the width of the cabin, which was just large enough to accommodate four. Two long bench seats folded open as beds, and above each were large brass catches holding two more foldaway bunks stowed from sight. Below the porthole was a narrow folding table clipped flat against the wall. *Surviving the nine-day crossing in comfort and peace*, thought Enoch, *will depend on my travelling companions' size and nature.*

And he didn't have long to wait before the second passenger arrived: a tall, well-built man with a fair, freckled complexion and faded ginger hair showing the first signs of greying and which looked as if it had been hacked short with a pair of blunt kitchen scissors. Enoch noticed the man wore heavy boots and the type of hard-wearing clothes common to agricultural labourers.

'Well, here we are then. I'm Dai Williams.' He dropped his heavy canvas bag and thrust out a strong, calloused hand while continuing to talk with alarming energy and cheerfulness. 'I'm Welsh, you see. A bit unfortunate, like, I know, but you'll soon get used to it,' he said with friendly humour and, with barely a moment to draw breath, he continued, 'How do you do? Are you alright, then? It's nice to meet you, really, it is.'

The Welshman gave the cabin a cursory glance. 'Not too bad. Not being funny or anything, but I've shared worse sheds with prettier sheep,' he said, laughing aloud. 'It's going to be nice and snug, and we'll definitely get to know each other by the time we reach Canada. But not too well, I hope!' Again, laughing at his own humour.

Taking advantage of a lull, Enoch said, 'I'm Thomas Price. It's good to meet you. I'm from Bristol.'

'Bristol!' Dai repeated enthusiastically. 'Now, then, you're just across the water from me. Almost neighbours, like. Now, what should I call you? Is it Tom or Thomas? Or do you have another name?' Again, he laughed aloud.

Enoch replied, 'Tom is what most people call me.'

'Well, Tom it is then. My name's David, but everyone calls me Dai. Except, of course, for me mam when I'm in a spot of bother. Then it's David! I expect your mam's just the same, calls you Thomas when you're in a spot of trouble, like… am I right?'

Enoch didn't reply. He was thinking about just how long nine days could feel.

* * *

Shuddering from the engines increased, and the ship's horns and whistles sounded. There was a distinct sense of sideways juddering. Dai looked through the porthole.

'We're moving,' he said. 'Come on. Let's go on deck and say farewell to the old country.'

Along the starboard railings, passengers waved excitedly as they shouted to those lining the dock wall. But as the ship made its way down the Mersey, the cheering onlookers slipped from view.

For many of those aboard, the next few hours would be a time of reflection, and for some, the separation from kin would feel like a bereavement. They may have wished it otherwise, but in their hearts, they knew they would never again see home. The boat was taking them, and they were going forever.

* * *

Making his way to the stern, Enoch found a sheltered bench from where he could watch the ship's wake churn and boil before rolling away in gentle curves. A lone seagull followed, hoping to find scraps thrown up by the ship's progress. The late afternoon sun cast long shadows across the water and back towards New Brighton and Formby Point. He thought of his three daughters, imagining them skipping hand in hand in the meadows surrounding their grandmother's home.

A week had passed since they had last been together, and already he missed the simple things he had taken too easily for granted: their warm touch, the softness of their lips kissing his cheek, their goodnight wishes, their laughter and constant questioning. Even their plaintive small voices pleading for a penny bun, 'Please, Father, please.'

Following the saving of baby Esther, Enoch had been busily making preparations to flee. He had been sure of his purpose. But now, alone in the gathering gloom, he was pricked by misgivings. Michael's words came to him, "leaving your girls behind won't be easy. Think hard on it". Perhaps Michael had been right – two years hard at Coldbath would not have been too much to bear. But he hadn't listened, *too damned cocksure*, he cursed. But there was nothing to be done until Canada, where he would send for Eliza the moment he stepped ashore. The family would be together by Christmas. He had promised it; never again would they be separated.

In his imagination, Enoch composed a letter to Eliza, describing how they would start afresh, building a new home, and prosper in business. With so many opportunities, their daughters would flourish and grow into young women to be proud of. Together, they would turn misfortune to their advantage.

As darkness encroached, he pored over the events of the past few months, pondering the cause of his misfortune. Although Dyson had done Toff's bidding to snare and summons him, Enoch considered only himself to blame for the way events had unfolded. He could have disappeared with Eliza and the children long before prison beckoned and done so in good order. He had been boneheaded not to have recognised the inevitability of his situation and had clung to the cause of avoiding bankruptcy for far too long. Perhaps Toff had wanted him gone sooner and was surprised, even annoyed, by his dogged persistence. Once Toff had recouped his loan and taken control of the business, he only wanted Enoch out of his way. It didn't matter if Enoch was in gaol, on the other side of the world or dead.

But how had he been so easily caught? It wasn't as if chicanery was any stranger; he had often practised his own scam, playing a role and delivering his lines convincingly. Although, compared to Toff's sophistication and menace, he was a mere amateur. Yet, the deceptions each played were much the same: using props to create an illusion so the audience might loosen its grip on reality and willingly suspend disbelief, allowing their emotions to weep in sorrow or celebrate in joy as the drama unfolded. Toff's troupe had played him like a fiddle. Bawtree's disarming pretence of expertise, flattery and pandering to conceit had snared his trust, and with trust safely bagged, then a fool and his money were easily parted, and what a fool he'd been. All the elements were there to see, if only he hadn't been blinkered by his overblown sense of importance. Conceited pride, this was the culprit.

Bitterness was in his throat, and he felt the chill air bite as the ship ploughed into choppier waters. Wrapping himself in a deck blanket, he pushed deeper into the shelter. His mood darkened as he watched the lone seagull turn back and the lights along the shoreline disappear as night enfolded him. His thoughts once more turned to home. A hot tear burnt his cheek as regret clawed at his innards.

'Are you all right, sir?' said a steward on discovering Enoch as he went about securing the last of the deck chairs. 'Evening meal will be served shortly, sir,' said the attendant cheerily. 'It's getting a bit cold to be out here, sir.'

Enoch nodded his appreciation at the steward's concern. 'You're right. I'll go below.'

SIX

The SS *Polynesian* made good speed and hove to just after dawn, anchoring a few hundred yards off the small port town of Moville on Lough Foyle. Enoch listened as securing cables clattered and ran off their capstans until she sat steady, bumping gently against a tug resting on her bow. This was her only stop before Quebec. If the remaining berths were to be filled, then this was where the passengers must board.

There was a sharp rap on the cabin door as breakfast was delivered: two thick rashers of bacon, two warm hard-boiled eggs, two bread rolls with butter and a flask of tea. The elegant dining room on the upper deck was available only to first-class passengers.

Dai, who had been up and washed for more than an hour, enthusiastically lowered and secured the folding table. As they ate breakfast, the noise of doors slamming, gangways being lowered, instructions barked and the general shuffling of feet in corridors could be heard throughout the ship.

Dai was talkative and quick-witted, turning any remark to his amusement. 'Right, we've had our bite to eat, now let's see what Londonderry has to offer,' he said, pointing skywards with his thumb.

On deck, they joined a group of men leaning against the starboard rail. It was a bright, cloudless day, and Enoch felt the warmth of the sun on his back as he looked out towards shore, which, surprisingly, remained some distance off.

'How the hell are they supposed to get on board?' asked Dai to no one in particular.

'They'll bring um up from Londonderry in a tender. Then we'll have a bit of fun watching um scramble up them rope ladders,' said one of the group of men. 'You missed a right proper laugh a few minutes ago. Half a dozen coppers trying to get onboard. One of um lost his cap in the drink.'

Several of the men, whose accents Enoch assessed as Cornish, laughed as they recounted the episode.

'They've got police on board?' asked Enoch, making the enquiry sound innocent.

'Aye! They're looking for a bloke on the run from London,' replied the man who had first spoken. 'I'll tell you this – if truth be told, those devils never give up. They'll chase you to the ends of the earth. I seen it round our parts.'

'You're right there,' said a second man. 'Take old Percy Lugg's boy from down Truro way. He were a wanted man, stole a horse, so they said. He went all the ways to Australia, but they still got him. Found him in the middle of nowhere prospecting for gold. Found a fair bit of it, so they say, and wasn't short of a bob or two by then, neither.'

Dai asked, 'Did they bring him back for trial?'

'Na. Couldn't be bothered with any of that rigmarole. They hanged him out there.' A peel of laughter rang out amongst the Cornishmen.

Enoch didn't speak. His mind was racing, his mouth dry, and his stomach was churning. *Is it possible?* he thought. *Would they go to the lengths of telegraphing the Irish police? How did they know I was on the* Polynesian? *Was I clocked by the two constables that passed me in Liverpool? Or was it the ticket clerk at Cowens?* There was nothing he could do now. He just had to sit tight and wait.

The group of men watched as more tenders arrived and left, each time discharging a dozen passengers. A few minutes after 10am, the police re-emerged, roughly bundling a dark-haired man into a waiting launch, his hands cuffed behind his back.

'I heard he's a foreigner,' said the Cornishman who'd told the story of Percy Lugg's boy. 'Mixed up with shooting the Russian Czar. A revolutionary, so they say.'

'Christ, I wouldn't want to be in his boots,' said Dai. 'They ain't going to be gentle with that poor devil.'

Much relieved, Enoch nodded. 'I'm going to the cabin. See if anyone's joined us.'

* * *

On entering the cabin, he was met by the two outstanding passengers unpacking their belongings from a tattered cardboard box. Each bore a striking resemblance and were obviously father and son. Their diminutive stature struck Enoch. The father was a little over five feet while the boy, who was no taller than any five- or six-year-old, had the face of a child twice that age. Enoch had seen the look amongst the waifs and strays begging on the streets of London.

'Hello there! How do you do? I'm Henry Keeley, and this

is my son, William. We're up from Donegal. I guessed you'd already took the bottom bunk, so we've fixed ourselves on top.'

'You're welcome to take my lower berth if it suits you better. I've no strong preference,' said Enoch.

But William, who was eleven and travelling for the first time, was adamant he wanted the top bunk.

Enoch introduced himself and told them of Dai.

'Well, that's a nice band we have,' said Henry. 'An Irishman, a Welshman and an Englishman, and all travelling to Canada. Now isn't that something?'

* * *

Enoch spent the rest of the day in the upper saloon reading Wilkie Collins, only returning to the cabin in time for the evening meal. He was feeling comfortable in the company of his new companions and, with only the Atlantic before them, hoped things would now be plain sailing.

The quality and quantity of the food was a pleasant surprise: sliced roast beef, Yorkshire puddings, carrots and potatoes, with treacle tart for dessert and four bottles of beer. All were hungry, and they ate in silence. Leaning back replete, Dai gave out a belch, saying, 'Pardon me for being rude. It was not me; it was my food.' William, who hadn't heard the rhyme before, thought it amusing and couldn't stop himself from giggling.

Henry, remarking in friendly banter, said, 'Well, Dai, let's hope we don't hit choppy water, or we'll all be enjoying your dinner.' Before adding, 'Shall we not finish the evening at the bar with a drop of good Irish stout? I hear there's music and dancing to be had.'

The mid-deck bar was the size of a large dance hall, illuminated by an ornate glass ceiling and chandeliers reflecting yellow light off the large, gilded wall mirrors. Comfortable armchairs and round tables with brass railings, thoughtfully attached to stop drinks sliding off in rolling seas, filled the room. Long bench seats upholstered in deep-red velvet lined the walls surrounding a polished, dark-mahogany floor, which doubled as a dance floor. All combining to give the ambience of opulence.

A hundred or more passengers were crowding the bar. Waiters in starched white jackets darted from table to table, taking orders and delivering drinks. Smoke rose and hung in the air, and somewhere in a corner, an unpractised amateur was trying to coax a tune from a piano. The impression was of a fashionable Parisian café with the atmosphere of a London pub.

The four Cornishmen from the morning's encounter had encamped in the corner nearest the bar and had, by all appearances, already imbibed more than enough. Enoch and the others made their way towards the familiar faces and occupied an adjoining table.

There was the excitement and energy of a first night party, and Henry and Dai were amiable company, neither being strangers to repartee. William sat quietly with a small glass of ale, taking it all in, watching the men enjoy what Henry described as "good craic".

One ugly moment threatened when a drunken Cornishman leapt to his feet, threatening to fight his compatriots over some insignificant slight. Enoch rose, ready to protect both himself and young William, who had sat beside him. But before things could develop, Dai leaned across and grabbed the Cornishman by his upper arm and, with the power of a steel vice ratcheting closed, was crushing muscle and nerve against bone, forcing the man back down into his seat. The Cornishman's anger subsided into incredulity as the strength drained from his lifeless arm.

Once the evening's gaiety resumed, Enoch turned to Dai. 'That's quite a hold you have.'

'Well, you know, Tom, when you're shearing hundreds of cantankerous sheep day in and day out, and having to wrestle every one of the damned animals, it kind of comes natural.'

* * *

The following morning, the ship, continuing through still flat seas, headed west-south-west towards Newfoundland. The exhilaration of the past few days, compounded by the pleasant social evening, had drained their energy, and listlessness fell upon the cabin.

Enoch spent the morning in the main saloon, reading the Wilkie Collins he'd brought for the journey. He was joined at midday by Dai, who had considerately brought him a cup of tea.

'Here you are, Tom,' he said, carefully passing him the cup and saucer. 'Do you enjoy reading?'

'Well, frankly, Dai, I've only just taken it up. I don't mind admitting this is the first novel I've read.'

'What's it about?'

Enoch, taking up his clay pipe and carefully charging it with black tobacco, said, 'A man marries using a false name. His first wife has been poisoned, and he's suspected of murdering her. His second wife then—'

'I once knew a bloke down in New Zealand,' interrupted Dai. 'Futter was his name. George Futter, from Norfolk. Hard worker, he was. He changed his name, started calling himself Albert Baker. Married a local native girl half his age, false name and all. Raised a family of young'uns, too. Then one day, Mrs Futter, his wife from Norfolk, unexpectedly turns up. Well, that really put the cat amongst the pigeons. Jesus! You should have seen his face. Poor old Bert. He went as white as a sheet, like he'd seen a ghost.'

Enoch was enthralled. 'What happened?'

'Well, she knocks him about a bit. Gives him a black eye an' all. She was a big woman, like, hands bigger than mine! Some said she was a coal hewer. Anyways, she moves in with um, the three of um living together, like. Imagine that – two wives nagging at you. I pitied the poor bugger. So, I tells him. I said, "Now you look here, Bert, I'm not trying to be funny or anything, but you wanna up sticks and move on." But he says he can't. He says he's gone and married twice. What they calls a bigamist. He says, if the law gets him, it'll be ten years' hard labour. So, I says, "Ten years' hard labour! That's nothing to a lifetime of torment!"'

Both men burst into raucous laughter, drawing disapproving looks from those in the saloon. Once the attention of the other passengers had returned to their own conversations, Enoch asked, 'Why choose the name Albert Baker?'

'Well, they says if you ever change your name, you should go with your favourite royal and the trade or calling you've always fancied. So, I suppose he liked Prince Albert and fancied being a baker. If it were me, I'd chose Owain Carpenter; I've always been handy fashioning wood, and the name has a nice ring to it.'

'Who was King Owain?' asked Enoch quizzically.

'Tom! Like most Englishmen, you know little of the majesty of Wales. Have you never heard of Owain Glyndŵr, the last Welshman to be crowned Prince of Wales?'

* * *

In shared conversation, Dai told of his upbringing and of his mother, who had died when he was barely twelve, and how his father had single-handedly raised him and his three younger brothers. Dai said, 'Our mam never spoke English; she was a proud Welsh speaker all her life and a staunch chapel-goer, too. She was a kind woman, was our mam, and, God knows, she had a lot to put up with.'

Enoch interrupted. 'Can you speak Welsh?'

'At home, that's all we ever spoke. In fact, I didn't learn English till I was nine, taught by our nan, I was. We lived on a remote hill farm in North Wales. It was a good hour's walk to school, in all weathers too. I tell you, Tom, it was bloody hard raising sheep on the side of a mountain, especially when snow came.' He broke off, deep in reflection.

'Anyhows, five years after our mam was taken, our dad passed on. Died from exhaustion, they said. Completely worn out, he was. Mind you, I think his heart broke when our mam went and left him to carry on alone. Even though he had us four boys, you could see the light had gone from his eyes.' Dai spoke with sorrow. 'So. There it is. It can't be helped. A week after we buried our dad, the landlord comes and tells us to move on. Said he had new tenants. So, us boys had to leave, orphans and homeless, we was. If it weren't for our nan… well, God only knows where we'd be.'

He paused and slowly examined his hands, turning them over as if looking for specks of dirt. 'I'm not gonna lie to you, Tom – it was hard for us boys. Anyhows, the three youngest got packed off to Canada to our uncle. That's where I'm headed now. I was the eldest, so I thought I'd try my luck raising sheep down under in New Zealand. Started with a smallholding and half a dozen ewes. Spent fifteen years building the herd, even survived an earthquake that knocked the house down. Pile of rubble, it was, but the neighbours rallied round, and we soon got it built back. But then disease came and took everything. Over two thousand head of sheep dead within the month. So, I had to sell up, you see. I had no choice. I couldn't pay the rent, and by the time the bank and lawyers had taken their share, well, there was nothing left.'

A melancholy mood descended, and Dai drew into himself. The memory had opened old wounds. There was a long silence before he brought himself back with a jolt. 'Never mind! It's no good crying over spilt milk. Gotta keep moving forward. What's done is done.'

Enoch nodded his agreement. 'I suppose so.'

More cheerfully, Dai spoke about joining his brothers in Alberta. 'We're moving to Argentina to start a new life with our cousins. They've built a homestead in Patagonia – lush green grass on gently rolling hillsides, and they're Welsh speakers too. It'll be like the old days back home on our old farm at Abergeirw.'

Reciprocating, Enoch told how, at age nine, his mother put him to work at the tannery where his father had died from throat cancer. 'What they call the tanner's disease,' said Enoch. 'When I'd reached twelve, she had me bound by indenture to a master tanner. I suppose she thought it was the right thing for me, but I had no intentions of following my father to an early grave in the piss sheds of a tannery. Anyway, when I reached nineteen, my master released me from my obligations, and I set off for London, but the streets ain't paved with gold, not like they said. I earned a pittance cutting whalebone for corset stays. It was hard graft and barely enough to keep body and soul together, so I earned extra, fighting bare-knuckle in the back-alley pubs. That was hard too, but there was friendship and camaraderie amongst us young lads – pugilist, the nobs used to call us.' Enoch smiled to himself. 'That's how it was in those days, Dai. The boys in the alleys fighting or robbing, and the girls were there earning too.'

Enoch had decided that any mention of his corsetry business would only lead to the disclosure of bankruptcy and prison, and any attempt at explaining leaving his wife and daughters behind would only arouse suspicion. He would say only that his wife had died in childbirth, and compelled by poverty, he put his daughters into the care of his mother. This was a safer yarn. No one would expect him to raise his daughters alone and would readily sympathise with him, leaving them with their grandmother, the wife of a Baptist pastor no less.

He told Dai he was striking out anew to begin trading whalebone from Saint John. Then, with admiration in his voice, said, 'Taking yourself off to the other side of the world took guts.'

Dai jabbed his finger. 'No, Tom. What you're doing takes guts. I was a young lad without ties or any fears. But you, you're leaving your daughters behind, who, from what you're telling me, are the apple of your eye. I'm telling you straight, Tom, I couldn't do it. It was hard enough parting from my brothers.'

'What choice did I have?' pleaded Enoch. 'It was that or the poorhouse, and God only knows where that would lead.'

'You could have found yourself a fair widow with a brood of her own. Good cooking and a warm, snug bed. You'd have been as happy as a pig in shit.'

'There ain't many like that,' said Enoch. 'Anyways, not as I've seen. Most begrudge you a beer at the end of the day and pull the blanket off you at night.'

'And spend your money on bonnets, too,' added Dai.

Both men laughed aloud.

Dai shifted himself forwards onto the edge of his chair as if to impart a secret. 'I'm not gonna lie to you, Tom. It's different out there in the new territories: New Zealand, Australia, places like Canada. They're raw with nature. Sometimes things ain't so easy, and most times it's bloody hard, but what you make, you can call your own. There's no high and mighty lording it over you, telling you what to do and when to do it. Nobody putting you in a pecking order, choosing whether you work or starve. Come on, Tom, speak honestly. Would you freely choose the gloom of a factory or toiling your guts out down the mines, only so the leisured classes can enjoy a life of idle pleasures? Go on, speak freely.'

In a grand flourish, Dai took to his feet. 'Don't let the bastards rob you – they need us, but we don't need them.'

Enoch caught him by the sleeve and pulled him roughly back into his seat.

Suddenly realising he was drawing attention, Dai said, 'Oh, Christ! Did I get out of hand? Sorry, Tom. I've embarrassed you? Welsh, you see. Talk too much. It's what our mam used to say, "Always showing off is our David."'

Enoch smiled. 'Well, that was quite a speech.' Then, lowering his voice, 'Now, be honest with me, Dai, are you one of them revolutionaries?'

Both men burst into laughter and, out of respect for their fellow passengers, retired for a beer before lunch.

SEVEN

The North Atlantic is perilous at any time of the year, with gale-force winds and the ever-present danger of icebergs. Even in summer, it can be hazardous, with sudden storms and hurricane winds. The Liverpool to Quebec sailing is the shortest sea route, with land out of sight for only five of the nine-day passage. And once Belle Isle, off the coast of Canada, draws into sight, the worst is over, and all that remains is the serenity of the scenic St Lawrence.

The steamship *Polynesian* was four hundred feet long and forty feet wide. The monotonous discordant percussion of its engine, accompanied by the dull beat of the ship's propeller, drilled achingly into the heads of each of its 612 passengers. But the constant din of propulsion wasn't the only cause for the clammy sweats and nausea. Below decks, the pervading stench of engine oil curdled with bitter coal dust clung suffocatingly heavily in the air, forcing passengers to seek refuge in the fresh salt breeze on the open promenade.

But it was the ninety-eight steerage-class passengers, crammed into the bowels of the ship's lower decks, who endured the worst discomforts. Their poverty and desperation for a new life condemned them to the foul conditions of the bilges, without hope of fresh air or the glimmer of daylight throughout their journey and sustained on only the meanest rations of bread, tinned meats and jam.

Enoch appreciated the privilege afforded by the open deck, where he took pleasure witnessing majestic sprays blowing high off the crest of crashing waves, set against the spectacle of billowing clouds scurrying eastwards across azure skies.

The flat calm of the first few days gave way to a boisterous, growling sea, ever-darkening through shades of vivid emerald to sinister deep indigoes, threatening menace with every giant wall of water slamming hard against the ship's sides of iron and wood.

As the swell grew mountainous and the wind strengthened, Enoch sought shelter below decks. Finding Henry Keeley and his son huddled together in the nearly deserted mid-deck saloon, Enoch enquired after the boy's welfare.

Henry was gingerly sipping from a cup of black coffee while his son lay restlessly next to him, his head snuggled on his father's lap. 'He needs to lay quiet for a while,' replied Henry. 'He's feeling dizzy when he stands.'

'It looks like a storm brewing,' said Enoch, settling himself into an armchair. 'What about you, Henry? Do you suffer with the seasickness?'

'I'm not sure that I do. This is my third crossing, and, touch wood, they've been without incident. This is William's first, so I've got my fingers crossed for him.'

'When was your first crossing?' asked Enoch, trying to make innocent conversation as a distraction.

'Six years ago, in '75. Me and the wife travelled to my brother in Boston. Our two daughters accompanied us, but we left William with his grandmother.' Henry was gently stroking away strands of damp hair from his son's brow as he spoke. 'He was a sickly child, and we thought it better to leave him until he grew stronger.'

'Did your brother travel with you?'

'No, he left for Boston two years before.' Henry noticed Enoch's quizzical look and added, 'It's a long story. My brother was a soldier with the Glorious Irish for more than twenty years, mostly in India. Anyway, he'd had enough of soldiering and wanted to settle with his sweetheart, Kate, a girl from our village, but the army wouldn't hear of it, said he'd signed for thirty years and, having cheerfully taken the Queen's shilling, that's the service she expected.'

'Jesus!' exclaimed Enoch. 'They wouldn't let him go?'

'Not a day short of thirty. So, he and Kate made a run for it to Queenstown, where they came upon a ship bound for Montreal.'

Henry took a drink of coffee, wiping his mouth with the back of his hand before checking on his son's comfort. Enoch did not speak, allowing Henry to continue at his own pace.

'You see, Tom.' Henry leaned forward, lowering his voice as if sharing a confidence. 'You see, Tom, he's a deserter. If he were ever caught, it'd be flogging and prison with hard labour. But the thing is, Tom, in America, they don't give a damn about no English laws. That's why he went south to Boston.'

'But if he was caught in Canada, they'd send him back to London,' queried Enoch.

'They would indeed, Tom. But in America, he's safe. Mind you, if he really wanted to lose himself, then New York's the place. It's a rabbit warren where you can just disappear from the face of the Earth.'

'So, why aren't you bound for Boston?'

'It's better for the boy. Fewer days at sea, and the train goes directly to Boston. It's a grand city, especially for us Irish, and there's plenty of work. Have you not considered it yourself, Tom?'

* * *

The storm worsened, and with it, the ship pitched and rolled in unpredictable ways. Saloon attendants hurriedly collected bar stools and chairs, roping and securing them to wall-mounted cleats.

With Henry carrying his ailing son, both men returned to the cabin, where they found Dai on his bunk, eyes squeezed tightly closed, slowly counting aloud. No sooner had they arrived than William turned a shade of grey-green and vomited freely. This was the trigger for Dai to rush for the bathroom, half bent and holding a hand to his mouth, but not fast enough.

Enoch scrambled onto an upper bunk, calling to Henry as he did so. 'You take my bed below. It'll be better for your lad.'

The sound of Dai retching was drowned out by stewards banging door to door, shouting instructions for passengers to don cork lifesavers and remain in their cabins. Only on the captain's order were women and children to ascend to the open deck.

As night fell, the ship filled with pungent smells of bile and the wailing of those in fear of impending death. And the ship's fabric did not escape the torment. Its wooden beams and iron structures moaned and screeched as they twisted under overwhelming forces.

The airless cabin became unbearably hot as the storm grew, yet Enoch shivered as clammy sweat clung to him. Spasms of pain cramped his stomach, pushing burning acid choking up into his throat. He felt the ship twist and judder as its riveted iron seams distorted and screamed under the immense pressures. Cold, salty water was now dripping from above.

Enoch thought of Eliza and wished they'd never parted. He should have done his time at Coldbath and been thankful for it. But regrets couldn't help now. Counting a slow tempo, one deep breath after another, he prayed for a new dawn and the salvation it brought. 'Please, God, don't let it end like this.' Repeating the mantra over and over, he fell into a sleep propelled by exhaustion.

* * *

It must have been around 5am when, through the porthole, Enoch glanced a distant star. Hope strengthened. He could just make out the faint edge of a passing cloud. Dawn was breaking.

As the sky lightened, vague silhouettes emerged from the darkness of the cabin. An hour later, Enoch realised that the wind had eased and the buffeting had lessened; the storm was abating – thank the good Lord.

Then, without warning, a sickening scream ran through the cabin, a siren shrill, so penetrating that Enoch doubted it was human. Turning sideways, he tumbled and fell heavily from his bunk; slipping awkwardly on the wet floor, he grabbed blindly at Henry's sleeve just as the ship lurched sideways, throwing Dai scrambling on all fours to Enoch's side.

Henry was rocking violently back and forth. 'Billy! Billy boy! Don't leave me, son.' It was a cry of despair.

Dai and Enoch groped about in the half-light until finding the body of the small boy cradled in his father's arms. Pulling the boy free from his father's grasp, Dai lay the scrawny lad on his bunk. In the early light, Enoch could just discern the features of the boy's face. His eyes had the stare of a dead fish, and his lips were little more than charcoal smudges on ashen paper.

Dai listened closely. 'Quiet! For God's sake, quiet!' A moment later, the only sounds were those of the engine's rhythmic thud and the cold arctic wind whistling over the ocean swell. 'Water! He needs water!'

Crawling on all fours through every conceivable mess, sticky and clinging, Enoch stumbled sideways into the washroom. Filling an enamelled mug, he shifted his hold from doorpost to wall to bunk, until passing the now half-empty cup to Dai, who, holding the boy like a sick lamb, poured into the boy's mouth. But he didn't swallow. The water lay there, lapping against neglected tombstones. Lifting the boy and tilting his head backwards, he poured again. There was no swallowing, no choking, no gasping.

Henry broke the silence with a pitiful plea for God's divine intervention. Speaking calmly and deliberately, Dai said, 'He's not dead, but he's close by.' He paused a beat before giving instructions. 'Tom, find a steward, and fetch the doctor and quickly. And you, Henry, rub the boy's chest with your warm hands.'

Still pitifully whimpering his invocations, Henry took hold of his motionless son.

'Here, wipe his face and wet his lips with this flannel,' commanded Dai.

Pulling himself clear of the door, Enoch found his way to the upper decks, where the crew fought to recover the ship from the night's tempest. Seeing an officer, Enoch demanded a doctor. 'We must have a doctor. A boy is dying. Quickly, now!'

The officer, who had the look of a man beyond exhaustion, replied with unruffled patience and courtesy, 'And which cabin is that, sir?'

'Twenty-four.'

The officer again spoke calmly. 'The doctor is presently attending the needs of a lady in childbirth. I will have him attend you with the greatest urgency.'

Enoch returned to find a funereal air about the cabin.

* * *

It was more than three hours before the doctor arrived. The boy's condition had changed only insofar as his rapid, shallow breathing was now audible to the careful listener.

Completing his examination, the doctor announced that William was suffering from nervous shock, dehydration, severe pain and a weak constitution. He promised to return later in the day and then, directing his instructions to no one in particular, said, 'In the meantime, continue with the current regime of rehydration, employing warm water drinks with a pinch of both salt and sugar.'

'Will he live?' asked the boy's father.

'We'll know tomorrow.' Casting his gaze around the cabin, the doctor added, 'I suggest you spend the intervening time cleaning this filth.' With that, he turned and left.

* * *

Throughout the day, the storm ebbed, and with each passing hour, with Henry gently cradling his son, signs of life returned. At first, weak tremors in his limbs, then the boy's eyelids flickered, as if he were trying to force them open; then colour flushed his pallid lips.

By 6pm, the boy was awake. His eyes were open, and he was conscious, but speaking more than a whispered word was an effort beyond his strength. The doctor returned at 9pm to administer an unexplained palliative, instructing that the boy drink plenty of water and sleep. 'And as for you, gentlemen,' the doctor said, 'I suggest only dry bread and water until breakfast. By which time your appetites will be raging.'

As the cabin door closed behind the doctor's departure, the three men gave out jubilant whoops of joy, slapping each other heartily on the back. They felt the unbreakable bond that had been forged between them, but their celebratory mood did not last as it gave way to tiredness. Dai slept noisily; Henry comforted his son; and Enoch lay thinking of Eliza. God had spared him an untimely death; this must mean something. He would send for Eliza the moment he docked.

EIGHT

At 10am on Monday, 2 May 1881, Enoch disembarked unnoticed onto the Rue Sainte Antoine in French-speaking Quebec. He was wearing his new boots, cravat necktie with a pearl pin and a tailored three-piece suit of dark-brown worsted, adorned with a recently acquired gold pocket watch and fob. He had the appearance of a man of business and importance.

Enoch found the Grand Trunk Railway office a short distance from the port, where he hoped to buy a ticket to New York.

Twenty or more customers crowded the small, scruffy office. They looked careworn, bedraggled and in need of a hot meal. Most held Canadian government travel vouchers and, from their guttural, coarse accents and agrarian clothing, Enoch guessed they were immigrants recently arrived from Eastern Europe.

The counter assistant was a large woman in her mid-fifties, with silver-grey hair drawn into a tight bun. She wore a high-necked black dress with a neat, white lace collar. Enoch was pleased to hear her speak some pidgin English, even though it was difficult to understand what was being said with such a strong Canadian-French accent.

After more than an hour of waiting, Enoch's turn arrived.

He spoke slowly. 'One ticket to New York.' He indicated the one with a raised index finger.

'When?'

'Today.'

'First class, or…' The woman glanced over his shoulder, nodding towards those crowding the office behind him. Enoch took the hint.

'Yes, first.'

'Fifteen minutes past the two. Arrive seven and forty next morning. Change Montreal for DH.' She wrote it down. 'American?' she asked.

'No. English.'

'Name?'

'Henry Mason.'

'Address?'

'St James Hotel, Broadway.' Enoch had seen the hotel displayed on an advertising poster and guessed it was one of New York's finest hotels. Too expensive for his pocket, but at least it was an address.

She handed him his ticket with a yellow form headed "Foreign Visitor Immigration Notice", on which his name, coach, seat number and hotel address were written. 'Give to *le contrôleur*,' she said, calling forward the next in line.

By this time tomorrow, he thought, *I'll be safe in New York, lost in its labyrinth of streets*. And he was pleased with his new name: Henry Mason. Buying his ticket had been the first time he had spoken it aloud. It sounded trustworthy and reliable and was easy to remember. Who would have cause to think that Henry Mason of New York was the same person as Enoch Price of London?

At the main post office on Fort Street, he posted a letter to Eliza. It simply informed her of his safe arrival. He then took a luncheon of soup and bread in a poorly appointed café opposite the train station. He had considered walking up the city ramparts to take in the view from the old citadel but decided against it. The effort required to climb the steep, cobbled streets would be too much; the voyage had tired and sapped his strength.

As the Cathedral-Basilica of Notre-Dame de Québec rang out 2pm, Enoch made his way through the station to the waiting train. Settling into his carriage, a lady of middle age joined him. Enoch recognised from the quality and cut of her fashionable clothes that she was of discerning taste and wealth. He watched as she made herself comfortable. Turning to Enoch, she said, 'Excuse me for being so presumptuous, but may I introduce myself?' She spoke with confidence in a refined American accent. 'My name's Kitty Morgan. I'm from Albany, New York State. It's so nice to meet you. Are you travelling far today?'

'How do you do?' he replied. 'I'm on my way to New York and then—'

'Well, that's so exciting. You must be English. Am I right?'

'Yes, I arrived this morning and—'

'That's wonderful. I've never been to Europe. I'd love to see London and Paris. Have you been to New York before? Do you have friends waiting for you?'

'I've friends who settled there some years ago and—'

'Well, that's nice. At least you've someone to meet you. I'm sorry, I didn't catch your name.'

'Mr Henry Mason and—'

'Henry. Well, I expect everyone calls you Harry. I always think Henry is too… well, you know, too formal. My name's Kathryn, but I much prefer Kitty. It sounds… well, less formal. Don't you agree, Harry?'

Before he could reply, Kitty continued. 'Now, you must tell me, Harry, what line of business are you in? We're in glass, for windows, not tumblers or spectacles, you understand. We make a lot of it; at least, that's what my husband tells me. He says we've glazed most of Manhattan; mind you, I'm not sure that's strictly true.' She gave a charming laugh, which suited her petite frame.

He noticed she had beautiful blue eyes, and from under her fashionable bonnet, he could see ample waves of pale straw-coloured hair.

'Tell me, Harry, have you ever visited Paris?'

'Briefly, I was there on—'

'Is it like Montreal or Quebec? Do you speak French, Harry?'

'No. Unfortunately, I—'

'That's a pity. My sister, Minnie, speaks French. I'm on my way to visit her; she lives in Montreal. She's married the most handsome French-Canadian gentleman. He does all kinds of things: property, banking and something with trees. What did you say your line of business is, Harry?'

Avoiding any mention of timber, he said, 'I manufacture ladies' garments and—'

'Ladies' garments! In heaven's name! Which ladies' garments, exactly?' she said extravagantly, teasing him.

'Bodices and corsets of the highest quality. I use only the—'

'Oh, my goodness. You do surprise me. I can't wait to tell Minnie. She'll be so envious. Imagine that! I met a man on the train who makes undergarments for us dear ladies. How exciting.'

The collector arrived, and Enoch passed him his ticket and yellow immigration form. Studying it, he read aloud as if talking to himself, 'Mr Henry Mason. The St James Hotel, Broadway.'

'No! Really! You're staying at the St James on Broadway?' exclaimed Kitty. 'Ladies' undergarments must be a profitable line.' She again smiled and gave a gentle laugh, then, turning to the ticket collector, said, 'He's called Harry, you know. He's from England.'

The man nodded. 'Yes, ma'am.' He didn't ask to see Kitty's ticket and moved on to the next carriage.

Kitty said, 'Listen, Harry, there's a great restaurant car on the D and H. Book a late dinner and get a bottle of wine, then take your ease in their wonderful dining chairs.' She paused a moment to delicately tuck a lace handkerchief into her cuff. 'Now, tell me about Paris. I want to hear it all.'

Kitty made herself comfortable, listening as Enoch spun a tale of Paris and the exclusive materials used in the bodices manufactured by his London & Paris Corset Company. Never having visited Paris, he imagined it to be like the best parts of London and, with some assistance from Michael's description and his recently read novel by Victor Hugo, he impressed Kitty with his familiarity of the city.

'Harry, you make it sound so wonderful. No sooner I'm home, I'm having my husband book a trip.'

Three hours after departing from Quebec, they arrived in Montreal, and Kitty alighted. 'It's been a real privilege meeting you, Mr Harry Mason. And it's been the most enjoyable journey. If ever you're in Albany, you must visit. It won't be as grand as the St James, but we'll make you welcome. And bring some of your beautiful garments.' Her captivating smile again crossed her lips, and with that, she stepped away, giving a brief wave.

Collecting his case and following other passengers, he changed platforms to the Delaware and Hudson Railway. As he settled into his new carriage, he was still thinking of Kitty Morgan. Were all American women so charming? "It's been a real privilege meeting you, Mr Harry Mason", she had said, making it sound so American. She had made him feel good about his new name. From now on, he would be Harry Mason.

* * *

For the rest of his journey, he was alone – the overnight train was obviously not a popular choice. As Kitty had suggested, he dined late and was the last when the stewards began tidying and setting the tables for breakfast. Making himself comfortable, he slept undisturbed.

At 5am, the train slowed to a juddering halt. Harry was shaken from his slumber by a steward offering him coffee. 'Excuse me, sir, but I think this is where you must return to your carriage.' He spoke politely but left no room for objection.

'Where are we?' asked Harry.

'This is Albany, sir. We have some business folk joining the train.'

The journey south towards New York was a slow, monotonous wake-up. Rattling along from the grey light of dawn towards bright morning sunlight, through deserted stations to crowded platforms, each becoming busier as the city drew closer and the working day nearer. The train was crowded by the time it arrived at Hoboken Ferry, where passengers transferred across the Hudson River to Christopher Street Pier and their onwards connection to Grand Central Terminal at the heart of Manhattan.

As the train drew to its final halt, the attendant walked through the coaches repeatedly announcing, 'New York! New York! End of the line.'

Everyone around Harry got to their feet, impatiently inching towards the exit. From his window seat, Harry could see crowds thronging the platform.

Harry was amongst the last to alight, and, as the crowd dispersed, a stillness returned to the empty platform where only the hiss and whistles of the resting engine broke the silence. The coach attendant, who had followed him out, said, 'Do you need some help, sir?'

'No. Thank you. I'm going to sit for a moment,' replied Harry, taking one of the nearby benches. *So, this is America*, he thought. There was a lot to take in, and already, he seemed a very long way from home.

NINE

A draught of cold, early morning air felt crisp after the stuffy warmth of the train. Pulling himself up from the bench, Harry followed the last of the passengers onto the concourse and towards great shafts of golden sunlight streaming in through tall, arched windows. He found himself in the marbled nave of an enormous cathedral. For a moment, he stood in awe, admiring the ornate walls and vaulted ceilings. Those jostling past seemed unaware of the grandeur of their surroundings, heads bowed, hurrying through the heavy double doors onto the bustling street and into the dusty air of the city.

The sidewalks were already teeming with movement and awash with noise and a kaleidoscope of colour. His first breath made him heady from the aromas of fresh baking, roasting coffee, boiling sugar and cigars. This was a city enthusiastic for the coming day.

Dragging his case onto the sidewalk, the sights and sounds swirling around him stopped him in his tracks. He was momentarily disoriented. Bewildered, he gazed from side to side and, feeling dizzy, staggered for support against the granite of the station walls.

'You okay, sir?' enquired a tall, middle-aged man wearing a bright-red top hat and matching commissionaire's frock coat, trimmed with gold braid. 'You look as if you're in need of an excellent hotel, sir? The Grand Union is the best in the city. We have a good bathhouse and barbershop, and there's a great restaurant serving a delicious hot breakfast, all at an affordable price. It's straight opposite. There it is, sir, just across the street.' With his white-gloved hand, the hotel doorman was pointing. 'I'll get a porter to collect your case, sir.'

Harry realised he hadn't washed since leaving the ship, and his new suit was crumpled and looked slept in. 'No. No, thank you. I need to get to Broadway. I'm looking for the Clyde Steamship Company at 290 Broadway, near Reade Street.' He was reading from an advertisement torn from the pages of a ship's magazine he had read during the crossing.

The doorman replied helpfully, 'Yes, sir. You need a streetcar going south on Park Avenue, or take the Harlem trolley. I can see it on the corner right this minute.' He indicated the junction opposite. 'There, sir. That's the one you need.'

Harry hurried across the crowded street, dodging between the many horse-drawn carts, streetcars and carriages. The cacophony of noise was deafening. Reaching the omnibus, he sat awkwardly with his case perched precariously on his knees and spent the ride staring out onto the bustling streets and crowded sidewalks. He closed his eyes, recalling the familiarity of London. He wished Eliza was with him.

'Hey! You, the guy for Broadway and Reade? This is it. This is where you get off.' The voice of the conductor brought him to his senses. Stumbling over his case, he fell to the sidewalk. Struggling to his feet, he admonished himself, 'Come on, Enoch, pull yourself together. You've gotta keep going.'

The Clyde Steamship office was open, and he was pleased to see that he was its only customer. He stood in the quiet of the shop, admiring the many colourful travel posters decorating its walls.

'You okay, mister?' enquired the clerk, an elfin young girl, perhaps no more than eighteen, with alabaster skin and raven-black hair woven into a plait.

Harry looked surprised. 'I'm sorry; I didn't see you.'

'Well, I've been here as plain as day ever since you came clattering the doorbell. You're English, if I'm not mistaken, and fresh off the boat by the look of you.' She spoke with a broad Irish accent.

Harry pulled the folded magazine advertisement from his pocket and handed it over.

'Jacksonville,' she said. 'Well, it's pretty in winter, so they say, but like the ovens of hell in summer, with flying bugs as big as blackbirds.'

Disappointed with the girl's response, Harry replied, 'But the article says it's a fast-growing city with plenty of opportunities to prosper.'

'You can't believe everything you read, not in this country.'

'Have you been there?' he enquired.

'God, no. Never been further than Staten Island, which I can tell you is a shithole compared to the beauty of Kerry.'

Harry laughed. 'Well, I'll give it a chance.'

'Next sailing is Friday at 3pm. Pier 36, South Street.'

Harry nodded and asked, 'What day is it?'

'Today is Wednesday, all day. And your next question is, where's the nearest boarding house? Or is it a hotel you'll be wanting?'

'A boarding house will be fine.'

'The nearest is Mrs Bennett's on Chamber Street. But to be honest with you, I wouldn't even send an Englishman there. You'll be better off making the effort to get yourself to Mrs O'Neill on Oliver Street. She's a horrible woman; the beds are hard; and it smells, but her cooking is good; the price is reasonable; and she's as honest as the day is long.'

'Will she take an Englishman?' asked Harry in good humour.

'If your money's good, she'll take in anyone: Italians, Poles, even Jews.'

Harry paid for his ticket and walked the few blocks along Worth Street towards Mrs O'Neill's lodging house.

Mrs O'Neill was a woman not to be trifled with. Short and stocky, with grey hair on her chin and small piggy eyes that glared defiance. Her arms, resolutely folded across her ample chest, were those of a dockyard porter. She showed Harry to a first-floor room, a partition of a larger room originally five or six times its size, but now just large enough for a narrow bed and space to stand. The great benefit of the room, which Mrs O'Neill pointed out more than once, was access to both daylight and fresh air through a sash window shared across a thin partition with the adjoining bedroom. A chamber pot, along with a washing dish and jug of water, were stowed under the bed. The privy was in the backyard. Breakfast and dinner were included. The front door was locked after dark at 9pm.

'How many nights?' she asked.

'Two.'

'Payment in advance. Dinner's at seven. Be prompt and only after you've washed and shaved. The barber is at the end of the street. There's no drinking, spitting or blaspheming on the premises; some of our guests are respectable young ladies.' With that, she closed the door and thudded heavily back down the stairs.

A few moments later, Harry followed her down and out onto the street. On the corner with Henry Street was a small diner. It didn't amount to a restaurant, but it served hot food and coffee. He ate cheese omelette, ham, fried potatoes and hot biscuits with gravy. The coffee was bitter and weak, but he drank plenty of it with several heaped spoons of sugar.

When he had finished, he crossed the street to the barber for a haircut, hot towel shave and his moustache trimmed into shape. He felt a sense of comfortable optimism as he wandered in the warm spring air back to Mrs O'Neill's. But as he climbed the dark staircase to his room, weariness descended over him like a heavy cloak; his boots filled with lead and his eyes with grit. He lay on his bed and slept soundly.

He woke late in the afternoon and, feeling revived, counted through his money. What remained was enough for another week, perhaps a little longer if he was frugal. Changing back into his worn travelling attire, he left for a stroll around the block.

The streets were crowded and busy. Both women and men sat on front stoops smoking clay pipes, and children ran like feral cats in all directions. Horse-drawn wagons congested the thoroughfares while pushcarts with canvas canopies, selling every conceivable item, lined the streets in all directions: fruit and vegetables, fish, meat, pots and pans, firewood, all manner of tools and clothing of every description. In places, groups of men gathered around a game of shell and pea, with every language spoken and shouted from one side of the street to the other. From time to time, gangs of roughs appeared from dark alleyways, cast their inspecting gaze across their patch before retreating into the shadows. *London was bad*, thought Harry, *but this was worse*. Here, the veneer of civilisation was indeed thin.

On the corner of Elizabeth Street, he passed a rickety boxwood kiosk selling tobacco, cigars and matches. A man with Hispanic features, no taller than four and a half feet, his head disproportionately too large for his body, stood lazily outside. Harry enquired about an ounce of Black Shag tobacco and immediately wished he hadn't. Without warning, the man grabbed him by the wrist with an unbreakable grip. Pulling him close, he looked up with a toothless grin and a deep, empty socket where his left eye had once rested. Harry pulled to free his wrist, but the man held him firm.

'What you want black shit for? You want best cigars?' The man spoke with a rasping Mexican accent. 'I you friend. You buy five best cigars one dollar. Good price?'

Keen to retrieve his wrist, Harry said, 'Yes. Good. I'll buy.' The exchange completed, the man released his hold. As Harry turned to leave, a newsboy stood defiantly blocking his way, a newspaper held outstretched.

'Your paper, mister. You can read while you smoke.'

Harry thanked him, paid and took the paper. Now fearing the consequences of any lateness for dinner, he hurried along Mott Street back towards his lodgings.

At 6.30am the following day, he was woken by loud banging. He had slept well, even though, as the Irish girl predicted, the bed was hard, and it smelled too.

'Breakfast in thirty minutes. Rise and shine.' It was Mrs O'Neill. *She ran a tight ship*, thought Harry.

Breakfast was good, as had been dinner the previous evening.

He spent the morning lounging lazily on his bed, reading his newspaper and smoking a Havana cigar. It was his first and he liked its fragrant and mellow smoke. His newfound pleasure of reading was heightened further when his attention was drawn to the sensational headline "Billy the Kid Escapes Hanging" reporting how the infamous outlaw had escaped hanging by shooting two sheriffs in a jailbreak in New Mexico.

Harry's attention was next drawn to an article about an upcoming world heavyweight prizefight between the world champion John L. Sullivan and the New York champion, John Flood, to be staged at a place called Yonkers on the Hudson River.

Harry thought of Michael and Conor. How he wished they could be with him to watch the fight.

By mid-afternoon, he decided to walk the short distance to Pier 36 in preparation for the following day. Walking along Henry Street, he was struck by the putrid smell of garbage littering the gutters and the barefoot urchins wandering aimlessly amongst the squalid filth. Through open windows, he saw hard-working men, women and children hunched over sewing machines endlessly whirring as they fed through the cloth. Their dark, sunken eyes in sallow faces were filled with despair. It reminded him of Izod's sweatshop at

Spitalfields, and, just as in London, these poor souls, driven from their homes by tyranny or hunger, had come in search of a better life. Only to discover that their newfound freedom was hardly any better, a bitter choice between starvation or endless toil as waged slaves, driven on by the slender hope of a brighter future for their children.

* * *

Turning at Montgomery Street, Harry began his return journey. By 4.30pm, he had reached the corner of Catherine Street when, without warning, he was kicked hard at the back of his knees. Losing balance, he stumbled forward. Gathering himself, he swung around just in time to see two small urchin boys, aged no more than eight or nine, disappear down a narrow alley. Before he could straighten himself, a thudding blow winded him. Pulling himself up to confront his assailant, he faced four skinny, cadaverous-looking teenage boys. Their bulging eyes, too big for their weasel faces, stared menacingly. The tallest of the boys held a knife at Harry's stomach.

'Your money, or I'll slit your guts.'

Harry felt the rage of indignation boil deep inside him, but before his anger could erupt, the boy grabbed him by the lapel and pulled him near. So near, Harry could feel the boy's lips touching his own. He snarled, spitting through blackened teeth, the stench of his breath sickening. 'Now!' he shouted. Harry's knees buckled as the blade cut into him. The other boys had their hands about him, plunging into every pocket, searching and grabbing at anything within. A second later, they were gone.

Harry was on his knees. Feeling at his stomach; his hands were wet with blood. He stumbled sideways, falling awkwardly against a wall. No one paid any attention as they hurried on by, some cussing him for obstructing their way.

Blood soaked into his trousers. He knew the bleeding must be staunched. Relaxing, he slowed his breathing. Pulling a rag from his pocket, he slipped it under his shirt to where he could feel the open wound. His fingertips gingerly explored the gash, the folds of cut flesh spreading apart on his touch. The blood was wet without stickiness; he was still bleeding. Clenching his teeth, he jammed the cloth into the wound, letting out a muffled scream before slumping against the wall. He needed help. Straining every sinew, he pushed himself up and staggered half-bent towards his lodgings. Turning into Oliver Street, an old woman pushed him to his knees.

'Drunken fool,' she shouted.

With the sheer force of willpower, he stumbled the final yards to where Mrs O'Neill was sitting on her front stoops. Seeing blood oozing through his fingers, she summoned help to have him carried to the kitchen and laid upon the large table. Stripping his clothing to expose the wound, she called to someone on the street to bring a doctor.

'How did this happen?' she asked.

'Robbed. Young boys cut me,' he replied in a whisper.

A small girl ran breathlessly into the kitchen. 'The doctor can't be found, Mrs O'Neill. Shall I run for the constable?'

'No. No police,' said Harry, gasping with the effort.

'Not that they'd be a fat lot of good,' said Mrs O'Neill, leaning over to examine his side. 'I'm going to clean your wound with spirit and iodine. Then I'll stitch you.'

'What about the doctor?'

'We can't wait. It's a clean wound, although, three inches to the right and you'd have been a goner.'

'Have you done this before?' asked Harry, sounding concerned.

'Plenty, and delivered babies and prepared corpses too. Don't worry, I'll go gentle, but by the look of you, you're no stranger to the infirmary.'

* * *

An hour later, Harry was sitting up drinking sweet black coffee.

'How do you feel?' she asked.

'Sore as hell. But I'm grateful; I thought I was going to bleed out.'

'Did they rob you of much?'

'A few dollars, a pipe, a cigar and a book. My money's safely upstairs. I've enough to keep me going 'til I find work.' After a brief moment, he said, 'You said you'd stitched before?'

'Nursing with the Women's Association in the Civil War.' She sighed deeply. 'There was a lot of suffering in those days, mostly young boys – it changed everything.'

'Do you mind me asking, and tell me to be quiet if you wish, but where's Mr O'Neill?'

'Killed at Fredericksburg, a captain fighting on the Union side.' She fell silent before adding, 'He was thirty-five. There was no need for him to have gone, but he insisted on volunteering. He said it was his duty to fight for justice. He was an honest lawyer and said, "How can I serve the law if I don't fight for justice?" That was twenty years ago.

'We've three sons. They're all married with families and have moved away – Boston, Chicago and California – all gone in search of a better life. They write from time to time, mostly at Christmas and Thanksgiving.' She broke off, reflecting on happier times. After a long silence, she said, 'I was born in this house. We were married opposite at St Nicholas. Mind you, I was a slip of a girl in those days, thin as a pencil, with beautiful golden curls and the voice of an angel, even if I say so myself. After the ceremony, my father put on a wonderful spread with plenty to eat and drink. My people were from County Clare. Father was proud of his new life. "We're all Americans now," he used to say. "The future's bright, and we'll never go hungry again." After he passed, Daniel and I made this our home.'

Her thick hand found a silver locket on a delicate chain around her neck. She caressed it gently and said, 'I still miss him, you know. I miss him every day.'

As she spoke, Harry heard the gentle voice of a young woman, now laced with sadness and regrets.

'I don't know your name,' she said.

'Harry Mason.'

'Well, Mr Harry Mason, with that gash out your side, you'll need to rest and stay awhile, you don't want infection setting in.'

'I've a ticket for the steamer tomorrow afternoon.'

She slowly nodded and then asked, 'And your wife?'

'I'm a widower this past year. I'm sad to say she died from consumption.'

'And the children?'

'They're with my mother, back in England: three girls, seven, eleven and twelve.'

'Do you think you'll ever see them again?'

'Soon, I hope. Once I'm settled, they'll join me. I've promised we'll be together by Christmas.'

'They'll need a mother, but a handsome man like yourself, with prospects too, you'll have no difficulty finding a wife.'

'First, I must find work.'

'There's plenty here,' she said in the way of an offer. 'And there's room for three growing girls – I can always do with extra hands.'

'I thank you for your kindness, Mrs O'Neill, but I can't. I've a plan, and I'm committed to following it.'

'I know,' she said. 'My husband was the same. Nothing could dissuade him from his course – he believed that whatever he did would turn out for the best. But I don't blame him. God rest his soul.'

TEN

The next day, Harry took a cab to Pier 36 on South Street and, walking hesitantly, boarded the steamship *Delaware*, which, at precisely 3pm, moved away from the quayside and out into the East River. The ship made good progress, hugging the eastern seaboard as it headed south.

Harry had a small but elegant cabin to himself. A rattan table and chair were positioned on an open verandah, allowing him the pleasure of watching the coast drift past, and it was here that he spent most of the voyage, smoking cigars, reading and writing to Eliza.

* * *

7 May 1881
My dearest wife,

You are my treasure. With difficulty, I seek to find words sufficient to tell you of my love and how much I miss you. My adorable Eliza, mere words created by the wit of man cannot tell you how often I think of you each and every day. An hour doesn't pass that you are not in my thoughts. Each morning and evening, I think of how we will soon be together in each other's arms.

My greatest sadness is not seeing our three loving daughters. I miss them greatly and expect they, in equal measure, miss their loving father too.

I cannot express the extent and depth of my sorrow at how life has led us to this temporary condition of separation. But we shall turn misfortune to our advantage.

This is a land of plenty and opportunity, and together we will seek a better future where we can prosper in peace and safety and find happiness together.

When I am settled, and in employment, I will send for you directly.

Now, let me tell you about my travels so far. Much has happened since…

* * *

He continued his correspondence over several more pages, telling of his experiences aboard the *Polynesian*, the journey to New York and his hopes for a new life in Florida. Satisfied with his letter, he put it to one side, ready for posting on arrival at Jacksonville. After a light lunch, he made his way to the upper deck to spend the remainder of the afternoon reading *Harper's Magazine*.

It was here that a well-dressed, middle-aged gentleman of slight build and dapper appearance, wearing a pale-blue linen blazer, cream flannels and a straw boater decorated with a striped ribbon of several colours, approached.

'May I join you, sir?' he asked.

Harry offered an open hand of invitation.

'I couldn't help noticing that you're a man of intellect and enterprise and an avid reader of *Harper's*.'

Harry nodded in appreciation of the compliment.

Having made himself comfortable, the man continued. 'I can recognise a discerning and successful gentleman when I see one. Someone who sees an opportunity where others do not.' The man removed a folded paper from an inside pocket, placing it with care on the table.

'I'm on my way to Jacksonville,' he continued. 'Where I'm to complete the sale of prime real estate, and I'm sure a man of your vision and ambition will want to hear of my good fortune and share in the luck that providence has sent my way.'

Drawing his chair closer, he said, 'I know I can trust you, Mr...'

'Mason,' replied Harry.

'It's good to meet you, Mr Mason.'

They shook hands. 'My name is Franklin, James L. Franklin. I'm well known in Jacksonville and widely acknowledged for my honest dealings and integrity of the highest standard. Only last year, I assisted the renowned Mr Henry Flagler, of whom I'm certain you have heard, buy over a thousand acres of the best land in Florida.'

Lowering his voice, he confided, 'I will be truthful with you, Mr Mason, and I wouldn't tell everyone this, but I've several wealthy businessmen waiting my return from New York. You see, Mr Mason, I've just signed four of New York's most prosperous investors to our prestigious venture.'

He broke off for a moment to check that Harry was

following along and his interest had been whetted. 'This is a rare opportunity, Mr Mason. A once-in-a-lifetime chance to get ahead. A month ago, I had over a hundred plots of prime real estate available for the discerning buyer, and to no one's surprise, they were snapped up within the week – I literally had to fight them off.

'And now I've only a handful left, and they're sure to go just as fast. Indeed, these plots are certain to be sold today. But here's the thing, Mr Mason.' He drew closer. 'It's guaranteed to make you money, a lot of money.'

Harry remained silent, paying close attention to the proposition being laid out before him, slowly shaking his head, more in incredulity than rejection.

Undeterred, the man pressed on. 'A thousand dollars gets you a fabulous riverfront plot on the banks of the magnificent St Johns River. You'll be the envy of your friends and associates. Six months from now, it'll be worth five thousand, and in a couple of years, over $25,000. Just think what you could do with that kind of money.'

Harry, who had yet to speak, could see the man was experienced at his trade and knew his patter well.

'I'm sorry, Mr Franklin,' said Harry, 'but my funds are running low, and although it's a tempting offer, I don't feel I can afford the outlay, and I wouldn't want to waste any more of your time.'

Franklin continued with renewed enthusiasm. 'I understand you perfectly, Mr Mason. But it's not a thousand dollars today; it's not even half that. This truly is the chance of a lifetime, an opportunity not to be missed.' Pausing barely long enough to draw breath, the man raced on. 'I know I can trust you, Mr Mason. I can see you're a gentleman of good standing. It's just three hundred dollars today, and you can take your time to pay the rest. My office is right on Jacksonville's waterfront. It's a great deal. Just three hundred dollars gets you a piece of the best real estate in the state of Florida. Sign this minute, and that riverside plot is yours to enjoy, all guaranteed by the federal laws of the American government.'

He unfolded an impressive-looking contract headed in bold, blue lettering "Land Entitlement Deed", illustrated around its margins with images of the United States flag and rampant mythical beasts. 'Your signature and three hundred dollars are all that's needed to get you ownership of this exclusive plot of Florida. In a year, you'll be a rich man.'

Harry thought for a moment, but before he could answer, the man chipped in again.

'Mr Mason. You're a successful man; that's obvious to see. This is a guaranteed way to own the finest property in the fastest-growing state in the Union.'

Franklin then brought his pitch to a crescendo. 'There's no time like the present, and there's no time to waste. Nothing ventured, nothing gained.' Then, lowering his voice to emphasise the finale, he said, 'But I must have your decision before one of these other folk snatch it right from out my hand. Your signature and three hundred dollars and it's yours. You know it's the right thing to do, so let's make a deal.'

Harry, who by this time had become a little irritated by the sales patter, leaned forward. 'I'll tell you what I'll do, Mr Franklin. I can see you're a fair and decent man. You lend me three hundred dollars to get me started, and in six months, I'll return your money and give you half my profit on top. That way, we both get rich. I know I can trust you. What do you say? Let's shake on it.' Harry extended his hand in agreement.

'Are you trying to be funny?' exclaimed Franklin, raising his voice. 'This is America, the land of freedom and opportunity, and this is how we do business.'

Harry, looking dismissive, relaxed back in his seat.

Standing abruptly, knocking his chair tumbling noisily backwards, Franklin's face was no longer filled with optimism but carried an expression of contempt and anger. 'And get yourself some decent clothes. Who the hell wears brown tweed in summer? You look like another dumbass immigrant.'

Harry smiled and nodded in sarcastic appreciation of the advice.

As the spiv left, Harry noticed an attractive, tall, willowy young woman in her early thirties approach.

'Excuse me, sir. And I apologise for my unannounced intervention.'

Harry rose, welcoming the well-dressed lady.

'Please let me introduce myself. I'm Mrs Handley, Bessie Handley from New York. I was just listening to that dreadful man trying to trick you. I believe his type infest these boats.' She hesitated before adding, 'I know this sounds rather silly, but I was ready to step in and stop his phoney talk.'

'Thank you, ma'am,' said Harry. 'I too have heard of these cheats plying their deceptions on the coastal steamers; I believe they're called carpetbaggers. Am I right in saying so?'

'Well, as near as makes no difference,' she replied.

Harry asked, 'Would you like to join me for coffee?'

'No, thank you. I was only concerned that you didn't part with your money. I couldn't have forgiven myself.'

'I'm grateful to you. My name's Harry Mason and I've not long arrived in this country.' He waited, uncertain how to continue. 'I don't want to appear rude, Miss Handley, but—'

'Mrs,' she interrupted.

'I beg your pardon, Mrs Handley, but how can I be sure you're not working as a double act with this man, hand in glove, as it were?'

'Mr Mason! I can assure you I am not hand in... to think that I... I've never been so... my intentions...' She ran out of words and indignation, blushing as she turned to leave.

'I apologise,' he said, hurriedly adding, 'it was a poor joke and in bad taste. Please forgive me; I shouldn't have spoken so rudely.'

Accepting both his apology and then his insistence on sharing coffee and cakes, she seated herself while the waiter laid the table. Harry told her of his recent arrival to New York, and she, in turn, explained that she and her five-year-old son, John, were moving to the more sympathetic climate of Florida for the benefit of her son's poor health.

As she spoke, Harry was drawn in admiration of her bright, amber-brown eyes and flawless complexion. Once the waiter had moved away, she said, 'I noticed you last evening, Mr Mason. You were dining alone. You seemed to be in some discomfort, with difficulty standing from your chair. I hope you don't mind me saying, but you looked rather alone.'

'Actually, I had the misfortune of being set upon by a gang of ruffians.'

She was aghast. 'In New York?'

'Yes, three days ago. I'm still feeling bruised.'

'New York is so overcrowded and, even though I arrived there as a girl from Ireland, these days there are far too many immigrants, who, I'm sorry to say, have neither the manners nor ways of a civilised Christian country. But let us not speak of such matters. Tell me, Mr Mason, have you chosen Florida for your health, too?'

'Well, Florida wasn't my first choice. I first considered travelling to the frontier territories of the Wild West, to Tombstone or Dodge City. But, in the end, I decided I would be of little use in a gunfight or best suited to riding the prairies in search of buffalo.'

They both laughed and relaxed into an amiable conversation about their hopes for the future. Harry told her he had read several articles describing Jacksonville as a booming frontier city, doubling every few years. And how the railways and agreeable climate made it an ideal place for respectable folk to vacation during the harsh northern winters and that jobs were plentiful and quickly found.

'Are you travelling alone?' she ventured.

'Yes, I'm quite alone in the world. I'm looking for a new start, somewhere I can settle and prosper.'

'Tell me, Mr Mason, if you don't mind me asking, where are you staying? Do you have a hotel or lodgings arranged?'

'I haven't yet decided, Mrs Handley, and to be honest, my resources are at a low ebb, so wherever I stay must be inexpensive.'

'This is unfortunate news.' She continued, matter-of-factly, 'I'm staying at the Nicholls Hotel until I find a suitable boarding house.' She stood, preparing to take her leave. 'Well, it's been a pleasure meeting you, Mr Mason. I do hope you recover soon. Perhaps our paths will again cross.'

That evening, he looked for her at dinner and scouted the public rooms and bars without success.

* * *

The following morning, the SS *Delaware* entered the St Johns River and moored alongside Hogan Street jetty.

Descending the narrow gangway, Harry turned into West Bay Street, a busy thoroughfare lined with boarding houses, bars, warehouses, dry goods stores and attorneys.

The European House, a bar in the Dutch style, at 80–82 West Bay, was the first bar of any size he came upon. The proprietor, who was about Harry's age, was hanging a notice on the wall: Barman Wanted – Free Room & Board. The man was powerfully built, with a thick bull neck and a barrel of a chest. His muscular arms were decorated with tattoos of ships and girls' names, and a large, thick blond beard in the Amish style compensated for a tanned, bald head.

'You interested?' the man asked. 'It's a good room, free food, hard work with no pay.'

'I'll take it,' said Harry.

'I joke,' said the man, speaking with a Dutch accent. 'I pay, but most drink it.'

'That won't be me.'

'Then you get to keep the money,' said the owner with a broad grin. 'Have you tended bar before? Ever been in a fight?'

'Yes and plenty,' said Harry, answering both questions. 'I ran a pub in London.'

'You're English? What's your name?'

'Harry Mason.'

'Mine's Nicky, Nicky Arend.' With that, he slapped Harry hard on the back and gave out a roaring laugh. 'It's your lucky day, Harry.'

* * *

Harry's room was at the top of the three-storey building. Sparsely furnished with a bed, chest of drawers, a narrow table with a chair positioned near a window facing south across the St Johns River. The view looked out towards an expanse of lush woodland of unfamiliar trees: tall, majestic palms, citrus groves, gigantic oaks draped in hanging folds of silver moss and emerald-leaved trees festooned in brilliant scarlet and lavender blossom.

In the emptiness of his room, Harry's mind turned to home, his favourite armchair and mantlepiece cluttered with clay pipes, candlesticks and the old, chipped toby jug given by his grandmother. There was nothing familiar here, no slippers, teapot or sepia photographs. He cursed aloud, suddenly realising he hadn't brought a photograph of Eliza and the children. How could he have forgotten? He would write, telling Eliza of his new address and instructing her to make preparations to join him.

Sitting motionless on the edge of the bed, he stared blindly into space. His breathing was shallow. Instead of prison, he had chosen exile to a foreign shore where he was nothing, an empty shell, with no history, no wife, no family, no friends, no possessions. He'd lost everything. The fond embrace of Eliza, the playful giggling of his daughters, the familiar banter with Michael and his pals from favourite haunts, where he was known and gladly shaken by the hand, where he shared a past and where a good tale could be told – all were ghosts in this empty room. He had been cowardly to run, and now he was to pay the price, and a high price it was.

For the first time since watching his father die, he broke down in tears. His chest heaved as if to burst; his heart was breaking. He was utterly alone, and to what purpose this suffering?

ELEVEN

The heat and humidity of the Floridian summer gave way to the cooler, windy autumnal weather of November.

Harry had been working for Nicky for over six months, much longer than intended, and he had settled into a comfortable routine of early morning chores followed by a second shift in the evenings. During his afternoon breaks, he read or explored the town, learning the names of streets, landmarks and popular shops. He wrote weekly to Eliza, describing the agreeable climate, tropical fruits and flowers and the bountiful supply of fresh food, especially the incredible array of meats and fish.

Although he frequently wrote imploring Eliza to join him, her replies were less often and confined to a few lines about the children and life at the Baptist chapel, signing off with her usual loving felicitations. When Harry pointed to the infrequency of her correspondence, she pleaded that letter writing was not her forte and was reluctant to ask his mother for help. She made no mention of joining him.

Although disappointed, Harry persisted.

***

25 November 1881

My dearest Eliza,

They say absence makes the heart grow fonder. I can testify to its truth and confess to being lonely without you at my side.

Life here is good, and there is an abundance of opportunities and prospects to begin a business. The girls will be happy and soon make new friends. My work goes well, and I save a little each week. The town is clean and the people polite and kind. There are many Irish, German and French here, and we are all treated equal and free. There are more Negroes than you might have seen in London, but they are cheerful, have their own places and do not trouble us. I cannot think of any hindrance that can keep us from again being together. I left you with sufficient money for your journey here. Please employ it for its intended purpose and decide on the date when you will join me. I can meet you from the ship and, if you wish, we can settle somewhere other than Florida. We can begin again in Boston, New York or even California, where they say the climate is like a perpetual English summer. I still hold to the expectation of us being reunited by Christmas Day and will be sorely distressed if I were to spend it without you.

I implore you to arrive soon.

Your affectionate and loving husband,

Enoch.

* * *

Harry set off for the post office on East Bay, the letter securely tucked inside his coat pocket. He was coming to the realisation that Eliza arriving by Christmas was a diminishing prospect, and his cheerless mood reflected his disappointment. He couldn't understand her reluctance. What was preventing her from travelling?

'Well, my goodness! If I'm not mistaken is that Mr Harry Mason?'

He spun around, startled at hearing his name. 'Oh, Mrs Handley. Good morning. You quite surprised me.'

'How are you, Mr Mason? Fully recovered, I hope?'

'I am well and in gainful employment.'

She hesitated. 'Oh, please don't let me detain you from your work.'

'No. No, not at all. I was on my way to the post office, but there's no urgency. I'd be most interested to hear your news.'

'I'm on my way to Rivas and Koopman's, a fine bakery where excellent confections and coffee can be enjoyed. Would you like to accompany me, Mr Mason?'

'I'd be very pleased to do so, Mrs Handley.'

'In which case, I'd prefer it if you were to call me Bessie, and I should very much like to call you Harry.'

Their conversation began politely according to the norms of etiquette; it was, after all, six months since their conversation aboard the SS *Delaware*. But by the time they reached the bakery, they were chatting as friends.

Harry hesitated before entering what looked like a rather elegant patisserie.

'What is it?' she asked, sounding concerned.

'Bessie, I appreciate your company, but… but I wonder whether it's proper for a married woman to be seen taking coffee with a stranger. It may become the subject of gossip and reach the ears of your husband.'

Bessie laughed and took hold of his arm. He felt a jolt of excitement. This was the first time she had touched him. Indeed, it was the first intimacy since parting from Eliza eight months before.

'For goodness' sake, Harry. You're not a stranger, and, anyway, I'm a widow. Does that put your mind at ease?'

'I'm sorry, but I thought—'

'Don't say another word,' interrupted Bessie, as she selected the most prominent table near the front window, pleased to be seen in his company.

'Have you found suitable accommodation?' asked Harry.

'I'm resident at Miss Helen Broward's guest house on East Bay Street. She is the most genteel lady who is well versed in music and literature and is very kind to my son. She has made us feel properly at home. I couldn't be better placed. And what of yourself? Have you found lodgings, and what employment have you secured?'

'I work at the European House on West Bay. I run the saloon and generally manage on behalf of the proprietor, and I've good accommodation provided on the upper floor. It's only a temporary position, of course, just until I can establish myself in business.'

'Well, that is encouraging news. What business do you have in mind?'

'I've an idea for a guest house, perhaps a small hotel. Something popular with more discerning visitors.'

'It sounds very enterprising and such an exciting venture.'

Harry said, 'I don't wish to pry or cause upset with my enquiry, but when you say you're a widow... well, what I mean to say is—'

To save his embarrassment, Bessie cut in, 'My husband died suddenly five years ago. Our son was born a week after his death. It was a terrible shock.'

'I'm so sorry; please forgive me for asking – it was impertinent of me.'

'Not at all, our good Lord sends these things to test us,' she said with a deep sigh. 'Our son is named John after my husband, a daily reminder. But you too must know what it is to lose a loved one. Is that not so?'

'Yes, indeed,' he said. 'It's painful to lose a loved one so young. You have my sincere condolences.'

'Oh, I've done with all my crying, Harry. My faith in the Lord has kept me strong, and I wouldn't want John growing up surrounded only by sadness. My husband was a good man and made adequate provision. I'm fortunate in being...' Stopping short, she changed tone and continued, 'Now, let's not speak of it again. We have a delicious cake and good coffee to enjoy. Tell me, Harry, how did you celebrate yesterday's Thanksgiving Day?'

'To speak frankly, Bessie, I wasn't sure what to make of it.'

'Oh, you poor man, you're in great need of instruction on our American ways. So, tell me, what plans do you have for Christmas Day?'

'Christmas! Well, to tell the truth, I've not given it a thought.'

* * *

Before parting, they strolled through the city's public gardens which decorated the river's edge.

Bessie said, 'It's such a pleasure to promenade in the fresh air without a care in the world, don't you agree, Harry?' Enfolding her arm in his, she said, 'Especially in your company.'

It was sometime later before Harry returned to his room, exhilarated by the unexpected turn of events. His letter to Eliza, still deep in his jacket pocket, would have to wait for the following day's mail.

* * *

Harry was in the habit of rising well before dawn, yet Nicky was always up and already working.

'Come on, Harry, wake yourself. It's a beautiful morning, and we have plenty to do. Are you ready to work hard?'

Harry shuffled slowly into the bar, 'I'm ready to work until I drop,' he replied with dry amusement in his voice.

'This is not good, Harry. I don't want you dropping like a lame mule. I need you working even harder tomorrow.' Nicky laughed and slapped his thigh, congratulating himself on his riposte. 'And my wife has invited you to share our table on Christmas Day.'

Harry was genuinely pleased to receive the invitation. 'It would be a privilege and something to look forward to. Please thank Agnes for her kindness; she's a generous soul.'

'I hope you like meat; we've a horse to eat.' Again, Nicky thundered with laughter. Then, in an instant and without warning, he turned serious, grabbing Harry by the arm and pulling him roughly to one side. 'Now, listen to me,' he said, sounding earnest. 'I want to talk to you, man to man. Can I give you friendly advice?'

Without waiting for a reply, he continued, 'Harry, I mean this. You've been grieving the loss of your wife for too long. You must go forward and think of life. It's not good to be alone; it makes you old.' With that, he released his grip and, turning away, shouted over his shoulder, 'You need a wife; our table has four chairs, not three.'

* * *

The following afternoon, a small boy with short, blond hair came shyly into the saloon. Nicky, who was alone and resting lazily on his broom, was surrounded by a cloud of golden specks, drifting in narrow shafts of warm sunlight.

Nicky watched the boy as a cat watches a mouse. Treading cautiously, the boy approached the giant with trepidation. With his arm outstretched, he gingerly handed over an envelope. The moment the letter was securely taken between the giant's thick forefinger and thumb, the boy turned on his heels and ran for his life.

The letter was addressed to Mr Harry Mason, care of the European House.

Nicky bellowed at the top of his voice, 'Harry! Harry!'

Harry, who was in his room, came running with urgency. 'What? What the hell is it?'

'A letter.'

* * *

Dear Mr Harry Mason,

Mrs Bessie Handley and her son John cordially invite you to Christmas dinner at 5pm on Christmas Day, hosted by Miss Helen Muland Broward, 48 East Bay Street.

Your attendance will be much anticipated.

* * *

'What is it?' demanded Nicky. 'Bad news?'

Harry said nothing.

Snatching the note from his hand, Nicky read it aloud. 'So, you old dog, you took my advice!' And, like a madman, Nicky danced and pranced, waving his arms wildly like a bear stung by a bee.

Harry watched as Nicky sent furniture scattering as he frolicked one way and then the next. Eventually, coming to a rest facing Harry, he said breathlessly, 'You're not pleased?'

'What about Christmas with you and Agnes?'

'To hell with that!' shouted Nicky. 'Next year we have four chairs.'

* * *

It was less than three weeks to Christmas, and Harry waited for Eliza's reply. Would she arrive before the festive celebrations? Her remarkable resurrection would undoubtedly change his situation. He couldn't bring her to Jacksonville; that much was certain.

Not for the first time, Harry planned his escape. He would meet Eliza in New York and travel cross-country to

California, where he was confident of finding work. This is where they would settle in the comfortable climate of the West Coast.

But as things turned out, Christmas Day arrived with no word from Eliza.

* * *

The table at Miss Broward's was set for eight. Joining Helen were her four sisters – Maria, Margaret, Florida and Caroline – Bessie Handley, her son John and Harry.

The house was decorated most charmingly with paper streamers and large yellow candles filling the room with a welcoming scent.

Christmas dinner was clam soup, baked fish with hollandaise sauce and roast turkey with oyster dressing. Dessert offered a choice of Christmas plum pudding with brandy sauce or Charlotte Russe.

After dinner, small gifts were exchanged, and on the advice of Agnes, Harry gave an embroidered handkerchief to Bessie and a wooden toy horse to her son. In return, Harry received a gift of Havana cigars. The company then withdrew to the drawing room for carols sung around the piano, followed by a round of amusing party games, the most popular being blindman's bluff, which caused hilarious shrieks of laughter. Everyone took their turn to be *it*, which involved being blindfolded and groping around the room, attempting to find the other guests. When Harry's turn arrived, there was heightened excitement. Especially when, perhaps too quickly, he caught Bessie in his flailing arms, and she, pretending not to escape his hold, drew raucous hoots and whistles. Never had he enjoyed Christmas with such lively company.

As the evening came to a close, he thanked Miss Broward for so generously welcoming him into her home and for such an enjoyable party. He was about to wish Bessie a happy Christmas before taking his leave when she led him aside and out onto the front porch.

'Aren't you forgetting something?' she asked, producing from behind her back a sprig of mistletoe. Holding it above her head, she moved closer and kissed him. Stepping away, she said, 'Thank you, Harry. It's been a wonderful Christmas, and we are certain of finding happiness in the New Year.' She gently squeezed his hand before returning indoors.

Back at his room, Harry's mind would not rest. Every moment of the evening, every word, every look, every touch was replayed over and over. Sleep would have to wait.

TWELVE

January was busy, with crowds of visitors coming ashore from the many steamships and paddle boats arriving from the north, with trains disgorging thousands more. It was as if most of Boston, New York and Philadelphia were escaping the snow and bitter cold of their northern winter, and the days quickly passed as Harry worked from before dawn until the early hours.

Several weeks passed before Harry again heard from Bessie. At the end of January, he received a note inviting him to attend choir practice at the Church of the Immaculate Conception on East Duval Street. Other than drunken, bawdy ditties, Harry had never sung, let alone in a choir, and he wasn't a Catholic, nor even a frequent churchgoer, and was reluctant to accept, but he didn't want to miss the chance to again see Bessie. He had four days to think it over.

The following day, a letter arrived from Eliza. The first since October.

* * *

20 January 1882

My dearest husband,

Thank you for your letter. I have used the money you kindly enclosed wisely. Although, I do confess to some indulgences for the children. You were in our thoughts and prayers at Christmas, and we hope your spirits were lifted.

Bertha has started work at Horlick's Bakery, a short walk from home on the Wells Road. Florence is at school but has the promise of employment with Frappell's Dairy, and Beatrice attends Mrs Hall's School for Young Ladies; your mother and John are generously meeting the fees. All our daughters attend Bible class and our chapel's Sunday school. Life here is settled and comfortable.

I miss you and wish you had never left us behind. I'm lonely, and my heart feels empty without you. Daily I think of joining you, but my fear of the crossing and venturing into the tropics and the unknown is an impediment too much. Your situation is of equal concern. You have yet to establish yourself in business or find a home of your own. A bartender is far removed from your intentions to trade whalebone and furs in Canada. As things stand, it is unlikely I will be able to join you until the girls are older and Beatrice has finished her education, at which she excels.

Such a lot has changed since the events of last year.

Love and best wishes from us all.

Always in our thoughts and prayers.

Your faithful and adoring wife,

Eliza.

* * *

How much longer did she intend waiting? Another year or two and the girls would be approaching womanhood. He could hear the domineering voice of his mother echoing from between the lines and felt his disappointment turn to anger. He did not reply.

* * *

Arriving for choir practice, Harry was both nervous and excited. But his enthusiasm was soon dampened on discovering that the men were separated from the women across the aisle, giving him only an occasional glimpse of Bessie, obscured amongst the opposite back row.

He felt awkward in the unfamiliar surroundings and was thankful when it was all over and he could escape back onto the street to wait for Bessie to join him.

Surrounded by a gaggle of chattering women, Bessie emerged onto the stone steps leading from the church entrance. Barely acknowledging him, her greeting was coolly formal as she passed without a second glance. But once out of sight of the others, she drew closer and brushed his hand as they walked. 'I'm so pleased you could make it,' she said. 'I've thought much of you these past few weeks.' Drawing closer, she said, 'It's such a beautiful day; shall we promenade in the park and have coffee at Rivas & Koopman's?'

Harry readily agreed and folded her arm in his.

With evident pleasure, she said, 'We must look quite the couple, don't you think?'

* * *

Choir practice, followed by coffee, became a weekly routine. However, on one such occasion nearing the end of March, just as they were preparing to leave the choir, they were surprised by the arrival of the avuncular Reverend O'Reilly. 'I see you two people have become close friends during our singing practice,' he said. 'And a fine thing it is too. Although I'm bound to say, Bessie, I'm disappointed you've not introduced your young man before now.'

Harry felt heat rising around the gills.

'I beg your pardon, Father,' she said. 'This is Mr Harry Mason. We met at Christmas, and I only noticed him attending choir a few weeks ago.'

'Well, I can see you're both getting along like a house on fire, and it warms the heart of an old man to see it.' Then, turning to Harry, Father O'Reilly said, 'It's good to meet you, Mr Mason. I do hope you'll be taking Mass with us next weekend, on Easter Sunday, a celebration of new beginnings.'

Harry, who had not given it a thought, said, 'Yes, of course, Father.'

'Good. I knew you wouldn't want to miss our special day.' With that, he bade them farewell.

Once outside, Harry cursed, 'Goddammit! Mass on Easter Sunday.'

'Harry, don't be so irreverent. Easter is the celebration of our Lord's Resurrection.'

'I know what it is; how could I forget? But I'm not Catholic, and I haven't a clue about Mass, let alone on Easter Sunday.'

'Don't worry. I'll tell you everything, and we can practise together.'

Bessie took great joy in introducing Harry to the ways of the Catholic faith, although secretly, Harry couldn't take it seriously: the bread and wine, the incense and candles, the Latin and the chanting. Yet, he never failed to enjoy his time with Bessie as they rehearsed the many rituals.

* * *

Early in May, Bessie received an urgent telegram informing her that her father had passed away and she must return urgently to New York.

In Bessie's absence, Harry filled his days with the distraction of work, but with the intense summer heat, business slowed to a trickle as the town emptied of visitors. By August, the sun burned fiercely, and thoughts turned only of keeping cool, either lazing on the banks of the St Johns River or with Nicky and Agnes aboard the pleasure steamer to Mayport Beach.

It was here that, after leisurely picnics, and while Nicky dozed listlessly in the dunes, Harry listened to Agnes talk of literature, philosophy and the arts. She was a sparrow of a woman with long, almost-white, blonde hair, pale, crystal-blue eyes and remarkable intellect. In the saloon, she said little; this was Nicky's domain, but on lazy, endless days on the beach, without the burden of daily chores, she spoke thoughtfully, in clear threads, which together wove into a rhythm of sense. Some days, they stayed on the dunes until late into the evening, until Nicky would raise himself up, stretch, yawn and say, 'You see, Harry, behind every successful man is a good woman.'

After one of their afternoon picnics, Nicky, without preamble or warning, asked Harry, 'When are you marrying Bessie?'

Harry, who was sleepily reading, said, 'What do you mean?'

'Harry, I've told you before. You can't prosper without a good wife.'

Having been caught off guard, Harry spoke without thinking. 'I can't.'

'What do you mean, you can't?' enquired Agnes, as she absent-mindedly tossed small, bleached seashells into the ocean.

'I'm not Catholic,' he replied, his mind racing to catch up.

'That doesn't mean you can't marry,' she said, turning to face him. 'You're both widowed and free to marry by licence at the town hall.'

'Bessie is committed to her church and wouldn't agree to a civil marriage.' Harry felt himself drifting into deep water and wished Nicky hadn't ambushed him.

'So, you've discussed it with her?' questioned Agnes.

'Not in so many words.'

More kindly, Agnes said, 'In my experience, Harry, a woman in love would rather be married than not, and the marriage can be sanctified in the sight of God by a blessing at her church. I'm sure Bessie would agree to that.'

In a last, desperate attempt to escape, Harry said, 'I'm nearly forty and ten years older.'

'Now you sound like you're making excuses,' scoffed

Nicky. 'Not Catholic, too old, not by license. Next, you'll be telling us you're already married.'

'Perhaps you should speak with the priest,' said Agnes, trying to ease his discomfort.

Harry reluctantly agreed and retreated silently into his own thoughts.

* * *

Trips to Mayport grew fewer as the heat gave way to the cool of autumn skies. Harry was alone on the back porch watching the last golden rays of a crimson sun gently dip below the horizon. Surveying thin trails of smoke, twisting in intricate swirls and loops from his cigar, he reflected on his passage from the hardships of cutting whalebone for Izod to the ease and splendour of Florida. It was idyllic. If only Eliza had followed, they would have found happiness and together would have prospered. Perhaps he should return to collect her and start again in California.

Agnes quietly padded by and, in the whisper of an angel, said, 'Halcyon days, Harry. Enjoy them while you can; they don't last forever.'

* * *

It had been over eighteen months since Harry arrived in Jacksonville, and Eliza was still undecided whether to join him. Even though he wrote often and regularly sent money, her letters came less frequently, and with each passing month, the prospect of her arrival became ever more remote.

With the support of his mother, Eliza had built an untroubled life of comfortable routines and steady progress, and Harry could imagine the difficulty she faced, trading agreeable habits for uncertain beginnings in a foreign land. But he couldn't wait forever; he had to decide. Was Jacksonville his home or a stepping stone, a way station on a longer trail?

* * *

Bessie returned from New York, and their habit of weekly choir practice followed by coffee resumed. On the last Thursday in November, Harry rose early to accompany Bessie to church before returning to Miss Broward's for the traditional Thanksgiving lunch. Those who had been seated around the table the previous Christmas were again assembled.

After everyone had eaten more turkey than they could comfortably accommodate and were about to withdraw to the sitting room, Harry gently tapped a spoon on an empty wine glass. The sudden chiming brought everyone's attention – the room filled with quiet anticipation as Harry began.

'Before we leave the table, I've something to say.'

There was a long, expectant silence. Harry turned to Bessie and, awkwardly getting down on one knee, said, 'May I take this occasion… to mark this occasion, I…' His voice broke off. Clearing his throat, he began again. 'Bessie, will you be my… I mean, will you marry me?' The room erupted into applause and congratulations.

Bessie helped him to his feet and, after kissing him, said, 'Yes. Yes, I will.' And then, after a moment, added, 'I thought you'd never ask. I'd almost given up hope.' The room again erupted with laughter and good wishes.

Their marriage was set for 23 April 1883. And on that date, widow and widower, Bessie Handley and Harry Mason wed by licence at the Duval County Court, where both solemnly declared that there being no lawful impediment, they would love one another until death did them part.

Two days later, Reverend O'Reilly blessed their union in the presence of God at the Church of the Immaculate Conception.

THIRTEEN

It was March 1886, and spring had arrived early. The jacaranda and poinciana trees were in full bloom, and their abundant lavender and scarlet blossom ushered in renewed promise.

Harry and Nicky were sitting on the saloon's back veranda, enjoying the late afternoon sun, spinning tales and weaving dreams of what the future might hold. Nicky talked of plans to extend his bar, with ideas of opening the upper two floors as boarding rooms, while Harry spoke of renting a house in the up-and-coming district of LaVilla.

'I've got to put Bessie and the family first,' said Harry. 'With George already two, and Bessie about to deliver our second, we need more room. And she hankers after a place of her own, reminding me daily that moving here was to be a temporary arrangement until we found a place of our own.

'I know you and Agnes have helped with an extra room, but I've promised Bessie we'll move, and I've seen houses for rent on Adams Street, and most come with a housemaid to wash, clean and cook for fifty cents a day.'

Nicky finished his beer and, comfortably satisfied, was at his ease. 'You know, Harry, I understand what you're saying. Women always want a home to call their own, but you can stay here as long as you want.' He gave out a long yawn as he relaxed deeper into his chair. 'It's five years since you stepped off the steamer on Hogan's Jetty. All the barmen before you found the work too hard and were gone within a month, and none fitted in like you have – you're more like family.'

'I like the work,' said Harry. 'It keeps me busy, and it's good craic.'

'What's craic?' asked Nicky, looking perplexed.

'Oh, it's what the Irish say when they're having a laugh with friends. It's like affectionate fooling around. It's difficult to explain. It's like when you take the piss and enjoy laughing about it, and nobody takes offence.' He could see Nicky was utterly lost. 'You don't understand, do you?'

'You English, steal everyone's language then twist it so nobody understands what the hell you're talking about.'

'I'm just saying, we have a lot of fun together.'

'This I can agree but not the pissing and laughing about it.'

Harry roared with laughter until tears rolled down his face. 'You see, you've done it again. This is what I'm trying to tell you.'

Nicky looked at him in all seriousness. 'What's funny? Can you please tell me the joke?'

'I'm sorry, Nicky, I can't. It wouldn't be funny.'

Nicky threw his hands up in exasperation. Both men settled as Agnes arrived with a plate of sandwiches and pickles. 'You boys sound as if you're having fun. What are you laughing about?'

Nicky said, 'I don't know, and he can't tell me.'

Agnes shrugged and, none the wiser, retreated to the kitchen.

After Nicky finished his sandwich, he asked, 'What about your daughters in England with their grandmother?'

Harry replied, 'I miss them, of course, and I wish things were different, but what is done is done.'

'What are their names?'

'Bertha, Florence and Beatrice, who we all call Annie, but don't ask me why.'

'How old are they?'

'Seventeen, sixteen and twelve.'

'Oh, they're women, not girls. It won't be long before they're married with children of their own.'

Harry didn't reply. He was thinking of what might have been.

'Do you hear from them?' asked Nicky.

'My mother writes from time to time, and I send money to help with clothes and shoes and other odds and ends.'

'They must be overjoyed with you marrying Bessie, having a new stepmother and half-brother too. Are they coming to stay? And with you in your own house at LaVilla, it will be possible, yes?'

'My mother is dedicated to them and would be heartbroken if they ever left her. Perhaps when she's passed, and they're older, then they might consider coming. Besides, with our own young family, I'm not sure Bessie is ready to take on three growing girls.'

'But she has her own son, and he must be eleven or twelve. I think the girls would be a help to her. You should suggest it; she might enjoy them being here.'

'We've talked it over, but she isn't keen. She has enough on her plate as it is. Perhaps when we have our own place.'

'How old is their grandmother?'

Harry hesitated as he thought about it. 'Sixty-five or sixty-six.'

'Oh. She is too young to be passing on,' said Nicky. 'I see her letters arriving from England.'

Harry nodded and, filling his mouth, bit extravagantly into his sandwich.

'Agnes has two daughters in Denmark,' confided Nicky. 'But that was over twenty years ago and now they have children of their own.'

'Does she miss them?' asked Harry.

'Of course. What mother wouldn't?'

'What about you? Do you have children?'

'Not that I know. But I imagine there must be hundreds scattered around the world, and I'm still young enough to have plenty more.' He laughed loudly at his own humour, slapping his thigh hard. 'Is this the craic, Harry?'

'Yes, I think you've got it,' Harry said, getting up from his chair. 'I'll fetch more beers and cigars.'

Harry was still smiling to himself as he disappeared into the saloon, reappearing a few minutes later, his hands laden. Nicky, who was still sitting comfortably in his favourite rocker, had dozed off.

In jest and to rouse Nicky from his slumber, Harry shouted, 'Well, what good company you are!' Putting the beers down with a clatter, Harry leaned across to hand Nicky a cigar. But Nicky didn't move. Harry shook him by the shoulder. His arm slumped limply to his side.

'Nicky! Wake up!' He turned Nicky's head towards him.

His mouth lolled open, and his eyes stared lifelessly back. He was dead. Nicky had passed away.

* * *

More than a hundred mourners lined the boardwalk as the cortege passed along Bay Street on its journey to Evergreen Cemetery.

Grey clouds threatened rain, and those around the graveside huddled together against the wind. Helen Broward and her three sisters were joined by their young nephew, Napoleon Broward, who was campaigning to be elected sheriff. Harry supported Agnes in her grief.

Nicky's death had been a shock to everyone in the Bay district. He had been larger than life: young, strong, vibrant and full of energy. Indomitable. His sudden demise didn't seem possible.

Stricken by grief, Agnes closed the saloon until after the Easter Sunday. Bessie, meanwhile, was confined after the birth of their second son, Charles.

* * *

The first day of May dawned unseasonably hot. Harry sat alone on the saloon veranda, precisely where he had been the afternoon Nicky had died, when Agnes arrived with two glasses of mint julep.

'I've received a reply from my daughters,' she said. 'I've decided to return home to Denmark, to the family farm at Esbjerg. I want to be near my daughters. There's nothing for me here.'

Harry said nothing as a host of questions crowded his mind. Then, after a long silence, he said, 'You're selling the saloon?'

'It's for you, Harry. A gift. I don't want it going into the hands of a stranger, someone who will tear it down and change things. That would betray Nicky and his dreams...'

She hesitated and took a deep breath before continuing. 'Without Nicky, the place has ghosts. I awake cold and alone; it's unbearable. I can hear his voice echoing in every room. I see him everywhere, and...'

Harry watched as her tears ran freely. 'It's not a place I can live,' she said. Then, stopping for a moment's thought, she continued, 'I'm taking our memories home, to where I grew up. I've grandchildren there now. I'll tell them about my Nicky, and together we can again find happiness.'

Harry couldn't grasp the enormity of what she'd said. Had he understood her? She was giving him the saloon. Was that what she'd said? How was he to thank her? Saying thank you wasn't enough and lacked the sincerity and gratitude demanded. They both sat in silence, each thinking of their futures.

After a few minutes, Agnes leaned over and gently touched his hand. 'Harry, I'm leaving at the end of the week. My attorney will send you the papers.'

'I don't know how to express my gratitude,' he said. 'It's beyond words... what can I say? It's more than—'

'It's what Nicky would have wanted. I have no use for it now, and I know you're happy here... you deserve it.'

'I'm... I'm sad losing Nicky, and now... and now I'm losing you too. I will miss you, Agnes. Your generosity is...' He struggled to find the words. Tears began to gather, and his voice was unsteady. 'I'm so sorry, Agnes...' He tried to say more, but he couldn't make the words come.

She stood to leave. 'Promise me you'll make a success of it for Nicky's sake.'

* * *

Agnes packed a few wooden boxes and had them shipped ahead. She spent her last evening with Harry and Bessie, reminiscing and telling them of her early life. Her long, blonde hair was plaited and braided into a traditional Danish crown, held in place with finely decorated combs of elk horn. She wore a plain dress which was well cut but worn. Around her shoulders, she had draped a blue-checked Danish folk shawl. Harry was struck by her simple beauty.

Over supper, she described her upbringing at Esbjerg, running happily barefoot and free in the wild flower meadows where the cows and goats grazed lazily in the warm, Scandinavian summers. As Harry listened, his mind drifted to his daughters, imagining them playing in the meadows around his mother's home at Highgrove Lodge. He missed holding their tiny hands and enjoying their innocent laughter. A sorrowful melancholy came upon him. *My God*, he thought, *what a heavy price I've paid.*

Agnes told them how her parents blamed her for bringing disgrace to the family when, at fifteen and unmarried, she had become pregnant. Even though her parents bitterly disapproved of the father, whom they said was a feckless boy, they nevertheless insisted they marry in the sight of God at their village church. But no sooner was the ceremony over, than her parents disowned her and refused them a room at the farm.

'Having been thrown out by my parents,' Agnes continued, 'we found a small, rented room in the nearby town. We struggled to make ends meet, sometimes going without food. My dear husband, Emil, did his best to find work, but at sixteen and without a trade, it wasn't easy for him. He was always moving from one job to the next, and sometimes, after a week's hard labour, they would refuse to pay him, telling him to clear out and not to return.'

Bessie interrupted, 'That's terrible. How could they do that?'

'It's not unusual, Bessie. If you're poor and powerless, what can you do? They can treat you like a slave if they want. They can do with you as they please. It happens all around us today; you must see it.'

She broke off and took some pickled herring on a small piece of black rye bread. Once she had finished eating, she continued. 'The following year, our second daughter was born, and my husband left in search of work. He was going to send for us once he was settled and in employment, but he never returned, and I've never heard from him since.'

Bessie was near to tears. 'For the love of God, can you ever forgive him for deserting you, penniless and fending for yourself?'

'There's nothing to forgive, Bessie. He was a boy. The burden of responsibility and suffering was too much for him. Perhaps it was guilt he was running from. Perhaps some tragedy overtook him.'

'Agnes! In the name of Jesus, you might have ended up destitute and begging on the street. He was a selfish coward to leave you like that.'

Full of indignation, Bessie turned to Harry. 'Harry? Imagine if you'd done such a thing.'

Harry averted his gaze, which remained firmly fixed on the tumbler of whisky he had been assiduously nursing. He could feel a hot flush rise and a sense of remorse twist in his gut. He couldn't speak. Instead, lighting a large cigar, he hid behind its smoke.

Agnes said, 'Women are left to bring up their children more often than you think. All families have their secrets, but people don't speak of them, not even within the family. Shame is an effective muzzle.'

'Emil is at fault and must be blamed,' replied Bessie. 'He left you in a terrible position. At the very least, he should have stayed at your side.'

'If blame is to be apportioned,' said Agnes, 'then it's my parents who must take a share. What were they thinking, turning their only daughter onto the street with no means of support, and an innocent grandchild too? Where's the Christian charity and forgiveness in that?'

Although the recollection brought anger to Agnes, she spoke quietly, as always. 'Things might have been different had we stayed on the farm. We could have made a living and been happy there.'

'How in heaven's name did you manage with your husband gone?' asked Bessie.

'I had no choice. I threw myself at the mercy of my parents, who reluctantly agreed to take me back. But they were resentful and at every opportunity spitefully reminded me I was the one who had sinned, and it was me who must atone for my wickedness.'

Agnes continued telling them how, after almost twenty years had passed, her father sent her on family business to Aarhus, a seaport on the Danish east coast. And it was at Aarhus that she first saw Nicky.

A wagon had lost a wheel, shedding its load of ale casks, blocking the market square. Several men had unsuccessfully struggled to reattach the wheel. Then Nicky arrived and, to loud cheering from the assembled crowd, single-handedly lifted the wagon. He was young and handsome with a shock of long, blond hair and was attracting the attention of all the girls gathered in the town square.

Agnes told how she had watched him from a distance. He was at least ten years her junior, but he was different from other men. As he looked up, he saw her watching and held her gaze. She looked on in trepidation when he strode purposefully in her direction, stopping only when he had reached her. At first, he said nothing, just staring in admiration. He told her later it was as if seeing the beauty of a jewel for the first time. Agnes told them how she could recall that moment as if it were yesterday. As Nicky stood there, her heart was pounding hard.

'I couldn't breathe,' she said. 'The first thing I noticed was the kindness in his eyes. His hands were strong, yet gentle. I knew he was a good man, and my heart told me I could trust him with my soul.' She paused, enjoying the memory. 'The first words he said to me were, "Tomorrow I leave for America – will you come with me?" Without a second thought, I replied, "I will." And the next morning, we were on a freighter bound for New York.'

'How could you have been so reckless?' gasped Bessie in disbelief. 'You could have been left penniless and alone, with no means of returning to your children.'

'I know it was a moment of madness, but we knew we were in love before any words were spoken.'

She told them she had read of love in poems, sonnets and novels, and how their Lutheran pastor often spoke of God's love, but it was different with Nicky. It was a compelling force like no other, and they had enjoyed ten wonderful years together, every day filled with happiness. 'It felt like the harmony of the vast, infinite universe beating rhythmically within me. It didn't matter what troubles the day brought, I was happy. I couldn't have been happier. I believe it was the will of God that had brought us together. God had intervened and shared his love with us.'

'Was Nicky of the Christian faith?' Bessie enquired.

'He believed in life. He was deeply in love with being alive.'

'Did your daughters forgive you for abandoning them, disappearing into the night without a word?'

'There's nothing to forgive, Bessie. What am I blamed for? They were grown women when I left, older than when I'd married and was a mother. We've written often, and they understood my suffering and have rejoiced at finding happiness with Nicky. And the irony is that it only happened because my father sent me to Aarhus. Such coincidences don't happen by chance; it was the hand of God, only He could have arranged it so perfectly. Nicky used to say that God had heard the love in my prayers and was deaf to my father's bitterness.' A smile crept across her lips as she recalled Nicky's words.

'And what of your parents?' asked Bessie. 'Have they forgiven you?'

'They still can't bring themselves to truly forgive,' replied Agnes. 'But they tell me I remain forever in their thoughts and prayers and that one day I will realise the error of my ways and muster the strength to acknowledge my sins and repent. Only then will God forgive me.

'The truth is, Bessie, throughout their lives, they've unquestioningly followed the doctrines of their church and the demands of their pastor. And they've made many painful sacrifices for their faith, but now, as they near the end of their days, I'm sure they wonder if it has been worth the suffering – has a place at God's right hand in the next world been at too great a price in this one?

'Nicky used to say that on the Day of Judgement, the only question God can ask is, "Did you leave the world a better place?" What more can he ask from his imperfect children?'

'You may be right,' said Bessie. 'We mustn't throw stones or pass judgement on others; we're all sinners trying to do our best in our own way. That's right, isn't it, Harry?'

Harry didn't raise his eyes from the table. He cleared his throat. 'Yes, my dear. We're all doing our best, but sometimes we can't help but make mistakes. Doing what we believe is right doesn't mean things turn out that way. But there can't be any blame in that, only the hope of forgiveness for the hurt we sometimes do others.'

FOURTEEN

Harry invested the same hard work and enterprise in his new saloon as when building his London corsetry business. Converting Nicky's spit-and-sawdust back bar into a respectable restaurant, selling only the finest brand of cigars and becoming the sole distributor of New York's renowned Rochester Beers and turning, as Nicky had intended, the upper floors into boarding rooms.

Moving to a rented house at 509 West Adams Street in the district of LaVilla brought blissful contentment for Bessie. She now had everything she had ever wanted: loving and healthy children, with the prospect of a larger family to follow, her own comfortable home with housemaids and a yard boy, a prosperous husband and the friendship of the congregation at her church.

Bessie adored children and, by the spring of 1888, was again expecting. Harry's business was flourishing, purchasing a second saloon and two boarding houses further along West Bay. This was the land of opportunity where success came unstintingly to those willing to work hard and apply their talents.

The last Saturday of July dawned hot and humid. The night temperature had not dropped below thirty-four degrees centigrade, and the early morning heat was unbearably sticky. Bessie hadn't slept, and her pregnancy made her irritable.

Harry stood listlessly on the front porch of their home as he emptied a pail of tepid water over himself. He asked one of the Negro boys to run an errand to Dr Holt, requesting he attend Bessie that morning.

The mosquitoes and summer biting bugs deterred the tourists, and the town quietly baked in the oppressive heat. Locals hid themselves away in darkened rooms, hoping for the hint of a breeze to ease their stupor.

Harry rested, leisurely reading in the shade of a large oak tree, over which Spanish moss hung in great folds like draped curtains. A plantation worker shuffled by, heading for another day's labour in the fields.

It was too hot for breakfast, so Harry had a jug of iced lemonade brought by Martha, the housemaid, who was already busy with her laundry chores.

As he sipped the refreshing cold drink, a cloud of dust rose lazily over Bay Street. Harry was intrigued to see people hurrying towards the waterfront, with horses and mules reluctantly kicked to a trot. He wondered if another steamboat had blown its boiler; there had been two the previous month, causing several deaths.

Doctor Holt didn't arrive until early evening, just as the midges swarmed and the cicadas rose to a cacophony. He looked tired and had been hurrying. Inviting the doctor to take his ease, Harry poured a glass of iced mint julep, which was gratefully accepted. After a minute, the doctor regained his usual calm composure.

'I've been at Sandhills Hospital most of the day, along with many of our town's physicians,' he said by way of an apology.

'Another steamboat disaster?' asked Harry.

'Not at all. It's a case of tropical fever, a Mr McCormick visiting from Tampa.' The doctor took a long draw of his drink. 'He's now quarantined.' Then, dabbing beads of sweat from his forehead and the back of his neck, he added, 'He's sure to recover in a day or two.'

But Harry sensed anxiety in the doctor's demeanour. 'Earlier, I saw people hurrying to the ferry from the direction of the Grand Union Hotel.'

'There's no need to concern yourself, Mr Mason. There's always those who...' He interrupted himself, perhaps realising he had already said too much. Changing course, he said, 'Now, tell me, how's your dear lady? Is she feeling the effects of this dreadful heat?'

* * *

The following Monday, Harry took his usual early morning stroll to his saloon on West Bay, but the hectic bustle along the way was far from usual.

He was greeted excitedly by his cleaner, Old Moses, a freed slave, who had worked himself into a state of agitation. 'Hey, mas'er! You hear da news? People dying like flies. Death is among us; he's a-visitin' and a-killin' wid da bad fella yellow jack.'

Moses handed Harry the morning newspaper, its front page announcing several deaths from yellow fever.

'I swear on the Bible, mas'er,' Moses continued. 'I'm a-clapping and stamping out loud. The wrath of God is a-comin' down on us. Ezekiel chapter six, verse eleven. He proclaims it, mas'er. I swear it's the gospel truth. Alas! Death is upon us and—'

Harry cut him short. 'Moses! For the love of God. It's superstitious nonsense. Pay no heed to stupid folk and their wilful gossip.' Harry spoke as a man who knew better. 'Now calm yourself and get back to work.'

Throughout that day, a palpable sense of anxiety spread across town. People nervously hurrying without a moment to spare. Perhaps, intuitively, they sensed impending disaster, the way animals feel an earthquake long before it shakes. Rumours of death from the fever grew by the hour; an unseen killer was on the loose, indiscriminately scything down rich and poor, white and coloured folk alike. Nobody was to be spared.

By evening, Harry's saloon was busier than usual, with men swilling copious amounts of bourbon in the belief that hard liquor killed the fever's microbes, whose nature it was to collect in the stomach before attacking and rupturing the organs of the body. It was a myth, but one Harry was in no hurry to dispel.

As was the habit for a Monday evening, his two friends, Dr James Fairlie and Henry L'Engle, joined him for drinks. Although far from being their intellectual equal, Harry looked forward to their bonhomie and appreciated the generous manner in which they had accepted him into their company.

Fairlie, a pharmacist, ran a drugstore on East Bay and was secretary to the powerful Jacksonville Board of Trade. He was tall and lean with short, spiky, grey hair and a ruddy complexion. An educated and erudite Scotsman, he'd been a prominent resident of Jacksonville since arriving with his wife Margaret and four children some fifteen years earlier.

L'Engle came from a distinguished, long-established southern family who had owned plantations before the war between the states. L'Engle was the city treasurer and president of the State Bank of Florida, which was situated only a few doors from Harry's saloon. All three men shared a love of single malt scotch whisky and assembled weekly to taste the most recently acquired examples from lesser-known Scottish distilleries. But their conversation that evening was not of scotch but of yellow fever.

As Harry set the table, he relayed the many rumours he had heard earlier in the day.

Fairlie, who retained his broad Scottish accent, said, 'Nothing's changed in the eleven years since the last outbreak. It was no different then.' Turning to Harry, he explained, 'Both of us were here,' indicating himself and L'Engle, who was sitting across the table lighting a large, Cuban cigar.

Fairlie picked up the latest edition of the evening newspaper with its sensational headline of deaths from the fever. 'This is scurrilous nonsense. The city council should calm people's anxieties, not stoke the fires of fear with careless talk of plague and pestilence. These days, we hear nothing but irresponsible scaremongering.'

L'Engle, who had been thoughtfully savouring the aromas of a peaty Lagavulin, said, 'It was worse the last time, and the town never suffered by it. But you're right to say it, James. It's groundless rumours that cause unnecessary worry amongst our lesser-informed citizens.' He paused to rekindle his cigar. 'The problem arises from the constitution. These days, citizens feel free to express an opinion on any and all matters, mostly about which they know little.' L'Engle had a commanding presence and spoke with authority in a well-mannered, whiskey-sippin' southern drawl. 'And they freely express their foolishness as if proven facts.'

Fairlie reinforced his point. 'By not furnishing truthful information, the authorities are misleading their readers and inviting them to employ their imaginations, cooking up their own so-called facts and filling their heads with half-truths or no truth at all.'

Harry joined in. 'But people like to make up stories, if only to entertain themselves and bring colour to their otherwise humdrum existence – they've seen little of the world and in their narrow lives they've nothing better to gossip on. You need only listen to their yammering at the bar, the more far-fetched the nonsense, the more willing others are to believe it. I've even heard the truth of mermaids and unicorns sworn on the bible.'

L'Engle agreed. 'That's true enough. And if there's a gain to be had, then the tale will be told all the more convincingly, and the more a lie is repeated, the easier it's believed. That's always been the way of things; it's how cheats and charlatans prosper.'

Fairlie pressed his point. 'If the authorities gave more information, supported by objective evidence, people would come to the truth by their own good reasoning.'

L'Engle looked askance and again took up the conversation. 'My dear James, I'm compelled to disagree. My experience tells me that good reasoning, or what we like to call common sense, is a rare commodity. Plain folk act from hot emotion or naked self-interest. When nonsense is asserted as fact, it's done for a purpose, usually malign, and it's the same with newspapers. The bigger the lie, the bigger the profit. Just ask yourself, who gains from these sensational and lurid scandals?'

Then, answering his own question, L'Engle continued, 'These damned Yankee owners in Washington and New York, that's who. And if they can sow discord amongst our southern states, then they like it all the better. A lie always has a purpose: to conceal a crime, avoid embarrassment or to gain an advantage. I'm afraid to say it, gentlemen, but these days, truth is a soiled commodity and traded without scruple. Words are mere tools to shape an end. Words can mean anything or nothing, as long as they achieve the desired purpose. It's the basis of all deception and is stock-in-trade for scoundrels.'

Fairlie said, 'What we need is firm leadership, someone who speaks honestly and stands his ground, not these double-dealing flimflammers, always scrabbling in the trough for the next easy dollar.'

Harry excused himself to fetch more cigars and a bottle of recently arrived Speyside Mortlach, a smooth and mellow scotch to contrast with the muscularity of the Lagavulin.

The saloon was noisy with excited talk of the fever. *If an infected person is here*, thought Harry, *then the contagion will be across the city by morning.*

On his return, Fairlie and L'Engle were still locked in discourse.

'Not all opinions are equal; indeed, not all votes are equal,' said L'Engle, turning to Harry. 'Now, Harry, let's hear what you have to say on the matter. Tell us truthfully, when it comes to casting your ballot, whose opinion do you trust? Is it your own, based on good sense and worldly experience, or that of your coloured boy, Moses?'

The conversation waned as attention passed to the cigars and whisky. Once each had sampled and given their verdict, L'Engle continued. 'Not every citizen has an equal vote, and the founding fathers intended it that way for good reason.'

Harry interjected, 'I thought government was of the people for the people.'

L'Engle took a long draw on his cigar. 'Well, Harry, in one sense, you're right. Every man has a vote, including the uneducated, the idle and the plain stupid, albeit, thank the good Lord, few have the enterprise to haul themselves to the ballot box. Just imagine the ruinous condition of our glorious southern states if our coloured brethren exercised their vote. It's why we have prudent constraints on who gets to cast their ballot. As I'm sure you'll acknowledge, having a vote and casting it are not the same. Few with good sense agree with the prospect of women or the Negro having a governing voice in our nation's affairs.

'You see, Harry, winning elections isn't only about votes. Take that damned Republican, Lincoln. A backwoodsman who sold snake oil to the gullible and those weak in the head. He stole the presidency with a third of the votes, relying on the electoral college to carry him into the White House. Even so, without any shame, the man wasted not a moment before claiming to enjoy the will of the people and declared war on our southern states; brother against brother.'

Harry could see this was a bitter memory for Henry, who was working himself into an ill temper.

'Let's have no more of this talk,' said L'Engle, placing his hand firmly on the table.

There was a moment of tense silence as the three men contemplated their whisky.

Harry broke their reverie. 'I believe I would make a good councillor, but not being born here—'

Fairlie interrupted, 'Not being born here is no impediment. I think you would make an excellent councilman. I'd certainly support you.'

'I agree,' said L'Engle. 'You're honest, trustworthy and God-fearing. I'll introduce you to my nephew-in-law, James Bowden – he was Mayor of LaVilla, following on from my nephew, Porcher.'

Fairlie laughed aloud. 'Well, why isn't that a surprise! What with your family owning much of the district and—'

L'Engle was indignant at Fairlie's interjection, 'Don't forget, James, it was our family of frontier pioneers who built this place out from the swamp. It's only right we have a say, especially in the face of this Yankee onslaught and their so-called reconstruction, buying our land and businesses at prices that amount to theft.'

Turning again to Harry, L'Engle said, 'We need good men like you, Harry. Bowden will see you right.'

Fairlie endorsed L'Engle's sentiments. 'Who knows, Harry, one day you might be mayor.'

Fairlie made a toast. 'I propose Harry Mason for councillor. All in favour, say, aye!'

All three shouted, 'Aye!', clinking their glasses.

'There, it's agreed,' said Fairlie.

Harry was touched and spoke in all sincerity. 'Gentlemen, I'm much obliged… I can't tell you how much I value your friendship. I shall never be able to repay your generosity and faith in me.'

Tapping Harry lightly on the shoulder, L'Engle, speaking in an avuncular manner, said, 'Harry, there's always a way to repay a debt.'

FIFTEEN

Next morning, Bessie ran breathless into the saloon. 'We can't stay! We must leave! Quickly, Harry! We've got to go! Martha's packing, and the other maids are getting the boys ready. The New York steamer leaves at noon and—'

'What the hell are you talking about? Calm yourself, woman,' exclaimed Harry.

'Yellow fever! It's come to kill us! The minister at Martha's church swore it on the Bible. Death has come to take us!'

'Stop it! Stop listening to Martha and her superstitions.' Collecting himself, Harry continued more calmly. 'What does Father O'Reilly say?'

'He can't be found. Some say he's already been taken and—'

'Bessie, listen to me. We're not leaving; everything's going to be fine. I've a good business, home and family. We're alright as we are and—'

Bessie collapsed into his arms. 'Harry, we can't stay. People are running for their lives. What about the children and our unborn? Please, Harry.' She waited for his response, but none came. 'Are we to stay only to attend our children's graves? Come, Harry,' she said, tugging at his arm. 'We'll be safe in New York. We can return when it's passed.'

'I can't just up sticks and leave; people will call me a quitter – they'll never accept me back.'

'Don't be ridiculous! These people you think so much of have already packed and gone.' Calming herself, she said, 'Harry, listen to me. You're respected. No one's going to think the worst of you for protecting your family. For goodness' sake, your children depend on you. Think of them first. What's the use of money when you're six feet under? Don't abandon us for selfish ambition.'

Harry said nothing. He was thinking of Agnes and what she'd said on her last evening. Was Bessie leaving any different from when he'd left Eliza behind? And then the same nagging question returned. Why had he left Eliza behind? He shook the thoughts from his mind.

Speaking quietly, he said, 'You're right, my dear, the children come first, but please understand why I can't go, at least not for now. I have to do what I think is right. If things worsen, then I'll join you without a moment's delay – I promise.'

'Harry, your place is with your family – stop being so pig-headed and cocksure of yourself.'

Harry held his tongue.

'For the love of God. I've buried one husband; I can't bury another. Don't leave me destitute and alone. Stop worrying about what others think of you...' Her voice faded. 'If they think of you at all.'

Her criticism stung. 'Bessie, these rumours make it sound worse than it is. We've good doctors and, after all is said and done, there's been only three deaths across the entire city.'

He could see she wasn't listening. He took her in his arms. 'Take the children and go. Don't worry about me – I'll be here when you return. I promise.'

He could feel her body tense and, again attempting to placate her, said, 'Fairlie, L'Engle, Colonel Daniel, they're all good men, intelligent men, and they know the facts, and they're all keeping their wives and children with...' He hesitated, thinking of how to continue, but Bessie broke in.

'Then they're bigger fools than you. The last time the fever was here, it killed hundreds. Half the women in my congregation are widows because of it, and now you want to make me one, too. You're like schoolboys playing at soldiers, daring to see who's the more reckless, who's the bravest.' She stamped her foot in frustration. 'You men are so stupid. Don't you ever give your women folk and your families a second thought?'

'Bessie, don't be angry, please. I have a chance to join their circle and become one of them. I don't want to be a saloon keeper all my life. I want to make something of myself, to be known and respected.'

'I can't listen to your nonsense. I'm sick of hearing about you making a name for yourself, and this idea of being one of them is childish. They'll never allow you in. They only pay you attention when they want something and drop you the moment they've finished with you. These men hold an iron grip on the city because they don't allow the likes of you into their circle. To them, you're just another outsider.

'Look at yourself. You're nothing more than an immigrant saloon keeper who has made a few dollars. For heaven's sake, don't let pride blind your good sense. Forget about these men and be grateful for what you've got. I'm the only one who has sworn a holy vow to be your wife, to stick by you in good times and bad.'

She waited as he weighed her words.

Continuing more kindly, she said, 'Harry, you've a good wife and beautiful children; you've good health and strength, a good home and business – we don't have a worry in the world. Isn't this enough for you? Do you want to throw it all away in exchange for your name on a headstone? Success isn't happiness, Harry. Happiness is success. Aren't you content with what you have?'

He wanted to sound indignant but kept his silence.

Then, scathingly, she added, 'Won't you be satisfied 'til everyone knows your name, stooping and bowing, begging and scraping and tipping their hats as you pass? Is this what you want? Lording it over those less fortunate? Because if it is, you'll be sorely disappointed.'

Her anger ebbed. She had exhausted her objections and spoke with a conciliatory tone. 'Harry, I pray the good Lord keeps you safe and has mercy enough to forgive your sinful pride.'

Not wanting to prolong the argument, he said, 'You must hurry if you're to catch the midday steamer.'

Bessie kissed him hard. 'Husband, don't come to harm and return to me soon.'

'I promise,' he said.

* * *

Harry woke to an empty house echoing around him. By late afternoon, a further five deaths were reported, adding to the four the previous day and the three the day before that.

Many of those who had stayed now abandoned their resolve. Concern turned to anxiety and then, in a flash, to panic. Like a herd of spooked cattle, they ran.

Carrying little or nothing, people abandoned their homes, leaving meals half-eaten. Roads choked with every kind of transportation. Steamboats, trains, wagons and coaches were all overcrowded, and, in desperation, people clung to the roofs of moving rail carriages.

Within thirty-six hours, the population of Jacksonville fell from 130,000 to fewer than ten thousand. Many of those remaining were from the coloured shanty towns, who, without the price of a ticket, had no choice but to stay.

The Board of Health declared a citywide epidemic. Saloons and places of public assembly were closed, with essential shops allowed to open only two half days a week. People were ordered to stay at home with windows and shutters closed.

The few hundred white citizens who had stayed gathered to elect Colonel J. J. Daniel as the leader of a volunteer citizens' assembly, known as the Auxiliary Sanitation Association, which was to take charge of the deserted City Hall. Henry L'Engle was appointed treasurer with James Fairlie its secretary.

* * *

At home, Harry sat enjoying a refreshing mint julep in the cool evening air. There was an eerie silence; not a sound could be heard on the streets or up from the river. A sharp rapping at the door roused him from his thoughts. Walking through the empty house, he found L'Engle waiting on the front porch – Harry had sent him a note volunteering to serve on the Auxiliary Sanitation Association.

Over brandy and cigars, L'Engle described the mounting death toll and the unfolding disaster, which was worse than anyone had imagined. President Cleveland had declared a statewide disaster and sent offers of federal assistance.

L'Engle asked two favours: would Harry donate to the Association, and would he become the town's superintendent, overseeing the LaVilla district? The first was easy – Harry gave fifty dollars. The second required explanation. What was he expected to do?

Producing official papers from a small attaché case, L'Engle said, 'You must recruit thirty labourers to clean filth from the streets, spread lime and other noxious disinfectants, light bonfires of pine and tar on street corners to purify the air. You're to make an inventory of everyone remaining in their homes, noting their health and putting yellow flags outside where the infection is suspected. Where necessary, taking the sick to the quarantine hospital established outside the city in the pinewoods of Sandhills. Black flags are to be hung outside the homes where the dead must be collected.'

Harry listened with mounting concern. 'Is it that bad?'

L'Engle ploughed on, 'You're to liaise with the military, who will discharge cannon every night to concuss airborne microbes. Routine militia patrols will prevent gangs from gathering or looting. You will receive daily food rations and pay at sixty cents a day for each labourer, sending daily accounts and reports to City Hall.'

He paused a beat before continuing. 'Your aim is to do whatever you must to halt this disease. It's your duty to serve.

The city will recognise those who give freely and gladly, not just of money but of their sweat, tears and sympathy in the assistance of others.' His sombre tone conveyed the gravity of the task ahead. Harry agreed. *This*, he thought, *is my chance to forge an unbreakable bond of comradeship as this band of civic leaders face danger and adversity together. At last, I will be one of them.*

More cheerfully, both men enjoyed a late supper of cold ham. Harry apologised for the meagre offering, explaining that Bessie was away visiting her sick mother.

Their conversation soon turned to theories of how the fever spread.

L'Engle set out the known facts. The districts nearest to the river were the worst affected. The pinewoods and along the ocean shore were free of the epidemic. 'We don't know the cause, nor do we have a cure, but we're certain that once the temperature drops and the first frosts arrive, the microbes will vanish just as quickly as they appeared.'

'But that won't be for another three months,' said Harry.

'And this outbreak is worse than last time. I was wrong when I said otherwise, and I apologise if I misled you.'

Harry shrugged. 'It matters not.'

'Harry, you've often spoken of your travels. As a man of the world, what does your experience tell you of this disease?'

'From my time in the Paris plagues and serving during the South African war, I'd say the culprit is foul water; just as typhoid enjoys its hospitality, this fever may be no different.'

'You may be right,' replied L'Engle. 'Typhoid killed more than any cannon or rifle shot in the war with the Yankees. By the way, Fairlie recommends igniting an ounce of gunpowder on a shovel before retiring. He says the acrid whiff of sulphur and ammonia deters the bugs.'

'And a good sleep, I'll wager!' replied Harry.

Laughing, they parted company in good spirits.

* * *

Moses, Harry's saloon cleaner, suggested a man called Nathan Cross to recruit Harry's team of labourers. Cross, a Negro in his early fifties, had been an overseer on the tobacco plantation where Moses had toiled as a slave before emancipation. Cross was a hard taskmaster but respected for his fairness. Moses told Harry, 'I never seen him whip a man without good cause, and he's more righteous than Noah himself. You can trust him, mas'er.'

Harry found Cross at the back of the rail yards sitting on boxes of rotting grapefruits, reading from a well-thumbed Bible. When Harry asked what he was doing, Cross replied, 'Waiting, boss. Waiting for the Lord to send something good my way.'

Harry liked him from the outset. He was laconic and reminded him of a friend and sparring partner back in the alleyways of London. Cross stood well over six feet tall and was heavily built, yet he moved with lightness and grace. His big, round face was a labyrinth of deep folds of pockmarked viscous tar, and with his deep baritone, he spoke softly and smiled constantly.

Cross knew every coloured labourer in the district and, within a few days, had assembled Harry's workforce. Cross drove the men hard but with care, as a shepherd with his flock.

The weeks that followed were tragic. Death descended heavily over the city, sending suffering to every home and every street, but Harry's labourers, mustering every sinew, never flinched from their task.

The work was harrowing, and the stench and agony of those afflicted offended the senses. At night, the shrill screams of the sick prevented sleep until death mercifully came to quieten their fevered brows.

The distress took a heavy toll on Harry, who despaired and considered the possibility that death would come for him too and was sure he'd never again see Bessie. She had been right; pride was a sin and ambition a curse, but now was not the time to lose heart – he had to fight on.

* * *

September began worse than August had ended. Acrid smoke drifted up from smouldering braziers of pine and tar burning on every street corner. A toxic film of lime dust and the disinfectant powder, mercury chloride, covered everything, seeping under doors, through window frames and into every nook and cranny. Fresh food was rationed, and what little there was had to be salted and boiled to a pulp before being safe to eat. Not that it mattered; most had long ago lost their appetites. People were frightened.

With his saloon and businesses shuttered, Harry had no occasion to meet with acquaintances. Fairlie and L'Engle, and many of the others who had stayed behind, busied themselves at City Hall. None having the desire to venture as far as La Villa, where Harry sometimes went a week or longer without seeing a white face, at least not one that lived.

Better than being idle and alone, Harry chose to work alongside Cross and his men, cleaning the streets and collecting the dead, whose racked and yellow bodies, caked in black vomit and dried blood, made him retch under his suffocating hessian hood, soaked in foul-smelling disinfecting fluids. The work was bitter and gruelling, but there was a camaraderie in their shared hardships.

Cross and his men laboured tirelessly without complaint in the dirt and stifling heat, remaining surprisingly cheerful and easily coaxed into song. Harry admired their sinewy strength and stamina, reminding him of the Irish navvies who had crowded the London pubs after fourteen hours digging heavy London clay for the new underground railways. Men, undaunted by hard labour and proud of it.

By the middle of September, the number of deaths increased into the hundreds, probably more, as most of the coloureds who perished were never listed. The Association had enough to record without adding coloureds to the tally.

At 10am on the morning of Friday, 21 September 1888, a date etched deep into Harry's memory, he received a message from City Hall directing him to send a buckboard two miles south across McCoy's Creek to Pine Street. Here, he was to collect the body of Charles Herrick, who had died the previous night. Harry could have chosen to stay behind but decided to go with Cross and take a ride into the countryside and lend a hand. As they drew near to Herrick's home, Cross pulled the wagon to a stop and listened.

Harry nudged him in the ribs. 'What the hell are you doing? Come on, get closer. We ain't carrying him this distance.'

'Something ain't right, boss,' said Cross.

Harry looked around. 'I can't see anything.'

'That's just it, boss. We come to collect old Mr Herrick, so where's his wife to meet us? Except for the birds, there ain't no sound.'

'Well, it's no good sitting here; let's get closer and take a look,' scolded Harry.

As they approached, a low humming replaced the birdsong.

Cross said, 'This looks bad, boss, real bad.'

Before Harry could reply, the cabin door swung open and a raw-boned youth, no older than eighteen, stepped forward. 'They're in here,' he called.

'They?' whispered Cross.

'And who are you?' called Harry.

'Alvia Herrick, I'm the eldest. It was me who went for help.'

Harry jumped down and sauntered across to where the youth was standing. 'When was that, son?'

'I walked into town two days ago. I told um Grandma and Pa, Mom and Pop and my little sister, Millie, were all lost to the fever.'

'You live here?' asked Harry, doing all he could not to vomit from the smell of putrid decay drifting across on the breeze.

'No. I'm over at Fairfield. I came to visit, see how my folks were doing. That's when I found...' He hesitated. 'That's when...' His voice choked and tears streamed as he covered his face and sobbed hard. After a moment, he said, 'I'm sorry, sir. I'm real sorry, but they're all...'

'It's okay, son. We're here now. Shall I come and take a look?' The stench of death was overpowering. A plague of flies swarmed and crowded the airless room, pitching and crawling over Harry's face and hands and into his eyes. Holding a cotton cloth soaked in creosote over his nose and mouth, Harry looked around the dimly lit room before retreating to where Cross and the others waited.

'What you see, boss?' asked Cross.

'There's five of them, all lying in the same bed. They've been dead for a week or more.'

'Jesus! What we gonna do?'

'What we've come for – collect the dead.'

The four labourers, who had been sitting idly on the back of the buckboard, frantically scrambled off and began shouting in protest.

'What the hell's got into them?' asked Harry.

'They sissy asses, chickenshit, sons of bitches,' said Cross. 'They say they ain't carrying no maggoty bodies for fear of catching something, and to tell the truth, boss, I ain't sure I can whip their black asses to do it; they real scared.'

'I ain't asking,' demanded Harry. 'I'm telling. Beat the bastards till they do what they're told.'

But before he could say another word, the four turned tail and ran for all they were worth, heading deep into a tangle of mangrove swamp.

Heavy with sarcasm, Harry said, 'Well, now it's just the two of us.'

Cross spat on the ground and strode off impatiently towards the cabin. 'I'll do the goddamn job myself. Those liver shits ain't never goin' work again – I swear it. I'll see um starve. I swear it. I'm goin' whip…'

Harry ran to catch him up. 'Come on, I'll give you a

hand,' he said, slapping Cross affectionately on the shoulder. 'Many hands make light work.'

The pair laboured together, moving the five bodies from the house, laying each under a blanket on the long, damp grass. Alvia crouched low on his haunches, watching, a blank stare frozen in time.

The bodies were so badly decomposed that without coffins, it would be impossible to get them into town in one piece.

'This land belong to your pa?' Harry asked Alvia.

'I don't think so. We only got here last year. Come down from Tiffin, Ohio. Pa thought there might be work here. I'm at the lumber yard and my little sister Millie, she's got a job at one of the hotels, but now...'

'I'm sorry, son, but the best thing is to bury them here, just for the time being. We'll give them a proper Christian burial when the fever's passed.'

The boy nodded his agreement.

Harry and Cross dug five shallow graves. But digging any deeper than a couple of feet was impossible. The ground was a wet bog and with every spit of soil, the graves filled with black swamp water.

On the return journey to LaVilla, neither man spoke, both absorbed by their own thoughts. The evening light was fading as they drew up on Adams Street. Harry turned to Cross. 'Let's go to my place and get cleaned up, have a whisky and get something to eat. It's the least we deserve.'

Cross said, 'Are you sure about this, boss?'

Harry shook his head with resignation. 'Nathan, I'm too fucking tired to give a damn about what they'll say.'

'Boss, I appreciate your kindness and your help, too.

I ain't never seen a mas'er do nigger's work before, but no good's going to come of us breaking bread.'

* * *

Conditions inside the city grew worse by the day, as fear of contagion terrified everyone. Vigilantes set siege to the city, with towns as far as Savannah, Macon and Tallahassee sending armed pickets to stand guard with orders to shoot anyone trying to leave. Rail tracks were ripped up, road bridges demolished and cables and chains laid to block boats from entering or leaving the St Johns River.

Bessie had been gone five weeks, and the two letters Harry had sent remained unanswered. When he enquired at the post office, he was told that all mail was held in quarantine at Waycross Junction, and it might be weeks before anything got through.

He was trapped and utterly alone.

SIXTEEN

Harry was exhausted and in despair. He'd given up washing and hadn't eaten properly for weeks.

The sun was already high when he woke. He'd slept heavily, and his head felt thick. The bottle of bourbon before bed hadn't helped, a nightly habit he had drifted into.

The previous night's thunderstorm made the air humid and turned the roads into thick mud. Dragging himself downstairs, he found that a handwritten note had been slipped under the front door.

* * *

Dear Harry,

I'm deeply saddened to tell you that our dearest and beloved friend Henry L'Engle succumbed to the fever at noon yesterday.

Yours sorrowfully,

James Fairlie.

* * *

Harry collapsed onto a chair. Winded by the news and struggling for breath, he slithered from the chair onto the floor and, crawling on all fours, made it to the front porch where, feeling sick, he retched and let out a primaeval screech as he curled himself into a foetal ball. He lay on his side, whimpering and gently knocking his head rhythmically against the wooden boards.

'You alright, boss? You ain't got the fever, have you, boss?' Cross was standing over him.

Harry rubbed his face and shook his head, trying to clear his mind of sleep, bourbon and bad news. 'Dammit. What the hell are you doing here?'

'We got trouble on Forsythe. You gotta git there real quick.'

'What trouble?' asked Harry.

'A white man, boss. They gone and done something stupid.'

Harry couldn't imagine what trouble there was but guessed it was serious from the look of Cross.

Grabbing his shirt and boots, Harry clambered onto a rickety buckboard drawn by a half-starved mule that Cross gently coaxed into a respectable trot. As they entered Forsythe Street, Harry saw a dozen of his men standing over the body of a white man lying prone on the ground. Their heads bowed, not in sombre respect but as guilty men.

Harry jumped from the wagon and shouted across, 'What's up? Another one lost to the fever?'

No one answered.

As he drew closer, he could see a dark pool of blood issuing from the man's head.

'Jesus Christ! What in God's name has...'

Stepping forward, Cross said, 'Boss, we find him doing bad stuff in Miss Gabby's house. She's gone to Chicago and her place is empty.' He stopped, waiting to see if further explanation was needed.

'Holy shit!' said Harry, struggling to find words. 'He's bloody dead.'

Cross said, 'We seen him, boss, with our own eyes. He was robbing real bad, pockets stuffed full.'

'Who caved his head in?'

'Boss, he put up a fight, real nasty, cussing and threatening and all. So… so you see, boss. Well, it's like this, boss.' Wringing his hands and shifting from foot to foot, Cross continued anxiously, 'Well, young Reuben here,' indicating a thin, lanky boy no more than sixteen, 'he goes and gives it to 'im. Gives it 'im real bad with the shovel… he didn't mean no harm. He didn't do nothing on purpose. He done it careless, by accident like…' Cross was struggling to excuse what had happened.

Harry let out a cry of anguish, a strangled scream, dragged from deep in his core. 'An accident!' he mocked. 'A fucking accident! What, he accidentally swung his shovel and accidentally bashed his fucking brains out?' Thick, foamy saliva bubbled at the corners of Harry's mouth. He bent double at the waist, both hands gripping his knees as he gasped for air.

The Negro boys took fright and looked skywards in search of salvation and began beseeching and praying out loud.

Harry straightened and took several slow, deep breaths. Speaking slowly, he said, 'Okay. Let's think about this. First off, who is he?'

'Dunno, boss,' said Cross, nervously. 'He got nothing on him to say. None of us never seen him before. He's a stranger, one of them drifters who's bin thieving and looting and all.'

Harry asked, 'Did anyone see you? Is there anyone still living in these houses round here? Anyone pass you on the street? Anyone with him?'

'No, boss. Everything round here's empty. We been checking all week. They gone and moved away, and the street been empty for days. We ain't seen a soul. I swear it.'

'Who's he with?'

'No one, boss, just him. Nobody's with him. We'd have seen if there was. He's one of them white trash come looking to see what he can rob.' After a long silence, Cross, barely audible, whispered, 'Boss, you... boss, you gonna tell da sheriff?'

'Tell him what?' shouted Harry angrily. 'Tell him a gang of niggers just beat the living shit out a white man on Forsythe, caved his brains in with a fucking shovel... but don't you go worrying none, sheriff, they done it all by accident. For Christ's sake!' Frothy spit again bubbled at the corners of his mouth and started to dribble.

Cross was shaking, tears dripping like raindrops to the dirt where the dead man's blood was now drying in the sun's heat. Already, flies were pitching on the corpse.

Cross, his head bowed and hands clasped tight, pleaded, 'We ain't gonna get no justice, boss. They gonna lynch us.'

'Justice! You boys ain't even gonna get the law. They're going to dangle you from the nearest tree.'

Several of the men fell to their knees, weeping and exhorting the Lord for mercy.

Harry turned and stepped away. They watched as he paced back and forth, cursing his luck.

'Okay!' he said at last. 'Get him stripped naked and burn everything. Then get him on the wagon. You boys are going to bury him out of town, up in the woods.'

'What about you, boss?' asked Cross.

'I'm coming with you. In for a penny, in for a pound. I gotta make sure you boys don't get caught hauling a dead...' He stopped himself from saying more. Instead, he continued issuing instructions. 'Cover him with a canvas. Rake that blood. Make sure everything's put back in Miss Gabby's house.' Then, resigned to the consequences of his design, he said, with dark sarcasm, 'Let's hope Miss Gabby hasn't sent a favourite nephew to collect her things.'

Gathering the men so close he could reach out and grab any one of them, he spoke with menace. 'Now you listen here, and you listen good. Not a word of this. Not to each other, not to your wives or mothers, not to your preacher. You tell nobody nothing, not even God. There ain't going be no whispering in confessional. You understand?' He stretched out, caught Cross by the scruff of his neck and pulled him close, so close they were breathing the same air. 'I hear of this from any quarter, and I'll string you up with my own hands. I swear it. I'll have you kicking your heels and doing a jig for the Devil.'

All listened in silence, nodding at every word, eyes bulging and mouths lolling open at every sinister gesture.

Cross spoke for them all. 'Yes, mas'er. Not a word, mas'er. We swear on the Bible and fear the wrath of the Almighty. None of us chokin' at the end of a rope for a loose tongue.

We're taking it to the grave, mas'er. Yes, sir.' Turning to those assembled, he said, 'Ain't it so?'

In unison, they agreed.

'How we goin' a repay you?' asked Cross.

* * *

The events on Forsythe Street frightened Harry. If discovered, he would hang alongside the rest of them. He made himself scarce and kept off the streets, running his work gang from home, where Cross collected his orders and reported each evening.

But the loneliness of the empty house echoing around him played on his mind, often catching himself talking aloud, lost in conversations with Eliza and Michael. At night, haunting images of the Herrick family kept him from sleep, and during the idleness of the day, he suffered tremors, his skin itched and red sores blossomed. Loneliness was crushing him, and he cursed himself for it.

To help break the tedium, he took to strolling the deserted streets, past his boarded-up saloons, to the Western Union telegraph office where, depending on whether an operator had turned in for work, he would send a telegram to Bessie. Sometimes there was a reply, but often there wasn't, and even when there was, it was never more than a few words of concern. On his return journey, he would loop round and stop at the Board of Trade, hoping to see a familiar face with whom he might converse and learn any news. But what little he gleaned only reinforced the view that the suffering was far from over.

* * *

At the beginning of October, while returning from the telegraph office, Harry was unexpectedly caught in a torrential downpour, one of many heavy showers that frequently punctuate the autumnal months. Instead of running for shelter, he stood, mesmerised by the spectacle of twenty or so young nurses cheerfully marching in formation, proudly and defiantly headed by Matron Caroline Standing of St Luke's Hospital.

Harry called out, 'Where are you from?'

Several shouted back through the beating rain. 'Tampa!'

'Good luck to you, and thank you,' he shouted back.

As he stood watching in admiration, James Fairlie, who was holding a much-needed umbrella, joined him. 'Volunteer nurses, Harry. They've walked the last ten miles; the damned driver wouldn't bring the train any closer.'

Harry was overjoyed to see his friend. 'Well, they're a sight for sore eyes,' he said.

Fairlie, shouting to make himself heard above the din of the rain, 'They're not the first. The Red Cross are sending nurses almost daily. Thank God for young people, that's what I say.'

'Selfless,' said Harry. 'But what makes them do it?'

'To do good in the world, I suppose, to do the right thing. But what of yourself? Are you keeping well? I don't think we've spoken since Henry's funeral. My goodness, this hideous business is taking a terrible toll.'

'I'm just pleased Bessie isn't here to see it,' said Harry. 'And what of your wife, Margaret, does she keep well?'

'I'm sorry to say it, Harry, but she suffers greatly with

depression. Constantly asking why God has abandoned us, and what have we done to deserve it? I struggle to keep her spirits up.'

The rainstorm swept along in waves, drumming deafeningly down on the umbrella. Fairlie shouted, 'I must hurry, another committee, but let's meet for dinner, or at least a glass of scotch.'

'Let me know when,' shouted Harry, as Fairlie turned and ran for the shelter of City Hall.

* * *

By the time Harry reached home, he was drenched through. Quickly undressing, drying and wrapping himself in a blanket, he retired to bed, where he remained undisturbed for the next three days.

In bouts of troubled sleep, the body of old man Herrick lay next to him, his putrefied corpse crawling with cockroaches. Screaming in terror, Harry leapt from his bed, falling naked and cowering in the corner of the room from where he could see that the face of the rotting corpse was not that of old man Herrick; it was his own.

Frantically, on all fours, Harry scurried about the floor in search of pen and paper. 'I must write,' he cried out. 'Don't take me yet,' he pleaded. 'I must tell her of my regrets.' In trembling script, he scratched out his plea:

My dearest wife,
Do not think ill of me. I intended you no wrong.
Forgive me for my selfish sins. I only did what I
thought was right.

The pen fell from his shaking fingers. The room brightened and became deathly quiet. He lay still, staring unblinkingly up to the white sky above, from where a swarming murmuration of corpulent, iridescent flies swooped down, changing as they fell to snowflakes, pitching cold on his face. Bright sunlight flooded through the long sash windows, and he felt her gently take his hand in hers and stoop to tenderly kiss his lips. She was warm and fragrant. 'Please,' he begged, 'please forgive me.'

* * *

It was Cross, who, worried by Harry's prolonged absence, raised the alarm at City Hall.

Next morning, Dr Broaddus, an elderly gentleman with impeccable manners, arrived. His dark, woollen suit with waistcoat and bow tie were of the finest quality. *More accustomed to scholarly learning than making house calls to the sick*, thought Harry.

'It's a great pleasure to meet you, Mr Mason,' the doctor said in a soft, southern drawl. 'Dr Fairlie was most anxious about your health and asked me to call by. Now, tell me, how are you feeling?'

Harry began by recounting his meeting with James when they had both sheltered under an umbrella. As he spoke, Dr Broaddus examined him, paying particular attention to his eyes and pulse. 'Any vomiting?' he asked.

'None,' replied Harry.

'That's good,' said Dr Broaddus, tucking a glass thermometer under Harry's arm.

'Have I got the fever?' asked Harry, not for the first time worrying about how he would tell Bessie. She had warned him not to stay and would never forgive him for being so mule-headed. His mind drifted as he puzzled over how he would tell her if he were already dead. He was brought to his senses by Dr Broaddus clearing his throat and asking, 'Do you have any aches or pains in your arms, legs or neck?'

'Sometimes, but I've had worse,' said Harry dismissively, with an air of casual nonchalance.

'Any pains in your stomach?'

'Yes, but I've not eaten for days.'

'What about headaches?'

'Not today.'

'When did you last have headaches?'

'The day before yesterday… or maybe it was the day before that.'

'Any delirium or night terrors?'

Harry shrugged.

'Nightmares, Mr Mason,' the doctor repeated the question, unsure if Harry had understood.

'No.'

'Let me see your throat. Open wide.' The doctor gently pushed a wooden paddle deep along his tongue, causing Harry to gag.

Eventually, after checking the thermometer and again taking his pulse and listening to his breathing, Dr Broaddus said, 'Well, Mr Mason, I don't want to alarm you, but it could be the fever. I can't say for sure.'

Harry's stomach tightened and twisted. A spasm gripped his innards. He was going to die.

The doctor continued, 'I don't want you putting too much store in what I'm about to say, but, in my humble opinion, and I may be wrong, it's more likely influenza worsened by exhaustion and self-neglect.'

'I've caught a cold!'

'Common illnesses continue, Mr Mason. They don't take a vacation just cos ol' yellow jack's in town.' He paused briefly. 'Hot soup and dry bread to begin, plenty of rest and plenty to drink, not of the alcoholic variety,' he said emphatically. 'Understood?'

'I understand, Doctor. I'm very grateful.'

'Well, let's keep our fingers crossed. If it worsens – high temperature, coughing blood or black vomit – get your boy to fetch help.'

* * *

After ten days' recuperation, Harry felt well enough to venture out. He had received an invitation from James E. T. Bowden, Henry L'Engle's nephew-in-law, to meet at the Board of Trade Rooms. No reason was given, but Harry assumed it must be to discuss his election to the city council as L'Engle had promised. Harry was excited at the prospect and hoped to see Fairlie after his meeting with Bowden – it had been more than two weeks since their chance meeting during the thunderstorm.

Making his way along Bay Street, Harry was pleasantly surprised to see several shopkeepers taking their shutters down. At the junction with Laura Street, a newsboy handed out copies of the Sanitary Association's free newsletter proclaiming, "End in Sight!". With only a handful of new infections, and with night temperatures falling, the news-sheet predicted the epidemic would soon pass.

Harry felt a surge of elation course through him – he had survived. The hellish nightmare was ending, and life would get back to normal. Bessie would return, and he could again think of the future. He felt joyous with the urge to tell someone, if only to hear himself say the words aloud. Harry called to a shopkeeper sweeping the boardwalk, 'The fever's at an end!'

'Good news, ain't it?' the man shouted back. 'Feels better than when war ended.'

'Yes. Yes, it does. It's good to be alive,' said Harry, turning to continue on his way. In good spirits, he looked skywards to enjoy the warmth of the sun on his face – for the first time in a long while, its embrace felt kinder.

The meeting with Bowden was scheduled for noon, and Harry had arrived in good time. The building was quiet. The committee rooms were empty and the side offices unattended. He checked the invitation to make sure he had the right day. Satisfied he hadn't made a mistake, he settled to wait on a long, polished, mahogany bench. He smiled contentedly to himself – it was coming to an end. *Thank the Lord*, thought Harry.

At precisely noon, a slight, unassuming man appeared at the far end of the hallway. He looked too young for his dated style of dress and had the movements of someone weakened by childhood illness. His thinning, fair hair and sallow complexion added to the appearance of frailty. *Unassuming, but not to be underestimated*, thought Harry.

'Mr Mason?' he enquired as he approached.

Harry stood and offered his hand in greeting.

'I'm pleased to meet you at last. Thank you for arriving so punctually. My name is James Bowden.'

Bowden wore small, round-lensed spectacles held in place by thin, gold frames. His ice-blue eyes flashed a sharpness, weighing and calculating every detail for effect.

Bowden said, 'I saw you at my uncle's funeral. Uncle Henry was a great man. An uncompromising Democrat and patriot who worked tirelessly for all the people of our city. It's a regrettable loss. He will be greatly missed.'

'I've felt his loss deeply,' replied Harry.

'As we all have,' said Bowden, extending his arm as an invitation for Harry to resume his seat on the long, mahogany bench. 'Shall we sit for a moment?'

Harry hesitated. He was eager to leave the public vestibule and retire to Bowden's private offices to learn of the proposals for election to city councillor.

Bowden continued, 'Mr Mason, it's Mr James Fairlie that brings us here today.' There was a directness in his voice.

'Indeed,' said Harry, momentarily thrown. 'I was hoping to meet him later this afternoon.'

'Mr Mason.' There was a long pause. The silence was uncomfortable. 'I'm aware of your recent illness and absence from superintending. Consequently, you'll be unaware of recent events.'

'Recent events?' From Bowden's measured tone and his cold, blank expression, Harry knew that pain was about to be inflicted. He felt sweat on his hands and a hollowness in his chest. He braced himself for the blow to land.

'I'm sorry to be the bearer of bad news, but, sadly, James passed away last Tuesday.'

Harry said nothing. He had hoped differently but knew the words before they came. Bowden continued in a ruthless monotone, sparing no mercy, like a surgeon cutting flesh. Better to get it over with quickly.

'His wife, Margaret, died three days before. I believe it broke his spirit.' Scarcely pausing a beat, he continued with the same ruthlessness, 'They will be forever in our thoughts and prayers.'

Harry nodded, barely able to control his rage. Henry and now James. His two friends, perhaps his only friends, viciously ripped from life and with it, any chance of a step up the ladder. Harry wanted to say something in a calm, dignified manner, as a gentleman might respond, but he knew he would only betray his selfish anger.

Bowden continued, this time a little more personally. 'Mr Mason. May I call you Harry? My uncle Henry valued your friendship and told me of the commitment he and James had pledged. I can assure you that I'll do whatever I can to fulfil their wishes.'

Harry, struggling to contain his disappointment, muttered a weak thank you.

Bowden continued, 'Harry, we all feel the pain of loss, but Jacksonville has suffered worse, and where life endures, there is always hope. Once business returns and City Hall resumes its usual schedules, then we'll speak again.' Bowden smiled easily. It was clear their meeting was at an end.

'There's always hope,' repeated Harry as he walked onto the sidewalk. But he felt empty and tired, the kind of fatigue that comes with defeat. No matter how many sacrifices he made, how hard he worked, how many chances he took, it always led back to the gutter. The injustice and brutal unfairness of it all. Cruel disappointment and self-pity swept through him, hurting worse than any grievous injury. He could feel his fists clenching until the knuckles ached. 'To hell with them all,' he said. 'Everything's been for nothing.' *If only I'd stayed with Eliza. If only I'd listened to Michael. If only I'd stayed at home.*

* * *

With the first heavy frost of winter settling overnight, Thanksgiving Day dawned white and crisp. It was the last day Jacksonville would ever record a case of yellow fever.

The city's quarantine was lifted, and with road and rail links restored, Harry reopened his saloon, changing its name from The European House to Mason's Bar & Restaurant. Harry was once again embarking on a new beginning.

Bessie and the children arrived on the first paddle steamer from New York, and Harry dressed for the occasion. But just as he was about to leave for the jetty, the first mail in several months arrived. There was a letter from England.

* * *

14 September 1888
My dearest Enoch,

We hope you are in good health and continue to prosper. It's been remiss of me not to have written with news of your daughters. Florence is wed and is expecting her first child. If it's a boy, she's chosen Enoch in honour of her dear father. Bertha is engaged to marry, although a wedding date is yet to be set. All three daughters are in employment as bodice stitchers, following in their mother's footsteps.

We've decided on a family photographic portrait at the new studio opening nearby and will send a copy at the first opportunity.

All goes well here.

Our family miss you, and you are always in our thoughts and prayers.

Affectionately, your wife,

Eliza.

* * *

It had been seven years since he had last seen his daughters. They'd been little girls – sweet, caring and innocent – and that's how he remembered them.

With no time to spare, he destroyed the letter and hurried to meet the steamer, but thoughts of England could not be so quickly banished.

* * *

The jetty was crowded with families reuniting, loved ones kissing and hugging and crying with tears of joy.

His two sons, George and Charles, had grown in the four months since he had last seen them, and his stepson, John Handley, was now a man; he had grown tall and broad and sported a well-groomed beard, set off by a new East Coast tailored suit topped with a natty straw boater. Bessie, large with pregnancy, stepped clear of the gangway and stood with her arms outstretched, waiting for Harry to embrace her.

'My goodness, you've lost weight!' she said.

Harry knew it from his trousers, drawn tight and held in place by both belt and braces.

'My dear husband, was there no time to eat?'

'It was fine, my dear. The newspapers always make things sound worse with their sensational nonsense.'

'Harry, don't blather me; I can see it in your face. You look tired and drawn, and you've a scruffy mop of grey hair. But it's no matter; now that our family is once more together, we will soon restore you to your old self. But, Harry,' she continued more seriously, 'you must promise never to part from us again.'

'I promise, my dearest. I swear to it.'

'Good, because tomorrow we'll celebrate Mass together and give thanks to the good Lord for His boundless mercy and compassion, and there, in the sight of the Almighty, you can swear your oath on the Bible.'

SEVENTEEN

The following day, Bessie learnt the tragic news of Fairlie and L'Engle's deaths, but Harry told her nothing of the suffering and filth, which by the time of her return had been cleaned away. The yellow and black flags had been taken down, the volunteer nurses returned home and the shops were again full of fresh food. And the streets were clean and smelled sweet from the gardenia, jasmine and pink mandevilla vines, all blossoming in profusion. Only the cemeteries and the eyes of those who had stayed bore witness to the sorrow.

* * *

At Christmas, Harry received a letter from the city council, thanking him for his loyal and courageous work. Attached was an invitation to join councillors at their Christmas drinks reception. Harry cheerfully attended but afterwards wished he hadn't. He found the councillors, to a man, dull-witted, self-important peacocks, without an original thought in their heads. Most spoke of how they had found themselves regrettably called away just as the epidemic struck and how they all envied him, wishing that they too had been there to fight for their city. They were contemptible. These were not his kind of people, and he was not one of them. Without the entertaining wit and intellect of Fairlie and L'Engle, the whole affair was a bore, and he resolved to abandon any ambition for elected office.

***

Harry's third son, Thomas, arrived in the new year, and to mark the occasion, Harry bought a newly constructed house with three reception rooms and six large bedrooms, located a little further along on West Adams Street at 914. Bessie could not have been happier than in her own home, caring for her children and running the household, which had increased from Martha, the housekeeper, to include a cook, two housemaids, a yard boy and a nursery-maid.

Keeping himself to himself and avoiding the usual business associations and social gatherings, he invested his time and money, acquiring two more boarding houses and a general store. He took pride and satisfaction in the rigours of hard work, which occupied his mind and kept his thoughts from loneliness and remorse.

***

Their fourth child, and Bessie's only daughter, Lily Beatrice, came into the world on a bright spring day in 1891, a year pleasingly marked only by family anniversaries and the usual public holidays. Life was comfortable and filled with agreeable routines, the contented life most men can only dream of. Yet, throughout this year, Harry was troubled by thoughts of Eliza, whom he continued to support with regular remittances. But it wasn't just Eliza that disturbed his mind. He regretted much, frequently imagining himself back in London, surrounded by happy grandchildren, relishing the respectability of an East End garment manufacturer. He missed the fellowship of his favourite pubs and the friendship of those to whom he was bound by an unspoken bond. He enjoyed reminiscing on the times when warming his hands at an open coal fire, toasting crumpet, drinking strong ale and laughing aloud as pals arrived, shaking him cheerfully by the hand, and he missed Michael and the raucous cockfights and thrilling bouts at blood alley.

He missed the granite certainty of England. Its features etched and chiselled over thousands of years, its countless peoples spread across every continent, ruled by an indomitable queen-empress. America was none of this. It was an adolescent in search of an identity. It was rootless, its people, disparate immigrants, drifting across prairies and mountains, moving from job to job, shifting from opportunity to opportunity, forever on the move to somewhere but never a destination. It was a country in flux, ephemeral and temporary, like cardboard scenery in a theatre, the stage crowded with countless acquaintances, associates and partners but rarely friends, of which he had none. Without noticing, he had grown old and cheerless.

Changing names meant nothing. No one knew who he was and cared even less. The country was indifferent, and he'd been foolish to think he could forge a new home or build a sense of belonging. It was a place where power and wealth dominated at every level, even friendship was understood as transactional, calculated in terms of its value. It was a country without foundations or any past; it had nothing to fall back on – like a book with its opening chapters torn out, it has only the promise of a good ending. Agnes had been right to return home.

Harry pondered how life had become a series of disappointments, with too many snakes and few ladders. Nicky and Agnes had been friends, and he'd found friendship with Fairlie and L'Engle, who had embraced and welcomed him, but in the end, all had led to sadness.

There was no point wishing for what might have been; his only course was forward. But this time, he would travel alone and confine himself to business. Business was impersonal, where everything was measured, counted and weighed without the hindrance of words or emotion. America was to be grabbed, harnessed and exploited – taken and enjoyed without thought for others – and to hell with what was right. Business suited America, where making your name and having more than enough was all that mattered. Success was the measure of happiness.

* * *

Harry bought another saloon at 107 West Bay and, the following month, a small boarding hotel on the corner of West Bay and Julia Street called The Acme.

Around the Bay district, Harry was regarded as a successful businessman and an example to others of what opportunity, enterprise and hard work could bring. He had, after all, made a name for himself.

Two or three times a year, Bowden brought political colleagues to dine at The Mason Bar & Restaurant, and sometimes he spoke to Harry about the prospect of becoming a councillor. Harry always played the amiable and lavish host, but he showed little interest in becoming one of them; he now ploughed a solitary furrow. Even so, there was an itch that irritated. Like a gambler, he just needed one more card, one more throw of the dice, one more spin of the wheel.

***

It was September 1893, while reading the *Jacksonville Evening Standard*, that Harry saw his chance. He noticed an announcement cancelling the world heavyweight contest between "Gentleman Jim" Corbett and the English champion Charlie Mitchell. The fight had been scheduled for December at Coney Island, but Brooklyn's Mayor, David Boody, had refused a permit.

The newspaper article described how the previous year, Corbett had fought the Great John L. Sullivan in front of ten thousand at the Olympic Club in New Orleans. The fight lasted twenty-one rounds before Sullivan, battered and bloodied, was knocked unconscious. Bat Masterson, the infamous Wild West gunslinger and Dodge City sheriff, was ringside, reporting in his new incarnation as a sports columnist for the *New York Morning Telegraph*.

Without a permit to fight in Brooklyn, the boxers urgently needed a new venue, but they faced another problem. Prizefighting had fallen out of popular fashion, with opponents arguing that it was barbaric and not conducive to the peace and dignity of civilised society. State governors in thirty-eight of the forty-four states had successfully mounted legal challenges to the so-called blood sport, and few cities showed any interest in hosting the contest.

Those in favour argued that it was a skill of science and art, pleasing to the aesthetic senses of cultured and discerning gentlemen. But the civil authorities remained unimpressed, fearing an influx of unruly spectators, cheap liquor, unregulated gambling and the assembled company of the worst criminals, thugs and prostitutes from around the country, all drawn to the bloody spectacle like moths to a flame, but Harry knew that this was the chance he'd been waiting for.

Using his acquaintance with Bowden, he made his pitch. Harry explained how the Corbett fight in New Orleans had turned a profit of fifty thousand dollars, and this was just the tip of the iceberg. Thousands more had been made from liquor, gambling, licensing, sponsors, hotel room tax and, what Harry called, telegraphic report shows. Bowden listened with interest.

Harry enthused, 'It's easy money. All we do is announce the time and place, and the newspapers do the rest. The money just rolls in; all we have to do is count it.'

'But do we have a venue, and will the governor and sheriff agree?' asked Bowden. 'And is it legal?'

The following day, the two men discussed their enterprise with Judge Henry B. Philips and the lawyer Clement D. Rinehart. After much deliberation, both men confirmed that there was no legal impediment to the fight being staged in Jacksonville.

Judge Philips said, 'The law is clear. It must be a gloved exhibition of pugilistic skill and science, regulated under specific and agreed rules of a properly registered athletic club. If it meets these criteria, then it's legal in the County of Duval and the City of Jacksonville.'

That clinched it – the fight was on.

* * *

As word spread, so opposition grew. Mayor Duncan U. Fletcher was vehemently opposed and encouraged a host of religious, moral and civic societies to organise and rouse public opinion to campaign against it. The Duval County Sheriff, Napoleon B. Broward, an old friend of Harry's, was adamant that it would never take place in his jurisdiction, and Florida Governor, Henry Mitchell, was so horrified by the thought that he pledged to send troops to prevent it.

'This matter,' proclaimed Governor Mitchell, 'is not a legal one. It's a matter of morality, common decency and the standards of behaviour expected from civilised people. It will be decided not in a court of law but by the court of public opinion. Together, the God-fearing people of Jacksonville will put a stop to this barbarity.'

Judge Henry B. Philips, who had been retained by Harry as his legal advisor, responded sharply, 'The rule of law cannot be cowed or intimidated by politicians or public clamour. It is the independence of the judiciary and the rule of law that shall decide matters in a free, constitutional democracy.'

This was the opening salvo between those in favour – the sports – and those who opposed – the puritans.

Bowden called a meeting of his business associates, and on 12 October 1893, the Duval Athletic Club was officially constituted. Six trustees were appointed, with Harry unanimously elected club president, with Bowden as treasurer. The next step was to bind both fighters under contract.

Harry and Bowden travelled to New York to meet the boxers and their respective agents at the Waldorf-Astoria Hotel, where Corbett resided in one of its grander suites. But after a week of haggling, they were no nearer agreeing terms, Corbett insisting that he would not fight for a cent less than fifty thousand dollars.

After an incredibly frustrating series of negotiations, Bowden, who had become exasperated by the process, exclaimed, 'I think they're playing us for fools. Someone's promised more money but hasn't yet put the cash on the table, and they're stringing us along until the money turns up, and there's nothing we can do except wait and pray. The question is, for how long?'

Harry said, 'We need to get someone on the inside.'

'Go on,' said Bowden, intrigued.

'Their room maid is in and out all day long, cleaning, fetching and carrying. She's a young, coloured girl, and they run her ragged.'

'So what?'

'She's earning less than fifteen dollars a month. So, for $150, she might prick her ears up.'

'You mean a spy,' said Bowden.

Two days later, Harry reported back, announcing excitedly, 'They've received a telegram from Carson City saying the deal's off. The maid says that when Corbett heard the news, he went crazy, throwing glasses, smashing tables and God knows what else. But listen to this,' said Harry, lowering his voice as if about to disclose a secret. 'Corbett's manager said, "We'll just have to take Bowden's offer. It's that or nothing."'

'I knew it!' said Bowden sounding vindicated. 'Carson City! The snakes! So, tomorrow we offer them a twenty thousand purse – take it or leave it.'

* * *

Mitchell agreed right off the bat, but Corbett faked ambivalence, insisting on minor changes to the contract. But after much theatre, Corbett gave way, and both fighters signed.

Harry wired *The Evening Telegraph* in Jacksonville. 'Corbett-Mitchell fight agreed. The greatest spectacle of the century coming to Jacksonville.'

All hell broke loose. Harry was inundated with requests from across the country, from East Coast gambling outfits offering to handle the betting arrangements to West Coast breweries offering to manage the beer and liquor commissions. Bowden was served with an arrest warrant for inciting an affray, which he publicly tore up in front of an excited throng of reporters gathered on the steps of the courthouse. Governor Mitchell obtained an injunction prohibiting Corbett and Mitchell from entering the State of Florida – the following day it was annulled by Judge Philips as unconstitutional. Mayor Duncan U. Fletcher issued a statement declaring that the city government would not allow the fight within its jurisdiction, but within hours, he was contradicted by the chairman of the city council granting the legal right to hold the fight.

Bowden appealed to the supreme court for an adjudication on the definition of a boxing competition and wrote to President Cleveland, canvassing his support. He didn't expect a reply from either, but it all added to the febrile atmosphere and generated thousands of column inches published across the nation.

The old Jacksonville racetrack, which accommodated fewer than eight thousand spectators in its heyday, was the largest venue available. Nevertheless, without regard to any practicalities, Harry arranged for the sale of eighteen thousand ringside tickets. He also sold special Jacksonville liquor and gambling permits, allowing the holders to ply their trade citywide during what he termed "fight week". Sheriff Broward responded by threatening to arrest anyone found possessing one of Harry's bogus permits.

Harry called a meeting of the local hotel and saloon owners to press home the commercial benefits afforded by the thousands flocking to witness the world championship. And how, in the spirit of partnership and to avoid malicious damage to their properties, he would provide, at a reasonable fee, additional protection to assure their safety. All agreed to pay.

Harry was less successful when propositioning the railroad owners, who politely but firmly explained that he would be ill-advised to persist in his demands. Harry took the hint. But even without the railways, he reckoned he had generated over two hundred thousand dollars, a small fortune.

EIGHTEEN

The fight was scheduled for Thursday, 25 January 1894.

As the date drew closer, the rivalry between the sports and puritans became increasingly acrimonious. Sheriff Broward deputised a team of volunteers to tear down the boxing ring the moment it was built. Harry, who had gotten wind of the plan, organised a gang of carpenters and blacksmiths to construct a prefabricated ring to be assembled in situ in less than two hours. His intention was to announce the precise location of the fight at the very last moment and have the ring built only after a crowd of several thousand had gathered, giving no chance for the Sheriff's men to tear it down.

Attempting to stop the fight from going ahead, Mayor Fletcher tried to persuade two of America's great railway tycoons, Henry B. Plant and Henry Flagler, to refuse train tickets to spectators journeying to the fight. They declined, saying they favoured free enterprise and had no duty to act as the government's policemen.

Two days before the fight, Governor Mitchell called up the Second Battalion of the Ocala Rifles with orders to use whatever force necessary to stop the contest, including live ammunition. This enraged the citizens of Jacksonville, many of whom had initially been ardent opponents of the fight. When the troops arrived, crowds booed and obstructed their progress at every street corner. Angered at the troop's reception, Governor Mitchell threatened to impose martial law and close the city, which only worsened the situation. Fearing wide-scale rioting and loss of innocent lives, the state supreme court ruled that a regulated boxing contest was lawful. This propelled Florida Circuit Judge Rhydon M. Call to issue an injunction proscribing any interference to the fight, with a sanction of two hundred thousand dollars. Governor Mitchell and the puritans conceded.

* * *

The town went wild. Extra trains were laid on from as far away as Mobile, Atlanta, Boston and even Kansas City. Those with hotel rooms sold them at four and five times what they had paid, choosing instead to sleep on the street and spend their windfall in the saloons. Mischievously, Harry provided free beer and fight tickets to every soldier in the Ocala Rifles, much to the annoyance of the governor.

On fight day, crowds gathered on street corners, filling every buggy, wagon and cab in town, excitedly waiting for news of the venue. Harry made the announcement at 11am: Moncrief Park, a sports field four miles north of the city. What followed was a chaotic stampede from town. By midday, fifteen thousand spectators had crashed through the gates and were fighting to secure a vantage point from which to view the spectacle. Harry's workmen laboured to assemble the prefabricated boxing ring and quickly hoisted a rudimentary canvas roof to protect the fighters from a light drizzle, which had begun falling shortly before noon. Bat Masterson positioned armed men around the ring with orders to shoot dead any spectator attempting to climb through the ropes.

Gambling was ferocious, with thousands of dollars bet on Corbett, the American favourite, to win. Harry seized the opportunity to circulate a rumour that Corbett was drunk and could barely stand. Sentiment changed in an instant, with a flood of new money piling in on Mitchell. Harry took a ten-cent cut on every dollar placed so had no interest in the fight's outcome.

Making his way through the throng of spectators to the fighter's locker room, Harry was pushed and shoved and came close to being trampled underfoot. The moment he arrived, Corbett, who was the younger and taller of the two men, standing at over six feet one inch and weighing 212 pounds, pulled Harry to one side. 'Are you the idiot who organised this circus? How are we supposed to get to the ring through this pack of animals?'

Mitchell, who stood five feet nine inches and weighed a mere 160 pounds, joined in, claiming to have been set upon by a mob of drunken spectators. 'You haven't got brains enough to give yourself a headache. If I'd known it was such a shithole, I'd have stayed away.' Folding his arms, he glared at Harry, adding, 'I ain't fighting. It's like a bloody fairground knockabout.'

Corbett, who had refilled his champagne flute, took a different tack. 'I don't mind fighting, but I want my money first.'

'Yeah! Me too! Money first!' demanded Mitchell.

Harry turned to the Englishman. 'Now you listen here, the world has come here to see you fight. Neither you nor Champagne Jimmy gets a cent until you've done your work. Make a run for it, and that mob out there will get to know you're a pissing coward, and when they get hold of you...' Harry made a twisting gesture with his hands as if wringing out a wet towel. 'That'll be your neck.' Then, turning to Corbett, 'And you can quit behaving like a spoilt brat too or you'll get your arse smacked.'

Corbett threw his chest out and took a step forward.

Harry clenched his fists. 'Don't stick your chin out at me, Jimmy boy. It's too big a target.'

Corbett's manager, Bill Brady, and trainer, Jack Dempsey, moved in to stand between them.

'Okay, let's all calm down,' said Brady. 'Look, Harry, you gotta admit, it doesn't look great out there. I'm gonna be honest with you, you ain't gonna get twenty-one rounds, not like with Sullivan in New Orleans. We wanna be out of here pretty damn quick.'

The roar of the crowd came in deafening waves, making it difficult to hear what was being said. Brady continued, raising his voice to be heard, 'Four or five rounds is enough. Let's agree on that. Jimmy wins, and in fair exchange, Charlie gets an extra five grand. Then we're all winners.' Turning to Mitchell, Brady said, 'What do you say, Charlie? Four rounds and an extra five in your pocket. Fair enough?'

Mitchell said, 'Bollocks! The purse and title are rightfully mine. I took Sullivan to thirty-nine rounds in Paris.'

Corbett piped up, 'But you didn't knock him out, did you? And if you ain't noticed, it's me you're fighting.'

Before Mitchell could continue bickering, Brady said, 'Okay, okay. So, let's play it like this. If you think you can take Jimmy, you go right ahead. But, here's the thing, if you go down before the fourth, you get the extra five and we all go home early. Think about it.'

Harry interrupted. 'You sort it out between yourselves. I just need to see both of you in the ring in ten minutes. Masterson's outside to get you through the crowd.' With that, Harry turned and headed for the door, shouting back as he left, 'Ten minutes!'

'I'll be there,' shouted Corbett. 'Not sure about chickenshit Charlie.'

* * *

Corbett was in the ring a few minutes later, but Mitchell didn't appear. Harry waited impatiently. The crowd was becoming restless. 'Where the hell's Mitchell?' Harry snapped when he found Masterson.

'Not sure, Harry. He left the locker room behind Corbett, and then I lost sight of him.'

'Sweet Jesus! He hasn't done a runner, has he?'

Masterson shrugged.

Harry was agitated, looking this way and that. 'Jesus Christ!' he shouted as if calling for divine intervention. 'If he doesn't show, we're in deep shit. We'll never get out of here alive.'

Masterson said, 'Calm yourself, Harry; no one's been shot... not yet at least.'

'Thanks, Bat, you're a big help. How the hell—' But before Harry could complete the sentence, a deafening roar went up. Mitchell was climbing into the ring wearing a scarlet silk dressing gown and was swirling a huge British union flag. Several thousand spectators booed the Englishman and screamed in protest. A man leapt from the crowd intent on snatching the flag, only to be knocked cold by one of Mitchell's seconds.

'What's the idiot playing at?' asked Masterson. 'He's gonna start a fucking riot wearing that British redcoat outfit.'

'At least we've got a fight,' said Harry, ignoring Masterson's remark.

'Who's gonna win, Harry? My money's on Corbett in the tenth.'

'I don't give a damn, just make sure you get them back to town in one piece.'

'Don't worry, I've ten guns and two fast coaches at the ready.'

Harry nodded, but he wasn't reassured.

Bowden pushed his way through to Harry's side. He was drenched from the rain, which was now falling heavily. 'We're still selling tickets. It's unbelievable. We've taken more than twenty thousand since noon. They're still fighting to get in, and I've heard someone's been shot dead at the gate.' He paused to get his breath. 'It's really great. Oh, and Sheriff Broward says he's on his way to arrest Corbett and Mitchell.'

'Well, good luck with that,' said Harry, pointing towards Corbett's corner. 'That's his deputies over there – most are too drunk to stand.'

Bowden slapped him on the back. 'We've done a great job, Harry.'

Nodding his appreciation, Harry said, 'Let's hope we live to enjoy it.' But the noise from the spectators was now so loud, Bowden had no idea what Harry had said.

* * *

At 2.20pm, the referee, Honest John Kelly, called the fighters together to shake on a fair fight. Neither did. Instead, they stood toe to toe, insulting one another.

The bell rang – round one – the crowd surged forward. Those at the front were in danger of being crushed as the fighters wasted no time. Corbett was a stylish boxer, employing honed skills to jab, hook and parry. Mitchell, who was renown as the hardest puncher, was fast, dodging, bobbing and weaving, forcing Corbett to miss and punch wildly into thin air.

Mitchell ducked low and, coming up fast under his opponent's guard, riveted home three pulverising rib-breakers. But as he stepped back from the attack, Corbett caught him with a scything left hook, opening a cut above the right eye. Mitchell grappled Corbett around the neck; there was a sickening clash of heads; and Corbett repeatedly smashed a short right into Mitchell's side. The referee struggled to separate the boxers as the bell signalled the end of the round. Honours even.

Round two was a furious affair, with both fighters punching and slogging it out without break or pause. Corbett's stylish approach gave way to rudimentary bludgeoning to Mitchell's head, while receiving in return sledgehammer blows, one after the other to the body. Corbett, momentarily winded, missed with an arching left uppercut. Mitchell stepped back half a pace and caught Corbett clean on the chin, sending his head lurching backwards. Mitchell hit him again, once in the neck and then full in the face as Corbett's head recoiled forward. Corbett staggered.

The crowd went wild, surging forward at every attack. Mitchell closed in to deliver a devastating combination, knocking Corbett sideways and opening a cut above the left eye. Allowing no time for his opponent to recover, Mitchell again pressed his attack with a punishing straight right jab to Corbett's chin, knocking him reeling against the ropes. But, before Mitchell could launch his lethal left to finish the contest, Corbett caught him with a stinging uppercut, quickly followed by a right-left-right combination to the head. Mitchell's knees buckled, and he hit the canvas hard. Struggling to get up, he perched himself on all fours, blood dripping freely from the gash above his eye. Mitchell was panting and shaking his head. Corbett hovered like a hawk watching its prey. Pushing Corbett away, the referee started the count but too slow for Corbett's liking.

'What the hell are you doing?' complained Corbett, breathing heavily and trying to wipe blood and sweat from his eyes. 'He's out! He's finished!'

Taking no notice of Corbett's protests, the referee continued his count at a pedestrian pace: 'Five-a... and-a... six-a... and-a...' When he reached seven, he stopped and ordered Corbett back to his corner. Only when Corbett had complied and was sitting on his corner stool did the referee recommence the count: 'Four-a... and-a... five-a... and-a...'

'You imbecile,' shouted Corbett as his team of seconds worked to close a cut over his left eye. 'That's the second time we've had five.'

Mitchell got slowly back to his feet.

But before the referee signalled the fight to continue, Corbett rushed at Mitchell. Right-left-right. Mitchell stumbled. Right-left-right. Right again. Mitchell's head rebounded from one shoulder to the other. Toppling forward, Mitchell was knocked sideways by a vicious uppercut, sending him heavily to the canvas. But Mitchell refused to stay down – gallantly struggling on one knee, gasping for air and head bowed, he prepared to force himself upright. But Corbett wasn't going to allow another long count. Striding across the ring, he hit Mitchell with a sickening right to the head, propelling him sprawling across the canvas.

The bell rang, ending round two. Corbett paraded triumphantly around the ring, arms raised aloft. But Mitchell wasn't yet finished. Staggering to his feet, he came at Corbett low and fast from behind, punching him with devastating force to the kidneys and to the back of the head. Dazed and taken by surprise, Corbett stumbled forward as he desperately wrestled Mitchell around the neck. Both sets of seconds ran from their corners to join the scuffle. Brawling broke out in all quarters of the crowd, provoking Masterson's men to draw their pistols and fire into the air. One spectator scrambled under the ropes, only to be kicked in the face by the referee. Harry and Bowden stood watching in disbelief as the whole arena erupted into pandemonium, in danger of deteriorating into a full-scale riot. Masterson clambered into the ring, firing his Winchester, one shot after another. The crack of rifle fire brought some sanity and sent both fighters reluctantly back to their corners.

There was frantic activity around Mitchell – smelling salts, iodine, grease, ice and water – his seconds slapping, patting and rubbing life back into their champion. The referee conferred with the timekeeper, and the crowd went quiet with anticipation of the fight being stopped. Corbett skipped around the ring, waiting for his quarry to reappear.

Eventually, after a long respite, the bell sounded to begin round three. Mitchell came out holding a solid-looking defence, but it didn't last long. Corbett came at him with the speed and agility of a cheetah. With his elegant style restored, Corbett deployed his renowned skill of picking his man off, penetrating Mitchell's guard with ease, each time sending his opponent's head rocking back. Three hard punches sent Mitchell once more to the canvas, but by the count of nine, he was back on his feet, ready to take more punishment.

Corbett chasséd and stalked his man, smashing him with one punch at a time, like a sniper picking his target. Mitchell lunged forward, grappling Corbett round the neck, hanging there like a bloody carcass. The referee pulled him off and, for several long seconds, stood between the fighters, giving Mitchell time to regain the semblance of composure. Corbett waited patiently, head slightly inclined to one side as if carefully eyeing a coconut on a fairground shy. As the referee stepped aside, Corbett hit Mitchell with explosive force, lifting the smaller man clean off his feet, sending him reeling backwards, tumbling sideways and falling dead weight on his face. He lay motionless for several minutes, his face so severely beaten and covered in blood, the English fighter was barely recognisable. There was no comeback this time. The referee raised Corbett's arm and declared him heavyweight champion of the world. The fight had lasted twelve minutes.

Masterson's men, weapons drawn, clambered into the ring as the crowd went berserk, tearing the ring to pieces, corner posts, ropes, bunting and shreds of canvas flooring, anything they could grab as a souvenir of the historic moment. In a tight armadillo, Masterson's men bundled and pushed both fighters through the frenzied mob and out to a procession of waiting wagons.

Mitchell was rushed to the Everett Hotel for urgent medical attention. Corbett and his entourage retired victorious to a champagne celebration at the prestigious St James Hotel, where Sheriff Broward was waiting his arrival. The champion was greeted with rapturous applause and cheering and, after signing souvenir programmes for the sheriff's deputies, was arrested and taken to the jailhouse on charges of unlawfully fighting by agreement.

Concerned for Mitchell's welfare, Harry went to the Everett, where he received news of Corbett's arrest and guessed that Broward would soon arrive for Mitchell.

Seeing Harry in the Everett's foyer, Broward said, 'I take no pleasure in this, Harry, but I've a warrant for your arrest.'

'For me!'

'For arranging a fight by agreement. I've got one for Mitchell, too.'

Harry and the sheriff knew each other well. Broward had spoken at Nicky's funeral, and Bessie had lodged with Broward's aunt Helen, where they had all enjoyed several Thanksgiving dinners together. Broward lowered his voice.

'Look, Harry, I hope you're not gonna make a fuss. It's just something I gotta do.'

'Don't worry, I ain't putting up a fight, nor's Mitchell, he's half dead. If you take my advice, you'll leave him with the doctor.'

'I gotta take him to the jailhouse, Governor's orders.'

'He's in a bad way. He ain't going nowhere. God knows, he can't even walk.' Harry continued in a sincere tone, 'Him dying in your jailhouse won't look good. Put a couple of men to guard him. I give you my word – he won't go on the run.'

Leaving Mitchell at the Everett, Harry accompanied Broward to the jailhouse, where he was welcomed by Corbett.

'Come on in, Mason, and help me celebrate,' said Corbett, who had made himself comfortable. 'The accommodation's a bit rough, but it's quite homely if you ignore the bars.' Corbett's left eye was badly cut and swollen closed. He had a nasty cut to his right ear and ugly swellings across both cheekbones. 'How's Charlie? I beat him up pretty bad.'

'He's not good, Jimmy. But the doc thinks he'll live.'

'Well, I'm sorry, but he got under my skin, and he hurt me real bad. I think he's broken a rib. The smarmy English. Oh! No offence, Mason, I forgot... here, have some champagne. I've already ordered dinner. The chef's bringing it from the St James, and the sheriff's gonna join us, too. Real nice fella, even if he's a little strange. Said he don't drink wine nor liquor. No matter, it means more for us, eh? We're having oyster mignonette, followed by *poulet à la moutarde* and then *entrecôte grillée*, with two bottles of the best Pétrus. Sound okay?'

Harry was impressed. 'What about court tomorrow?'

'Oh, that!' Corbett charged their glasses. 'This Clicquot is pretty good stuff.'

'My favourite,' replied Harry. 'But what about court?'

'Bowden has straightened things out. He reckons I should make the afternoon train.'

'Bowden?' queried Harry, as he made himself comfortable on one of the straw bunks.

'He says the judge is his aunt's nephew, or his wife's cousin or... well, who the hell knows, I just know he's straightening things out.'

* * *

Next day, Corbett and Harry strolled leisurely to the courthouse in the bright, morning sun, Corbett stopping from time to time to sign autographs and wave to well-wishers. As they crossed the street, Bowden sidled up to Harry and whispered, 'Judge Philips has dissolved The Duval Athletic Club – it's no longer a legal entity.'

'Good,' said Harry. 'Meaning what? I'm not guilty of arranging the fight?'

'You're in the clear,' said Bowden. 'And tell Corbett he can collect his cheque for $28,000 at Barnett's bank.'

The hearing began at 10am. The public gallery was packed, mostly with fashionably dressed young ladies from Jacksonville's well-to-do families. Witnesses were called, and Sheriff Broward swore on oath that the contest involved drunkenness, disorderly conduct and rowdy behaviour, with guns being discharged.

Corbett's defence lawyer asked, 'Tell me, Sheriff, how many drunks did you arrest in Jacksonville last Saturday night?'

Broward replied, 'Four.'

The lawyer continued his questioning. 'Tell the court, Sheriff. How many drunks did you arrest at the boxing competition yesterday?'

'None.'

'So, Sheriff, you'll agree that your town on a Saturday night is immeasurably more disorderly than a harmless boxing exhibition?'

The court collapsed into laughter.

Masterson took the stand and gave a long, rambling speech, citing his experience as a US marshal and, more recently, as an international sports correspondent. In his opinion, it was a lawful assembly of educated and discerning gentlemen, come to witness an exhibition of athleticism and skill.

Mayor Duncan U. Fletcher arrived to give evidence but was excluded by the judge, ruling that he would only accept testimony from those who had been present and had actually witnessed the fight. Fletcher admitted that he had been at home with his family and saw nothing of the contest.

With no other witnesses, the case against Corbett was dismissed and charges against Mitchell and Mason dropped.

Bowden greeted Harry outside the courthouse, shaking his hand vigorously. 'Well, partner, I think we did a great job.' There was a patronising and disingenuous tone to his voice. It reminded Harry of the spiv he had met on the steamer coming south from New York.

'Where's my cut?' asked Harry.

'Don't worry, partner. It's all being taken care of.'

Harry didn't trust Bowden's effortless smile and turn of phrase. He felt uneasy as cramp grabbed his guts, and his fists began to tighten.

'What do you mean, being taken care of?'

Masterson, who was carrying his Winchester, interrupted. 'Well, gentlemen, it's been a pleasure,' he said, handing each a business card. 'You know where to find me for the next time.' He thrust out his hand and grasped Harry in a tight handshake. 'Let's hope our paths cross again, Mr Mason.'

Harry said, 'Before you go, Bat, mind if I ask you about your rifle? Was it the one that shot the outlaws out there in the Wild West?'

'Hell no! This one's shot nothing bigger than a rat. Here, have it,' he said. 'Take it as a souvenir.'

Harry took the rifle. 'Thanks, I might have cause to use it. There's plenty of vermin around these parts.'

NINETEEN

Harry arrived early at the private banking office of Bion H. Barnett, which, compared to the bank's grand, marble lobby, was surprisingly small and unassuming. Behind the simple oak desk, surrounded by weighty ledgers, sat a serious-minded gentleman with old-fashioned manners. Wearing half-moon, tortoiseshell spectacles and a conservatively tailored dark-blue business suit, he looked the image of rectitude.

Barnett welcomed Harry warmly and invited him to take his ease in a well-padded armchair. Without prompting, a secretary arrived with coffee. As she poured, Harry glanced around the room. Golf mementoes and a polo trophy sat proudly on a sideboard, an onyx ashtray with a stubbed Partagás Cuban cigar was close at hand on the desk and on an otherwise bare wall, hung a simple framed pen and ink sketch of the bank's founder, who, Harry guessed, was Barnett's father.

After brief pleasantries, Barnett began, 'I expect, Mr Mason, you've come about your money. Well, I can give you every assurance that things are in good order and properly accounted for.'

'That's good to hear,' replied Harry. 'And I apologise if I sound disrespectful, but the last time I was confidently assured my money was safe, I ended up out of pocket. So, if you don't mind, I'd like to know the details to my own satisfaction.'

'Very prudent, Mr Mason. I couldn't agree more.' Barnett collected a green, leather-bound ledger from his desk drawer. 'I have here, Mr Mason, a record of all transactions concerning the Duval Athletic Club. You may of course inspect it at any time. It contains all incomes, expenditures and miscellaneous payments, listed both by date and in alphabetical order.'

Harry listened as every word was carefully sculpted from the air. The man intrigued him; his accent was not southern, nor was it east coast. Indeed, he sounded almost aristocratically English. 'Shall I continue, Mr Mason?'

Harry nodded. 'Please do.'

'After all deductions, and a small provision set aside for future contingencies—'

'Such as?' interrupted Harry.

'Legal representation, government or state taxation, insurance indemnity, damage or injury claim, unexpected late invoices, and so on. The kind of unplanned incidentals which must always be provided for.' He paused momentarily, waiting further questions. 'After all deductions and distribution of agreed fees to the club trustees, the remaining surplus is to be divided between the two principals: namely, yourself and Mr James Edwin Theodore Bowden, who I believe is known to close friends, of whom I include myself, as Jet.'

Barnett gave a detailed description of how income and expenditures were recorded, which, to an accountant, may have held some fascination but to Harry's ears was an unnecessary distraction. What was his share and had Bowden short-changed him? This was what he wanted to know.

Barnett continued, 'The dividend payable to yourself is...' again pausing to double-check for accuracy and running a finger slowly across the ledger, 'yes, here we are. $96,352.84.' Looking over the top of his spectacles, Barnett tentatively enquired, 'Is this in line with your own calculations, Mr Mason?'

Harry said nothing. A rush of excitement had taken his breath. He really wanted to hear Barnett repeat the number – this was a colossal sum and vastly more than he had anticipated.

Sounding concerned, Barnett said, 'I can provide every assurance, Mr Mason, I've carefully verified the accounts myself.'

'It's very satisfactory, Mr Barnett, and is indeed broadly in line with expectations.'

Reassured, Barnett continued, 'I assume you will wish to open a personal account here at the Barnett Bank, where we can securely deposit your money and provide all the advice and benefits attached to Florida's largest bank.'

Matter-of-factly, Harry said, 'I'll deposit $95,000 and take the odd extras as cash.'

'It will be my pleasure, Mr Mason, and may I congratulate you on such a bold enterprise. You've certainly put Jacksonville on the map, and your success is nothing less than remarkable and is the talk of the city, indeed, the length of Florida. I can say, without fear of contradiction, that with assets enough to support any number of business opportunities, your acquaintance will be much in demand.'

Barnett wasn't wrong. The following three years were a whirlwind of social and business engagements. Harry built a spacious Atlantic beachfront house at Ponte Vedra, which he used during the summer months for entertaining, inviting those guests who might prove to be useful.

Bessie became a significant donor to the Church of the Immaculate Conception and a founding member of the Daughters of Isabella. She enthusiastically involved herself in local fundraising and other charitable good works. Bowden nominated Harry for membership to the influential Jacksonville Board of Trade, while Judge Philips enlisted Harry into the exclusive Florida Yacht Club and introduced him to the classy Seminole Social Club, where Jacksonville's wealthiest socialites and political elites gathered. Harry was pleased to become a benefactor to the Daniel Memorial Orphanage & Home, named in honour of Colonel Daniel, alongside whom he had fought the yellow fever epidemic of 1888.

Of all his new acquaintances, it was Bion Barnett who interested him most. Yet, while Barnett willingly spent time with Harry at his office in friendly conversation, Barnett always refused Harry's invitations to meet socially. Nevertheless, Harry did learn of the tight family connections between Barnett's wife, Carolina, and Bowden's wife, Laura, both nieces of the late Henry L'Engle, and how their extended families passed summer vacations together with the Stocktons at their cottage on the fashionable island of Aquidneck.

In the spring of 1897, Harry received an invitation to lunch with Bowden at the St James Hotel, where he found Bowden already seated at a corner table in the hotel's elegant dining room, its gilded mirrors and French crystal chandeliers reflecting the pristine white linen tablecloths and extravagant silverware. Many of the tables were already occupied, and a murmur of polite conversation filled the palatial surroundings. Bowden looked pleased with himself and welcomed Harry to what he called Florida's finest restaurant. Harry was cautious; extravagant expenditure on lavish entertaining was out of character for Bowden, and Harry had an uneasy feeling that something was afoot and raised his guard.

'Harry, I'm going to come straight to the point because I know you'll be wondering what this is all about.'

'It hadn't crossed my mind, Jet. I thought you were simply treating me to a good lunch.'

Bowden stuttered for a second, unsure if Harry was being ironic. 'We've something important to say. It's an opportunity we're all excited about.'

'Well, you've certainly set the stage,' said Harry, rapidly forming the impression it was a sales pitch. So, disrupting Bowden's choreographed patter, he interrupted. 'Have you ordered?'

'What? Oh, no, not yet. I'm waiting for John and Telfair to arrive.'

'The Stockton brothers are joining us?' It was increasingly looking like an ambush. 'Is there anyone else you've invited? Should we move to a larger table?'

'Sorry, Harry, I forgot to mention there's going to be four of us.'

At that moment, the Stocktons arrived. They were buoyed and in good humour. Harry knew John, with whom he had partnered in the purchase of several plots of land. He was fifteen years Harry's junior, bright, amiable, with a good head for figures. He had arrived in Jacksonville in 1870 with his widowed mother and five siblings, including his younger brother, Telfair. Their father, a Confederate colonel, had been captured during the Civil War, who, on his death, had bequeathed sufficient funds for the family to buy a small boarding house, from which to eke out a living. Both John and Telfair had inherited their father's fortitude and were fiercely ambitious. Harry knew of Telfair's reputation as Jacksonville's most successful real estate agent, but they had never been properly introduced.

John spoke first. 'Harry! It's good to see you. Let me introduce my brother Telfair.' They shook hands and seated themselves around the table. Telfair looked serious and was dressed to match. He was stockier than his brother and moved more slowly and with less enthusiasm. His eyes were languid and gave the impression of being preoccupied on important matters, and he had the manner of a man who didn't tolerate fools.

Harry beckoned the sommelier; he was already thinking about how to let them down gently, whatever their proposition might be. 'If this is a celebration, perhaps we should order champagne. Shall I choose?'

John spoke for the three of them, 'Please do, Harry. But rather than the usual, let's have something special.'

Harry chose two bottles of Krug Grande Cuvée. Feeling

that he had in some small way regained the initiative, he said, 'Okay, I think we're all set. So, tell me, why are we here?'

It was John who took the reins. 'Harry, first, let me apologise for not writing and putting you in the picture. A group of us who care greatly about our city – members of the Board of Trade and other key investors – have come together to promote new business opportunities. So, I suppose this is the starting point for what I want to say.' He paused and took a sip of champagne. No one spoke, waiting patiently for him to resume. 'We all want to seize the opportunities presented by these fast-changing times to modernise our city, creating new jobs, building homes, new roads and bridges, more electric lighting and telephones. A prosperous city attracts new business and more visitors. You know this, Harry, better than most. After all, it was you who brought the Corbett fight and plenty of business with it. Even people in Washington took notice of what you did for our city.'

He paused as the maître d' approached, and Bowden unceremoniously waved him away. John continued. 'Sometimes, Harry, the city council is a little slow at getting things done. They've become complacent and, if we're not careful, Jacksonville will be left behind as new resorts develop around us. Until now, we've been the centre of the railroads and steamers bringing people south, especially during the winter months. These days, many are passing us by, journeying further south to Daytona, Palm Beach, and even as far as Miami. And Flagler is laying tracks for his new railroad around Jacksonville, bypassing us altogether.' He stopped and took his time to finish his glass of champagne. Dabbing his lips dry with his napkin, he continued, 'It's why we need you, Harry. We need your persuasion and business acumen to help develop our city.'

There was a long silence as they waited for Harry's response.

'I don't see how I can help,' said Harry. 'It seems you need Henry Plant or Flagler. They're the ones with the railroads, the hotels, the great tracts of land and the money to get things done.'

John Stockton continued, 'Harry, we need you on the city council. Jet and I are already members, but we need you to help sway decisions in the right direction. Clement Rinehart is running for councillor this year, and Jet is up for mayor the year following. Together, we can get the construction permits and funding to build new roads and housing.'

Bowden interrupted, 'Harry knows Rinehart. He was our lawyer with the Corbett fight.' Harry nodded in recognition of the fact and John continued, 'Duncan Fletcher has given his support, and Judge Cromwell Gibbons is on our side too, and with you, we'll have a powerful group taking the city in the right direction.'

Harry remained silent. He hadn't thought of political office since the yellow fever and the loss of his friends, Fairlie and L'Engle, but that was ten years ago, and things had changed – now they were coming to him.

Bowden chipped in, 'Councillor Harry Mason! You have to admit, Harry, it has a nice ring. Your name will be known far and wide. What do you say?'

Bowden's demeanour gave every indication that he expected Harry to accept enthusiastically, but Harry remained impassive. He was wary, like a trout eyeing a fly. Was it real, or was there a barb cleverly concealed?

Eventually, Harry spoke. 'Even with six of us, we wouldn't have a majority on the council.'

'The other councillors will bend like reeds in the wind,' replied John Stockton. 'Many are Democrats, and the others you'll easily talk round with your way of pointing out which side their bread's buttered.'

Harry was torn. He had become used to being his own master. Now he was being invited to dance to their tune.

Telfair called the waiter. 'Let's order and talk more over lunch.'

Turning to face Bowden, Harry said, 'Why now? Why after all these years?' He already knew the answer but wanted to hear it.

The waiter took their order and brought plates of amuse-bouche while they waited.

Telfair resumed the conversation. 'I'll be honest with you, Harry. The fact is, and this may sound disagreeable, and I wouldn't blame you for taking offence, but the truth is, we've never needed you before.' He paused, expecting Harry to be angry or at least show signs of annoyance, but Harry remained unmoved. What other explanation could there be? Their decision wasn't personal; it wasn't based on sentimentality, family or friendship; it was business, the necessary action required at the time.

At one of their first meetings, Harry recalled what Barnett had said, "business is for the head: reason and facts. Politics is emotion and beliefs. Like religion, it's a leap of faith, and Telfair's no preacher".

Telfair continued, 'The thing is, Harry. We're not getting our own way these days. Too many fossil politicians, outsiders and newcomers getting elected. You know the type: Yankees, Republicans, the plain stupid and narrow-minded, storekeepers who get excited at selling a few bushels of corn or a barrel of pork to the city authorities. Our ambitions are grander; we're talking about state and federal contracts worth millions.'

Harry sat back, carefully straightening his cutlery and aligning the table condiments. 'You want me to make up your numbers, vote when I'm told, get your building permits and federal funding.'

John Stockton interjected, 'Harry, that's unfair. You see the bigger picture, you take risks and get things done for ordinary people, and people admire you for that, and with everything you've achieved, they trust what you say.'

Telfair cut in, 'We need your persuasive talents, Harry. You put things the way ordinary folk see things as plain common sense. You tell a good story and, if you'll allow me, you're charismatic with it. You'll be a great asset to our city.'

Harry ignored the flattery. 'And what do I get, other than a fancy nameplate?'

'The job's what you make it,' said Telfair. 'It's not just roads and housing. There's banking, shipping, transport, electric power, liquor and gambling. There's no limit to it. The world's your oyster. Speaking of which...'

The waiter arrived with their first course of shellfish. Once the waiter had delivered their plates and returned to the servery, Telfair continued. 'Harry, this is an important decision, and I don't want you rushing it, but I can't enjoy this beautiful lobster until I know your answer. Are you in?'

There was a long silence. John Stockton and Bowden poured themselves another glass of champagne. Harry could feel the excitement swirling in his gut and tingling at his fingertips. A seat on the council was what Fairlie and L'Engle had promised. It's what he had once wanted so badly he'd risked his life for it, and here they were, pleading him to be one of them. Harry wanted to say yes, but he had to consider the cost. What was being proposed was business, and he'd seen the way the Stocktons operated; nothing came for free. He would have to work tirelessly for their benefit, but he could make as much as the opportunity allowed, so long as he didn't tread on their toes. As he contemplated the trade-offs, exhilaration surged through him, not that anyone noticed.

Speaking plainly, with a deadpan voice, Harry replied, 'Okay, I'll do it.' Adding begrudgingly, 'But only for as long as it pays.'

Telfair shook his hand. 'Thank you, Harry. It means a lot to me personally.'

Bowden raised his glass. 'You won't regret it, and don't worry about a thing; I'm running your campaign. We need to get you registered and start on your publicity. Remember, Harry, politics is a serious business.' Then, lowering his voice, 'But it's the best entertainment in town.'

* * *

Later that afternoon, Bowden met Harry at his Acme Hotel.

'The first thing we need,' said Bowden, 'is a biography, something for the newspapers. Something straightforward, something about who you are and what you've done in your life. Something about the real you, so people feel they know and can trust you.' He took a notebook and pencil from his leather case. 'Tell me about yourself. Just talk away while I jot down a few notes.'

214

Over several glasses of bourbon, Harry relayed tales of his life. When he had finished, Bowden said, 'Okay, let me read this back, and you tell me if I've captured the real you.'

Reading aloud, Bowden began, 'Harry Mason, a Democrat, married, born in Bristol, England 1846. Started work aged nine. At thirteen was apprenticed to a tanner. At nineteen, entered the British Navy and, a year later, after seeing action at sea, brought himself out the service and went to London, where he engaged in mercantile pursuits importing silks and fine jewels from the Orient. In 1870, went to France, enlisting in the French Army to fight under General Trochu during the Franco-Prussian War, being badly wounded defending Paris. Returned to London and again engaged in commerce. 1876, went to New Zealand to become a sheep farmer, later moving to Patagonia to farm and mine. Later travelled around Cuba before coming to Florida in 1880. After experience in the lumber trade at Cedar Key, establishing himself in Jacksonville, where he devoted himself to civic duties, tirelessly helping those suffering during the yellow fever epidemic. Yes, I think that covers it,' said Bowden, taking a long swallow of bourbon. 'Democrat, family man, soldier, sailor, patriot, businessman, hard-working farmer, pioneer, a man of the world, civic duty, compassion for others, trustworthy, truthful, God-fearing and honest. Perfect. I will craft some words and get posters printed and sent out.'

Bowden, clipping a cigar, said, 'You've had a full life, Harry. I envy your many experiences. You're a true pioneer, exactly what Jacksonville needs.'

Rolling up his shirt sleeve, Harry exposed the burn scars suffered when saving baby Esther. 'You shouldn't be envious of me; experience comes at a cost. It's me who envies you with your close friends, many relatives, settled family life, grandchildren and home.' Then, opening his shirt to expose the stab wound sewn up by Mrs O'Neill, 'A Prussian bayonet. I wouldn't wish the horror of battle on anyone.'

* * *

Bowden managed Harry's election campaign, arranging everything from business dinners and drinks parties for journalists to street processions and marquee rallies with free beer and suckling pig for all comers. Harry gave a few speeches, but mostly he shook hands and made promises and, as anticipated, was duly elected on 15 June 1897 to serve as city councillor for the eighth ward of Riverside and Ortega.

As chairman of the Public Works Committee, Harry lost no time persuading the other councillors to invest in building projects, including new waterfront jetties, electrification of the city's street railcars and new road and rail links to Riverside and Ortega, all of which he personally supervised.

As well as his civic duties, Harry was busy on his own projects, acquiring the buildings that made up the plot on the north-west corner of West Bay and Julia Street, which he renamed Mason's block. He then embarked on an ambitious extension of his Acme Hotel, raising it two floors and building new shops around a spacious piazza topped by an impressive octagonal copper roof that dominated the skyline. And, by charging the labour and material costs to the council's civic development fund, all was happily accomplished at no expense to himself.

* * *

By the turn of the century, Harry was vice-chair of the Board of Trade, chairman of the Electric and Power Authority and held directorships with the Jacksonville Waterworks Company, the Independent Day Steamboat Line, the Stockton Brothers' development company and the North Jacksonville Street Railway.

With considerable influence over Jacksonville's economy, Harry used his position to negotiate a citywide permit and licensing system, allowing corporations from across the country to operate monopolies. The flow of revenue to the council – and to his own coffers – was considerable. Other than the industrial titans of rail, lumber and banking, few businesses operated without his patronage.

However, it was a man new to the city who brought Harry the most remarkable opportunity. Nathaniel Webster, a wealthy investor and scion of an established Massachusetts family, had spent a small fortune buying and refurbishing the Everett Hotel, where the boxer Charlie Mitchell had retired after his bloody fight with Corbett. The Everett was an enormous eight-storey brick and stone building with a dominating clock tower and 180 rooms on an extensive plot at the corner of Julia and Forsythe, located opposite Harry's smaller Acme Hotel.

Webster had bought the hotel at the top of the market and funded its lavish renovation with a substantial mortgage from Penn Mutual Life Insurance. However, because of a dip in visitor numbers and a faltering economy, Webster was encountering difficulties meeting his repayments. Hoping to bring the hotel back into profitability, Webster proposed selling forty-nine per cent of the stock to Harry for $150,000, a fraction of the hotel's valuation, and inviting Harry to take control of day-to-day management for a significant annual fee.

Harry could easily afford Webster's generous offer, but instead, he approached Penn Mutual, informing them of Webster's predicament and offering to buy the debt at a fair price. Penn, however, turned him down, preferring foreclosure instead, putting the Everett up for public auction on 1 November 1900. Harry was one of only two bidders, acquiring the hotel with his bid of fifty thousand dollars. Within six months, he had subdivided the property, opening two remodelled stylish hotels, the Everett and the Aragon, sitting on half a block of prime real estate worth close to a million dollars.

The audacity of his predatory raid shocked Jacksonville's business community, most of whom held stressed mortgages of their own.

TWENTY

Precisely twenty years since stepping onto Hogan Street Jetty and finding work at Nicky's saloon, Harry was a millionaire many times over.

As Bessie joined him for breakfast, he presented her with a large bouquet of scented blooms. The previous evening, they had talked of building a grand mansion on the exclusive Riverside Avenue, near where John Stockton had recently completed his new home.

Harry said, 'I'm stopping off at the saloon on my way to the bank before having lunch with Telfair. I want to ask him about his new development at Avondale; he's had a few of the best up-and-coming architects bid for the design; hopefully, he'll give me a recommendation for our new mansion. He's already mentioned a young architect, Frank Lloyd Wright, from Chicago. He says he's all the rage.'

'I'm stopping at the saloon too,' replied Bessie. 'I've a few things to collect for the church bazaar; I'll follow you in the buggy.'

As Harry left the house, there was a spring in his step. He was enjoying these easy times.

* * *

At the saloon, a letter from England had arrived, the first in more than a year. Harry's spirits were dampened, and all thoughts of a new mansion turned instead to England and a previous life. He prayed it wasn't bad news.

* * *

22 April 1901
Dearest Enoch,

We're all in good health. Bertha has three sons and Florence three daughters, and Beatrice is to marry this summer. Your mother and John have retired from the Baptist mission and now live quietly in Somerset. I'm accommodated comfortably with Florence and her husband, Edward, who is gainfully employed at a local woodyard with hopes of starting his own business. I occupy myself with stitching corsets, which brings in some pin money. The purpose of my letter is to enclose a news cutting concerning Toff. There are now no reasons for you not returning home. There is plenty of well-paid work available, and Edward says he can find you a suitable position at his yard.

Your remittances are gratefully received and allow us an occasional treat. We all look forward to hearing from you and hopefully seeing you soon.

Always in our thoughts and prayers.
Affectionately, your loving wife,
Eliza.

***

Six grandchildren, but again no mention of their names or an enclosed photograph. He unfolded the newspaper clipping from London's *The Times*.

***

Railway Death – Kingston upon Thames. Workmen repairing the track approaching Hampton Wick Station found early Monday morning the body of Mr Gabriel Toff (fifty-six years). Mrs Toff had reported her husband missing the previous Friday when he failed to return home from London's Guild Hall after attending the Lord Mayor's annual charity banquet. The pathologist told the inquest that cause of death resulted from a single fracture of the skull, likely caused by falling from a passing train. The police reported that there were no other signs of injury or suspicions of robbery. Mr Toff, who is well known for his many business interests, had received criticism from government inspectors and social reformers for the squalid, overcrowded and insanitary housing let at high rents to the East End's poorest, many being recent immigrants to the city. The coroner recorded a verdict of accidental death.

***

Harry wondered how Eliza had come by the clipping. Perhaps Michael had sent it. At least Toff had got his comeuppance. Although, it was an unusual occurrence for him to fall from a train at the station where he routinely alighted for his Kingston town house. Harry made a note of Eliza's new address and, as always, destroyed the letter and cutting. He was still thinking of the newspaper report when Bessie, who had arrived in the buggy, emerged from the back parlour carrying a large bundle of clothes, over which she struggled to see. 'Any news?' she asked.

'No. Just the usual business. I was going to—' Harry suddenly stopped mid-sentence and, inspecting the bundle of clothes, said, 'These are mine.'

'You never wear them, and they're too small for you. I'm taking them to the charity bazaar, and I'll be grateful for a donation too. And why ever did you want this old opera top hat – have you ever worn it?'

Harry took five dollars from his wallet, which he considered more than generous. 'Five! I need twenty,' said Bessie with a hint of derision.

Harry begrudgingly handed her a twenty-dollar bill. 'I'll keep an eye open for well-dressed beggars.'

'Don't be so mean. You're beginning to sound like Bowden. Anyway, you can afford to clothe the whole town and, besides, my ladies expect it of me.'

'I thought charity began at home.'

'Which reminds me. I'm meeting my dressmakers on Friday for new gowns for the summer season. So, I'll be at home all day and would be grateful not to be disturbed.'

'I've business meetings with John Stockton and Bowden at Barnett's bank on Friday.'

Bessie wasn't paying attention. She turned and nimbly chasséd out to the waiting buggy.

In the quiet of the back parlour, Harry thought of Eliza's letter. Toff's death changed nothing. Harry was fifty-seven, married with four children; his youngest, Lily, had just turned ten. Eliza and England were from a different time and a different life. He had made a name for himself in Jacksonville and had worked hard to climb the ladders of success. Yet, Harry couldn't help a sense of longing come over him in this moment of reflection. He pictured London's damp, grey, winding cobbled streets with row upon row of tightly built yellow brick houses. The glow of London's gaslights peering through the fog that swirled and mixed with the sour smell of coal smoke rising from the thousands of rooftop chimneys, the palaces, the parks and lakes, the markets and its pubs, the docks crowded with ships from every outpost of the empire. His memories were fond ones, but they were those of youth long passed.

The menacing sound of a giant moth flapping noisily against the windowpane snapped him back to the present. He would write, asking Eliza for a photograph and the names of his grandchildren, and even though having only recently sent a remittance, he would again send money. It was the least he could do.

* * *

Friday, 3 May was a bright, calm day. The temperature was comfortable and didn't yet have the oppressive humidity of high summer. Harry walked the three short blocks from the Everett along Forsythe to Laura Street, where, opposite City Hall, Barnett's granite bank stood solid and respectable.

The board meeting was punctual and businesslike. Barnett reported that, while substantial investments in land purchases had yet to realise any annual return, the asset values continued to climb.

At 1pm, Harry suggested they finish for the day and cross the street to a small restaurant for lunch. As they stepped from the bank, their gaze was drawn skywards to an enormous pall of black smoke billowing up to cloud the sun. The distinctive smell of burning wood pervaded the air. 'That's a sizeable blaze,' remarked Stockton.

'God, I hope it's not Cummer's lumber yard,' replied Barnett. 'I carry the insurance.'

'No,' said Harry, 'that's somewhere in the north-west corner. I'd guess near Hansontown. It'll be one of the coloured shanties going up in smoke.'

Mayor Bowden looked worried. 'I'm wondering if I ought to return to City Hall and find out what's going on.'

Stockton suggested they first luncheon and allow Fire Chief Haney time to get things under control. 'He's a good chief and knows what he's doing. My goodness, he costs us enough, and his men are forever training. Let's give him a chance before interfering.'

A light lunch of pâté and salad followed by grilled fish was promptly served. As they ate, several more customers arrived complaining of the smoke, which seemed to have thickened. By the time the four men emerged onto the sidewalk, the smoke was towering several thousand feet into an otherwise clear sky. It was drifting east, enveloping the city in a blanket of smut and flakes of white ash. People hurried in all directions while shopkeepers quickly brought their displays in from the sidewalk.

'Holy Mother of God,' said Harry. 'Half the city's going up.'

Barnett was already halfway across the street, heading back towards his bank.

Bowden, with urgency in his voice, said, 'I must get to City Hall.' As he turned, his two companions latched on, following close behind.

A few minutes later, they reached the grand foyer of City Hall, and as Bowden crossed the threshold, two grave-looking officials in formal business attire with stiffened winged collars approached. They spoke calmly in low, measured tones. Harry overheard one say, 'Mr Mayor, we have a fire in the north of the city which is spreading at an alarming pace. We must speak privately.'

Bowden nodded. 'Councillors Stockton and Mason will join us.'

The two clerks explained that a spark from an oven had ignited Spanish moss and horsehair, laid out to dry by workers at the Cleveland mattress factory at Beaver and Davis Streets. Chief Haney attended quickly, but a stiff, north-westerly breeze sprung up, blowing embers high up over the heads of his fire crews, setting light to a row of tarred pine shingle roofs. From there, it spread rapidly, engulfing a dozen blocks north-west of Beaver and Julia Streets. No deaths or injury had yet been reported, but Chief Haney believed this was only a matter of time.

The senior of the two officials added, 'Chief Haney believes the fire cannot be contained and expects everything north of Beaver Street to be lost, including the gasworks. Hogan's Creek is the only natural barrier to halt the fire's expansion.'

Harry asked, 'If the wind turns south, will the city be lost?'

The colour drained from Stockton's face as he slumped onto a chair.

The official replied curtly, 'The wind is blowing east, Councillor Mason. There is no reason to believe it will turn south. Chief Haney is building firebreaks the length of Beaver Street and has asked Waycross, St Augustine, Brunswick and Savannah to send every fire crew and volunteer they can muster. He hopes for seventy or more men within the hour. He plans to contain the fire north of Beaver.'

There was a long silence before the mayor spoke. 'And if the wind does turn south?'

'Then only brick and stone buildings will survive,' said the official in dire tones.

'And the safest place to evacuate?' asked Bowden.

Again, the official replied with the same seriousness. 'North of Hogan's Creek, out towards Springfield or south towards Riverside or, in extremis, south across the St Johns River. You could request Governor Jennings send troops if you think it prudent, Mr Mayor.'

Bowden turned to the two councillors. 'What do you say, gentlemen?'

Harry spoke first. 'Chief Haney's right. Once the wooden buildings are alight, they'll blaze like tinder and won't be saved. Firebreaks and dousing those buildings still standing is his only hope.' Harry stopped for a second to collect his thoughts. 'Evacuating south to the jetties will be a mistake. There simply aren't enough ferries or barges to take that mass of people. The poor devils will be trapped between drowning or burning on the quayside.'

No one spoke. Stockton sat with his head in his hands.

Harry continued. 'My experience of the great fires of London is that most people will save themselves. I don't believe there's much to be done until the ashes have cooled. We have to trust Haney and his men.'

Stockton straightened himself and cleared his throat. 'I'm sorry, Mayor. I don't take pleasure in saying this, but I think it's every man for his own. Only when his property is secured and his family safe can he afford to turn his attention to helping others.'

Bowden turned to his two officials. 'Thank you, gentlemen. Please inform Governor Jennings of our perilous state. Tell the press I'll address them at three-fifteen. Inform Captain Garner at the Board of Trade that I must speak with him urgently. In the meantime, gentlemen, make whatever arrangements are necessary to protect yourselves and your families. My only solace is that the damned Yankees burned and razed our great city, not once but twice, and each time we rebuilt it bigger and better, and we'll do it again. Cannon, fever or fire will not cower our great city.'

Rousing oratory, thought Harry. The mayor was already rehearsing his speech to the press.

Deep in thought, Harry and Stockton left without further delay.

Stockton said, 'Harry, you and your family are welcome at our home on Riverside. You'll be safe there.'

'Thank you, John. I'm grateful.'

The heat and smoke were now bowling down between the blocks. Harry's only thought was to get home to Adams Street and warn Bessie. He could only hope that his stepson, John Handley, who was working at the saloon on Bay Street, would have the good sense to clear the decks and secure the place without waiting to be told.

Harry ran the few blocks to the Everett Hotel, where guests and staff were in a state of anxiety. He instructed Mr Norman, the general manager, to make preparations in case the fire turned south and bore down on them. Guests were to assemble in the public rooms in readiness to evacuate south to Riverside. If the worst came, then the strong boxes and safes were to be emptied and, along with all other valuables and silverware, loaded and carted south, where Norman and his staff were to stand guard overnight.

Having reassured and commanded his staff into action, Harry took a buggy at full trot to Adams Street, where Bessie, oblivious to the danger, was in the parlour with her dressmakers, serenely posed on a low pedestal being measured and pinned.

Without politeness or ceremony, Harry burst in, 'Hurry! You need to get out! There's no time to waste! Take the children and get out! Now!'

There was a stunned silence as Bessie and her dressmakers looked on in astonishment. Reluctantly stepping from the stool, Bessie asked flippantly, 'May I ask the urgency?'

Annoyed by her haughty complacency, Harry lost his temper, 'For God's sake, woman! Are you blind or plain stupid? Half the city has gone up in smoke. People are running for their lives. Bloody hell, woman. Stop this nonsense and get yourself and the children out before you all burn to death.'

The seamstresses ran from the room while Martha, their loyal housekeeper, fell to her knees and, clasping her hands in prayer, began wailing, 'The Devil's come to take us. Lord have mercy and save us from the fires of Hell.'

Pushing Martha out of her way, Bessie dashed onto the porch. Rolling clouds of black smoke obscured the sun, leaving an eerie, yellow-magenta gloom, the colour of a raging prairie storm. Coming to her senses, Bessie barked at Martha, 'Get the children and pack as much as you can carry. And don't forget my jewellery, especially my rings and brooches. Where's the yard boy? Harry!' she called with urgency. 'Where shall we go?'

Harry appeared from the back of the house. 'The boy's bringing the buckboard now. Load as much as you can and get to John Stockton's place on Riverside. Stay there until I arrive. Hurry now and save yourself and the children while there's still time.'

'Aren't you coming?'

'I must attend an emergency meeting of the council,' he lied. 'I'll join you the moment I'm finished.'

'Don't waste time talking, and don't do anything stupid. We need you with us.'

'I promise, my dear,' he replied in softer tones. 'I won't stay a moment longer than necessary.' He kissed her and the children goodbye. Placing his hands firmly on the shoulders of his eldest son, George, who had just turned sixteen, he said, 'You're in charge now, son. I need you to be brave to look after your mother – can I trust you to do that?'

George nodded. 'Yes, sir.'

Harry ushered them onto the front porch. 'Quickly now. The sooner I leave, the sooner I'll return. You must be on the road within fifteen minutes; leave whatever you can't carry.' With those final words, he left in his buggy.

Tiny flakes of white ash began falling like snow.

Harry drove the horse hard, racing back towards Forsythe Street and his three hotels: the Everett, Aragon and Acme.

The guests at the Everett had not waited, preferring instead to evacuate of their own accord. Most, struggling with suitcases and bags, joined the tide of humanity trudging south towards the waterfront and piers, from where they hoped to escape by ferry across the river. The only guest remaining was Mr James Munoz, a wealthy businessman on vacation from his home in Venezuela. In his mid-thirties, he was tall, thickset and muscular, with a large moustache and shock of well-groomed, jet-black hair. Mr Norman, the hotel manager, had insisted Munoz make haste and seek refuge from the fire. In reply, Mr Munoz had, in his best broken English, been equally firm, insisting that if an adventure were to be had, then he would stay to be a part of it.

TWENTY-ONE

Dashing from one hotel to another, Harry organised those who had chosen to stay, mainly because they had no family or anywhere else to go – the hotel was their home. All except the French chef and Mr Norman were coloured boys: waiters, porters and bellhops.

Valuables were collected and moved to safety. Every effort was made filling buckets with dirt and baths with water in readiness to quench falling cinders and burning flares. Six of the strongest men were chosen to work the hotel's water pump and two hoses. Gathering his men in the Everett's elegant ballroom, Harry thanked them for their loyalty, promising that none would be without work, irrespective of the day's outcome, and swore an extra month's wage of thirty dollars for every man who stayed until morning. As Harry finished speaking, a single round of applause rang out from the back of the room. It was Mr Munoz, who had been listening unobserved from the shadows of a deep curtain recess.

'Bravo! Bravo!' he called. Everyone assembled took this as a cue to join in with their own rapturous shouts of approval.

Mr Munoz congratulated Harry on his courageous stand and offered his help, which Harry accepted, inviting Munoz to go aloft with him to the hotel's rooftop. The Everett was amongst the tallest buildings in Jacksonville. From its large observation deck, perched high above its tiered wedding cake clock tower, exceptional views could be enjoyed across the city and south towards the St Johns River.

From their vantage point, the landmarks of City Hall and the courthouse to the east could be clearly seen. To the north was the St James Hotel and Hemming Park with its marble column bearing the dominating statue of the Confederate soldier, and to the north-east was the Church of the Immaculate Conception and the Episcopal Church of St John. Looking south, the two men could see across the St Johns River to Villa Alexandria, the largest of the magnificent Jacksonville mansions. With over 140 acres of lush parkland, its citrus groves and arboretum of rare trees gathered from the far corner world, it was home to the wealthy Mitchell family.

But it was the raging inferno to the north which held their gaze. Its extent and enormity were shocking. Vast tongues of bright-red flame flicked, leaping skywards, spewing thick, black smoke in towering plumes high into the air. A searing wall of fire over four blocks wide was creeping east across Laura Street. In its wake, stretching six blocks back to its genesis at the mattress factory, everything was laid waste to ugly, blackened smouldering rubble. Half-collapsed brick walls stood like rotten, broken teeth, dotted here and there with thin, crooked fingers pointing skywards, where once-substantial brick chimneys had proudly risen.

Even at almost a mile distance, Harry felt the blistering heat of the fire. Sparks and glowing embers rained down from rolling clouds like eruptions from monstrous volcanoes. From time to time, gusts of wind sent bundles of blazing material rocketing on soaring currents of hot air before falling back to earth like the fiery tails of comets, only to set ablaze buildings two or three blocks behind the firebreaks. Both men watched in awe as this hellish scene unfolded.

Penned in by sheets of flame shooting fifty feet into the sky, Chief Haney and his men fought hard to contain the roaring beast, but for all their purpose, it looked a hopeless effort. Unrelenting, the fire advanced eastwards, ripping into Main Street.

By good fortune, the fire had passed wide of both the St James Hotel and the Church of the Immaculate Conception as it turned north, away from the jetties, City Hall and the castellated stone walls of the armoury. If the inferno continued on its trajectory, it would soon weaken and burn out on the swampy banks of Hogan's Creek, and that would be an end to it.

At the junction of Ocean Street with Ashley, teams of firefighters created a second firebreak, demolishing houses with charges of dynamite. But as quickly as the houses fell, so the fire leapt mockingly over their work. Yet the bravery of these fighters never wavered, nor did they cower as the buildings around them burst spontaneously into flames, flashing from one building to the next, showering sparks and ash onto adjoining streets.

To the west, where the catastrophe had started, the fire had done most of its work and grew weary. Its low belly flickered as it picked over charred remains in search of morsels of tinder. Tired and starved of fresh fuel, it was dying. Even so, its hot, smouldering edge crept ever closer to Adams Street and Harry's home, which, at the death of it, was its last victim before petering out. Harry watched, unmoved. *Thank God Bessie and the children are safe*, he thought, and compared to the egregious losses suffered by others, his injuries were slight; his hotels, saloons, and villa at Ponte Vedra remained untouched.

The observation deck on which the two men stood shook as the tower clock chimed 4.30pm. Two hours had passed since Bessie had left for Stockton's, where Harry hoped soon to join her, knowing that his properties were safe.

A moment later, a gust of cool fresh air struck Harry in the face. Taking a deep breath, it felt refreshing and pleasant, a welcome relief from the hot, stifling smoke, but before he could exhale, the horror of it dawned. The wind had turned and was now blowing due south towards him. This fresh, invigorating breeze fanned the glowing embers like a blacksmith's bellows, roaring the fire back into action. Within seconds, it had again built to an inferno, destroying buildings as if made of paper and card. The blaze was worse than before, launching itself across Beaver Street, smashing into Ashley, then south into Church Street. Ten blocks disappeared in the space of minutes. Haney and his crews were seen in Newman Street running for their lives, pumps and horses abandoned. At Main Street, they regrouped to face the onslaught, but it was futile. The Church of the Immaculate Conception exploded and crashed to the ground as a pile of burning debris. At this rate of advance, it would take less than an hour before the fire levelled City Hall, the courthouse and armoury. Nothing could withstand its force. Neither brick, stone nor walls of granite provided any defence to its renewed ferocity. Harry and Munoz watched in horror as three blocks north, a pencil-thin tornado of roaring gases and jets of hot flame whipped and twisted hundreds of feet upwards. This whirlwind of fire dipped and wrapped its flowing skirt around the elegant St James Hotel before ripping it out by its roots, the whole block vanishing into the sky as a flash of blinding heat.

Munoz grabbed Harry by the arm. 'My God, it's coming! Mr Mason, we must leave. The Devil himself is upon us!'

But the fiery orb mesmerised Harry's attention. Munoz slapped him hard.

'No!' screamed Harry. 'I can't lose again. I must fight.'

'Mr Mason, if we stay, we'll die.'

At that moment, their attention was drawn to a commotion in the street below. Freshly arrived from Savannah, fire crews were careering up from the train station, bells clanging and horns hooting. Two large steam-driven pumps on heavy wagons, each pulled by six snarling, chestnut drays, sped wildly along West Bay Street. Harry and Munoz were transfixed as forty firefighters followed close behind, jogging in close order towards the danger. The two spectators allowed their gaze to follow the parade to the intersection with Laura Street, where Haney and his men had reassembled. Long hoses were being hurriedly unreeled and connected to the nearby jetty hydrants.

'Look, Mr Mason. They are preparing an action to fight. Here is where your hotel is saved,' said Munoz, wrapping a firm hand around Harry's wrist, dragging him away from the decking and pushing him hard through the trapdoor of their crow's nest. Munoz came behind, helter-skelter down the wooden stairs they went, through the clock tower and into the foyer where Harry's staff had gathered. Every one of them terrified and ready to desert. Munoz, commanding them in melodramatic style, said, 'Come, gentlemen. Take up your buckets and follow. We will save our hotel.'

Outside on the street, Harry urged his men on as hot embers showered down, scorching holes in their clothes and catching their hair. Harry and Munoz jumped into a buggy and drove furiously towards Haney and his congregation of firefighters. The heat was so fierce, the buggy's canopy burst spontaneously into flames. The horse, its eyes bulging in terror, reared and kicked, frantically whinnying in distress. Harry leapt forward, releasing the traces, allowing the terrified creature to escape at a wild gallop along West Bay.

Harry's band of porters, bellhops and kitchen boys ran to make up the distance, frantically pulling their hoses on two dog carts found abandoned on the sidewalk. In their grey and burgundy-striped uniforms, they had the appearance of a gang of crazed convicts.

At the junction of West Bay and Laura Street, Haney's men were hampered by crowds of panic-stricken refugees packing the jetties in the hope of salvation across the river.

Harry and Munoz continued on foot until, amid the chaos, they found Haney, looking exhausted and close to collapse from his endeavours.

Shouting to make himself heard above the roar of the fire, Haney was surprised to see Harry. 'What the hell are you doing? You need to get back.'

Barely able to hear himself, Harry shouted, 'We're here to help. I've thirty men. Where do you want us?'

'We've pumps and a good supply of water,' Haney explained. 'This is our last stand. We'll drench three blocks on the west of Laura. If we stop the fire jumping, we might save what's left of the city.'

Instructing Harry, the fire chief continued, 'Get behind Oldham's Livery. Draw water off the Coral Dock hydrant. Dump it on Southern Express. The Savannah crew are on Western Union. My crew on Barnett's Bank. If you see me pull back, drop everything and run.'

'Yes, Chief.'

'You're a good man, Councillor,' said Haney. 'Not many put the city before themselves.'

Harry nodded, aware that Haney had unwittingly deployed him to protect his own saloon. He led his men along the alley which ran south off West Bay between the Southern Express building and Harry's bar, the spot where, twenty years before, he had met Nicky and where, only a few hours ago, his stepson boarded its windows and doors. From the alley, Harry gained access to the rear of Oldham's Livery and Coral Dock, where he put his men to work with hand-to-hand bucket chains and stirrup pumps and where Munoz discovered a twin hydrant with two fifty-foot hoses.

But before the men could start their work, the fire reared up, lurching forward to threaten what remained of Laura Street. The inferno was now growling, boiling and crackling worse than any sound Harry had ever heard. Its wrath knew no bounds. A man, screaming in terror, ran past, his hair and coat ablaze. He had gone no more than a few paces when he stumbled to his knees as flames engulfed him. Firemen grabbed and rolled him in the sandy dirt, but his face had gone.

Harry doused himself in a horse trough; the water was hot. A moment later, Munoz opened the hydrant, shooting a jet of water high into the air, raining down like a sudden tropical downpour. A loud cheer went up from the men; their spirits lifted.

After two hours of hard struggle, the fight was locked in stalemate; the fire's progress had been stopped from going further south by the St Johns River, and progress west across Laura Street was contained by a contingent of firefighters and steam pumps. Yet still, the conflagration threatened more destruction.

Ankle-deep in mud, churned by the sprayed water, the men slid and fell each time they changed position or shifted to gain a better purchase on their pumps. Harry climbed precariously onto the roof of his saloon. From there, through the haze of smoke and orange glow, he could see tall spouts of water from the Savannah steam pumps. Both the Western Union and Barnett's Bank looked intact. In the opposite direction, the Everett stood serenely undisturbed in the gathering dusk. It may have been wishful thinking, but Harry sensed the wind had eased.

Returning to his men, he urged them on. 'We're winning! Keep fighting, men! Don't lose heart.'

Munoz joined him. 'Is it the truth?' he asked. 'Are we really winning, Mr Mason?'

'I believe we are, Mr Munoz. One more round and I think we'll land the knockout punch.'

The men were near exhaustion, but with renewed strength, they fought on, their hands raw and bleeding. Several of the

Negro boys struck up a rhythmic chorus. There were no words, just a deep bass sound which, without any instruction, united the men's efforts to a single cause. As the work went on, the wind noticeably eased, and the men felt the change.

* * *

At 8pm, Chief Haney sauntered through the alley towards Harry and his men. There was no urgency in his gait.

'It's out!' he shouted, raising his arms in victory.

A cheer went up.

He approached Harry and Munoz with an extended hand, which they shook enthusiastically, slapping each other on the back.

'We've done it, Mr Councillor,' said Haney. 'You and your men have been of great assistance. The city will be forever grateful. But now you can leave it to us – get yourselves some well-earned rest.'

Harry nodded, grateful that his hotels and saloons had been spared.

Munoz crossed himself and looked to the heavens. 'Our Lord is gracious and merciful and smiles down on us. He answered our prayers, Mr Mason, and has saved us from the fires of hell.'

But there are plenty his mercy didn't save, thought Harry, *and none of them wicked souls, not by any measure*. But instead, he said, 'He certainly moves in mysterious ways; I'll give you that much. But tell me, Mr Munoz, are you pleased you stayed?'

'To tell the truth, Mr Mason, I was very afraid the devil had caught me and was certain of my death. If not for your brave stand, Mr Mason, I would have run away.'

'And not for you, Mr Munoz, I would have lost everything and slid back into a pit of snakes. I shall be forever indebted.'

'Snakes! Where is this pit of snakes?'

'All about us,' replied Harry, putting his arm around Munoz's shoulder. 'Come, my dear friend, let's refresh ourselves.'

Exhausted by their efforts, Harry's gang of porters, bellhops and kitchen boys had collapsed and were lying prostrate in the sodden mud, where, like corpses mown down on the field of battle, they lay motionless. But like a miracle of the resurrection, Harry roused them up to rejoice in their victory. Abandoning their pumps and hoses, the merry company tramped happily to the Everett, where they ate heartily on cold meats and bread and cheese and drank copious amounts of beer. Filthy, dirty, caked in mud, blackened by soot and ash, clothes riddled with scorch marks and stinking like smoked herring, Harry's band of brothers retired unwashed to the hotel's comfortable beds and clean white linen. And Harry had not a care for what people might say.

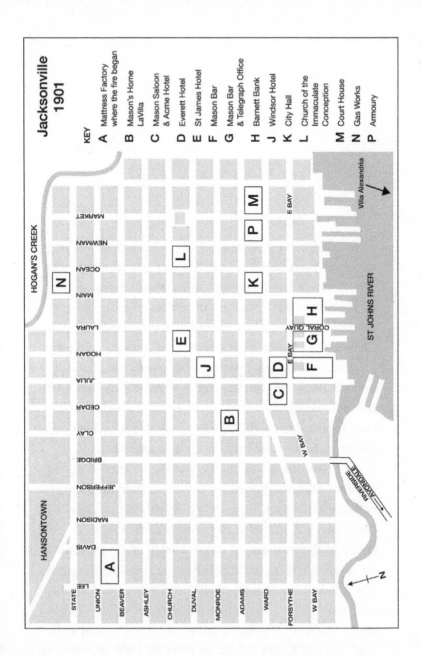

Jacksonville
1901

KEY

A Mattress Factory
   where the fire began
B Mason's Home
   LaVilla
C Mason Saloon
   & Acme Hotel
D Everett Hotel
E St James Hotel
F Mason Bar
G Mason Bar
   & Telegraph Office
H Barnett Bank
J Windsor Hotel
K City Hall
L Church of the
   Immaculate
   Conception
M Court House
N Gas Works
P Armoury

TWENTY-TWO

At first light, Harry sent news to Bessie before climbing the clock tower to survey the landscape fashioned by the fire. It was total desolation. Jacksonville appeared now as a photographic negative in shades of charcoal-grey. A blanket of white ash lay unbroken block after block. Charred, blackened tree stumps and stunted telegraph poles stood as evidence of a previous civilisation. Yet south towards Riverside, the stark monochrome gave way to a kaleidoscope of rich colour. The emerald, lush oaks and tall, leafy royal palms, with flashes of pink bougainvillaea and mauve wisteria, stood magnificent and untouched.

Mr Norman and a dozen waiters, all turned out in pristine uniforms, greeted Harry as he entered the Everett's morning restaurant. Only their blistered, cut and swollen hands gave any hint of their previous day's labours. At the centre of the near-empty room, a table of six gentlemen sat enjoying a breakfast of bacon, eggs, blood pudding and newly baked bread with English marmalade and strong, fresh roast coffee. The aroma was warm and welcoming. On seeing Harry, they stopped eating and stood to wait as he made his way towards them, weaving through the expanse of white, starched linen tablecloths, sparkling crystal and polished silverware. He recognised Mayor Bowden, Captain Charles Garner, Chairman of the Board of Trade, Judge Duncan U. Fletcher, Chairman of the Democratic Party, and Telfair Stockton.

Bowden approached and shook him warmly by the hand. 'Good morning, Harry. Let me introduce you. You know, of course, Charles, Telfair and Duncan.' Then, turning to the two men Harry had not previously met, Bowden continued, 'This is Mr Joseph Parrott, general counsel and vice president of Mr Henry Flagler's East Coast Railway.' Harry had heard much about Parrott from their mutual acquaintance, Admiral Cogswell. Parrott was short and stocky, with fair hair and penetrating pale-blue eyes. Although an influential industrialist and capable lawyer, the graduate of Yale spoke gruffly in short, unsophisticated sentences. Harry found him uncouth and recognised Cogswell's description of someone who would browbeat any opponent until he got his way.

'Finally, let me introduce Colonel Charles P. Lovell of the First Florida Infantry, who is representing Governor Jennings.'

Harry welcomed the assembled men to his hotel and invited them to continue their breakfast. 'Whilst we eat, you can perhaps tell me the purpose of your visit, gentlemen.'

Bowden began, speaking as if addressing a town hall meeting. 'Yesterday, the city suffered a grievous calamity. A hundred and fifty blocks burnt to the ground. Three thousand buildings were destroyed. Every church, hospital, theatre and bank levelled to the ground. Only Barnett's bank survives, narrowly escaping destruction, in no small part due to the heroism of Chief Haney and his men. Every hotel, except thankfully yours, Harry, was destroyed, including the St James and the magnificent Windsor. The conflagration has left fifteen thousand of our citizens homeless and destitute. And now it falls on us, as the civic leaders of this—'

Colonel Lovell interrupted. He was tall and thin, yet with a muscular build and square jaw. Resplendent in his dark-blue uniform and gold braid, the colonel cut an impressive figure. He spoke firmly with a no-nonsense Midwest accent. Carrying his rank and authority with ease, Harry guessed he must be from a military family on the Union side.

'Thank you, Mr Mayor, for your kind introduction. Perhaps I can come straight to the point.' Turning to face Harry, he addressed him directly. 'Mr Mason, Governor Jennings has imposed martial law on the city of Jacksonville and county of Duval. I'm here to take whatever action is necessary to maintain law and order and keep the peace. I have temporarily relieved Mayor Bowden and the council of their civil authority and will retain control until normality is restored. Specifically, Mr Mason, I can requisition whatever property I require to carry out my duties. In this regard, I have, and I do this with the greatest respect and consideration to yourself, requisitioned this hotel and the adjoining Aragon building. They will be returned to you in good order once I hand power back to the mayor.'

After a long silence, during which nobody flinched, Harry asked, 'How long do you anticipate being here, Colonel?'

'A month, perhaps longer. I will take a floor for my own use.'

'Will you billet your men here?'

'No. Troopers will bivouac on open ground in Hemming Park. Only I and my four senior officers will accommodate ourselves here. Our board and lodging will, of course, be paid in full.'

'Shall I be allowed to remain?' asked Harry.

'I rely on you being here, Mr Mason. Your assistance will be invaluable and very much appreciated. And, I assume, with your own home destroyed, you will bring your family to join you. The mayor will require space for offices and meetings, as will other civic bodies, including Captain Garner's Board of Trade, Fire Chief Haney and the sheriff, whose jail has been destroyed. All will need accommodating.'

Bowden said, 'I'm sorry, Harry, but needs must.'

'Not at all, mayor. You know I always put the city before my own interests. As a loyal patriot, it's my duty to accommodate Colonel Lovell in the best way I can, and I will be pleased to do so.'

Captain Garner spoke for the first time. 'The Board of Trade will need five rooms, Harry, and I'm hoping you'll agree to the ballroom as our temporary council chamber. The council will be—'

Mayor Bowden interrupted. 'On behalf of the council, I've established a new organisation known as the Jacksonville Relief Association, or JRA. It will coordinate the rapid reconstruction of the city. The JRA will need ten rooms for its executive committees, possibly for several months or even a year. At least until City Hall is rebuilt. I hope you feel you can accommodate our needs, Harry.'

Harry nodded but said nothing. He was already calculating the costs and opportunities.

Bowden continued, 'Thank you, Harry. I knew we could count on you. I've arranged for the JRA's inaugural meeting to assemble in the ballroom at 10am today, where I'm expecting Jacksonville's prominent business leaders, storekeepers and news reporters to attend. I've received telegrams from the president and Governor Jennings, pledging federal support and funding.'

Harry said, 'It's my honour to help the city in whatever way I can, and, as chairman of the council's Public Works Committee, I'm delighted to become a member of the JRA's executive committee, where I'll gladly put my experience of reconstruction gained from the London fires and New Zealand earthquakes at your service.'

Colonel Lovell said, 'That's an excellent proposal, Mr Mason. I'm sure Mayor Bowden will be pleased to accept your generous offer.'

Bowden said, rather begrudgingly, 'Of course, Harry, it goes without saying. Your experience is always invaluable.'

Colonel Lovell offered his hand to Harry and said, 'It's been a pleasure meeting you, Mr Mason. Your reputation as a man who gets things done travels far ahead of you.' With that, the colonel took his leave.

* * *

The ballroom was packed to capacity as Bowden opened the inaugural meeting of the JRA with a long-winded speech foretelling future glories awaiting a new Jacksonville as it rose like a phoenix from the ashes. At the conclusion of his soaring oratory, he called upon all citizens to come together in unity. Muted applause rippled up from the audience.

As Bowden finished speaking, Harry seized the moment and leapt to his feet to deliver an enthusiastic call to arms. 'The first thing the people want is food and clean water,' he shouted, banging his fist hard on the lectern. 'They want shelter and clothing. Thousands have nothing more than the scorched rags they stand in. They deserve action, not words. They want our committee to do something, to do whatever is necessary to ease their plight.'

A huge roar of approval reverberated around the hall.

Having captured the audience, Harry continued. 'I propose,' he shouted, 'that we start a collection. Half the city is burnt to the ground, yet the other half stands untouched, carrying on as if nothing has happened. Trains run and steamboats dock. There's plenty of food to be bought. So, let those of us who can, buy it and feed the hungry. We'll build shelters for the homeless and clothe the destitute – then we can talk of future prosperity.'

A great bellow of approval rang out. People were on their feet, stamping and cheering him on.

'I'll start the ball rolling,' shouted Harry, taking a wad of dollar bills from his wallet and waving them aloft. 'Here. $250.'

The crowd were roused to a frenzy.

'Come on! Come on! Give your money to help those in need,' encouraged Harry.

Bowden, who felt sorely upstaged, tried to regain the initiative. 'I'll give a hundred dollars,' he shouted, but before he could reach into his pocket, Parrott was on his feet.

'Mr Flagler commits five thousand dollars here and now and will send another five if necessary.'

Harry took a hat from a man on the front row and began stuffing it with dollar bills. He toured the ballroom like a churchwarden collecting alms at the offertory and, by the end, had gathered over fifteen thousand dollars.

Bowden quickly dispensed with formalities; Charles Garner was elected chairman and seven sub-committees were formed. Harry was appointed to assist Parrott run the commissary, distributing and receiving donations of fresh food, dried goods, clothing, household equipment and tools.

* * *

The catastrophe shocked the nation, with help pouring in from every corner of the country. Ships and barges loaded with building materials arrived daily. Trains crammed with public donations of tents, blankets, towels, chairs, cutlery and prefabricated water closets came by rail.

With the loss of their home on West Adams Street, Bessie and the children settled into family life at the hotel. Harry, meantime, was occupied running his saloons, which were packed from dawn until the small hours with migrant labour swarming to the city in search of work. And, seizing advantage of the colossal sums of federal funding flooding into the city, Harry was busy with council work too, approving building permits and lucrative public-funded contracts, many favouring his own and partner companies.

Each morning, Harry made the short walk to Parrott's temporary offices on Ward Street to discuss the commissary, which, pleasingly, took little time, which suited both men, as neither much liked the other.

It was their mutual animosity that surfaced during a board meeting of the JRA. Joseph E. Lee, the only black judge in Florida, had been appointed to the committee to represent the Negro community. He had on several occasions raised troubling concerns at the lack of help going to the coloured suburbs, particularly the shanty Hansontown. In reply, Parrott explained that white neighbourhoods came first, and those less deserving would have to wait their turn. Then he added, 'The only assistance I can spare is my deputy, Mr Harry Mason, who might wish to spend less time propping up his saloon bar and more time helping the judge.' Harry agreed to help, but Parrott's slight had not gone unheeded.

Judge Lee and a local coloured builder named Joseph Blodgett met with Harry at the Edward Waters College for Freed Slaves, where Lee was principal dean. Over the following weeks, the three men organised shelters, a tented village, feeding stations and a clinic for the shanty town communities. It was here that Harry renewed his acquaintance with Nathan Cross.

Harry discovered that the obstacles to providing urgently needed supplies to the coloured communities were red tape and official procrastination, much of which was wilful. Harry, however, assured the judge that he would use his influence to pull strings and speed up essential deliveries.

* * *

Just before dawn, two men walked to the jetties clustered along the St Johns waterfront. Even though only the faintest grey light broke the sky, porters and stevedores were busy unloading ships and barges laden with supplies. The two men stood in the deep shadow of the warehouses lining the wharves and watched. No sooner were goods brought onto the quayside than they were manhandled onto wagons and carted away. One man was in charge. He was heavyset, wore a bowler hat, corduroy trousers and a leather waistcoat over an open-neck shirt. He was continually shouting instructions, pointing, directing and, from time to time, stopping to inspect paperwork or sign dockets brought by porters.

As dawn broke, spreading a cool-yellow light across the scene, one of the two men stepped from the shadows and walked casually towards the man in charge.

Noticing the figure approach, the man said, 'What can I do for you? If it's work, you're out of luck.'

'I'm Harry Mason, and it's more about what I can do for you.'

'And who might Harry Mason be when he's at home?'

'I apologise. Let me introduce myself properly. I'm Councillor Mason, owner of the Everett Hotel, chairman of the Public Works Committee and member of the Jacksonville Relief Committee and, most importantly, I have a really big say in who works here and who doesn't. And to whom am I speaking?'

Harry had grabbed the man's attention.

'George Briggs. What can I do for you, Councillor Mason?'

'As I said, George, it's what I can do for you.'

There was a loud clatter as one of the porters dropped a wooden packing crate.

'You clumsy fool!' shouted Briggs as he strode over, giving the porter a hard clout behind the ear. 'Do that again and you're out.'

'Sorry about that, Mr Mason. What is it you're after?'

Harry pulled a roll of ten-dollar bills from his pocket. 'I'm interested in buying spillage and damaged goods. Boxes that might have been dropped accidentally on purpose, if you know what I mean. And I'll pay well.'

'What goods you looking for?' asked Briggs.

'Food, building materials and tools, bedding and household goods. Practical things, Mr Briggs. It's for a good, charitable cause.'

'How much do you want?'

'Two cartloads a day.'

'How much you paying?'

'Twenty-five dollars a cart. My man will arrive before dawn each day.'

'How will I know him?'

'You won't mistake him. He's big, black and the meanest cuss you ever set eyes on. You can collect your pay-off on West Bay at my saloon.'

Briggs, nodding his agreement, stuck out his hand to shake. 'You're a gentleman, Mr Mason.'

Harry ignored the gesture, turned and left. Cross, who had been watching from the shadows, ran to catch him up.

Harry said, 'That's your man. His name's George Briggs. Find out who he is and where he lives. Arrive before dawn each day with two heavy carts and make sure he gives you the best stuff. Take your time loading and don't draw attention. Take the carts to Judge Lee to share with the needy.'

Cross nodded. 'What if he rats on us?'

'He won't. He knows what'll happen if he opens his big mouth.'

TWENTY-THREE

Life was hectic as the city rebuilt; hospitals, schools, banks, churches and civic offices were all under reconstruction.

Bessie, who was occupied raising funds for the restoration of the Church of Immaculate Conception and busy assisting Bishop Kenny and the Daughters of Isabella rehouse the many homeless Catholic families, saw Harry only briefly each morning over a hurried breakfast.

In the evenings, Harry often dined with Telfair Stockton, Mayor Bowden and Admiral James Cogswell, who kept himself fit and trim, despite eating like a horse, and was always good company, amusing those assembled with one entertaining anecdote after another. Over brandy and cigars, Telfair invariably spoke of real estate investments. His current project was building a street railway to run from the rail depot and waterfront warehousing to the coloured shanties of Hansontown, convinced that moving a plentiful supply of cheap labour to the jetties and railway yards where it was needed for heavy haulage work was a sure-fire moneymaker. Telfair was ready to invest but needed Harry to grease the wheels and sell the proposal to the council.

It took only a few weeks for Harry to approve generous public funding and a thirty-year monopoly licence for Telfair's North Jacksonville Street Railway Company and, taking advantage of the opportunity, issue numerous building permits for new housing, shops and a recreational field to be known as Mason Park.

* * *

By August 1902, Harry was riding a crest of popularity, especially amongst the shanties clustered along the Kings Road and around Hansontown. His street railway and Mason Park were opened with great pomp and ceremony by Mayor Duncan U. Fletcher, who had succeeded Bowden in the civic office. The Board of Trade lauded Harry as Jacksonville's businessman of the year. The city council nominated him as their honoured representative at the state governor's Tallahassee summer ball, staged that year to celebrate the coronation of the British King Edward VII.

And it was at the governor's summer ball that Harry renewed his acquaintance with Napoleon Broward, the erstwhile sheriff of Jacksonville, who, several years before, had arrested him after the Corbett v Mitchell boxing contest. Broward, who had been elected to the Florida State House of Representatives, had obviously prospered since his days as sheriff. But Harry, who had always considered Broward dull-witted, was surprised beyond astonishment to hear Broward's intentions to run for state governor, with his sights set on becoming a senator in Washington.

Returning from Tallahassee, Harry wasted no time meeting with Bowden, John Stockton and Mayor Duncan

U. Fletcher, who together made up the nominations committee of the Democratic Party. Harry came straight out with it, confidently nominating himself as their next delegate for election to the State House of Representatives. But Harry's proposal was met with outright rejection, and he sensed considerable annoyance at his presumption.

The following day, while dining with Bowden, Harry asked, 'What the hell happened yesterday?'

'They don't think you're ready,' said Bowden, cutting ravenously into a medium-rare sirloin.

'Not ready!' exclaimed Harry, putting his cutlery down with a clatter. 'Come on, what's the truth of it? It's not my turn, is that it? Or they've got someone else lined up?'

'The thing is, Harry, Duncan intends running.'

'And he's asked you to run his campaign.'

'Not in so many words.'

'Duval County has two seats; why can't we both run?'

'Judge Cromwell Gibbons is already nominated, and Duncan wants to join him at Tallahassee.'

'Cromwell Gibbons, the Yankee from Connecticut?'

'I'm sorry, Harry. It's not up to me. You'll need to wait a few years.'

'A few years! I'm fifty-seven. Another few years, and you'll be telling me I'm too damned old.' He paused before asking, 'What if I ran as an independent?'

'You'd have no chance. The only way to win in Florida is on a Democrat ticket, and that means Duncan endorsing you.'

'So, I need Duncan to step aside?'

'He won't do that, Harry. Come on, be reasonable and wait a year or two.'

'Everyone's got their price.'

'Money won't do it this time; you know how strait-laced Duncan is.'

'Yes. I remember him trying to stop the Corbett fight and then trying to give evidence against me. Well, he failed on both counts, and he'll fail this time too.'

'Harry, don't do anything rash; your turn will come around, and after a term in the House, we'll put you up for governor.'

Harry changed the subject. 'Another thing, just how long are the mayor and his entourage camping in my hotel?'

'Harry, don't be spiteful. Evicting Duncan won't improve your chances. Be patient. John Stockton is busy rebuilding City Hall, which will be finished by early next year.'

* * *

A week later, Harry was at the construction site of the new City Hall, where he knew he would find John Stockton in the surveyor's hut, poring over the plans.

Stockton greeted him amiably. 'Harry! Welcome to our new City Hall. Have you seen the plans?'

'No, I've not had the pleasure.'

'By the way, congratulations on getting the trolley park at Hansontown named in your honour. The coloured folk must be pleased with what you've done for them.'

'Unfortunately, John, these people are never satisfied and are even less grateful.'

'What the hell now?' asked Stockton, sounding irritated.

'They don't like the way white folk are getting new brick houses while they're getting nothing.'

'Nothing! Goddammit! They're getting plenty of work, and everyone, even them, will benefit from a busy, modern city. You know that better than most. After all, it was you who gave them their street railway.'

'It's not about work, John. It's about housing. They're getting nothing better than shacks and dirt floors. They're saying that when the next fire comes, it'll be them that burn, not the white folk.'

'These damn people are maddening. You can tell them that once we get downtown rebuilt, they'll be next. And that's a promise.'

'I've tried, John, but I can't deny what they see with their own eyes.'

'Harry, you have to make them understand that they'll all have brick houses with slate roofs, all in good time. For goodness' sake, none of us can afford another fire.'

'I know it, John, but it's hard for them to believe it when they hear Broward talking about segregation and pushing them outside the city limits.'

'Broward needs to keep his mouth shut. In any case, he finishes at the legislature this year, and I can assure you, none of us will be sorry to see the back of him.'

'Well, as I understand it, he's running for governor.'

'What! Believe me, Harry, his term's over.'

'Well, I only say it because there's wild talk of trouble brewing.'

'What trouble?' asked Stockton, sounding concerned.

'A mob, like the one that burned Alabama. They're mad as hell about how the city's reconstruction is making them poorer while white folk are getting richer off their sweated labour.'

* * *

Later that afternoon, Mayor Fletcher arrived hurriedly to the Everett, where Harry, anticipating the mayor's arrival, was in the lobby casually leafing through the hotel's newspapers.

The mayor spoke with urgency. 'Harry, I'm coming straight to the point. Stockton's relayed your conversation. If this is true, we must stop it.'

'Good afternoon, Mayor,' said Harry, slowly lowering his newspaper and carefully folding it. 'I only relayed to John what I'd heard on the grapevine. As for stopping it, I suggest you consider calling a meeting with our black civic leaders – pour oil on troubled water. By the way, may I offer you tea or coffee?'

Ignoring Harry's offer of refreshments, Fletcher unbuttoned his jacket and perched himself on the edge of a leather sofa. 'Can you gather your coloured folk, their preachers and whatnot? I'll meet with them on Saturday afternoon, a conciliatory meeting to take the steam out the situation?'

'At your office?'

'Good God, no, not there. Somewhere less…'

'You could meet at my new Mason Park,' suggested Harry. 'I'm sure they'll be pleased to see you there. Although, I must caution, Mr Mayor, there's always the possibility that things could flare up – you know how volatile these people are. It might be wise to have Police Chief Vinzant with half a dozen officers on hand.'

'That's a good idea, Harry. Please make the necessary arrangements.'

'I will, Mayor – you can leave it all to me.'

Harry told Cross what the mayor had in mind.

Cross looked puzzled. 'There ain't no trouble, boss. There's more than enough work and plenty of food for everyone.'

'But the mayor doesn't know that, does he?' replied Harry. 'And there's something else I need you to do.'

Cross listened carefully.

Harry then went to Judge Lee to arrange for the mayor's meeting with black civic leaders at the Edward Waters College, near where it overlooked Mason Park.

Then, at his saloon on West Bay, Harry found his tame news reporter slouching on his regular barstool. After several more whiskies, Harry dropped details of the mayor's upcoming meeting. Harry's last stop was to Chief Vinzant to inform him of the mayor's request for extra officers to be in attendance.

* * *

Saturday dawned with the oppressive humid heat of August. Harry took a stroll along the water's edge to a small, riverside café where he ate an early lunch and made pencilled notes. He then took a horse and trap to Mason Park, where Judge Lee was awaiting his arrival.

As Harry drew to a stop, Judge Lee hurried over. 'Councillor Mason, am I pleased to see you. There are rumours of a protest gathering.'

'A protest gathering?' said Harry, sounding surprised. 'I've heard nothing of it, but I'm sure the police have everything under control.'

'Some hotheads have got wind of our meeting, the reason for which I have to admit is puzzling.'

'As I understand it, Judge, the mayor wants to discuss progress of the reconstruction work.'

'But why now, and why here?'

***

By 2pm, a gang of thirty or so coloured men had assembled at the park gates, with an equal number of white ruffians menacingly watching from across the street.

'What the hell's going on?' demanded Chief Vinzant when he found Harry near the college entrance. 'I've only got six men here, and there must be more than a hundred of them. You said this was going to be a peaceful powwow, not a full-blown race riot.'

'I don't think violence is on their minds, Chief. They're only interested in hearing what the mayor has to say.'

'Like hell! This mob's here for trouble, and worse still, there are a dozen Klansmen on their way. The last thing I need is another lynching.'

'Chief, if you think there might be trouble, you must act quickly to assemble reinforcements. It'll be best to telegraph the governor and request that the militia are called out. You don't want to be caught off guard.'

'You're right. I'll be back as soon as I can. Hold the fort while I'm away.'

***

By 3pm, the crowd had swollen to more than two hundred, and scuffles were breaking out.

Mayor Fletcher arrived looking pale and unsure of himself. 'Oh, my God! I didn't expect this. You were right, Harry, things are worse than I'd thought. And Chief Vinzant tells me the Klan is here. I'm sorry, Harry, but I'll have to cancel. I can't be seen involved with this kind of—'

'Is cancelling wise, Mayor? If you leave now, it might inflame the situation. People will think you're running away.'

'I see your point, Harry. Perhaps I'll speak privately with Judge Lee.'

* * *

The afternoon editions of the local newspapers splashed headlines of violent clashes between police and protesters, with rumours spreading of rioting and marauding Klansmen. Crowds of excited onlookers flocked to Mason Park, hoping to witness the spectacle of brawling or worse.

Chief Vinzant returned with an extra four officers and, pushing his way through the assembly, found Harry. 'The governor's as angry as hell and wants to know why in God's name the mayor didn't have the courtesy of telling him he was fomenting a riot. Anyway, he's agreed to send twenty militia and promised a platoon of Ocala troopers in an hour or two.'

Somewhere in the distance, a gospel spiritual was being sung in opposition to an accordion squeezing out the old Confederate "Dixie".

Harry saw Bowden jostling his way through the crowd, being pursued by several newspaper reporters. Vinzant excused himself to deploy his men.

'What the hell!' said Bowden, arriving red in the face.

'Mayor Fletcher is to address the coloureds,' replied Harry, as if stating the obvious.

'Why? What in God's name is he thinking?'

Harry, raising his voice so that all those in earshot could hear, replied, 'The governor's mobilised the militia. He's called out the Ocala Rifles. They're to fire a volley to disperse the mob.'

'Oh, my God! No, we can't have that. That'll be the starting pistol for a race riot, Klan lynchings, arson, martial law and God only knows what else. Jesus! Fletcher is going to get us all—'

But before Bowden could finish, Harry saw the reporters, who had written every word, scurrying off, notepads in hand.

Judge Lee joined them. 'Mayor Fletcher has returned to City Hall. He says his departure will avert any unpleasantness.'

'He's leaving us holding the baby, his damned baby!' exclaimed Bowden. 'If this carries on, we can expect…'

His mouth dried, but Judge Lee continued where Bowden left off, 'Bloodshed, arson and looting. This is indeed a serious circumstance we find ourselves.'

'I'll address the crowd,' said Harry and, without hesitation, clambered onto a nearby buckboard and, through a megaphone usefully at hand, delivered his rehearsed speech.

'My name is Harry Mason. You all know me. You trust me to keep my word.' The general hubbub died away as

Harry drew the attention of the crowd. 'I swore I'd bring you work, better pay, new schools, new parks, street railway and opportunities for your families. And, as God is my witness, I've made good on my promises. Harry Mason is a man of his word.'

Speaking with conviction, he drew approving shouts. 'I've listened, and I've heard. I respect what you say. I will build you new homes. Homes of brick and slate. Fireproof homes where you and your families can live in peace and safety.'

His impassioned plea was in the manner of an evangelical preacher rousing his congregation to a crescendo of whoops and hollers of approval. 'Now, go about your work and build a better today. Go to your homes and prepare for a brighter tomorrow. Go to your churches and give praise to the good Lord.'

As Harry finished speaking, cheering and applause rose from the assembled throng. Well-wishers jostled around, pledging their support and shaking him enthusiastically by the hand. But Harry's attention was fixed on Cross and his men moving deftly amongst the crowd, encouraging onlookers to leave and to be on their way. Soon, only a handful of white hooligans remained, who, without any prospect of trouble, turned and slunk off. Thirty minutes after Harry's speech, Mason Park was all but deserted.

Bowden grabbed Harry by the hand and heartily patted him on the shoulder. 'My God! Let me be the first to congratulate you. It's no exaggeration to say you've single-handedly saved the day. I've never seen anything like it.'

'I agree,' said Judge Lee, who had watched in admiration. 'I must compliment you on your oratory. You certainly know how to turn a congregation.'

* * *

At breakfast next morning, Harry was absorbed in the newspapers.

Bessie, interrupting his concentration, said, 'It says here you're the hero who saved the day.'

'That, my dear, is a gross, sensational exaggeration, but it won't do me any harm. However, the headline I most enjoy is this one, "Mason for state legislator". It describes how Fletcher ran from the field with his tail between his legs, while I calmed the angry crowd, averting a riot and returning peace to our city. I couldn't have written it better myself!'

Bowden, laden with various newspapers under his arm, rushed excitedly into the breakfast room. 'My God! Have you seen this, Harry?'

Suddenly becoming aware of Bessie, Bowden stopped in his tracks. 'I beg your pardon, Bessie. Good morning to you. I hope all is well with you and the family are—'

She stopped him. 'I'll leave you two to your intrigue. I've more important things to do!'

Bowden helped himself to coffee. 'The governor is furious with Fletcher but is singing your praises. What I don't understand, Harry, is how it all started. Fletcher says that you told Stockton; Stockton told him; he told you; you told him and… well, he's in a state of confusion.'

'The truth is,' said Harry, 'Fletcher's political judgement is flawed. He can't be trusted with high office. You witnessed it yourself yesterday, and everyone else will know the truth from the newspapers. I've said it all along; he's not the right man for the House of Representatives, and I'm pleased to hear you're saying so too.'

'You're right, Harry. John and Telfair and the others are saying the same.'

'So, you'll run my campaign for the House?'

'It goes without saying, Harry. Everyone's behind you.'

TWENTY-FOUR

Duncan Upshaw Fletcher reluctantly stood aside, endorsing Harry as the Democratic Party candidate. Bowden managed the campaign, and both Harry and Cromwell Gibbons were elected to the 1903 Florida House of Representatives.

Gibbons was elected House speaker, and Harry spent the spring at the state capital assisting him on the Democratic legislative programme.

Returning home at the beginning of summer, Harry found Jacksonville's reconstruction well advanced and, much to his delight, the city council had removed itself from the Everett Hotel to establish camp at the Western Union building.

Returning to his ideas of building a new home on Riverside Avenue, Harry discovered, much to his disappointment, a scarcity of materials and labour, most being diverted to the city's rebuilding. And there was an absence of good architects prepared to work on private commissions, favouring the many prestigious municipal projects.

* * *

The evening before Independence Day, Harry and Admiral Cogswell dined together, marking the fifth anniversary of the naval victory off Santiago de Cuba, in which the admiral had played a notable role aboard the USS *Oregon* during the Spanish-American war.

Cogswell was an outstanding raconteur, and Harry enjoyed his company. After a meal of exquisitely prepared French cuisine served in the Everett's private dining room, the two men settled down to cognac and the finest Partagás cigars.

Cogswell said, 'I've a small favour to ask. I don't want to burden you with my petty domestic problems, but I know you're a man of integrity and I can trust you with complete confidence. Indeed, as a fellow military man, I have no hesitation in saying that I would trust you with my life.'

Harry nodded in appreciation of the plaudit. 'Whatever it is, James, I promise not to let you down.'

'It concerns my nephew, David,' said Cogswell. 'The son of my sister, Bianca, and her husband, John Mitchell. I expect you know of him, Senator John Lendrum Mitchell?'

'I've never made his acquaintance,' replied Harry.

'A scholar and a military man from a prominent Milwaukee family. Indeed, his father, Alexander, who was a good friend to my father, was a wealthy banker and important in Washington. My sister married John nearly forty years ago, back in '65. They had seven children, although tragically, only two survived into adulthood, and the eldest of the two, Alexander II, sadly passed away when only seventeen, leaving their only child, David.'

'I don't see how this is any business of mine,' said Harry, feeling uncomfortable.

'I will come to that in due course; bear with me for a moment longer.'

After finishing his brandy, Cogswell continued his account. 'Some say Bianca became unbalanced after losing an infant in childbirth and blamed John for the misfortune. Whatever the reason, she turned on him, making wild accusations of drunkenness, cruelty and adultery. At the time, and this is now several years ago in '77, it scandalised society, resulting in their acrimonious divorce. It was an upsetting time for everyone.'

'Where's your sister now?' asked Harry.

'Sadly, she died alone and heartbroken in '82, soon after her thirty-sixth birthday. She's buried at home in Milwaukee – it was very distressing.'

'I'm so sorry. It's always tragic to lose a loved one.'

The admiral poured himself another brandy and, swirling the amber nectar around the glass, was savouring its aroma. 'A year after the divorce, John remarried and moved to France with his new wife, leaving his four-year-old son, David, to be raised at Villa Alexandria by his grandmother, Martha Reed Mitchell.'

'The huge mansion across the river?' asked Harry.

'Yes, it's very grand, practically palatial. Martha built it as her winter residence and furnished it at great expense; that was in the days when money was plentiful and of no concern. She passed away last year at the good age of eighty-three. In its heyday, the house had a hundred servants and hosted many fantastical weekend parties, but by the end of her life, she lived alone and with no more than a yard boy. You see, Harry, as with many great fortunes, it was fleeting. The Mitchells owned a prosperous bank and had countless railroad and mining interests, but it all went in the great depression and silver crisis of '93. In straitened circumstances, Martha sold up and left Milwaukee for Florida, where she made Villa Alexandria her home. But without her husband, who'd passed some ten years before, she found things difficult and withdrew from society. Partly, I believe, from the shame of being financially reduced and partly embarrassed by her son's scandalous divorce.'

Harry asked, 'Who lives there now?'

'I'm coming to that. On Martha's death, my nephew, David, inherited the villa and has lived there ever since.'

'And his wife?' asked Harry, becoming intrigued at the turn of events.

'This is the nub of it,' continued the admiral. 'David married a vivacious young beauty called Kathryn. I expect you know her as Kitty Sutton, Joseph Parrott's stepdaughter, Joseph having married Kitty's mother.'

Harry was now paying full attention. 'Your nephew, David Mitchell, is Joseph Parrott's son-in-law?'

James nodded, taking a long drink of cognac and again refilling his glass.

Harry asked, 'So, where's Kitty?'

James resumed his tale. 'David and Kitty have a son, Alexander III, named after his distinguished grandfather. Alex is being raised by Kitty's parents, principally by Parrott's wife, Helen, a dear, kind woman.

'Soon after Alex was born, David fell from a pony while playing polo, suffering a nasty head injury which left him prone to bouts of both rage and depression in equal measure. Kitty, still a young woman, complained that David was no longer the man she'd married and couldn't cope with his moods and wanted more from life than caring for a cripple. In the end, she ran off with another man.'

'My God! This is tragic.'

'And this is where I come to my point. David is financially ruined, receiving only a small allowance from his father. The crux of it is that David has many vices – drink, gambling and loose women and many debts to match – and he's asked me to lend him $24,000.'

Harry said nothing. The twists and turns of the admiral's tale had arrived at its destination. His nephew wanted money and a lot of it. More than a retired admiral could afford.

After a long silence, Harry said, 'You'll have to gift him the money, because he'll never repay you.'

'That's why I want your advice, Harry. If I don't give David the money, I fear he'll sell the villa and end up homeless as well as penniless. John Stockton has offered him fifty thousand for the villa and has agreed to allow David to continue living there for as long as he wishes. But David has refused the offer.'

'How much is the property worth?' asked Harry, curious to discover that Stockton was involved.

'Half a million, perhaps more. The villa includes 140 acres of prime real estate. A small town could be built there.'

'What about his father-in-law, Parrott? Wouldn't he lend him the money?'

'Parrott's a parsimonious devil. He won't forgive Kitty for the shame and embarrassment she brought him and has threatened to disinherit her. Parrott begrudgingly offered to lend David the money on condition that the villa's title deeds were surrendered as collateral. David says he would rather starve than hand him the deeds.'

'What does your nephew intend doing with $24,000?'

'I assume the same as before.'

'Well, it seems you've answered your own question, James. You wouldn't do any worse than find a drunken street beggar to give your money. Either way, it ends up running down the gutter.'

Cogswell stared forlornly into his brandy.

'How old is he?' asked Harry.

'David? He's thirty-four.'

'My God! By that age, we'd fought and seen good men die. And what does your wife say about it, or haven't you told her? No doubt she'd put your money to better use.'

The admiral said nothing.

After a long pause, Harry continued, more frankly than before. 'I'm sorry, James, but giving him money would be foolish. However hard that sounds, you can't deny the fact that he has the biggest mansion in Jacksonville surrounded by acres of prime real estate.' As Harry continued, he became increasingly annoyed. 'He won't countenance exchanging a small plot of his own property in favour of wine, women and song but will happily piss your hard-earned cash down the drain.'

The pair sat in silence. Eventually, Cogswell stood to leave and, shaking Harry by the hand, tears began flooding his eyes.

'Thank you, Harry, I knew I could trust you for honest advice, but I'm duty-bound to help him. He's my sister's boy, and he's had a miserable life one way and another. His mother died when he was a child; his father abandoned him; he suffered a grievous head injury; his wife left him for another man; he's been forced to give up his young son into the care of his mother-in-law; and his grandmother, who raised him and loved him dearly, has passed away. He's alone in the world with few friends, no money, no employment and little purpose in life.'

Harry said nothing, and they parted in a disconsolate mood.

TWENTY-FIVE

Harry was elected to the State House of Representatives for a second term and kept chairmanship of several important city council committees. And, to the dismay of many, Napoleon Broward became Florida's nineteenth governor.

Abandoning all thoughts of building a mansion on Riverside Avenue, Harry made the Everett's newly refurbished presidential suite his home, enjoying its sumptuous grandeur which reminded him just how far he had travelled from Harold Street, with its single cold tap and shared outside latrine.

Life was good. Harry's stepson ran the saloons and boarding houses while his eldest son, George, who was as bright as a button, was assistant manager at the Everett. Harry's second son, Charles, a stout and successful athlete, spent most of his time competing on the sports field with dreams of participating at the 1908 London Olympic Games. Thomas, who was sixteen, attended musical school, working hard to fulfil his mother's dream of him becoming a classical pianist. Lily, who was fourteen, had all the rebellion of a tomboy, taking every opportunity to antagonise her parents.

Harry wasn't close to his children, not in the same way he had doted on his three daughters in England. Bessie kept her brood close by and bossed over them like a mother hen. To Harry's mind, she spoilt them with indulgences they hadn't earned, and when he objected, he was shooed away and scolded for interfering, and with no inclination to push in where he wasn't wanted, he turned his attention to his one genuine pleasure of making money.

Bowden pestered Harry to run for state governor, promising him the full weight of the Democratic election machine. But Harry was too busy acquiring property, buying stocks, joining the boards of major companies and accumulating mountains of cash, which swelled the deposit vaults of Barnett's Bank.

And it was during one of his regular business meetings with Barnett that Harry broached the topic of joining the bank as a partner, suggesting changing its name to the Barnett & Mason Bank. Horrified at the thought that his illustrious institution, established by his loved and esteemed father, could be shared with the likes of Harry Mason, Barnett patiently set out the facts, whereby even the most significant investor could not disturb the bank's foundations.

However, encouragingly as always, Barnett suggested Harry consider starting his own bank, pointing out the many advantages, including authority under the National Banking Act to issue his own dollar bills, which could include his name and image in the design.

'Just think of that, Harry,' said Barnett, fuelling Harry's interest. 'The Mason dollar bill. The Mason greenback. Now, *that* would get you noticed. And, if you don't stray from the golden rule of banking – never risk your own money, only other people's – you've every reason to succeed.'

* * *

Harry lost no time instructing his lawyer, Rinehart, to license his new bank. Harry was duly elected chairman, with Judge Henry B. Philips appointed the bank's president. Initially, Harry insisted the bank carry his name above its portals, but reluctantly and a little disappointed, he was persuaded that the Bank of South Jacksonville would attract broader appeal.

* * *

Soon after registering his new bank, Harry invited Mr John J. Heard, founder of the colossal Heard National Bank, to join him for lunch. The purpose was to discuss a loan to build Florida's first skyscraper hotel, to be named the Hotel Mason.

Heard, who harboured ambitions to become Florida's wealthiest man, had let it be known that he was keen to invest in prestigious construction projects. Over several bottles of Chateau Margaux, of which Harry sipped abstemiously, he persuaded Heard to lend him $260,000 secured on a promissory note issued by the Everett Enterprise Corporation, an empty shell company established to give the appearance of financial solidity. Repayments of Heard's loan was agreed at six per cent in ten equal stages between 1920 and 1925.

Harry immediately put a hundred thousand dollars to work as operating capital for his own bank, investing the rest with Barnett at an annual 6.75%. Harry's first foray into the world of banking and his contrivance at making free money had been successful. He could now see no end to the possibilities for more.

And the more money Harry had, the more he got. There wasn't a person in Jacksonville who didn't know and respect his name. His decision to abandon London was at last vindicated. If success was happiness, then this was it.

* * *

More good news arrived when his eldest son announced his engagement to Georgia Dix Nelson, the socialite beauty and soprano opera singer with the Peabody Conservatory of Baltimore. Georgia was descended from the Dix family of Accomack County, Virginia, one of the first European settlers to arrive at Jamestown aboard the ship *Thomas* in August 1635 and was widely regarded as American aristocracy. George and Georgia were married in July 1906 at the Church of the Immaculate Conception, followed by celebrations the like of which Jacksonville had never seen. Harry could not have been prouder.

* * *

Going from strength to strength, Harry secured his third term as House Representative, and it was at the state capital that he heard how Henry Flagler, founding partner with John D. Rockefeller of Standard Oil, was experiencing difficulty disposing of his two-hundred-bed Continental Hotel at Atlantic Beach, a remote location fifteen miles east of Jacksonville. Harry saw an opportunity. He could easily steer the city council to build new road and rail connections between Jacksonville and Flagler's hotel, opening the possibilities to develop a new coastal resort.

Flagler had built the Continental on three thousand acres of coastal land gifted by the Federal government and, although he'd invested two hundred thousand in the project, most of the labour used in its construction had come at little cost through the penal authority's convict leasing scheme.

Harry planned to meet Flagler in New York, where he proposed to offer $125,000 cash, confident that Flagler would take the money rather than leave his hotel empty and rotting.

As Harry completed his travel arrangements, Daniel T. Gerow, an old friend and Republican rival who was Jacksonville's postmaster general, interrupted him. He was carrying a letter from England addressed to Mr Enoch T. Price, care of the European House.

Gerow said, 'I apologise for troubling you, Harry, but I think this is for you.'

Harry missed a beat as his jaw slackened.

'It arrived a few days ago,' continued Gerow. 'I thought of you because of your English origins and, if memory serves me well, one of your saloons was once called the European House.' Gerow handed Harry the envelope for closer inspection. The handwriting was not Eliza's, and it wasn't addressed in her usual manner.

'Do you know who this Enoch T. Price is?' asked Gerow. 'I've never heard the name before, and I was hoping you might help.'

'There was a man of that name lodging at the European,' replied Harry, quickly regaining his composure. 'He moved to Boston, but I'm sure he left a forwarding address. It'll take me a while to locate his details. Can you leave it with me?'

'I appreciate your help, Harry. I knew you were the right man to ask. I said to my wife only this morning. I said, if anyone knows, it'll be Harry Mason.'

* * *

The letter was from Harry's eldest daughter, Bertha, the first she had written to him.

* * *

24 March 1907
Dear Father,

I hope you are well and enjoy a happy and settled life in America. We all miss you and think of you always. I know this letter must come as a surprise, being the first I have ventured to write since the occasion of our parting when I was only twelve years old. Much water has passed under the bridge since then, but, in all truthfulness, the love of your three daughters remains as solid and undiminished as ever. You are our father, and this fact cannot be altered or denied and, as each day passes and we mature into women, our separation from you becomes ever more difficult to bear, especially as we have so much to share with you. I write in the certain belief that you will again allow us into your heart.

Mother is well, except for the pain she suffers from arthritis, most severely in winter. Her fingers are no longer nimble enough to stitch or write. As for myself, I am married to Bill Davis, a soap-cutter by trade. Our eldest, Teddy, is fourteen and works with his father.

My sister, Florence, married Ted King, and they have seven children. Their eldest is eighteen, while the youngest is just five weeks old. Beatrice has recently wed Fred Shearn, a docker at the city port; they are yet to have children. We all live nearby at Totterdown, where we have many relatives and friends. We are a happy band, and your kind remittances over the years have helped support us in an agreeable situation. We sincerely thank you for your generosity.

Your mother still lives but is frail and unable to leave the house where she lives in the village of Keynsham.

I write in the hope that you might permit me to visit. It would bring great joy to see you and renew the bond between father and daughter. I am happily disposed to travel to New York and make my way to Florida. All I require are dates which suit your circumstance and the cost of any lodgings should your own be insufficient for my stay; a narrow bed and washstand will be adequate for my needs.

Please agree to our meeting and let me know what arrangements to make. It will be a delight to see and kiss you once again. I have so much to share with you.

Please reply soon.

Your loving and devoted daughter,

Bertha.

* * *

Harry felt an emptiness and an aching deep inside. 'My God, what a price I've paid.'

He replied by return post.

* * *

3 April 1907
My dearest Bertha,

I am overjoyed to receive your letter. To see you and hear news from home would indeed be a pleasure. I happen to be in New York on business for two weeks at the end of May. Please arrange to arrive on or soon after the 15th. If you can stay for a week or longer, it would be most convenient and give me the greatest joy.

I prosper and can afford a modest hotel for our stay. New York is a magnificent city which we can enjoy together. It is more agreeable to stop there than endure the long and arduous journey south to Florida, where the weather in May is too hot and overbearingly humid to afford any comfort and is an area plagued by mosquitoes that bite viciously.

Whatever the cost of your fare, and please don't buy the cheapest available (steerage), I shall refund you in full, as I do not wish to see you out of pocket. Let me know the date and shipping line, and I shall meet you on your arrival.

I look forward to our reunion with happiness and anticipation.

With fondest regards,
Your loving father,
Enoch.

* * *

Harry told Bessie of his plan to travel to New York to meet Flagler and remain to conclude their business for a week or two.

TWENTY-SIX

Although Harry had heard much of the renowned Mr Flagler, this was to be their first meeting, scheduled to take place at Flagler's grand brownstone offices on Fifth Avenue with East 11th Street, a few blocks north of Washington Park, where Harry had taken two rooms at the Hotel Earle.

On his arrival, Harry was greeted by an English butler who showed him into a comfortably appointed sitting room where only the solemn ticking of a large grandfather clock could be heard. In his imagination, Harry had assumed the oil magnate and titan of America's railroads would be at the centre of a hive of frenetic activity, with telegrams arriving by the minute and ticker tape machines noisily reporting up to the second stock movements. Instead, it was as quiet as the grave. At the chimes of 11am, the butler reappeared and led Harry through to an inner sanctum. It wasn't an office but an opulent private apartment decorated in the French baroque style. Flagler, a man in his late seventies, was immaculately dressed in a beautifully tailored light-grey suit, a pristine starched white shirt with a high-winged collar and a neat, navy-blue bow tie. His hair was silver-grey and cut short, and his manicured moustache had turned snow-white. He was seated behind a large pedestal writing desk surrounded by shelves of rare editions bound in the most beautiful calf leather. 'Good morning, Mr Mason,' he welcomed Harry in a kindly manner. 'I'm delighted to at last meet you. Your reputation around Jacksonville is an enviable one. I hear you've made quite a success of the old Everett, and your saloons are nothing less than gold mines. And I envy you living on the Florida coast, one of my favourite locations, notably St Augustine, although I expect you miss the charm of London town.'

Harry was taken aback and flattered to find that the great Henry Flagler knew so much about him, before realising that Parrott was Flagler's man and would have reported every detail.

Flagler continued, 'Well, Mr Mason, you've come to persuade me to give away my Continental Hotel for a fraction of its worth.'

Before Harry could answer, Flagler said, 'I'm about to have a cup of tea. Will you join me?'

The butler reappeared. 'Two cups of our Assam blend, both with a little milk.' Then, turning to Harry, he said, 'Tell me, Mr Mason, how do you find your work at the House of Representatives? More rewarding, I imagine, than city councillor?'

Harry cleared his throat. 'Each gives me the opportunity to contribute to the advancement of the city and improvements to the lives of our citizens.'

'I couldn't agree more. Civic duty is a noble endeavour and important for the good of our nation. Speaking for myself, however, I've never found the time nor inclination. Business is my passion. If I can add to the advancement of humankind by the production of a single tool, then I shall have made my contribution to the world.'

The butler arrived and served tea in an elegant set of bone china.

'Now tell me, Mr Mason, how much will you pay for my hotel? Don't be coy, we are both men of the world, come straight out with it.'

'A hundred thousand cash is a fair offer. The hotel will need—'

Flagler interrupted. 'Come, Mr Mason, you disappoint me. Let's not dilly dally like hog merchants haggling at market. I understood you came with an offer of at least $125,000.'

Harry was momentarily knocked off balance. Was the $125,000 a guess, or did he know more? 'I'm prepared to go a little higher,' said Harry, now thinking on his feet. 'With certain conditions, I would go as far as $150,000 if repayments are spread over a handful of years.'

'I'm only guessing,' said Flagler, studiously stirring his tea, 'but I assume you intend to subdivide the Continental's acreage into smaller plots, selling each for home development. As for the hotel, I presume you'll create a limited company to sell stock to investors and then run the hotel as their third-party agent. The entire enterprise will cost you nothing and has the beauty of giving you control of the cash flow, which is always an attractive advantage. Your plan is a good one and will provide a handsome profit. But tell me, Mr Mason, why shouldn't I do this myself?'

Unsure how to proceed, Harry didn't rush to answer. 'Well, you've obviously considered such a plan and found it not to your liking. Cash would be better employed further south at your Palm Beach development. Selling the Continental will remove a loss from your books and a drain on your time and reputation.' Harry hesitated before adding, 'And you have no interest in a failing hotel that doesn't fit your plans for the Southern Keys.'

'Perhaps you're right, Mr Mason, but I can't employ cash if it's drip-fed by instalments. I want to sell the hotel, not rent it.'

Harry felt the moment ebbing from his grasp and had the sensation of déjà vu, as when being taught basic logic by Isaiah, the furniture maker, in his tiny office on Curtain Road.

'Now, Mr Flagler,' said Harry assertively, trying to wrestle back the initiative, 'it's your turn to haggle over the runt. How much do you require to sell?'

'I like you very much, Mr Mason. You have a way about you that is rarely found these days in modern America. It's a pity we didn't meet thirty years ago; I think we would have gotten along very nicely.' He paused a second before saying, 'To induce me to sell, I'll require two hundred thousand with twenty per cent of every plot sold for home development.'

Harry was stunned. 'That's too much for my pocket; I'd be handing you any profit for years to come.'

'But imagine this, Mr Mason, if you persuaded the city council to fund the construction of a new road and rail link to Atlantic Beach. Well, my goodness, your opportunities would be limitless. Why, before you know it, you'll be developing a whole new resort, perhaps even a new town.'

'I'm sorry, Mr Flagler, I couldn't contemplate the kind of deal you're proposing.'

'Even though it's more than you want to pay, it's a reasonable and profitable offer. And you can borrow on preferential terms from your bank, or, as you've so ingeniously done, from the generosity of the Heard National Bank. I'm confident that a courageous investor such as yourself will find a way to complete our mutually beneficial transaction.'

Harry was puzzled. How did he know so much about his affairs?

Flagler continued, 'Let's part on amicable terms and give ourselves a month to think it over.'

They shook hands warmly.

As they parted, Flagler said, 'It's been a pleasure meeting you, Mr Mason, and if I can ever be of help, then contact me without delay because, I can assure you absolutely, I won't hesitate to enlist your support should ever I need it.'

Harry stepped back onto Fifth Avenue. Their meeting had lasted forty minutes, yet he was drained and felt his shirt damp and clinging to his back. Harry wandered north to the St Regis Hotel on the corner of East 55th, where he ordered a large glass of the finest scotch before again considering Flagler's proposal. If every plot sold, Flagler would net a tidy sum. But with Flagler developing his Palm Beach and Miami resorts, competition would be stiff, and with the Continental needing an expensive refit, it didn't sound like the giveaway Harry had hoped for. But with a month to think it over, he pushed all thoughts of it from his mind and turned his attention to his daughter's arrival.

* * *

The following day, Harry made his way to the Hudson River jetties. He was excited yet apprehensive at the thought of meeting his eldest daughter for the first time in twenty-six years.

Bertha's disembarkation was for 10am, but he grew anxious after more than an hour of waiting. Perhaps she had passed without either recognising the other. Then, as he was about to enquire, he spun on his heels. A petite young woman was asking for directions. It wasn't her looks that Harry recognised; it was her voice that transported him back to Harold Street. 'Bertha! Bertha!' he called.

The young woman turned to face him. 'Father?'

'Bertha. Can it be you?'

For a moment, both looked unsure before throwing their arms around each other. Releasing their embrace, Bertha took her handkerchief, wiping away tears of joy as those around them smiled in approval at their happy reunion.

Harry said, 'Well, here you are. You have the looks of your mother. Her eyes and smile too.'

'And you've not changed either, Father.'

'Oh, if only it were true. I'm larger around the middle and thinning on top, and what's left is going grey. Come, enough of this. Let's get you settled, and then you can tell me about your journey and how long you intend staying.'

'For two weeks, Father, if this is convenient?'

'It's perfect. We'll fill every minute together. You've so much to tell me, and I'm longing to hear it all.'

Harry felt a surge of intense happiness and was momentarily filled with thoughts of abandoning everything to return home to his daughters and Eliza.

As the cab crossed town, Harry watched as Bertha marvelled at the sights of enormous, towering monolithic skyscrapers.

'Impressed by the city?' he asked.

'My goodness, Father, it's better than I imagined. The buildings are so tall, and the ladies in their stylish fashions carry themselves with such confidence. I can hardly believe my eyes. It's so different from home.'

When they arrived at the Hotel Earle, its splendour took Bertha's breath.

'Father, can you afford this? Please don't go into debt on my account. We should move to somewhere less expensive; I am happy with a small room in a boarding house.'

'My darling girl, I've a small business which allows me an occasional extravagance, and your arrival is an auspicious occasion to be marked.'

Over lunch, they ate little as they spoke enthusiastically, which continued unabated throughout the afternoon and again through dinner that evening.

Harry had fabricated his story and was sure of sustaining the fiction for the duration of his daughter's stay. He would not tell her about Harry Mason, his new family, his hotels, political successes or his considerable wealth. Harry didn't know if she would be sympathetic and understanding or respond with disappointment, outrage, or even disgust. He wanted his daughter to think only the best of him and return home with fond memories.

Bertha described the past twenty-six years, from the day they departed for Bristol and how they cried for days when he didn't follow. She told him of growing up in Totterdown and the Sunday school at the Baptist Chapel. She spoke of her sisters, their work, marrying and his grandchildren, the eldest of whom was eighteen and courting. Harry listened as Bertha talked hour after hour, and in every word, he heard his beloved Eliza.

***

At breakfast next morning, Bertha spoke joyously of their reunion and the splendours of New York. 'I've never slept so well,' she said. 'My room is larger than our whole house, where five of us must live. It has electric lighting, its own lavatory with a bath and scalding water the moment I turned the tap. There's even a telephonic device. Everything here is modern and of the future.'

'America is a new country with grand ideas,' replied Harry. 'This hotel is one of its smallest. Some hotels have two, three or even four hundred rooms, with restaurants and ballrooms, even heated indoor swimming pools.'

'Oh, my goodness! Have you ever stayed at such a hotel, Father?'

'I did once. Maybe we'll visit one. Would you like that?'

'Father, I enjoy everything we do together, and I love your American manner of speaking; you sound sophisticated and so important.'

***

Over the following week, father and daughter visited the tourist sights of New York: the Statue of Liberty, Coney Island Amusement Park, Broadway, shopping on Ladies'

Mile and excitedly to the new twenty-storey Flatiron skyscraper, amazed by its height and shape.

Most afternoons they visited Central Park, leisurely promenading the Mall and sitting by the Boat Pond to enjoy ice cream from one of the many pushcart vendors. It was here that Harry asked about his friend, Michael.

Bertha said, 'I'm afraid to say it, Father, but he's in prison. He beat a man to death. Mother says he'll hang.' Breaking off for a moment to feed inquisitive ducks from a ten-cent bag of crumbs, she continued, 'Did you know that Mr Toff is dead? Mother thinks he was murdered, but the police say it was an accident falling from a train.'

For the first time, Harry sensed melancholy take hold of him. 'Why didn't your mother join me? I asked her enough times, even pleading with her.'

'I can't say, Father. She never speaks of it. I once overheard her say to Grandmother that you wore her out, and she longed for a quiet life without constant worries.'

Harry fell silent for several minutes before speaking. 'How did I wear her out?'

'I suppose she is happier without fearing who might knock at our door. Sometimes, when reading the scriptures on a Sunday, she would say that happiness came from knowing that tomorrow will be filled with the certainty of peace and safety.' Bertha took a long pause before continuing. 'We were girls, Father, she didn't tell us much, except to say that one day you would return home.' Bertha waited before asking, 'Did you ever think of returning home?'

'Yes, my dear, many times.'

Bertha leaned forward and, covering her father's cupped hands with hers, said, 'Why didn't you come home to us?'

'I don't know,' he said, shrugging at the futility of further excuses. 'Truthfully, I wish I'd never left.'

Both stared out across the park, watching a group of children playing happily with a hoop and stick.

Gently squeezing his hand, Bertha said, 'Tell me about your life here. Have there been happy times?'

Harry sensed her acceptance, perhaps even forgiveness.

He told her about his ocean crossing, his stay at Mrs O'Neill's, and his work as a bartender with Nicky, and how, after a few years, he had saved sufficient to start a small corset factory but lost everything in the great fire of 1901. 'Fortunately, the insurance paid enough to start a small liquor saloon.'

Bertha said, 'Did you find someone to share your life with?'

The frankness of her question startled him. He saw Bertha as his little girl, and here she was talking to him as a friend and equal, the way Michael or Agnes might have quizzed him. But her question led to a way of telling her about Bessie, a moment of honesty to share and explain everything, a blessed release from the dishonest charade he danced. But his nerves failed him. He was afraid.

'No, there wasn't anyone.'

'You've been alone all these years? Dear Father, my heart breaks for you. I'm so sorry to hear this news; weren't you ever lonely?'

'And what of your mother?' he asked, wishing to change the subject.

'She is happy. Her life has been fulfilled looking after us girls, and now, with so many grandchildren, she's busier than ever.'

It hurt to hear his daughter speak so joyfully of the loving family he had left behind; it was a happiness he yearned for.

She hugged him and spoke cheerfully, 'Come, Father, we are at last together, and one day soon, you'll return home. But, for now, let's enjoy ourselves and visit one of those hotels you've spoken of. The ones with ballrooms and swimming pools. The Astoria or Ansonia, is that what you call them?' She kissed him and threaded her arm through his, and with renewed enthusiasm, they put the past behind them and once more continued their tour together.

* * *

Harry returned to Jacksonville, telling Bessie only of his disappointment at not clinching a deal with Flagler and how his time spent in New York had been wasted. But Bessie showed little interest and seemed not to have noticed his absence.

He wanted to tell her of Bertha, but that was impossible. He was trapped between two worlds: one he wanted and the other he couldn't do without. With wealth, privilege and power, his life was filled with comfort and rich experiences, yet, paradoxically, he felt impoverished and alone without a soulmate with whom to share his bounty. And again, the same question returned. Why hadn't he taken Eliza with him? Together, they would have built a prosperous, happy life.

TWENTY-SEVEN

It was the hottest day of the long summer of 1908. Harry was lazing on the white sand beach fronting his Ponte Vedra house, enjoying the cool sea breeze and the shade of an oversized striped umbrella when a messenger boy arrived by bicycle carrying a note from Judge Henry Philips.

* * *

Regret to inform death of Admiral Cogswell this day, 12 August. Return immediately.

* * *

It was a shock. Cogswell couldn't have been older than sixty. Harry recalled the evening when they had last dined when he had confided his nephew's misfortunes.

Harry gave the messenger a lemonade drink and two dollars for his trouble of cycling the fifteen miles from Jacksonville. Two hours later, wearing a panama, a linen shirt and cream flannels with two-tone tan brogues, Harry strode into Judge Philips' office on East Bay Street.

'Well, this is sad news,' said Harry. 'When did it happen?'

'During the night. The doctor says it was heart failure.'

'But why the urgency in your message?' asked Harry. 'Is something amiss?'

The judge, sounding irritated, replied, 'His wife, Annie, came to see me this morning. You're named as Cogswell's sole executor, and he's scrolled across the face of his will in red lettering, "I trust only Harry Mason to settle my affairs".'

Harry was bemused. 'Sole executor. I don't understand.'

Judge Philips continued, 'I've looked through his inventory. He owns nothing more than a lame horse, a donkey, two cows and an apple orchard, with debts amounting to fifteen hundred dollars. There's not even enough for a decent burial, and him being a military hero and all. Annie's the sole beneficiary of nothing, not a bean to live on. God only knows what he meant by saying you're the only one he trusts.' The judge spoke as if cross-questioning at court. 'Harry, you must tell me, has anything untoward occurred between you and the admiral? You must declare it, now.'

'I swear, Judge, I've no idea what it means. I'm as much in the dark as you.'

The judge handed Harry the will along with a portfolio of papers. 'Take these. As sole executor, it's your moral and legal duty to carry out his final wishes and, please, Harry, do what you can for dear Annie and their son, Francis. The dear boy only graduated from naval academy last month.'

* * *

Harry did not disappoint, arranging an elaborate cortege with an ornate hearse adorned with a canopy of black ostrich feathers and drawn by a team of four jet-black stallions. An entire naval honour guard in ceremonial dress led the procession of mourners, including the admiral's old comrades, Lieutenant General Arthur McArthur and General Charles King, who were amongst his distinguished pall-bearers. Annie cried uncontrollably throughout.

Setting about his duties as executor, Harry collected as many of the admiral's private papers, letters and accounts as he could find. Cogswell was surprisingly not a good record-keeper, with correspondence and bills crumpled at the back of drawers, stuffed down the sides of armchairs and lodged behind plant pots. Much of what Harry found were debts, including unpaid accounts from the butcher, the baker and the grocery store, some dating back over six months. Harry settled them all.

After failing to bring order to the various documents, Harry enlisted the help of his accountant, who sent him a young lad with neither the look nor manner of a bookkeeper, let alone an accountant.

In his disappointment, Harry greeted the young man rudely, 'Do you shave yet, son?'

The young man replied, 'I beg your pardon, sir. My name's Frank Wilson.'

'I hope you're at least a clerk?' enquired Harry curtly.

'I'm an apprenticed accountant, sir. I've just completed my studies in law and mathematics. I apologise if I'm a disappointment to you.'

Harry calmed his irritation and took a kindlier tone. Leading Wilson to a long, mahogany table where he had laid out Cogswell's papers, he said, 'I'll leave you to it.

I've already given myself a headache puzzling over these damned things.'

* * *

Returning several hours later, Harry enquired, 'Well, lad, any progress?'

Showing Harry a file indexed with slips of different coloured papers, Wilson said, 'What's intriguing is that this series of documents appear related, but I don't see how. One, dated 1903, names a man called Parrott. Another, dated a year later, refers to Huling or Holing, and there is a reference to D.M. and a property called the Mitchell House. There's also a roughly drafted contract for thirty thousand dollars signed by two people: Admiral Cogswell, dated 25 March 1908, but I can't make out the second signature. Does any of this make sense to you, Mr Mason?'

Wilson had captured Harry's attention. 'Show me again, young Frank.'

Together, they began to connect the pieces of the jigsaw. Harry asked, 'Do you enjoy filet mignon and French champagne, young Frank?'

'I've no idea, sir, I've had neither.'

* * *

Over dinner, they talked of their discoveries. In 1903, Joseph Parrott lent David Mitchell $24,000 in return for the title deeds of Villa Alexandria. Parrott agreed to return the deeds to Mitchell on repayment of the loan. Parrott, unsure he would ever see his money returned, hedged his risk with an insurance policy underwritten by a Mr George Huling, payable on Mitchell's default or premature death. Parrott then lodged the title deeds as collateral to secure a substantial loan from the Mellon National Bank of Pittsburg, which Parrott repaid three years later in 1907, at which time the bank returned the deeds. In 1908, making a healthy profit, Parrott sold the deeds to Admiral Cogswell for thirty thousand dollars.

Harry said, 'So, Cogswell gave away his life savings to protect his nephew.'

Wilson replied, 'Well, the admiral didn't give away his money, not in the sense that he got nothing in return. The deeds will always have value as a tradable document to be bought and sold. The admiral would have gotten his money back, either when Mitchell repaid the loan, albeit he believed Parrott held the deeds, or by selling it on the open market should Mitchell default, so there was little risk of the admiral losing his outlay.'

'But the admiral would never have sold,' replied Harry. 'The admiral was concerned for his nephew's welfare. He bought the deeds to stop Parrott evicting Mitchell, which, no doubt, he would have threatened.'

'Mr Cogswell's concern for his nephew was indeed laudable,' said Wilson. 'But it has left his wife in a precarious position.'

'You're right, Wilson, but he didn't intend any harm to Annie. When the admiral bought the deeds, he had every expectation that his nephew would, in good time, repay him. Then, with the villa's deeds returned safely to Mitchell and the admiral's savings repaid, no one would be any the wiser. But then, discovering his heart was failing, he realised time was not on his side and had placed his wife in a terrible position. With no time to remedy his predicament, he thought that I might recover his money, and that's when he scrolled my name in red.'

'Why did he think you could help?'

'Something he once confided.'

'Well, he was right to trust you,' said Wilson. 'You now only need sell the deed to recover the money.'

'But that would betray the admiral's intentions to stop his nephew's eviction.'

After a moment, Harry said, 'There must be a way to get Annie her money while allowing Mitchell to remain in the villa. Tell me about this Huling character, the insurance man.'

'His contract was with Parrott, who no longer has an interest, so he and Parrott are out the picture.'

Thoughtfully, Harry said, 'So, the deed belongs to the Cogswell estate and its sole beneficiary, Annie Cogswell.'

'It's not just the document she owns,' said Wilson. 'It's the villa and its grounds.'

'But we don't yet have the deed.'

'No, but there's a receipt amongst the admiral's papers for a deposit box at the Barnett Bank. My guess is it's there.'

* * *

Wilson had guessed right. The following day, Harry collected the deed and headed south across the St Johns River to visit Mitchell.

Villa Alexandria was indeed on a grand scale and just as Cogswell had described it. With its private chapel, a dining hall to seat fifty and each of its four large reception rooms elaborately decorated in the theme of a different country: Japanese, French, Italian and Gothic English. But before Harry reached its front door, an unkempt individual appeared from a side porch carrying a shotgun.

'Are you David Mitchell?' asked Harry.

'If you want money, you can get in line with the rest.'

Harry repeated his question.

'I'm Mitchell, and you're trespassing on my property.'

Mitchell was thin and much shorter than Harry had expected.

'I'm here to discuss the deeds to this property,' said Harry, sounding reasonable.

A reasonableness that was not reciprocated. 'This is my house, built by my grandmother, so you can shove your worthless deeds up your ass. Now get the fuck off my land!'

'I'm sorry to say it, Mr Mitchell, but it's not your property and—

Mitchell raised his gun and took aim. 'You blackmailing bastard. Get off my land, or I'll shoot you dead.'

* * *

Harry relayed the morning's events to Judge Philips. 'I sympathise with what you're trying to do, Harry. But there may not be a legal remedy to your quandary. The courts regard possession as nine-tenths of the law, even for a squatter. To get Annie her money, the deed must be sold, and Mitchell has to leave.'

* * *

That evening, Annie arrived at the Everett in a state of anxiety. Her rent was months in arrears and the storekeepers were refusing her credit. Harry reassured her he was close to recovering her inheritance and, in the meantime, would settle all outstanding accounts.

Harry tried several times to reason with Mitchell, but each time Mitchell refused to speak, once discharging a shotgun over Harry's head. He wrote to Mitchell's lawyers with a range of conciliatory proposals, including selling a small parcel of the estate for housing development, allowing Annie to receive her inheritance and Mitchell to remain in residence. But not once did he receive a reply.

Harry even stooped to ask Joseph Parrott for help, but he only laughed, saying that Mitchell was a wastrel, and he wouldn't countenance spending another dime on him. Parrott asked Harry, 'Has the Mitchell family offered to buy the deeds of their mother's house?' Answering his own question, he said, 'No. I didn't think so. They're not interested in Bianca Cogswell's debauched offspring. They don't acknowledge him as a true Milwaukee Mitchell, not after the disgrace of the divorce and his father marrying the Becker girl. If it weren't for Helen and me adopting his dear child, Alexander, the poor mite would be roaming the streets as an urchin. No. I'm afraid, Mason, you've found yourself another lost cause.'

Obsessed by his duty to fulfil the admiral's dying wish, Harry devoted every waking hour to the task. But there were consequences to his persistence. His absence from council business lost him the chairmanship of influential committees; Telfair dissolved their partnership; and Harry's eldest son, George, took control of the hotels and ran the bank. Bowden, worrying that Harry was suffering a mental breakdown, begged him to see a doctor. Bessie, however, showed little sympathy, complaining that he was no better than a fool. Harry took no heed of either; he was locked in a fight that he would not concede. Harry doggedly pursued Mitchell for three years, but the task deteriorated into a stalemate; Mitchell bunkered at the villa while Harry lay siege.

* * *

In the fall of 1911, after another exhausting and futile attempt to settle in court, Frank Wilson made a chance remark that gave Harry an idea.

Wilson said, 'It seems to me, Mr Mason, that Mitchell is playing Antonio to your Shylock. You must demand your pound of flesh.'

'Wilson, I've no idea what you're talking about. Who is my Shylock?' asked Harry.

'It's Shakespeare, Mr Mason. Sometimes you have no alternative than to be ruthless in taking what's yours.'

* * *

Harry placed an advertisement in national and local newspapers.

* * *

Sale by auction. Title deeds to Villa Alexandria, a substantial mansion (currently unlawfully occupied) *standing in 140 acres of prime real estate. The sale will take place at 10am on Thursday, 1 December 1911 at the Everett Hotel, Jacksonville. Reserve bid $30,000.*

* * *

The response was overwhelming, with enquiries flooding in from around the nation.

On hearing of the proposed sale, Mitchell instructed his lawyers to stop the auction by all legal means.

At last, I've got their attention, thought Harry.

On the morning of the auction, real estate agents from as far afield as New York, Chicago and Boston crowded the Everett's ballroom. Rumours of half-million-dollar bids abounded, but Mitchell's lawyers had not been idle and had gotten a Federal court injunction. Moments before 10am, court officials, assisted by several deputy sheriffs, arrived with a writ forcing Harry to abandon the sale or face arrest.

Undaunted, Harry tried again. This time scheduling the auction for 10am on Monday, 1 January 1912, thirty-one years to the day since being summoned before Judge Hazlitt in London's bankruptcy court.

Again, realty agents arrived, albeit fewer than before, many discouraged by a heavy blanket of snow that had settled over the northern states. Again, Mitchell got an injunction, but this time Harry had prepared.

The court's officers, as before, served an injunction stopping the sale. But Harry, acting with urgency, lodged an emergency application to annul the injunction with Judge Philips at his private chambers. Only Harry and his lawyer, Rinehart, were present when the judge, hearing the appeal uncontested, granted the application cancelling Mitchell's injunction, thereby allowing the auction to proceed unhindered.

At 4pm that afternoon, the auction was reinstated in the small buffet room at Harry's Acme Hotel. As sole executor, Harry was not permitted to bid, but this legal exclusion did not apply to his son George, who was the only one present when the sale began, opening the bidding at the reserve price of thirty thousand dollars. The auctioneer, in exaggerated comic style, invited further bids from the otherwise empty room. Calling fair warning, he shouted, 'Ladies and gentlemen, is there another bid in the room? Going once! Going twice!' Then, after a moment of silence, the auctioneer brought the hammer down. 'Sold! Sold fair and square to the gentleman, Mr George Mason.'

That evening, George sold Villa Alexandria to his father. The contract of sale was witnessed by former Mayor James E. T. Bowden and lawyer Clement Rinehart, and Mrs Annie Cogswell was pleased to receive the auction's proceeds.

Mitchell, however, refused to leave the property and continued living at the villa as if he were still its owner. In some ways, this suited Harry, who was not yet ready to take occupancy, and the fewer people who knew how he had gained ownership, the better. Above all, Harry was delighted to have honoured the admiral's last wishes, keeping his nephew from becoming homeless and ensuring Annie was financially secure.

* * *

Having discharged his obligations, Harry returned to his ambition to build a million-dollar skyscraper hotel, the most opulent and tallest building in Florida. If all went to schedule, the Hotel Mason would open on New Year's Eve 1913.

Buoyed by the idea of owning the grandest building in Florida, Harry returned to his old confident self, enthusiastically latching on to the latest craze for silent movies. And when the major studios began leaving New York to set up operations in the Sunshine State, Harry brought political pressure to promote Jacksonville as "The Winter Film Capital of the World".

For his part, Harry offered attractive discounts to accommodate the movie world's celebrity stars at the Everett, staging glitzy cocktail parties for politicians, movie moguls and their young starlets. It was here that Harry befriended stars such as Mary Pickford and Lillian Gish, even playing a cameo role alongside Laura Lyman in *Pedro's Revenge*, filmed outside Harry's South Jacksonville Bank. He was having a ball, not that Bessie approved.

Even though Mitchell continued living unhindered at Villa Alexandria, he nevertheless plagued Harry with a blizzard of litigation in his attempts to retrieve ownership. But in April 1912, the final straw arrived when Mitchell summoned Harry to appear before the state's supreme court. In a fit of pique, Harry vowed to force Mitchell's eviction, at whatever cost.

Writing to Bat Masterson at *The New York Morning Telegraph* offices on West 52nd Street, where the erstwhile gunslinger wrote his daily sports column, Harry asked for help.

TWENTY-EIGHT

Harry was surprised to see how much Masterson had changed. His youthful, svelte figure had given way to a middle-aged paunch. He had lost much of his distinctive black hair and no longer sported a heavy Pancho Villa moustache. Gone were his Western clothes and Stetson and in their place was a natty, russet-brown, checked East Coast styled suit, which made him look more of a dandy politician than a deadly gunfighter. Harry felt rudely disabused of the image he had harboured for so many years.

Over dinner and several whiskies, the two men talked amiably of the championship fights Masterson had reported on from ringside and how he often visited the White House, arranging boxing contests for the president's entertainment.

'Well, Harry, it's good to see you looking so well,' said Masterson. 'But you haven't travelled all this way to reminisce, so, tell me, what's the job?'

'I've a squatter I want rid of.'

'You mean…' said Masterson, making a cutting gesture across his throat with his thumb.

'No, I mean, evicted.'

'Why come to me? What about the sheriff or a court order?'

'I've tried all that,' said Harry, 'but there ain't a court in Florida who'll side with me. They say he's got squatter's rights. The only way is to drive him out.'

'What about the Winchester I gave you? That'll scare the damn fool.'

'Except he's the one taking potshots at me! I need someone like yourself to bring him to his senses.'

Masterson laughed and slapped Harry hard on the shoulder. 'You've not lost any of your English humour. Look at me, I couldn't get a gun belt around my middle. Besides, I'm a respectable reporter and businessman living on the swanky Upper East Side.'

'But you know lawmen or bushwhackers who'll help.'

'Bushwhacker! For Christ's sake, Harry, those days are long gone. This is the twentieth century and modern America; you gotta give up reading those nickel-and-dime cowboy books. What about a private detective agency, have you tried Pinkertons?'

Harry shook his head.

'If you take my advice,' continued Masterson, 'you're better off handling it yourself. If it involves tangling with the law, then trust only yourself.'

* * *

Harry made his way south across town to Nassau Street, where he'd seen an advertisement for the Bell Detective Agency, trading under the reassuring banner Sound, Swift & Successful. Harry relayed his story, just as he had told

Masterson, and the agency agreed to send two agents to quickly resolve matters in his favour.

On his return to Jacksonville, Harry received a telegram. "Agents arrived. Staying Palmetto. Contact soonest".

The Palmetto was an anonymous, down-at-heel hotel on Market Street. The desk clerk directed Harry to two men slouching at the bar. Both were in their late thirties. One was tall and gaunt, with dark hair cut so short it drifted into a stubble beard. His partner was heavier and was wearing a threadbare waistcoat and jacket that had been slept in, many times by its appearance. They looked like roughneck drifters, not the silver-buckled, self-assured gunslingers Harry was expecting.

Introducing themselves as Brewer and Green, obviously not their real names, the heavier of the two, Mr Green, said, 'We're here to get a squatter off your property.'

'His name's David Mitchell,' replied Harry. 'I'll take you to the house tomorrow. It's south of the river.'

Green replied, 'That won't be necessary, Mr Mason. We'll deal with things in our own way. Better you're not around, if you get my drift.'

Brewer said nothing. *The silent type*, thought Harry. Of the two, he looked the more menacing with his hollow cheeks and mean stare.

Green continued, 'Be here same time tomorrow. That's the last you'll see of us.'

Harry had a bad feeling. Back on the street, he worried at what he'd set in train, recalling Masterson's advice about not trusting strangers. He didn't know these men from Adam, and he didn't like how they had spoken. He considered calling the job off but then convinced himself that a New York agency wouldn't send cold-blooded killers to evict a squatter.

The following day, apprehension played on his mind. If things turned nasty, the job was better done by someone he knew, or better still, he did the job himself. But the die was now cast, and all he could do was wait.

That evening, Harry hurried across town. Apart from the two agents, the bar was empty. Harry could see they were on edge, Green shifting uncomfortably as Harry approached. The bravado of yesterday was gone. 'What the hell's happened?' demanded Harry.

'Everything's fine,' Green replied. 'Nothing to worry about.'

'What in God's name have you done?'

'We just need more time—'

'Is he dead? Have you killed him?'

Both men looked stunned by the accusation.

'No. No, for Christ's sake. Do you think we're killers?' replied Green, now looking more anxious than moments before.

'So, what the fuck's happened?' pressed Harry.

'It's like this, Mr Mason. Things didn't go as intended,' replied Green. 'When we got there, we took a look around the back. That's when he jumped us.'

'Who, Mitchell?' asked Harry.

'No, an old Negro. He comes up behind pointing a shotgun, says we're robbing the place, and he's in his rights to shoot us. So, we tell him we're detectives come to speak to Mr Mitchell, and he says he doesn't give a shit if we're the Pope come to bless him. That's when Mitchell appears. So, we told him that an interested party wants him off the property. He says, if it's you, Mr Mason, then you'll have to go get him off yourself.'

'What did you do?' queried Harry, now troubled by the way events were unfolding.

'That's when the nigger lets go of a shot over our heads.'

'So, you shot him?'

'No. We ain't armed.'

Harry was dumbfounded. 'You ain't armed! What the hell were you going to do, sweet talk him out?' Things were now unravelling fast, and Harry wished he'd handled things himself. His fists clenched hard as his anger rose.

For the first time, Brewer spoke. His voice, surprisingly high-pitched, was out of keeping with the menace of his looks. 'There's been a misunderstanding, and we're real sorry. We usually serve subpoenas, sometimes following husbands for suspicious wives, and we thought this was another routine job, a chance to take it easy in the sun, maybe pick oranges and—'

'For fuck's sake, a misunderstanding. I paid good money to get this job done by people who know what—'

Green interrupted, 'There's no cause for concern, Mr Mason, we're going back tomorrow and then—'

'Tomorrow!' exclaimed Harry. 'Tomorrow's too damned late. You've spooked him, and he'll be with the sheriff ready and waiting for you. It's gotta be done tonight, and this time it's got to be done right. Have either of you halfwits got guns?'

Brewer nodded. 'In our room.'

Harry stepped forward, poking Green hard in the chest, and as he gasped for air, Harry pushed him hard against the wall. 'Now you listen to me, you great lump, and you listen real good. Be at the ferry in two hours, and don't think of running, or things will go real bad for you. Got it?' snarled Harry.

Harry cursed himself. He should have listened to Masterson and done the job himself.

* * *

At the allotted time, the agents were waiting nervously on the jetty when, out of the low river mist, a ferry came silently into view. Harry, who had been watching from the shadows of the quayside sheds, stepped into the light. He was accompanied by Cross and two heavyset Negroes, one of whom was Ruben, the boy who, twenty-four years before, had brained the man on Forsythe Street. Harry was carrying Masterson's Winchester.

'Let's go!' he said, and the six men boarded the ferry.

* * *

Villa Alexandria was set back from the road, shrouded by huge rhododendron bushes and large, overhanging oaks. As the gang approached along a dark, narrow, wooded path, they could just make out a dim, yellow light coming from the villa's ground-floor windows. The men concealed themselves amongst the thick shrubbery.

Green said, 'With respect, Mr Mason, I think it's better waiting until daylight when we can reason with the man.'

Harry ignored him and whispered to Cross, 'You and your men get close enough to throw small stones at the windows.'

Moments later, Harry heard the ping of gravel bouncing off glass. The front door swung open, and a shaft of light crossed the porch. Mitchell stepped out with a shotgun. 'Who's there? Show yourself.'

With that, a shower of small stones clattered hard against a side pane. Mitchell instinctively moved back, just as Harry spied his yard boy creeping silently from the back of the house.

Mitchell raised his gun and shouted, 'Come out, or I'll shoot!'

More pebbles clattered against the windows.

There was a flash, and a loud report rang out, quickly followed by a second. 'Next time, I won't miss!' shouted Mitchell.

Green whispered to Harry, 'He can see us. Let's get the hell out of here before we get shot.'

Harry hissed back, 'Damn you! Lie low and fire into the air.'

Mitchell fired again. Lead pellets rustled through the branches over Harry's head.

Harry snarled at Green, 'Come on! Get shooting!' Harry moved sideways and took up a position behind a large oak.

Reluctantly, the two agents let go of two or three rounds. Almost immediately, Mitchell replied with blasts in the direction of the detective's muzzle flashes. This time, the lead shot came so close, Harry could hear the detectives squirming as they dropped flat, pushing their faces hard into the damp soil.

Brewer squealed. 'Jesus! That was close. I'm getting out of—'

But before he could move, another volley echoed out from the shotguns.

'Keep firing!' Harry demanded.

But neither did. Harry perched himself on one knee, raising his Winchester and, aiming high, fired off a volley of shots. His ears were still ringing when he heard Mitchell cry out in pain, 'I'm hit! The bastard's got me.'

Harry could see Mitchell writhing in agony on the porch; his yard boy was trying to drag him into the house. The two detectives took their chance and ran off into the darkness.

Cross appeared at Harry's side. 'You okay, boss? What we goin' a do?'

'Wait. See if help arrives.'

Both men lay in the thick, lush undergrowth, silently watching.

Mitchell was crouching, half-leaning against the open doorway. His man had fetched water and bandages from the house.

'For Christ's sake, I need a doctor,' shouted Mitchell. 'Go! Go and get help!'

Harry watched as Mitchell's man ran into the darkness in the same direction the detectives had vanished only moments before. He turned to Cross. 'Get your men and walk up to the house, slow and curious like. Say you were passing when you heard shots and cries for help. Look as if you've come to help, then carry him back to the ferry and into town for a doctor. Once you've dropped him off, go to the Everett and tell George to come with half a dozen men.'

'What if he dies before we get to a doctor?'

'Let's hope he doesn't, but if he does, say that you were...' Harry stopped and, after several seconds, said, 'I don't know, Nathan.'

Cross nodded his understanding. Harry watched as the three Negroes gently carried Mitchell's diminutive frame back towards town.

* * *

It was after 1am before George arrived with the hotel's detective and an assortment of kitchen porters and bartenders. Once the villa's windows and doors were securely battened, Harry instructed George to find out what had happened to Mitchell. He was then to tell John Handley to bring enough food, bedding and supplies for a few days.

George nodded nervously. 'Are you going to be okay, Pa?'

'Sure I am. Tell your mother we've got our new mansion!'

* * *

Dawn broke bright and clear. The first to arrive was Police Chief Vinzant with two of his officers. Harry greeted them warmly.

Vinzant said, 'For God's sake, Harry. What in the name of sweet Jesus happened here? Mitchell's got a bullet in his shoulder; luckily it was a ricochet, or it would have killed him. And now I find you're here and moved in with a group of your coloured boys.'

Harry said, 'Where's Mitchell?'

'He's with Doc Fernandez on West Bay.'

Harry didn't miss a beat. 'I saw Mitchell late last night on Laura Street. He looked pretty bad. I guessed he'd left the place open, so I took my chances to get over here and take

312

my property back. You know I've been trying this past year to evict him.'

Vinzant remained silent for a long while. 'So, it wasn't you who shot him.'

'Christ, no. You know I don't have a gun. Anyway, who does Mitchell say shot him?'

'He doesn't know. But says if he had to guess, he'd say it was you.'

'He would say that,' replied Harry, scoffing at the thought.

'Know anyone else who might want to kill him?' asked Vinzant.

'Yes, plenty. Mitchell's got a bunch of enemies and as many bad debts to match.'

'Mind if I take a look around?' asked Vinzant.

'Go right ahead. You'll find Mitchell's shotgun and a dozen spent cartridges inside. Looks like he was at a shooting gallery.'

'I hope it wasn't you, Harry. Because whoever it was is going to jail for a long time, attempted murder.'

'The sooner you catch whoever it was, the better,' said Harry. 'Let me know if I can do anything to help.'

* * *

In the days and weeks following, Harry set about occupying the villa, using Cross and his men to clear ditches, cut back undergrowth, clean out the boating lake and renovate the dilapidated tennis courts.

Harry was shocked to find that Mitchell had been living like a hermit, using only the kitchen and a bedroom. The furniture and velvet drapes had all been wrapped in dust covers, with most of the valuable ornaments and objets d'art packed safely in wooden crates. Only a portrait by John Neagle depicting Mitchell's grandmother in her youth remained on the wall in the hallway.

Wanting the villa seen and marvelled at from across the river in downtown Jacksonville, Harry had electricity cabled in and strings of coloured garden lights festooned through the trees and around the grounds like an enormous fairground.

Bessie, who liked the house, began furnishing the rooms to make it a comfortable family home.

TWENTY-NINE

It was a month before Harry again saw Mitchell, who, still recovering from his wound, arrived at the villa wearing a bandaged shoulder sling. Accompanied by his lawyer, he said, 'I know it was you, Mason. Coming like a coward in the night to murder me. And it was you who sent those drifters to threaten me. Well, you're not getting away with it. I'm having your sorry ass kicked off my property and thrown in jail where you belong.'

Harry remained impassive. 'Chief Vinzant and the city attorney reckon I've no charges to answer. I don't know who shot you, and I'm sorry you got hurt, but it wasn't me. I've a dozen witnesses who swear I was at the hotel having dinner at the time.'

'You can buy as many witnesses as you like, Mason, but I'm taking you to court, and I'm going to find out everything about you. Mr Harry Mason, or whoever you are.' Mitchell was now spitting his words. 'I'll expose you for the scoundrel you are and push you back to the gutter where you belong.'

'Have you come here with a purpose or just to insult me?'

Mitchell's lawyer stepped forward, handing Harry a file of depositions and a notice of prosecution for trespass, theft and deadly assault.

* * *

After careful consideration, Harry's lawyer, Clement Rinehart, spoke. 'Well, Harry. They've done a pretty good job. There's enough here to have you stand trial; whether there's enough to win a prosecution, well, that's a different question. In my opinion, your chances of acquittal are much improved if we get Duncan Fletcher to defend you, and with Judge Philips and myself as second counsel, you'll have a formidable team.'

'Why Fletcher?' asked Harry. 'We aren't on the best of terms since I knocked him out the race for House Representative and he tried jailing me over the Corbett fight.'

'Harry, this is no time for sentiment. Get this wrong, and you'll be locked up with hard labour, and you know what that means.'

Harry looked pensive. 'Yes, I do.'

'Fletcher's an established US senator and the best defence lawyer in Florida. He's highly respected and will defend you as if you were his son. You can rely on that.'

* * *

Harry was arraigned for trial before Judge W. B. Young at Jacksonville Courthouse on Tuesday, 3 September 1912.

Besides the usual newspaper hacks, many fine ladies from Jacksonville's high society had arrived at the courtroom with every expectation of a good day's entertainment. Around the upper balcony, the city's hoi polloi were packed to overflowing, and in the coloured section, Harry could see Nathan and Ruben.

Stanton Walker was leading for the prosecution, a brilliant young lawyer not long out of the University of Florida, where he had graduated best in his class.

Walker opened proceedings with a fiery address. 'The prosecution will show that Harry Mason is a common cheat and swindler or what these days we call a con man. In his many criminal enterprises, the defendant is a ruthless and dangerous man. He will go to any lengths to dishonestly gain the property of others, including intimidation, grievous violence and murder. Nothing is beyond this liar and trickster to deprive his innocent victims.'

Duncan U. Fletcher sprang to his feet. 'Objection, Your Honour!'

Judge Young spoke in a flat tone, 'Overruled, Senator.'

Walker continued, 'The man before you, who calls himself Harry Mason, arrived amongst us as a penniless, foreign immigrant in 1881, a stranger of uncertain provenance. Through the generosity of one of our most revered tavern owners, he began work as a bartender. Yet, within a year, his employer, aged only thirty-eight and in rude good health, died in mysterious circumstances. And then,' Walker paused for effect, 'and then, suspiciously and with no good explanation, Mason inherited his employer's business.' A gasp rose from the gallery. 'And this, gentlemen of the jury, was after he had forced the poor man's widow to flee the United States without means of support or prospect of work.'

Walker waited for the point to make its mark before continuing. 'A little over a year later, Mr Nathaniel Webster, an upstanding citizen, an honest businessman, an esteemed member of our Masonic Lodge and owner of the landmark Everett Hotel, went to the defendant seeking business advice and a helping hand. But instead of helping, Mason drew the good Mr Webster into a web of lies and dark deceit, cheating him of his hotel and forcing Mr Webster into unwarranted bankruptcy.'

Fletcher again sprang to his feet. 'Objection, Your Honour! This is absurd. These are not matters of fact. It's gossip, speculation, irrelevant and wilfully designed to harm the reputation of my client.'

'Overruled.'

Walker continued, 'Already we see a pattern of fraud and lies. There are countless other examples, but I want to turn to Villa Alexandria and the murderous attack and criminal deception played on my client, Mr David Ferguson Mitchell. My client is a gentleman from one of the founding families of this country. His great-uncle, Mr Harrison Reed, was governor of this state; his grandfather was a friend and counsel to Abraham Lincoln; his father was a senator and war hero who fought bravely for our freedoms.

'Mr Mitchell is an honourable man who, through no fault of his own, has been robbed of his home, personal possessions and many family heirlooms of immense sentimental value. He was robbed at gunpoint by this man you see here today, the man who currently goes by the name of Harry Mason. A man who hides in the shadows behind a cloak of wealth and respectability, surrounding himself with clever lawyers and sharp accountants. But, gentlemen, behind this facade of respectability is nothing more than a common itinerant criminal of dubious origin.'

Fletcher rose to his feet. 'Objection! Irrelevant! None of this amateur oratory has any relevance to the charges of trespass and assault. It's slanderous nonsense.'

The judge, in a weary and tedious voice, said, 'Overruled.'

Fletcher, who remained standing, said, 'Your Honour, with all due respect, is there any point in me raising further objections?'

'I can't advise you either way, Senator, but in my humble opinion, you'd do better resting your legs and saving your breath.'

Walker resumed, 'Mason obtained ownership of Villa Alexandria through a rigged penny auction where he paid less than a cent on the dollar of its actual value. Nevertheless, Mr Mitchell, a true and honest gentleman, even though cheated of his property, refused to surrender his home to Mason and his gang of outlaws. So, what did Mason do? Well, I will tell you, good gentlemen of the jury. He sent two thugs to threaten and badly beat Mr Mitchell in the hope of frightening him out of his home, a home built by his grandmother, Mrs Martha Reed Mitchell, a generous benefactor to St Luke's Hospital and All Saints Episcopal Church.

'And being a true American patriot and an honest son of Jacksonville, Mr Mitchell, though in grave fear of his life, refused valiantly to yield to Mason's blackmail and violence. It was then that Mason, according to his vile character, took the law into his own hands and, with a gang of desperadoes, shot my client, intending to kill him. The only way Mason could take possession of Villa Alexandria was by force and, in that enterprise, to murder Mr Mitchell. Yes, to murder him in his own home in cold blood.'

Fletcher again rose to his feet but, thinking better of it, resumed his seat.

'As we all know,' continued Walker, 'Mr Mitchell is a much-loved member of our community. Any of us here would be hard pressed to find a man or woman who will say a bad word against him. Only Mason has a motive to shoot him dead.' Turning sharply on his heels, Walker pointed an accusatory finger at Mason, exclaiming, 'Look! See now how Mason hangs his head in shame. Gentlemen of the jury, you see with your own trusted eyes, the demeanour of a guilty man. This matter must be decided without further delay. Harry Mason is a guilty man!'

A round of applause and loud cheering rang out from the public pews.

Harry shifted uneasily. The gallery was rapidly turning into a lynch mob.

Duncan U. Fletcher addressed the jury: 'Well, that was quite a performance. I must congratulate my young and aspiring colleague. Although, having listened to the most fantastical fairy tale ever rehearsed, I suggest his future is in the theatre and not the courtroom, a place where we deal only in facts and the law. Gentlemen of the jury, not a single sentence of what you have heard from our novice attorney is true or even half true. Indeed, let me speak plainly. Every word was false. So, let us return to the truth and put Mr Walker's fictions behind us.

'The first fact, supported by over twenty sworn witnesses, including testimony from the city mayor, several eminent civic leaders and many important businessmen, is that

Mr Mason was enjoying a dinner of roast duckling in the crowded main restaurant of the Everett Hotel at the time of Mr Mitchell's shooting. This is the truth. An unsurmountable fact. Fact number two. The two so-called roughnecks who came to threaten and badly beat Mr Mitchell is a figment of his imagination. Neither the authorities or the defence team have ever found or named these so-called thugs. Police Chief Vinzant will testify on oath that Mr Mitchell has never reported being beaten, threatened or molested by anyone, let alone by a pair of unknown desperadoes. This is the truth. An unsurmountable fact. Fact number three. On 1 August 1904, Mr Mitchell sold Villa Alexandria by way of a mortgage for $24,000 to Mr Joseph R. Parrott, a well-known railroad executive and friend of Mr Henry M. Flagler, one of our nation's richest men. The fact is, Mr Mitchell has been living unlawfully, rent-free, as a squatter in Villa Alexandria for the past eight years. An indisputable fact.'

A buzz of shocked voices reverberated around the courtroom.

Fletcher continued, 'The plain fact is that Mr Mitchell cannot suffer trespass or be robbed of something he does not own. Since the time Mr Parrott bought Villa Alexandria in 1904, the title to the house has been purchased and sold on at least two further occasions, including once to a Pittsburg bank. It is also a fact that Mr Mitchell cared not two hoots for the house so lovingly built by his grandmother. He sold the house thoughtlessly to Mr Parrott for one-twentieth of its actual value and now, regretting his folly, is trying to persuade you, twelve gentlemen of the jury, to make good on the wilful neglect of his legacy.

'Fact number four. Mr Harry Mason, a city councillor of thirteen years standing, an esteemed member of Florida's House of Representatives for eight years, the owner of the Bank of South Jacksonville and several prestigious hotels and other businesses in our city, does not carry a gun, does not own a gun nor has he ever fired a gun. And this fact is confirmed on sworn testimony by Police Chief Vinzant. So, gentlemen, if we are to believe the theatrical story spun by Mr Walker, then his client was robbed of property he does not own, was beaten by men who do not exist, was shot by a man who could not have been there and who does not own a gun.'

A ripple of laughter rang out from the crowded spectators.

'The facts speak for themselves. Mr Mitchell has concocted a fabric of lies to blacken the good name of an innocent man. Mitchell was evicted from a house where, as a squatter, he had no right to be and on which he has paid not a cent in rent for the past eight years. Finally, a question I'd like Mr Mitchell to answer. What happened to the $24,000 he received from Mr Parrott? Was it invested wisely or spent recklessly? Perhaps it's a question best answered by those of us here today who know the appetites and true character of Mr Mitchell.'

* * *

After three days of witness testimony and legal argument, the jury retired to consider their verdict. Twenty minutes' deliberation was sufficient for the jury to return a not guilty verdict.

But before discharging Harry from the dock, the judge made his closing remarks. 'David F. Mitchell resided upon the land, known as Villa Alexandria, as a home long after the assignment of the Cogswell mortgage to Harry Mason and did not finally leave the premises until he was, on the said premises, shot at and wounded by a person who, in my opinion, had no right to interfere with Mitchell's occupation of the premises, and that person is—'

Fletcher abruptly interrupted the judge mid-sentence, 'Your Honour, is this a judicial finding and a matter of court record or merely your personal opinion that you are now expressing?'

'It is, Senator Fletcher, my opinion that—'

'Thank you for that clarification, Your Honour. In which case, it is of no importance and even less interest. I thank you for your patience and wisdom in hearing this case, and may you enjoy the remainder of your day.' With that, Fletcher turned his back to Judge Young and heartily shook the hand of Judge Philips, who had assiduously assisted throughout. The remainder of Judge Young's remark went unheard as the court noisily rose and news reporters crowded around the acquitted man.

Mitchell, jostling his way through the throng, approached where Harry, Senator Fletcher and Judge Philips were congratulating each other.

'Don't get carried away,' said Mitchell. 'I'm a sore loser, and I haven't finished with you yet. I've private investigators in England discovering who you really are. Soon we'll know the truth, and then I'll have the satisfaction of seeing you penniless and behind bars, where you belong.'

Harry drew back his fist. Fletcher stepped briskly between them and, addressing his remarks to Mitchell, said, 'I've noted your threat to my client, and it does not bode well for your own liberty. I suggest, sir, you take care with your tongue.'

THIRTY

Christmas 1912 was a glorious affair. Harry staged two days of extravagant festivities at his refurbished villa, inviting townsfolk to come and freely enjoy the spectacle. During the mornings, a funfair and Barnum & Bailey circus entertained children and parents alike. In the afternoons, famous stars of stage and silver screen put on vaudeville and comic slapstick shows. Harry hosted formal dinners in the extravagantly bedecked banqueting hall, where he lavishly wined and dined movie moguls, politicians and business leaders and took particular pleasure in reading aloud a personal handwritten letter from President Woodrow Wilson, tendering sincere apologies for his absence.

* * *

Buoyed by his popular success, Harry began the new year by engaging a promising young English architect, Harold Frederick Saxelbye, to design his new Hotel Mason. It was Saxelbye's first commission in Florida and would incorporate the most modern design and building techniques. Saxelbye was thirty-one and newly arrived in Jacksonville. He had been born and brought up in Yorkshire, England, before emigrating to New York, where he had worked on several of the city's latest high-rise skyscrapers, including the Flatiron on Fifth Avenue. He was enthusiastic and full of innovative ideas, and Harry was prepared to indulge him.

'Mr Mason, if I'm to accept your commission,' said Saxelbye, 'I must have clear instructions.'

'Your objective, Mr Saxelbye, is to make my hotel the tallest and grandest hotel in Jacksonville, ensuring everyone knows my name. When folk arrive from New York, it must be my hotel they demand to stay.'

'But at what cost, Mr Mason? I must know your budget.'

'Whatever it costs, young man. Use your imagination. Let's not be miserly!'

* * *

Harry felt optimistic about the future as he relaxed over several large glasses of scotch with Bion Barnett in his private office when, for no apparent reason, Barnett raised the subject of an enduring legacy.

'Harry, you've made more money than can be spent in two lifetimes and yet, here you are, and I hope you won't think me indelicate, but here you are nearing three score years and ten. What in Heaven's name are you going to do with it all? You can't take it with you; there are no pockets in a shroud. Perhaps you're leaving it for your children and grandchildren to enjoy?'

'I'm planning on spending it, every last penny,' replied Harry cheerfully.

'Well, you'd better get a move on, because as things stand, assuming you never make another dime and live another ten years, you'll need to spend two thousand dollars a day for the rest of your life, and that's a lot of money to burn through,' said Barnett, quickly calculating. 'That's a hundred dollars every waking hour – for most men, a hundred dollars is their entire year's salary.'

'What are you doing with yours?' asked Harry. 'You've more than me by a long chalk.'

'Mine's tied up in trusts for following generations. But they'll have to make the Barnett Bank ever more successful if they want to get their hands on it. It's a kind of golden treadwheel. In a hundred years from now, the Barnett family will gather at Christmas to toast me, saying, thank God for good old Bion! It's my way of leaving my legacy. Mind you, I'm not skimping on my own pleasures. I've a beautiful yacht and a delightful villa in France, where I vacation most years with the family.'

Harry fell into thought. 'Perhaps I should make a will?'

'You must,' replied Barnett. 'It's fun playing King Lear, deciding which of your children love you most.'

* * *

It was this conversation that galvanised Harry to commit well over a million dollars to his new hotel. His name would be emblazoned at the pinnacle of the building for generations to come. He would bequeath the hotel to his eldest son, with the proviso that he build Mason Hotels in every major city, a chain stretching across the country from New York to San Francisco. John Handley would inherit the saloons; he deserved no less. His other children – Charlie, Tom and Lily – would all receive annual endowments. Bessie would have Villa Alexandria and decide its future in her own will, most likely leaving it to her only daughter.

Eliza deserved to be included. He owed her that at least. Even though he had regularly sent money, she hadn't benefitted from his wealth as much as she ought. Even a modest gift would change her life immeasurably. He would bequeath her land alongside the Moncrief Shell Road, which would be worth half a million dollars in a few years, especially when it was incorporated into the city of Jacksonville. But writing Eliza's name into his will might raise complications, and what use would the land be to her? No, he would visit, taking her cash as well as the deeds to parcels of real estate. Yes, this is what he would do. Once the new hotel was opened, he would travel to Bristol and be reunited with Eliza and his daughters, and together they would enjoy life, just as he had done with Bertha in New York.

* * *

Harry spent 1913 working from dawn until well after dusk, visiting daily the site of his new hotel, discussing with Saxelbye the seemingly constant design changes, insisting on only the best materials and the most modern innovations. Besides all-steel and stone fireproofing, the hotel was to have electricity throughout, elevators to the upper floors, telephones, hot water and a private bathroom in every suite. It would boast a freshwater swimming pool in the basement with Turkish steam rooms and the most exceptional roof garden to be found in all the southern United States. There was to be an indoor garden conservatory and tearoom, a private theatre, three restaurants and a large conference hall to seat three hundred. Guests arriving by train or steamer would be met by liveried staff and transferred directly to their rooms.

Articles extolling the grandeur of Harry's new hotel appeared in travel and fashion magazines across the country. By the end of October, two months before opening, every room was booked for the entire following year.

The New Year's opening party was the most spectacular and glamourous ever seen in Jacksonville, with a rooftop firework display drawing crowds in their thousands, packing the streets and filling the parks and riverside gardens, all welcoming 1914 with a bang.

* * *

As the excitement of the new year subsided, Harry's health failed him. His heart was weak and his breathing shallow. Building the hotel had been a monumental achievement and had all but finished him. His physicians feared he might succumb to pneumonia, prescribing complete rest with a diet of thin soups and vegetables. Meat, liquor and cigars were all forbidden, and he was relieved of all business meetings and visitors.

* * *

As Harry recuperated, a letter arrived from Bertha.

* * *

12 April 1914
  Bristol, England
  Dearest Father,

  I write to share our joy at this time of year. On this Easter Sunday, we have given our heartfelt thanks in celebration of the Resurrection of Christ, who willingly gave his life to save us from sin.

  There is much talk of war with Germany, and as the dark clouds gather, our Prime Minister, Mr Asquith, says we must pray for peace but prepare for the worst, and I seek and indulge your kindness for your eldest grandson, Teddy. He is nineteen and unsuited to soldiering, and I fear dreadfully for him. It would be safer if Teddy were to stay with you. He can work for his living, helping in your saloon, or find a job bringing in additional money to assist with your household expenses. If it came to war, then I'm sure it wouldn't last for long; the newspapers say for only a few months at most.

* * *

The remainder of her letter was of petty gossip, signed off…

Dearest Father,

  Please write saying when and what travel arrangements Teddy should make to join you.
  Your affectionate and loving daughter,
  Bertha

* * *

The thought of Teddy arriving filled Harry with foreboding. His reply was swift, explaining that her fears were unfounded. Germany would never begin a war against the vast British Empire. However, if, in some exceptional circumstance, war were to break out, then, of course, Teddy would be welcomed, but crossing that bridge was yet a long way off, and Teddy was safest remaining at home.

* * *

Freed from the demands of the hotel and business, Harry's days passed slowly, and his thoughts once more turned to Eliza. Acknowledging his advancing years and declining health, he decided to travel to England at the earliest opportunity, sailing first class on the new Cunard RMS *Aquitania*, the most modern and luxurious ship in the world. He wrote to Bertha, informing her to expect his arrival, at which time they would discuss Teddy's future, which Harry had decided would not include Florida.

When Bessie discovered Harry's travel plan, her fury could not be contained.

'Why, in the name of the Holy Mother, do you want to go?' she demanded. 'You've just recovered from death's door and are in no fit state to journey halfway around the world. Are you going back to die? Is this what it's all about? To be buried in your family plot, leaving me a widow in reduced circumstances. Is this your hare-brained scheme?'

'My dearest,' said Harry. 'Calm yourself. No good comes of hysteria. I can assure you I'm in good health and will return before Christmas.'

But Bessie was having none of it.

'Is it to see your daughters for the last time? Well, there's no good reason why they can't come here and bring their families, too. I will make them more than welcome. I insist you send for them this very moment.'

Harry remained silent. He knew that he couldn't give her a good reason to travel.

Bessie continued, her anger unabated. 'I've never understood why you haven't invited your children before. With their mother passing when they were young and you leaving them in the care of their grandmother, I would have thought as a loving father you'd have snatched at the chance to bring them here. No. No. Instead, you've barely spoken of them since our marriage, and now, when you think you're dying, you want to assuage your guilt for the manner in which you so cruelly deserted them. You want their forgiveness. Go on, admit it.'

'That's not true,' said Harry, trying hard to contain his rage.

'It is, too!' insisted Bessie, spitting her words. 'Before George was born, I asked you more than once to bring your daughters to join us. I would have loved them as if they were my own. I asked you again and again, and then, when we moved to our new home on Adams Street, I pleaded with you to bring them to make our family complete. But no. Oh no, you always had some flimflam excuse why it wasn't the right time. Said it would upset their grandmother or interrupt their education, or one was suffering from poor health. You always had a good reason to put it off until finally, I gave up asking. My biggest regret is not insisting on having your daughters with us here. If I'd had any sense, I should have gone to fetch them myself. I would have given them every opportunity and a good Christian upbringing, which is more than you ever did for them. God only knows why you've denied them all these years. It's as if you have a burning secret, a Pandora's box; that's what it is. You're frightened of something.'

Guilt was clawing at his guts. He had to steer her away from the truth. He spoke in softer tones, explaining how he wanted to see old haunts and to visit friends. But Bessie could not be mollified and dismissed his claims as utter nonsense.

'I don't believe a cussed word of it,' she said. 'It's over thirty years since you were last in London; any friends you had have long forgotten you or, more likely, are dead and gone. Everything's changed. You've changed, and the world's changed around you, just like this place with its electric lights, motor cars and telephones, even its flying contraptions. You'll be going back to a different place, a country where you'll be a stranger.'

But Harry was adamant.

'If you won't have your daughters here,' continued Bessie, 'then I'm coming with you. You're not gallivanting around London in your state of health.'

The prospect of having Bessie in tow forced Harry to show his temper. He was travelling alone, and his mind would not be changed.

THIRTY-ONE

The assassination of Archduke Ferdinand in Sarajevo on 28 June went largely unreported in America, as did much of the subsequent July political crisis enveloping Europe.

On Wednesday, 5 August, as Harry stepped ashore from the early morning St Johns River ferry, he was dumbstruck by the billboards lining the wharf, reading in horror that Britain and Germany were at war.

Barnett was passing by and, seeing Harry reading the news, said, 'Good morning, Harry. Shocking news, isn't it?'

'Yes, Bion.'

'The price of cotton has dropped from eleven to six cents a pound. My advice is sell your cotton stocks and buy steel and armaments – it could prove profitable.'

'I'm sorry, Bion,' said Harry, without sounding at all apologetic, 'but I must hurry.'

An hour later, Harry was in his office waiting impatiently for a telephone connection to Senator Fletcher in Washington, when Bessie burst through the door, slamming down a bundle of newspapers with such force the table inkwell and pens scattered across the floor.

'That's it!' she said. 'You're not going to England.'

There was a long, astonished silence before Harry said, 'Bessie, my dearest, you worry unnecessarily. War in Europe won't affect London. You've no cause to—'

'I'm not stupid, Harry Mason. It says right here that the Russians, Germans, French and goodness knows who else are killing each other in their thousands, and you think I've nothing to worry about. You're a damn fool.'

'Bessie, you're in shock, and, like any woman might be, you're getting yourself unnecessarily emotional. I promise I'll be back before Christmas.'

'Stop it! Stop your nonsense. Stop your lies and promises. You're not going, and that's an end to it.'

* * *

Eager to hear news from Washington, Harry hurried to City Hall to speak with Bowden. But Bowden, who was busily campaigning for a second term as city mayor, was in high spirits and showed little interest.

'I don't see the problem,' he said. 'If the old empires want to destroy each other, what does it matter to us? America's the future, and in any case, the *Aquitania* is a luxury liner; no one's going to sink her, not even the kaiser.'

Returning disheartened to the Mason, Harry found George's in-laws, Lillian and Captain Howell Atwater, waiting expectantly in the lobby. Howell was tall and slim with, even at his advanced years, an unmistakable military bearing. In 1861, at the outbreak of the Civil War, Atwater abandoned his studies at Yale and volunteered with the First Connecticut Cavalry. He saw action on the Union side at Bull Run, Fredericksburg, Antietam and

Appomattox and was still widely regarded as a patriot and hero.

Lillian called out, 'Harry! Harry! Thank goodness. We've been looking for you high and low; we've been so worried. George says you're going to Europe.'

'Not Europe, Lillian, merely a brief visit to London.'

'But what of the war? Is now a good time for you to be travelling?'

Atwater interjected, 'War's a cruel affair, Harry. The further away from it, the better. You've seen it yourself and know there's nothing noble in the butchery of young men.'

'I understand the suffering, Howell, but I'm not going to war. London's the safest city in the world, and it'll all be over by Christmas.'

Atwater gave a wry smile. 'When our war between the states began, every young man, north and south, me included, ran to join up, fearing it would be over before any of us had a chance to show our courage. Four years later, with half a million dead and another million maimed and limbless, we hurried home, hoping never to hear the sound of battle again.

'At the start, we were fighting with single-shot rifles. By war's end, we had machine guns and siege cannons so big they needed a mule train of more than a hundred beasts to drag them into position. That was fifty years ago, so God only knows what science has been bent for the needs of modern warfare. Harry, if you'll allow me, my advice is to stay at home with your family, where you belong.'

* * *

Later that morning, Harry was in his office, alone and dejected, when Saxelbye unexpectedly arrived. 'I just want to say goodbye,' he chirped cheerfully. 'And thank you for the opportunity of working on your incomparable hotel. It's been a privilege and has set me on the road to a successful career, which I'll resume once I return.'

Harry was taken aback. 'Why? Where are you going?'

'To war, Mr Mason, to war. I'm off to fight for king and country, like any true Englishman. I'm going home to Yorkshire, where my brother, Frank, and I are volunteering. We're joining the East Yorkshire Regiment. We're going to teach those filthy Hun a bloody good lesson.'

'When are you leaving?' asked Harry with a lame, timid voice.

'Tomorrow morning. Just think of it, Mr Mason, a month from now, I'll be in France, fighting at the front. Who knows what glories await us!'

Harry felt the urge to dissuade and warn him of the dangers, but he couldn't bring himself to say the words.

'Well, wish me luck, then,' said Saxelbye. 'When I'm back, we'll have cocktails, and I'll tell you about the fun you missed.'

'Good luck,' said Harry, still stunned by the news. 'Look after yourself, son, and come back soon. We need you here.'

After Saxelbye had said goodbye, Harry remained in his darkened office with heavy shades drawn against the bright afternoon sun. George arrived with a tray of coffee and freshly baked pastries.

'George, tell me honestly, what should I do?'

'Father, it's a serious undertaking travelling at this time, especially at your age and recent illness. To speak truthfully,

I'm against it. Why not postpone your visit until the war is over? You've said yourself it won't last beyond Christmas. Delaying your trip until spring won't do any harm.'

Harry conceded. 'You're right, George. A few months won't do any harm.'

* * *

The summer of 1914 dragged on into fall. Harry, preoccupied with thoughts of the war, spent most days searching *The Washington Post* and *The New York Times* for reports of the conflict. But each day brought only worsening news. Britain and France were being pushed back by the rampant armies of the kaiser, with casualty numbers beyond imagination – thousands were being killed daily.

* * *

At the beginning of September, *The New York Times* published a vivid account of the Battle of the Marne, in which several Yorkshire regiments suffered grievous losses. Harry was overcome with the disturbing thought that Saxelbye had been killed. Images of his death came in reccurring nightmares. Harry felt trapped in the grandeur of his daily existence. His frustration and helplessness hurt like any physical pain might and even more so, knowing that in Flanders, boys spilt their guts while young men around him were carefree, happily enjoying life.

He wrote to Bertha, informing her of his travel postponement, promising to arrive in spring once the war was over. He also penned a letter to the British War Office in London, enquiring about Saxelbye. Other than Saxelbye's name and regiment, he had no additional information and had little hope of receiving a reply, but the act of writing made him feel as if he was doing something useful.

A month passed before a response arrived. His hands trembled as he opened the envelope. It was written in pencil on rough, inexpensive paper.

* * *

3 October 1914
Dear Mr Mason,

Thank you for your concern and kind enquiry about my welfare. I am well and still in one piece. We've had the rough end of the stick of late but have now halted the Hun and get the better of him. I cannot, in all truthfulness, tell you that conditions here are comfortable. Each day I dream of the wonderful times we shared together. Halcyon days. But now I am engaged in a noble enterprise and mustn't complain about the damp blanket on which I sleep, the rats, lice and fleas that infest my body, the mediocre food or the constant threat of sudden, bloody death. The fellows around me are of the highest calibre and continuously keep us amused with their cruel, gallows humour, which cheers us gleefully in these direst of circumstance.

Since the Battle of Marne, during which we lost our colonel and major, along with half the company, in a courageous yet suicidal charge on a machine gun nest, we have been in daily scraps. I'm sure the war will be over by Christmas, if for no other reason than there won't be a soldier left alive to fight on.

We now exist in trenches cut deep into dark-red clay, reinforced by countless sacks of earth and timber struts. The architectural aesthetics are not pleasing to the eye, but the functionality of preserving life from the numerous snipers has worked sufficiently well until now. My brother, Frank, keeps well and is rumoured for promotion after the next big push.

Please write and let me know of Jacksonville's news and describe your day-to-day life: the weather, trees, flowers and birdsong. It helps to know that not all the world is an image of hell. And if you can see your way to sending cigars and a good book, I will be eternally grateful. The address of my battalion and army number are below.

Dreaming of the St Johns River and cocktails at the Mason. I hope to see you soon.

Kind regards,

Harold F. Saxelbye (Lieutenant).

* * *

It was another eight weeks before Harry received Bertha's letter.

* * *

10 December 1914
Dear Father,

We are disappointed to hear you've delayed your return home.

Things do not go well, and I fear the war will go on for another year.

Teddy has found casual work at a woodyard. The work is heavy and not to his liking, but he is safe at home for the time being.

The army is presently only recruiting volunteers, of which there is no lack of young men. But I fear that conscription will soon come. The thought of letting dear, kind Teddy go to war horrifies me, and I dread the day when he receives his papers and is taken from me.

This war touches us all. My sister's boy, Dorson, serves with the Bristol Glosters and is soon to be posted. Our nephew, Alfie Warren, also with the Glosters, has received a wound that keeps him safely in hospital.

We must be careful with our food and other essentials. There are shortages of sugar and meat, and we are told that coal for warmth this winter will be in short supply. Father, if there was a time when the family needed you at home, it is now. Mother has taken to crying herself to sleep and wonders what kind of world she has brought us into. The sooner this torment ends, the better for us all.

Dearest Father, please send tinned and dried foods and perhaps a sweet delight for Christmas dinner when we will gather, including our soldier boys, to celebrate the birth of our saviour, Christ. We all pray you will join us soon, once more reuniting and making our family whole.

You are always in our thoughts and prayers, and we wish you every happiness.

Love from your three devoted daughters,
Bertha.

THIRTY-TWO

On 7 May 1915, the German submarine *U-20* torpedoed and sunk Cunard's passenger liner, RMS *Lusitania*, sister ship to the RMS *Aquitania*, with 1,200 civilian lives lost, including over a hundred Americans, many of whom were women and children.

Harry was sure this would bring America into the war, with much-needed support for the hard-pressed British and French troops. But to his dismay, the tragic loss of civilian lives only hardened American opinion against entering the war.

Socialists and labour unions led the chant with, "a rich man's war is a poor man's fight", while a coalition of pacifists, neutralists and non-interventionists campaigned for America's isolation with a rallying cry of "safe in our vastness". And the Midwest farmers, many of whom were of German descent, promoted widespread distrust in the political and East Coast elites, dismissing anti-German news reports as lies and conspiracies.

Harry's own political affiliations were strained when the Democrats favoured staying out of the war with their protectionist slogan, "America first". Few shared Harry's pro-British interventionist ideas, and he found himself isolated from business and political colleagues alike, some of whom doubted Harry's American allegiances.

***

Harry also felt excluded from his family. Bessie enjoyed hosting her circle of wealthy socialites and, since their row over his planned visit to England, avoided him as often as possible. George was fully occupied managing the hotels while John Handley was busy running the saloons and boarding houses. And, with the help of his mother, Charles had taken employment as an apprentice to Telfair Stockton at his real estate office. However, much to the disappointment and irritation of Bessie, Thomas abandoned his studies at the conservatory, opening instead an automobile garage selling new Cadillacs and Oldsmobiles, none of which interested Harry. In defiance of her parents, Lily moved to California the day after her twenty-first birthday and was now living in San Francisco with her husband and three children. She had always been a free spirit and, as a teenager, turned any conversation with her father into a querulous shouting match.

The constant comings and goings, and incessant din of Bessie's morning committee meetings, afternoon charity teas and evening soirées drove Harry to distraction and eventually from the house. Each day, soon after breakfast and before a gaggle of Bessie's clucking hens arrived, he left the house to make the journey by pony and trap to his retreat at Ponte Vedra. Here, in the peace of the ocean beach, he spent his time reading and writing letters, often to Saxelbye and Bertha, to whom he sent boxes of canned foods and other small luxuries.

Concerned for Harry's self-imposed solitude, Bowden and Rinehart made occasional visits, encouraging him to participate in various civic projects. But Harry had no time for trivial local affairs. His thoughts were preoccupied with the war in Europe. Until, that is, a visit in the summer of 1915, not long after Bowden's re-election as mayor, pricked his imagination.

Rinehart suggested Harry employ a housekeeper.

'For goodness' sakes, Harry,' Rinehart said. 'You shouldn't be journeying to and from your beach house each day, bringing packed luncheons and spending so much time alone. It's not good for you. God only knows what would happen if you fainted or had a nasty turn. With a housekeeper around the place, you could stay overnight once or twice a week. She could clean and cook and keep an eye on you and provide company, too.'

Harry wasn't taken with the idea. 'I don't need a goddamn nursemaid fussing about the place. I'm happy as I am, and I've plenty to do. Besides, I'm not alone; a maid and yard boy visit to keep the place looking spick and span.'

'Well, I only mention it because I know of a young English woman who is looking for such a position. She's a schoolteacher from London and is keen on literature and politics and, by all accounts, is an accomplished cook and plays the piano too.'

'You say she's from London?' asked Harry, his interest roused. 'What's her name?'

'Miss Jones,' said Rinehart. 'Eleanor Jones. Last week

she applied for the job as assistant to Miss Fischer at the public library but was abruptly turned away.'

'Fischer? The big German woman living on East Bay?' remarked Harry.

'That's her,' said Rinehart. 'Her parents were German émigrés.'

Bowden barged in, 'Sounds too damned German for my liking, and she's fat, too. No wonder she's a spinster. If you ask me, she turned the Jones girl away because she's English and quite a looker.'

Rinehart continued, 'Since the sinking of the *Lusitania*, there's been a lot of anti-German sentiment around town. A German butcher on Main Street had his windows smashed and "go home" painted across his door. And the saloonkeeper running the German place on Ward Street was beaten pretty badly. They called him a saboteur. He was lucky not to have been lynched.'

Harry ignored Rinehart's remarks. 'How do you know her?'

'She's been lodging with my sister since arriving from New York.'

'I'd like to speak to her.'

'Well, now that we've got your attention,' said Bowden, turning the conversation, 'there's another problem.'

Harry showed little interest and spoke flatly, 'Is this going to take long, Jet? Because if it is, I'll get some drinks and cigars, or have you taken up smoking cigarettes?'

Once Harry had returned with a tray of drinks and settled himself into his favourite armchair, Bowden began, 'It's about next June's election for state governor and who is running as our Democratic nominee.'

Harry interrupted him, 'Don't tell me it's old Sheriff Broward again!'

'God, no, not at all. He died some years ago. Didn't you hear? He got elected to the US senate then died just before taking his seat – it was damned unfortunate.'

Harry shrugged his disinterest.

Bowden continued. 'It's a man called Sidney Catts.'

'Never heard of him,' said Harry sharply, already becoming bored with Bowden's narration. Pushing himself up from his chair, Harry crossed the room to the large sash windows overlooking the beach, from where he could watch a colony of sandpipers patrolling the water's edge.

'He's for segregation and white supremacy,' said Bowden. 'A month or two ago, there were lynchings that he refused to condemn. Said it wasn't his place to interfere in local justice. And he's anti-Catholic and a Prohibitionist, too.'

'Anti-Catholic! How the hell can you be against Catholics?' asked Harry, still following the sandpipers.

'He says the Pope is stuffing convents and monasteries full of weapons in readiness to seize power and take the White House. He's been campaigning to have the Sisters of St Josephs arrested for teaching Negroes to read.' Bowden paused a moment to light a cigarette.

'What the hell is Catts doing on a Democratic ticket?' asked Harry, growing irritable and turning to face Bowden.

'We tried barring him,' said Bowden, getting up from his armchair to join Harry at the window. 'The point is, he's a southern Baptist. He's good at whipping up a frenzy with plain folk and country hicks. He's tapped into their baser instincts, blaming their hardships and everything wrong in the country on the Jews, the Negroes and the Rome Church.'

'He hates anyone who doesn't cheer for him at his rallies,' interjected Rinehart. 'And blames corrupt politicians, liquor interests and bankers for every misfortune, and the crowds love him for it. He's a real hater is our Mr Catts.'

Bowden continued, 'He's campaigning under the slogan, "vote for Catts to kill the rats" and advocates that America is only for true Americans, first, last and forever. His supporters are all for it, chanting, "if you ain't with us, you're against America" – un-American is what they're calling it. We got a tiger by the tail, Harry, and it won't be long before he's eating us for breakfast.'

'Who's running against him?' asked Harry, now sounding concerned.

'That's a bigger problem. It's William V. Knott,' replied Bowden apologetically.

'Bill Knott! The most boring auditor in Florida?'

'That's just it, Harry. As state auditor, Knott has decided not to go on the campaign trail, saying that he'll let the facts speak for themselves. Says the truth will out.'

'Well, he's a bigger fool than I thought,' replied Harry. 'He'll lose by a straight knockout with that kind of stupidity, and as us Democrats have never lost in Florida, Catts is certain to become the next governor.'

'That's what worries us, Harry, and we thought that maybe… well, you might…'

'You're not suggesting I run for office?'

'Well, now you mention it, you could—'

'No! But if I can help with a donation or a fundraiser, then of course.'

'Donations are always welcome, Harry, but the fact

remains – we gotta stop Catts. If we don't, he'll ruin the party and us with it.'

'Can we call in some favours?' asked Harry.

'I've tried that, but no one's interested. Catts is very popular, and our people fear for their own necks.'

'Bloody hell! I thought we paid them to make problems like Catts go away?'

'I'll try turning the screws again,' said Bowden, but with little conviction.

'For Christ's sake. When's the vote for nominations?'

'Next month.'

Harry slumped back into his armchair, threw his head back and stared in frustration at the ceiling. After a moment, he gave out a long sigh. 'I'll think it over. In the meantime, don't forget about that English girl.'

* * *

The Democrat's nomination campaign was raucous and bad-tempered. While Knott was holed up in his bunker, poring over his accounts and allowing surrogates speak on his behalf, Catts was on the campaign trail, touring every town, hamlet and farm in his new Ford Model T, shaking hands and rallying crowds to his colours.

The day after the count, Bowden hurried to Harry's beach house, where, for the first time, he was greeted by Miss Jones.

'What's the result?' demanded Harry.

'Catts won by a few hundred votes. He's going to be our next governor, meaning Prohibition, saloons closing, Catholic churches boarded up, coloureds chased out of town, and that'll be just the start of it.'

'Over my dead body!' said Harry dismissively. 'I'll discredit and bankrupt him long before any of that happens.'

Bowden continued, 'Our only hope is with Fletcher's appeal to the supreme court for a recount.'

'Where are the ballot papers stored?' asked Harry.

'For Duval County, they're in the vaults at City Hall. If there's a recount, they'll be taken by railroad to Tallahassee. Why do you ask?'

'There's more than one way to skin a cat. Excuse the pun,' said Harry. 'But I need you to do something for me.'

* * *

Harry was relaxing on the veranda, watching Atlantic waves crashing against the shore, when Bowden arrived with a list of everyone involved with transporting the ballot boxes to Tallahassee.

Bowden was jubilant. 'Good news, Harry. The supreme court has ordered a recount on grounds of voter fraud.'

'Good,' said Harry, carefully searching through the list. 'Here it is. Here's our salvation. George Briggs, chargehand for the removal team. I need you to send a sealed letter by trusted messenger to an office on Fifth Avenue, New York.'

* * *

The following week, Nathan Cross arrived at Harry's beach house, followed shortly afterwards by George Briggs.

Harry went straight at Briggs without ceremony. 'You're to replace one of your men with Mr Cross here. Then you're to keep your mouth shut and look the other way. Understood?'

Briggs nodded.

'You'll be well rewarded. Am I clear?'

'Yes, Mr Mason, very clear.'

'Good,' said Harry. 'Miss Jones will see you to the door. Cross will bring your payment to your home.'

Briggs, sounding concerned, said, 'You know where I live?'

'There ain't nothing I don't know about you, Mr Briggs. You can rest assured of that.'

Once Briggs had gone, Harry turned to Cross. 'I need you to swop the ballot boxes before they're loaded onto Flagler's mail train. Once they're loaded, the guard will take care of everything. You're then to burn the original votes.' There was a long silence before Harry said, 'They'll hang you if you get caught, and there's nothing I can do to stop them.'

'It doesn't matter none, Mr Mason. I know whatever you do is for the best. I ain't never seen you do a bad thing yet, and I'm happy helping with the Lord's work. Anyways, I reckon I've had more lives than any cat.'

'Well, let's hope on this occasion it'll be the cat who loses a life.'

* * *

The state electoral commissioners, closely watched over by armed guards, recounted the votes more than a dozen times before declaring, by the narrowest margin of just twenty-three votes, that William V. Knott was the winner of the Democratic Party nomination for Florida state governor.

Catts knew he'd been cheated, blaming all the usual suspects for stealing the election, accusing Harry of orchestrating a dark, anti-democratic conspiracy. Nevertheless, undeterred by his loss, Catts switched allegiances and joined the radical Prohibition Party to challenge Knott head-to-head.

Knott persisted in his belief that campaign razzmatazz, empty promises, inducements and campaign lies had no effect on the opinion of ordinary, hard-working folk. 'Plain facts are enough to determine a fair outcome,' he said. 'When it comes to American democracy, we can trust in God and the people to exercise honest decency and good sense when casting their ballot.'

When the election came in November, Catts won convincingly. For the first time in Florida's history, a Democrat had lost an election. It was a bitter blow, and Harry took it badly. Everything he and many others had worked so hard to achieve had been needlessly thrown away.

With a radical Prohibitionist and white supremacist as governor, Harry could expect no quarter, but he was not yet ready to concede the fight.

THIRTY-THREE

Harry settled into a comfortable routine of spending several nights each week at his beach house, each morning taking a stroll along the vast expanse of white sand, watching beachcomber birds scouring the shoreline while thunderous ocean waves crashed before rolling gently up the beach.

In the afternoons, he relaxed in the coolness of his library, where Miss Jones read aloud to him. She had an eclectic taste in literature, from contemporary American novels to the English classics of the eighteenth and ninetieth centuries. Her voice was soft and melodic, with a familiar Thames estuary accent. After nightfall, over tumblers of whisky, they would talk amiably of London, with Harry regaling her with tales of cockfights, bare-knuckle contests and the seedy underworld of London's East End pubs. Sometimes, they argued over socialism, the war and women's suffrage. Harry enjoyed the sense of enlightenment rekindled from when he had listened to Agnes on the dunes at Mayport. Above all, Harry felt protected in Eleanor's company, the same way as when at home with Eliza, and she reminded him of his daughters, whom he liked to imagine as spirited and independent.

One evening, not long before Christmas, Harry and Eleanor, each with a large goblet of Rémy Martin, sat warming themselves around a log fire that burned brightly in the grate. They were enjoying their reminiscences of London's Christmases past: hot mulled wine with roasted chestnuts and carols sung as snow fell lightly on decorated, bright-green holly wreaths. Harry relaxed into the ease of contentment. In just a few short months, Eleanor had become special to him, bridging the chasm he felt for his daughters in a way he had never shared with his children here. As their excited chatter faded away, both drew into their own thoughts of home.

Eleanor spoke first. 'Harry, I've a confession to make. I'm burdened by a secret I've harboured for far too long. I've never spoken of the true reason I left London, not to anyone. The shame of it keeps me silent. But now, here with you, I feel I can speak freely of my guilt, a guilt which tortures me cruelly, but finding the words to begin is not easy.'

Harry, speaking light-hearted, said, 'Perhaps another cognac will fortify your courage.' But as he leaned across to charge her glass, he noticed her hands pale and trembling. 'My dearest Eleanor,' he said, now speaking with concern, 'a problem shared is a problem halved. Whatever troubles you won't seem so awful once you speak it aloud. I've seen too much of life to be shocked by any guilty confession, even of bloody murder.' He watched as she composed herself, and then, drawing on inner strength, she began.

'What I've done,' she said, taking a moment to draw breath, 'what I've done is horrible. Many say it's a wicked sin. But I will speak truthfully, even though I fear you will be repulsed and have every right to be so.' Turning to face him and holding his gaze, she said, 'I trust you, Harry Mason, and believe you will neither judge nor condemn me.'

Speaking plainly, she told how she had fled London after being discovered with the woman she loved, the wife of a prominent politician.

'We met at an exhibition of fashionable London artists. I noticed her the moment she entered the salon. Tall and slim, with warm, chocolate-brown eyes and russet-red hair. She had a presence that drew me to her and an orbit from which I could not escape. That afternoon, we talked of our many shared interests: literature, the theatre and politics. She was witty in a carefree, easy way, her mind twisting one way and then swiftly turning the other. She was my superior in both status and intellect.'

Harry listened, enthralled. Eleanor spoke with such affection as if lost in a trance.

'The following week, I received an invitation to visit Millicent at her Bloomsbury home. We had tea and spent the afternoon in conversation. I can't now recall what was said, but as I listened, something possessed me – it took control of my senses. I reached across and softly touched her hair and, as she turned towards me, she leaned in to kiss me. I made no move to resist. Never before has such a scandalous thought entered my mind.'

Eleanor sipped nervously at her brandy. 'You see, Harry,' now whispering, 'I don't know how I can bring myself to utter these words, but the truth is, we became lovers. Not in a sordid sense but in a noble way, the way a woman might love her dear husband.'

Harry said nothing for fear of disturbing her discourse. But his silence made the air feel thick, and Eleanor began to regret she had spoken so openly.

'Please, Harry,' she pleaded. 'Don't think badly of me. Don't cast me out, even though you have every right.'

'Your secret,' said Harry, trying to ease her discomfort, 'is one hidden and denied across the ages and today is concealed by more souls than you might like to imagine.'

'It seemed so natural,' continued Eleanor. 'It seemed so right, as if it was meant to be, and we pledged ourselves to each other. And, perhaps too innocently, I believed we would be together forever; two souls as one.'

'Yet, here you are, alone.'

'Indeed,' replied Eleanor with a sigh. 'One evening, instead of attending parliament, Millicent's husband burst in on us. His temper could not be constrained, and in his rage, he beat us grievously.' Eleanor covered her mouth as if once more witnessing the violence.

'And to escape, you sailed for New York,' said Harry, as if stating an obvious fact. 'You're not the first, nor will you be the last.'

'But travelling alone,' replied Eleanor, 'was a cowardly betrayal of our betrothal of love, and I cannot forgive myself. It's a constant regret that we did not flee together. I can never recover from my loss. Every day, I feel her absence, an ever-present torment of sorrow. Harry, please, I beg you, don't rebuke me.' Pleadingly, she took his hand. Her tearful eyes were on his, searching for the faintest hope of clemency.

Reassuringly, Harry offered a gentle smile as he watched her struggle to contain her sadness. 'Eleanor,' he said. 'I understand your loss.'

He knew all too well the suffering of being separated from true love – gender wasn't important; the sickening emptiness it brought was the same.

'If you seek my advice,' he continued, 'then I urge you to return to London and bring your... to bring Millicent here. You can change your names and begin a new life together. Americans don't give a damn for the past; they concern themselves only with the present. And if money is the issue, then I will gladly fund your expenses. It's the least I can do to see you happy.'

'Harry Mason, you're a good and decent man, but I can't turn back the hands of time. What is lost is gone forever, and I can never forgive myself for leaving without her.'

'Don't reproach yourself. It's never too late to right a wrong.'

'Even if it were possible, living a lie and pretending, hiding the truth and disguising one's true self, brings neither happiness nor freedom.' With a cry of anguish, she held her head in her hands and sobbed. 'What have I done? In God's name, what was I thinking?'

Placing a reassuring hand upon her shoulder, Harry spoke softly. 'I beseech you, Eleanor, please don't repeat the mistake of others. You must return for the one you love.'

'My dearest Harry, I would give anything to have my love beside me, but Millicent, humiliated and shamed, cast herself from Westminster Bridge.'

Unable to continue, Eleanor fled to the kitchen, from where Harry could hear the anguish of her tears.

He thought of Eliza, and his heart ached too. His unspoken secret had kept him alone, and again he felt the pain of separation from home.

A few minutes passed before Eleanor returned to the fireside. 'Keeping it locked inside,' she said, 'has been suffocating. Lies have made a prisoner of me.'

Her eyes were red and sore. 'Thank you for listening,' she said. 'My grief has lain heavy on my heart. Now, for the first time, I feel the weight lifted. It's a blessed release to speak freely.' Hesitating a moment to dry her eyes, she continued. 'In some ways, and this may sound strange, but I welcomed the nagging pain of remorse. It was a daily reminder of Millicent and our love for each other.'

'My dear girl, the ones we love remain vivid and constant in the memory. You've no need to punish yourself.'

She sighed and turned to face him. 'In time, I hope to find contentment and peace, but happiness? Never.'

'We all learn to live with our mistakes, and in a lifetime, there are many regrets that must be endured, but happiness will return.' Then, fumbling for his fob watch, and after needlessly adjusting its hands, he continued, 'Me fleeing London was not so very different.'

He began slowly, telling Eleanor of the London courts and his narrow escape from incarceration. He told her of his three daughters and how leaving them behind had broken his heart.

'And what of their mother?' asked Eleanor.

'My wife, Eliza?' said Harry, standing to put another log on the fire, for the first time, realising that he had spoken her name without caution. 'We married on her nineteenth birthday and found poor lodgings at Bethnal Green. That was fifty years ago, although it seems like only yesterday.' He paused, uncertain how to continue.

'And you loved her, dearly?' asked Eleanor.

'Yes, from the start.' He fell silent as he drifted into a distant world. Then, startled by the spit and crack of a burning log, he again spoke. 'To begin, we had only a small, damp room with the narrowest of sinks and a meagre hearth for warmth and barely a crust to share between us. But we were pleased to have our own place and did what we could to make a cosy home for our daughters, and though we had next to nothing, we were happy. And, to speak truthfully, our days were not without laughter and pleasure.'

Harry shifted himself to poke at the fire. Staring unblinkingly into the flames, he said, 'Eliza knows me better than I know myself, and yet, with all my faults, she loves me all the same, and I miss her for it.' Returning to his armchair, he began clipping the end from a cigar. 'It was a mistake not bringing her with me. I admit it.'

'Why didn't you?'

'A question that haunts me still. Whatever the reason, it eludes me now. Eliza was to join me once I'd gained employment, but she never found the strength to follow.'

'What happened to her?'

Harry drank deeply from his glass of brandy. Now was the moment for the truth. It required only the courage to push the words across his lips. He felt a knot twist and tighten in his stomach and a dryness catch his tongue. Yet he would confess it all, telling of his enduring love and selfish betrayal and the pain of regret and all the falsehoods that had followed. He had only to say the words.

'By the time I'd established myself in Jacksonville...' he was struggling to summon the strength, '...raising our daughters alone had taken its toll on Eliza, and in weakened health, she was reluctant to make the crossing.'

'But you returned for her?' asked Eleanor.

'I would have done so willingly, but circumstance conspired against me. And now, as I grow older, my regrets gnaw at my very soul. A day doesn't pass when I don't think of her, and often I've considered returning and... and... well, like you, I wish I had done things differently.'

'She has passed?' Eleanor enquired in a gentle voice, coaxing him to say more.

'There was nothing I could do.' He moistened his lips as if to continue, but his courage had deserted him.

* * *

Christmas was a dull affair. Bessie had still not yet forgiven Harry for his intentions to travel and was sour about the time he spent alone with Eleanor, spitefully insisting she remain at the beach house alone for the Christmas holiday.

1917 began much as the old year had finished. The war in Europe dragged on; George planned a second Mason Hotel, grander than the first; Charles wanted to quit Stockton's and find work as a sports coach, a notion his mother forbade him to ever mention again; and Thomas, free of the conservatory, was happily selling cars.

* * *

Harry was taking his morning coffee in the shade of a large palm in the Mason's roof garden when Bowden unexpectedly arrived. He looked dispirited and spoke in his flat, official tone.

'The state legislature has passed Catt's liquor Prohibition laws. We're finished!'

Preoccupied with a flush of vibrant cerise azaleas, Harry showed little interest.

'Harry, listen to me. He's closing every saloon and bar in the state.'

Harry spoke dismissively. 'It's all hot air. It'll never happen.'

'It's already happening. Both Congress and senate are pushing legislation for a constitutional amendment ending liquor sales forever. For God's sake, Harry, wake up.'

'Forever! That's madness.' Turning from the azalea, he was now paying attention. 'These people are stupider than I thought. Do they expect people to drink milk? Are we now celebrating with jugs of cold water? It's the end of civilisation in this damned country.' Harry was in full flow. 'These Washington hypocrites and Bible-bashers have forgotten that God approves of a drink, and Jesus enjoyed a glass of wine too. Remember the marriage at Cana. My God, what has the world come to? Butchery on an industrial scale in Europe, and all Americans can worry about is a glass of beer. Congress should commit troops to Europe, not stop an honest man from having a drink at the end of a day's work.'

'I don't think America will join the war, Harry. There aren't any votes in it.'

'Well, if Germany wins, America will be next; you mark my words. The kaiser's ambitions know no bounds. He's already sinking American shipping with impunity, including civilian liners, with God only knows how many American women and children drowned, and what do politicians do? Worry about the price of cotton, tallying up their losses in nickels and dimes while… while Britain and France count the butcher's bill in blood and guts.

'I thought you Americans prided yourselves on being God-fearing, courageous defenders of justice and liberty. You certainly brag and have enough flag-waving parades about it. But when it comes right down to it, you're no better than stay-at-home mummy boys, shit-scared to take a swig of whisky or join a good Christian fight. What happened to your moral fibre? Still favouring the bully brawl, Winchesters and cannon against savages with bows and arrows?'

Bowden looked shaken at Harry's outburst. 'I'd better get back. I've a meeting to attend.'

As Bowden hurried from the garden, Harry shouted after him, 'Don't let me keep you from another talking shop.'

Just as Bowden hurried away, Howell and Lillian came into the garden. Seeing Harry's ill temper, Lillian asked, 'What in heaven's name has upset you?'

Heavy with regret, Harry replied, 'Begging your pardon, Lillian, but I've offended an old friend and driven him away. I lost my temper and shouldn't have spoken as I did. I'm getting old and at a loss as to how I can help my country in its time of need.'

'I'm sure your friend understands and will soon be back. That's what friends do.'

THIRTY-FOUR

The spring weather was warm and gentle, with not a breath of air to disturb a clear, blue sky.

It was early afternoon, and Harry and Miss Jones were at leisure after enjoying a picnic luncheon beautifully laid out under a large, colourful sun canopy on the sugar-white dunes surrounding the beach house. Eleanor read aloud from Zane Grey's *Riders of the Purple Sage*. Harry listened intently as he watched a solitary white egret strutting over the water's edge in search of prey.

In Harry's mind, this counted as idyllic, and he wished every day could be the same. But at that moment, the noise of a distant motorcar making its way along the dusty shell track leading to the house disturbed his reverie. Harry guessed it was Bowden and Rinehart come to while away their afternoon. The car stopped, and a few minutes later, Thomas appeared at the low, white picket fence edging the dunes. Following close behind was Bessie, angrily shaking her parasol back and forth. Uncertain why, Harry felt a sharp stab of guilt hit him in the guts.

'Is this how you spend your time, carrying on behind

my back with this slip of a girl?' Bessie, red in the face, remonstrated as she closed in.

Harry leapt furiously to his feet and, stumbling through the pillows of soft, white sand, shouted back, 'You've no rights coming here.'

'I'm sick of gossip about you and this... and this trollop. It's all around town and at my church too. Have you no shame?'

Thomas slouched off, disappearing back to the car.

'What are you talking about? Miss Jones is a respectable English gentlewoman, and a schoolteacher too, and with more wit than—'

'Respectable!' interrupted Bessie, who was now crazed enough to strike Harry with her parasol. 'Well, it doesn't look that way with her hanging about the place like a common floozy.'

'Don't be ridiculous. She's here because I'm driven from my house by the endless noise of that gaggle of brainless clucking geese you're forever entertaining.'

'So, this is about my ladies, is it? It's my fault you're with her day and night, and God only knows what nonsense you both get up to.'

'I'm here escaping your madness.'

'You're hiding something. I know it. It's not normal spending days on end out here in the middle of nowhere. And what about me? Do you ever give me a second thought? Not to mention my position in respectable society.'

'I'm here, woman, to get some damned peace and quiet and enjoy myself, reading, writing, and... and the simple pleasure of watching the ocean. And you ought to know better than listen to the malicious gossip of mindless, wagging tongues.'

'Well, I want her gone, and I want you back home where you belong, at home with your family. And I'm not leaving without you.'

Harry stood defiant, hands firmly planted on his waist. Miss Jones remained silent, hardly daring to breathe.

After a long silence, Bessie's anger began to subside. 'At home, you can have all the peace you want.' And then, in a more conciliatory tone, 'I'll meet with my ladies at the hotel, and you can have the villa to yourself. I know how you enjoy the peace of your rose garden.'

Harry stood his ground, but he knew his days at the beach house were at an end.

Bessie continued, 'You can invite your friends to the villa, hold your business meetings in the smoking room and afterwards take luncheon on the south lawn.' Bessie's shoulders dropped, and her countenance became almost pitiful. 'We can do as before and come here together at weekends – just the two of us – you used to enjoy that. Please, Harry, come home, where you belong.'

He was cornered, and Harry knew he must now choose.

Bessie continued, 'I'll arrange for you to have your own housemaid to see to your needs. We can hire a butler, an English one if you wish. I'll make sure you have every comfort. My maid Minnie will be pleased to wait on you.'

His heart sank. Exchanging Eleanor for old, lame Minnie, what kind of exchange was that? But he knew his brief flight of freedom was over. He was to be caged in the grandest home in Jacksonville.

Before following Bessie back to where Thomas waited with the car, Harry turned to Eleanor and, with the saddest look of resignation and apology, said, 'Go to Rinehart; he'll arrange everything.'

She nodded her understanding before turning away to watch the lone egret continue its search.

* * *

A week later, on 2 April 1917, President Wilson declared war on Imperial Germany, telling Congress that America would no longer tolerate her shipping destroyed and citizens killed by German aggression. Nor would a German-Mexican army of alliance be allowed to invade the southern states of America. Congress cheered him to the rafters. This was the news Harry had waited for, but strangely, he took no pleasure from it.

* * *

Harry was breakfasting in the library when Minnie arrived with the morning papers.

'Can I git you some fresh coffee, Mr Harry?' she asked. Minnie was an old woman with a kind soul. She had begun work as the children's nanny some thirty years before and was both grateful and fiercely loyal to her employer. 'There ain't much light in here, Mr Harry. Can I open the blinds and let the sun in?'

Harry shook his head.

'Can I bring you some cookies, Mr Harry? They're fresh-baked by cook? They smell real good. Is there anything you need, Mr Harry?'

There was nothing Minnie could do to assuage his

melancholy. Without the company of Eleanor, each day was desolate.

* * *

Within weeks of President Wilson's declaration, twenty-four million American men aged between twenty-one and thirty had received conscription papers.

Charles, who was approaching thirty, grasped the opportunity to escape the stifling oppression of Stockton's real estate office. Arriving home with his draft papers and uniform tied in a cardboard box, Bessie was horrified and flew into a rage.

'You damned fool,' she screamed at him. 'What has gotten into you? You're not joining the army; I can assure you of that, young man. You can return that uniform right this minute.' Grabbing hold of him by the shoulders, she tried pushing him out the door. 'This is your fool of a father's fault. He's the one putting ideas in your head, putting you up to this stupidity. God only knows how hard I've worked to get you that job with Stockton, and this is how you repay me by throwing it back in my face. You're just like your father – ungrateful – and after all I've done for you.'

But Charles would not surrender his escape so easily. 'I'm not taking my uniform back, and I'm never going back to Stockton. I only stuck the God-awful job to please you. I've hated every minute, so now it's my turn to do what I want. Being in the fresh air, playing sport, travelling and enjoying myself with men my age. I might as well have been dead in that coffin of an office.'

Bessie turned to Harry, who, having heard raised voices, came to investigate the commotion. 'You're his father; you tell him. Go on, don't just stand there; tell him straight – tell him he's not going to the army. If he doesn't want to work for Stockton, then I'll find him another job; he can work with his brother at the garage or start his own business, but he's not going to the army, and that's an end to it.'

Before Harry could speak, Bessie continued, this time pointing her dagger finger at him. 'It was you who started this nonsense, always talking about America joining the war. Well, now you can see where it's led, so you can tell him yourself. If he goes to the army, he'll never get another cent from either of us. See how he manages without—'

Charles interrupted, shouting back at his mother. 'You can't stop me. It's the law. All able-bodied men are being drafted. All my friends are joining up, and I'm not being the coward left at home tied to my mother's apron strings, so you can stop bullying me. For God's sake, I'm thirty. I'm a grown man capable of making my own decisions, and if there's one thing this war's done, it's brought me to my senses and given me a purpose in life. I'm going to do something I want, and it's my duty to America because that's who I am; I'm not an immigrant – I'm a true American. This is my country, where I was born; it's where I belong. So, it's no point trying to pester me out of it. For the love of God, I only want—'

In a flash, Bessie stopped him with a raised hand. 'Don't you take the Lord's name in vain in this house!'

But Charles continued defiantly. 'For God's sake, Father fought defending Paris before he was twenty. So, neither of you are in a position to tell me what I can and can't do. I've joined the army, and that's all there is to it.'

'How can you talk to me like that after all I've done for you? Fed and clothed you, a good education, a good job, a good home, waited on you hand and foot, provided for you and given you everything you've ever asked for, and this is how you repay me?'

'Well, Mother, I now understand why Lily left at her first chance. While I've been entombed in that office, she's been out there free to roam and follow her heart, seeing the world, having fun and now married with children. And what have I done? Nothing. Well, now it's my turn to see the world.'

But Bessie was unmoved. 'If you leave, you'll never be welcomed back. You'll never sleep under this roof again.'

'Fine, see if I care.'

Harry raised his hands to pacify further argument. 'Let's all calm down. He's a man, not a boy, and it's his decision.'

'Thank you, Father,' said Charles, taking a deep breath.

'Mother of God!' exclaimed Bessie. 'You never miss a chance to contradict me. Always siding against your own wife. Well, I'm telling you this, Harry Mason, if my child comes to harm, it'll be you who burns in hell. You mark my words. I'll never forgive you.'

Ignoring Bessie's outburst, Harry turned to Charles. 'There's one thing I insist on. It's that you go as an officer, a lieutenant. You must allow me to help you join with a rank. You'll be ten years older than most recruits, and you'll make an excellent leader.'

Charles nodded his agreement, happy to have his father's support on any terms.

Harry wrote to Judge Philips and Senator Fletcher, asking them to nominate and support Charles for the June intake at West Point Military Academy.

As things turned out, Charles was amongst the best cadet officers of his class and, in September 1917, was posted to France with the Twenty-Sixth Infantry Regiment.

* * *

The day following his son's proud departure aboard a troopship out of Norfolk, Virginia, Harry sat comfortably reading in his library, where Minnie had brought him coffee, when his peace was abruptly disturbed by Bowden bursting in, looking terribly dishevelled and in a state of anxiety.

Harry said, 'What in God's name has happened to you? You look as if you haven't slept. Here, sit yourself down and have some coffee.'

'Haven't you heard?' said Bowden, ignoring Harry's offer. 'Last night's riots at the Union Depot?'

'No, but you don't surprise me. Was it the mass lynching down at Gainesville that set them off?'

'It certainly didn't help,' said Bowden, his face red and puffy from a sleepless night. 'Now they're in a goddamned stampede to go north. Chief Roach dispersed a mob rioting at the rail depot. Unfortunately, some bones got broken, and a young girl was trampled, and now the newspapers are blaming me. I can't believe it.'

'I told you Roach wasn't the right man to take over from Vinzant. He's too quick to rile.'

'Look, Harry, I need your help. It's not just the lynchings; we've got gangs of tough-looking white labour agents stirring up trouble. They're here from Pittsburg, New York and Chicago, recruiting to fill the labour shortages up north caused by this damn war effort. They're taking on as many hands as they can muster to harvest Connecticut's shade tobacco crop, which is coming in early this year, and they're offering a dollar eighty a day.' At last, Bowden took a gulp of coffee. 'The Reverend James told me only this morning he awoke to find his entire parish had flit during the night, and both Pennsylvania Railroad and New York Central are signing workers. They're recruiting over a thousand men. Can you believe that? A thousand men!'

'Calm yourself and take the weight off your feet,' pleaded Harry. 'Can I get you some breakfast?'

'Goddammit, Harry. This is serious. It's turning into a fucking exodus. The Jacksonville turpentine and sawmill operators reckon they'll close their factories if they lose any more hands, and the citrus fruit and tobacco plantation owners say their crops will rot in the field for want of labour.'

'Remind me,' asked Harry, 'what's their daily rate?'

'Fifty, sometimes seventy, cents a day.'

'Well, there's your answer.'

'It ain't that simple,' Bowden said, as his hand found the back of his neck, kneading the stress he found there. 'The Farmers Alliance can't afford to pay more and are demanding I stop their labour from going north. I've told Roach to close the rail depots and arrest any blacks assembling in groups of three or more, and I've signed an order requiring labour agents to have a city licence, or they'll get arrested too.'

'What do you want from me?' asked Harry.

'You've got influence with these people. They trust and believe what you say.'

Harry said nothing.

'Come on, Harry, reason with them. Organise a rally at the Union Depot; give a speech; persuade them that going north isn't the answer. Tell them the work isn't permanent. Tell them they're not suited to the cold, northern climate. For Christ's sake, tell them there's six feet of snow in winter, and they'll freeze to death. Tell them the labour agents are cheating them. Tell them their true home is right here with us, where they belong. Promise a pay raise. Say something, for fuck's sake.' Exhausted, Bowden collapsed into a chair.

Harry remained silent.

'Please, Harry. Look, I know we've had our ups and downs, a crossed word here and there, but we've always pulled together when it mattered. You can sway these people; I know you can. At least do something,' Bowden pleaded. Then, in a more moderate voice, he said, 'I've asked Judge Lee to try and bring his people to their senses.'

'Well, maybe they've already seen sense,' replied Harry. 'They're just looking for a safe place to live and work for a fair wage. It's what we all do, isn't it? You can blockade the railroads and build a wall all you like, but it won't stop them from trying; they'll still find a way of getting north.'

'For Christ's sake, Harry, those leaving are making it worse for the ones left behind.' Bowden lit a cigarette and again paced the room. 'I'm setting up a citywide commission led by the coloured lawyers, Judson Wetmore and John Ballou, and I've written to Senator Fletcher and Governor Catts for their help.'

'Governor Catts! Catts, for fuck's sake! Have you taken leave of your senses and forgotten he's a segregationist? He doesn't even want coloureds in town and turns a blind eye to every bloody lynching. And as for the government in

Washington, well, they're not going to get involved in any southern race troubles; they've learnt that lesson once too often.'

Stubbing his cigarette hard into an ashtray, Bowden said, 'What do you suggest I do? I can't just let them leave. For God's sake, Harry, we need nigger labour if our city is to profit and progress into the future.'

'Well, I can tell you one thing – violence and coercion ain't going to stop them, that's for sure. I'm sorry to say it, but you need to stand in their boots, see how things look from their side of the fence.'

'What the hell are you talking about?'

'I'm talking about the police shooting a dozen or more coloured men in just the past few weeks. Tell Roach and his men to stop beating on them; they're having it hard enough already.'

'What do you mean, hard enough? It's factory owners and farmers like us who are suffering from their damned uncivil disturbances.'

'Look, Jet, they're compelled to work for fifty cents a day, not enough to feed one mouth, let alone raise a family. Then the farmers and factory owners trick them into debt and use the law to bond them until the debt's paid off, which is never – that's slavery by any other name, can't you see that? Where are the incentives to keep them here? Would you stick around if it were you? Because I can tell you, I would have gone a long time ago.'

Bowden looked aghast.

Harry continued, 'Come on, Jet, don't pretend you don't know what's been going on. Tell me honestly, do you pay your housemaids and laundry girls?'

'Of course, I do. Thirty cents a day.'

'Well, some of our good friends don't even pay that. They take their liberties and treat them cruelly.'

Bowden was indignant. 'This is the twentieth century, not the 1850s. Jacksonville's a modern, vibrant city with opportunity and a bright future for everyone. It's a world port; it's the New York of the South – it's the renaissance and future of America.'

'For fuck's sake, Jet, don't go believing your own fancy words. If it's so damned good, explain why thousands are risking their lives to go north? You've passed laws to deter them, and when that failed, you coerced and beat them half to death or lynched them for trying. Where's the freedom and greatness in any of that?'

'I'm the elected mayor, and the voters demand I put an end to this exodus, and that's what I'm going to do. It's the law, and it's the right thing to do. It's for the good of the city, for the good of all of us, including you.'

'Well, I'm sorry, Jet, the will of the people or not, I won't help you. They're doing no more than looking for a better life and hope for a decent future – they're pursuing happiness, like the rest of us. In any case, their help is needed up north working on the war industries supplying our boys in France.'

'Jesus! Are you going to allow this damned foreign war ruin everything?'

'You're a good friend, Jet, and for the sake of old times, I'll speak with Judge Lee and the labour agents, see if I can't slow things down and make it a bit more civilised and peaceable but only on condition you rein in Roach and his men.'

THIRTY-FIVE

Harry spent the remainder of 1917 busily corresponding with business leaders, politicians and movie celebrities, promoting Government Liberty Bonds supporting US troops in Europe.

Charles regularly wrote from France, with letters frequently arriving from Saxelbye, Bertha and Eleanor, who had moved to California, becoming a respected columnist on the *Los Angeles Examiner*.

The following spring, Harry received three letters in the same week. The first from his son, Charles.

* * *

4 May 1918
France
Dear Pa,

All goes well. My regiment is the best amongst the American troops. We work together and look out for each other. The twenty-sixth is one big family, indeed a band of brothers. My only regret is not joining sooner. My fellow officers affectionately call me "the old boy".

Last week we enjoyed much-deserved leave and spent three days in Paris, and now I understand why you loved being here. It's the most beautiful city – spring is magical. The trees are in blossom, and their scent makes one's heart turn to thoughts of love. Speaking of which, the girls here are beautiful and not at all prim, calling out to us in the street with words of endearment, even rushing to hug us as we pass on the sidewalk. Many of our boys swear they'll marry and stay.

At camp, we are preparing for our next big push. The fighting is bloody, and we have lost many officers, some of my closest friends. But we are not deterred and grow in determination to end this war quickly, even if it means sacrificing our lives in the effort and will do so willingly.

We eat well and have excellent equipment, for which we thank the American people back home. The English and French are brave and fight to their last man, but how they do it is beyond our comprehension. Four years of war has taken a toll on both men and equipment. A few weeks back, we fought alongside the Scottish regiments. It's no exaggeration to say they are insane, preferring to walk into battle playing bagpipes and wearing skirts, which they call kilts, and covet the honour of doing so. They are feared by the Hun, who call them "women from Hell"! But they are all wonderful boys who drink copious amounts of whisky and swear and blaspheme in a fashion that none of us doughboys have heard before. There are soldiers from every nation, including India, who shun steel helmets, favouring simple, cloth turbans. They are fearsome warriors with enormous black beards and walrus moustaches.

Last week we overran an enemy position taking several hundred prisoners. Most seemed pleased to see us and surrendered willingly. We found them in a shocking condition; their uniforms torn to shreds, their boots ripped, some without soles, and they were filthy and covered in lice. We had marched them no more than two hundred yards when their order broke down, falling upon their knees, begging for food and water. It was a pitiful sight, and it's hard not to have the greatest sympathy for these poor fellows.

We have battles ahead but are in good spirits and eager to get the job done.

Give Mother my love and tell her not to worry. This war won't last much longer.

I'll be home for Christmas.

Your loving and devoted son,

Charlie (Lieutenant).

* * *

The second letter was postmarked Yorkshire, England, but was not written in the usual hand of Saxelbye. Opening it carefully, Harry took a deep breath.

* * *

7 May 1918
Mrs C. Saxelbye
Kingston upon Hull
East Ridings of Yorkshire

Dear Mr Mason,

My sons are Norman Frank and Henry Frederick. With great sadness, I write to inform you that my son Norman was killed in action while leading his men into battle. His brother was at his side, who, thank the good Lord, was mercifully taken prisoner; his exact whereabouts are yet unknown.

I write to thank you for your regular correspondence to Henry and the many gifts you have sent, which he has shared with his brother and the other men. He often spoke of you in letters home, describing the enjoyable times he spent with you in Jacksonville. I will write again as soon as I have news of Henry's whereabouts.

Yours sincerely,
Clara Saxelbye (Mrs).

* * *

The poor woman, thought Harry. And how bravely stoic, amid her grief she made time to write with thanks for the few cans of peaches and cigars. Harry stared blankly into space. Her son's sacrifice was total and her loss infinite.

* * *

The final letter was from Bertha.

* * *

8 May 1918
Bristol, England
Dearest Father,

This war drags on interminably. There is no good news. If it weren't for your food parcels and gifts of money, I'm sure we'd have died from hunger. The government has reduced our rations to two eggs and two ounces of butter, cheese and meat a week. There's no coal to be had, so Teddy's bringing wood shavings and waste scraps from the workshop to keep a fire on the coldest nights.

Our losses are heartbreaking. Your grandson, Dorson, has been wounded and is in a hospital near Boulogne, waiting for a ship home. Dorothy's husband is in the mountains of Northern Italy, suffering from TB and mental exhaustion. Her sister, Norah, grieves the loss of her husband lost at sea. Florence's husband was gassed in the trenches and is in a sanatorium near Bournemouth. The doctors say he'll never work again.

Everyone we know has lost someone. Grief and despair are on every street. Dear Mrs Smith, at number 24, lost her three sons in the same week, and her husband is away in the trenches of France. None of us can begin to imagine how she keeps going. I'm sure I'd have thrown myself from the Clifton Suspension Bridge before now.

Teddy has received an anonymous letter with a white feather enclosed. He is now marked as a coward and spat upon in the street. Two weeks ago, he arrived home with a bloodied nose and black *eye after being attacked on our doorstep. Once this war is over, he must start a new life in America. The government says jobs should be reserved for those who fought and not those who sheltered at home. I've told him he must change his name and settle with you in Florida. We depend on you affording him sanctuary.*

We all miss you.
Your loving daughters,
Bertha.

* * *

Every American newspaper ran graphic and sensationalised accounts of death and suffering on the battlefields of Europe, which Harry read and reread, hoping to glean news of his son. But the more he read, the more inflamed his imagination became. At night, he lay awake, picturing his boy lying dead and alone in a foreign field.

Despite his worst fears, time pressed on, and with each new dawn, Harry gave thanks for the absence of bad news. And each afternoon, at the Church of the Immaculate Conception, Harry pleaded and bartered with God, swearing oaths of devotion and extravagant philanthropy in exchange for his son's life, sometimes offering his own in exchange.

* * *

Winter came early, and as dawn broke on Monday, 11 November, frost lay heavy and jagged across Jacksonville.

The sound of banging and the maid's voice cursing as she struggled to slide the bolts on the front door woke Harry. Pulling his dressing gown around him, he shuffled his way downstairs. Through the window, he saw Bowden waiting with a Western Union messenger boy; both looked cold and impatient. A terrible twisting yanked at his stomach – was this the telegram he feared?

'No! Please, God, no!' he cried in anguish.

Bessie followed close behind. 'Please, God, don't let it be our Charlie.'

As the heavy door swung open, Bowden rushed forward, throwing his arms around Harry. 'It's over!'

'Is it Charlie? What's happened?' demanded Harry, pulling free of Bowden's hold.

'War's over! Germany surrendered!' cried Bowden, doing a jubilant jig. 'We've won.'

The telegram boy stood, watching in silence. Then, stepping forward, he handed Harry a buff plain telegram marked urgent.

* * *

Home soon. Charlie (Capt.)

* * *

Crossing herself and mouthing prayers of gratitude, Bessie fell to her knees, kissing her rosary and thanking the Holy Mother for Her infinite mercy. Harry collapsed onto a side chair and wept hard as his heart burst with joy. The shackles had been broken and at last he could breathe.

Three days before Christmas, Charles arrived home to a rapturous hero's welcome and, to everyone's surprise, was accompanied by his French fiancée, Amélie. His proud parents feted their son with a gala Christmas dinner and a New Year's garden party, attended by his sister, Lily, who arrived from California with her husband. The family was again complete.

* * *

Charles spoke only once of his wartime experience, telling his father how each day was filled with horror. 'I watched my men fall, scythed down like wheat. Every brother slaughtered in the fields of Soissons.'

Harry held his son tight as their tears ran freely. 'You're home, son. You're safe at home.'

'But why me? Why was I spared?'

Searching for an explanation, Harry said, 'God was watching over you, son. Every day we gave prayers for your safe return.'

'But why did God mark my boys for death but not me?'

'He saved you for a purpose, son.'

'No, Father. He saved me as a punishment. To relive the horrors each day and every night. To carry the pain of guilt, turning any happiness life might bring to bitter ash.'

'Why would God punish you?'

'For coming home, Father. For leaving them behind. They trusted me; they depended on me; and I left them behind. I wish I was dead too.'

'Don't speak like that, son. You've your life ahead of you,

full of happiness to share with a beautiful wife and children of your own.'

'I can't stop thinking of all those lives that won't be lived, young men, nineteen and twenty, lying dead in the mud of Flanders. I promised I'd bring them home.'

After a silence that seemed to last forever, Harry said, 'Your mother wants you to celebrate Mass with her tomorrow with Bishop Curley.'

'I can't. I'm sorry, Pa, but I can't. I lost my faith in the bloody mire of Europe.' Pausing to compose himself, Charles continued in a whisper, 'God wasn't there, Pa. He wasn't with us. He abandoned us. Not just Americans: soldiers on all sides and from every nation; He abandoned us all. I can't believe an omnipotent and merciful God would allow such wicked suffering and death. He left us behind.'

Charles fumbled for a cigarette, his hands trembling as he struck a match. 'It's foolish to think God favours America over other nations or chooses one man before another. It simply isn't true. He's a cruel God, indifferent to the world and without any care for His children. We called on Him for salvation, thousands, perhaps millions of us on our knees begging Him to save us, to save our innocent lives. But He turned his back and was deaf to our prayers. I'm sorry, Pa, but I can't thank the Lord for that, not after what I've seen and done.'

Harry looked bewildered and spoke softly, 'You were always in our thoughts and prayers, son. What more could we have done?'

After a moment's silence, Charles said, 'If it pleases Mother, I'll pray with her tomorrow.'

'That's kind, son; she'll be glad of you at her side.'

THIRTY-SIX

January 1919, the National Prohibition Act outlawing the manufacture and sale of liquor came into law. Sydney Catts, Florida's Governor, enthusiastically began closing every bar and saloon in the state, using armed force where necessary.

Harry knew he had a fight on his hands, but he wasn't yet ready to throw in the towel.

* * *

The new year was unusually cold, with biting winds blowing in from the northern states. None of which improved Harry's temper as he shuffled, leaning heavily on his cane, across the Italianate marble floor of the Mason's lobby. He cursed his rheumatism, which had worked itself into every joint and pained his knees and hips. As he reached the heavy oak door marked in gold lettering, "General Manager – George H. Mason", his trusted accountant, Frank Wilson, emerged, struggling under the weight of several ledgers.

Harry greeted Wilson with as much goodwill as he could muster.

'Good morning, sir,' replied Wilson. 'Can we speak privately?'

'Sure we can; find me after lunch.'

A moment later, Harry stepped across the threshold into the familiar office, where George wasted no time with pleasantries. 'I'm telling you, Pa, this damned Prohibition will ruin us. We're going to lose a quarter of a million, perhaps more. And I'm talking hard cash, folding dollar bills.'

Harry pulled up a chair. 'Just because politicians have gone insane, it doesn't mean we have to follow. There's no way I'm losing that kind of money, and I'm sure as hell not being robbed by Catts and that mob of lying, Bible-bashing crooks ruling the roost in Washington. They can line their pockets making highfalutin speeches and playing their holier-than-thou games on Capitol Hill, but for us down here in the real world, life goes on as before. The people want a drink, and as sure as hell, we're going to get it to them.'

'Pa, I'm not sure you understand. Catts is sending cops to close us down and says he'll make arrests and send troops if needs be.'

'I don't give a damn what Catts says. There's plenty of ways of doing business, and if the government force our hand, then we'll do our trade with the bootleggers.'

'Bootleggers! Jesus! You're not seriously proposing working with… with outlaws? I run a decent and respectable hotel, not a smuggling outfit. There's no way I'm going to jail; I've a wife and children to think about.'

'For Christ's sake, George, nobody's going to jail over a glass of beer. I'll keep the sheriff and police sweet while

Bowden takes care of Mayor Johnny Martin and a handful of his tame judges.'

'What about your reputation? City councillor and all.'

'To hell with that. Politics and business are two sides of the same coin. People have short memories and don't give a fig about reputations. They think only of what's in it for them and cheer the loudest when there's a handout in the offing. Reputations are built on how the story gets told, not on what gets done. And besides, there's no joy knowing you're being fleeced by lesser men than yourself.'

Harry paused a second before changing tack. 'Anyway, it's only a couple of hours in a fast cutter from Nassau and not much more from Cuba, where a case of rum costs twenty dollars and sells here for a hundred. We can ship thirty or forty cases a trip, and once we get organised, we can expand that to three or four hundred. I know plenty who'll be willing to run the straits; Johnny Doyle and Lefty Moore are up for it.'

'Doyle! Have you lost your senses? He's just out of jail. I can't be seen with the likes of him. And how the hell do you know these people anyway?'

Harry relaxed back into his chair, rolling a cigar gently between forefinger and thumb, listening carefully to its freshness. 'Jacksonville's the gateway to the north, son. We can supply as far as Atlanta and Charlotte, maybe even Richmond. Charlie knows how to keep one step ahead of these rookie federal agents, who haven't a clue about the swamps and shallow keys. Tom can organise the transport, leaving you in charge of sales. Wilson will handle the money.'

'For Christ's sake's Pa, listen to yourself. We'll be no better than common crooks.'

'You're wrong there, son. We're respectable businessmen. We'll run it like our other businesses with smart lawyers and clever accountants who'll keep things looking straight and legitimate. Who knows, Prohibition may be a godsend, making us richer than we ever dreamt.'

George was hesitant. 'I don't like it, Pa. We got a good life here; we're respected. Why risk it all, getting mixed up with the likes of Doyle? We should wait to hear what Charlie has to say.'

'Of course, he knows how to get things done, being an army captain and all.'

'He's in bed with a heavy cold,' said George.

'Then we'll wait until he's back on his feet. In the meantime, I'm meeting with some gentlemen from Atlanta who are interested in coming on board with our new enterprise. Anyway, whatever happens, we're not letting those fanatics in DC ruin us.'

* * *

Wilson found Harry napping in his private office. 'I'm sorry for disturbing you, sir, but I think this is important.'

'Come on in, Frank. Everything these days is important.'

'I've received a letter from the Bureau of Internal Revenue. As you'll recall, the Sixteenth Amendment, ratified in 1913, gives the government powers to levy a tax on wealthy individuals and, as a result, they've—'

'Frank, I know about the Sixteenth. What you're telling me is the government want my hard-earned money.'

'They do, sir. They claim that over the past five years, your unpaid taxes amount to $96,000.'

Harry looked at him agog. 'They want to rob me of how much?'

'Ninety-six—'

'The bastards!'

'Naturally, we'll appeal, but considering their claim is over five years, it's actually less than twenty thousand a year. We could delay payment for a while, but you might risk a federal violation and—'

'But if I pay, they'll be back for more?'

'I suggest we move money to the British Bahamas and Canada, reroute cash around the cash registers, making sure nothing gets recorded. We'll declare losses and reduce your personal income to a few hundred dollars a year, all of which can be explained by Prohibition. You'll be the richest man in Jacksonville with not a dime in tax.'

'That's smart, and how do you propose we sell liquor?'

'I suggest we convert part of the lower basement and build a new, discrete entrance at the rear of the—'

Urgent knocking followed by Mr Pratley, the lobby manager, gingerly poking his head around the door, interrupted their conversation.

'My sincere apologies, sir,' said Pratley, 'but a Mr Mitchell is demanding to see you. He's in the lobby with his attorney and says he'll call the cops. I've told him you're not to be disturbed, but he insists, and he's making quite a scene.'

'What does the damn fool want?'

Mr Pratley eased himself into the office, closing the door silently behind him. 'I beg your pardon, sir, but he says his London enquiries have uncovered the truth.'

Harry's mind was racing. Toff was dead. Had Mitchell found Eliza or discovered Dyson, or had he got hold of *The*

London Gazette reporting his bankruptcy? Had his passage on the *Polynesian* been traced? How had he connected Enoch Price to Harry Mason, who first appeared in conversation with Kitty Morgan on the train from Quebec? Then it struck him. It was his biography so boastfully given to Bowden for the election campaigns. It had been too detailed and linked him to Bristol, and from there, it wouldn't have been difficult to trace his mother and from her to Eliza. Damn it! He'd been the author of his undoing, and now his past had caught up with him.

Even though Harry had prepared and rehearsed for this moment, his blood ran cold and, without thinking, he cracked his knuckles. Then, as his confident poise returned, he grinned broadly and let out a gasp of amusement. 'Well, I've no idea what the idiot is talking about, but I'm not missing the opportunity of throwing him out by the scruff of his neck.'

Harry crossed the lobby to where Mitchell stood defiantly.

'I've discovered your sordid little secret,' announced Mitchell, triumphantly. 'Your name's not Mason after all.' Mitchell was speaking loud enough for the whole lobby to hear. 'You're a phoney, a swindler, a scoundrel, a flimflammer, and we both know it. You're on the run from the law, and I've cornered you.'

Harry felt his mouth dry and wanted to moisten his lips and swallow hard. But he didn't. Instead, he kept the hint of a smile and the air of a man who held no fears.

But Mitchell didn't falter. 'There are no records of a Harry or Henry Mason, neither born, baptised, nor married in London or Bristol. It's all fiction. Neither did you enlist in the

British navy nor fight with the French army. You're a liar and an impostor! There's no record of you landing in New York, and, as for Cedar Keys! Well, they've never heard of you.'

A crowd of several dozen hotel guests gathered to witness the stand-off. Harry was aware that all eyes were now on him. A brief moment of silence seemed to last minutes.

'If it's not Harry Mason you address, then to whom do you speak?' asked Harry calmly.

Mitchell ignored the question. 'I'm warning you, Mason, or whoever you are. If you're not out of my villa by tomorrow, I'll publish and expose you for the dishonest fraudster you are.'

In that brief moment, Harry knew with certainty that Mitchell was bluffing. He was playing a long shot, hoping to rattle him and dislodge the truth. With a sweeping gesture of dismissal, Harry said, 'Tell whoever you like. Publish and see if I care. There's not a soul alive who'll believe your foolishness. You're a sad loser, Mitchell – you've lost everything you once had in abundance, and now insanity has taken hold of your mind.'

'Damn you!' shouted Mitchell.

There was a gasp from the assembled onlookers.

'Own up!' pressed Mitchell. 'You're nothing but another immigrant on the run. At least I've a family name and an honourable past to be proud of.'

'You're a fool, Mitchell,' said Harry. 'Now get off my property before I throw you off.'

To Harry's surprise, a ripple of applause rose from those gathered around. Pratley appeared with the hotel detective. The crisis had passed.

Back in his office, Harry collapsed heavily into a chair. 'Bloody hell! Fuck it all! Am I never to be free?' But there was no one to hear his plea. He may have avoided hard labour and left poverty in his wake, but the truth still dogged him.

As Harry poured himself a large whisky, George appeared at the door like a ghostly apparition, his pallor drained and ashen.

In mocking theatrical style, Harry said, 'Sorrows come not as single spies but in battalions – it's Shakespeare, you know, George. So, what ails you now? Not that cretin Mitchell. Don't believe a word he says; he's quite mad.'

George ignored Harry's poor attempt at levity. 'It's Mother.'

'Well, spit it out. What's she on the warpath about now?'

'She collapsed at church and has been taken to St Luke's Hospital.'

* * *

The diagnosis was not favourable. The best physicians from Washington and New York were summoned, but their conclusion was the same. She had nine months.

A bed was made available at the Women's Hospital in New York, where the most modern care was possible, but Bessie refused to go, preferring to stay at home, near to her children and beloved church.

One evening, as Harry was making her comfortable, he was shocked to discover how the disease had emaciated and laid waste to her body. Noticing his alarm, she took his hand. 'My dearest husband, I'm in God's care and have no fear of death.' Resting her head, she whispered, 'Harry, you're a good husband, and I've much to be thankful for, and I want you to know that—'

'Rest, my dear, don't tire yourself,' he interrupted, busily straightening the quilt and propping pillows around her.

'All these years, you've been my rock and fortress,' she whispered. 'You've always worked hard to keep our family together.'

'Please, my dear, don't tire yourself,' he pleaded.

'I've loved you dearly from the beginning, from the day we first met on the steamer coming south. A day doesn't pass when I don't thank the Lord for your presence and strength in our lives and for your endless kindness and unquestioning love. And now, as I—'

'Enough,' he interrupted sharply, with the sudden realisation of just how much he had squandered.

'Pray with me,' she murmured. 'Only God can forgive.'

* * *

George and Thomas visited daily, and Lily arrived from California. Charles, who was convalescing from a bout of influenza, stayed away. He and Amélie were living in the nearby suburb of Avondale in an upmarket villa generously loaned by Telfair Stockton until their marriage, which Bessie was determined to attend.

Bessie fought to keep her spirits strong, struggling against pain which deprived her of sleep and appetite. Regular morphine helped during the mornings when Bishop Curley and members of the Daughters of Isabella visited. She enjoyed their company and prayed with them at the villa's private chapel. In the cool of the late afternoons,

Harry kept her company on the west lawn overlooking the tranquil St Johns River, where together they watched sailing boats drift silently by.

It was one such afternoon when George and Thomas unexpectedly arrived, both looking ill at ease.

George spoke with a tremor in his voice. 'It's Charlie, Pa. We've come to collect you because… well, because—'

'Because what?' asked Harry irritably. 'Can't you see I'm with your mother?'

Averting his gaze, George pressed on. 'I'm sorry, Pa, but something terrible has happened.'

'What's happened?' demanded Harry.

'I'm sorry, Pa, but… but he's passed away.'

Harry shook his head. 'Passed away? Who? What are you talking about?'

George tried to explain. 'Charlie died this morning. The doctor says that—'

Thomas interrupted. 'Spanish Flu has taken him, Pa. He died at home with Amélie at his side. When we—'

'Flu! He's just back from the war. He's marrying in a few weeks and—'

'Father, please,' insisted Thomas. 'We've come to drive you to his house – I'm sorry, but the Lord has taken him from us.'

It took a while before Harry realised their meaning. There was a long, numbing silence before Harry whispered, as if in respect for the dead, 'Your mother's resting. I'll tell her I'm just popping out.'

***

The hour-long journey to Avondale was driven in silence, Harry staring blankly through the car windshield. Disconnected thoughts tumbled through his mind: *Charlie was too young to die; there must be some mistake; he was crucial to the success of our bootlegging; his last letter from France had tempted fate, and he should have been more careful about what he wished for, and what about the wedding? The arrangements were made and invitations sent. What will Amélie's parents think? The embarrassment of it all... young men don't die of flu, and he's only just back unscathed from war – why in Heaven's name would God save him from violent death only for him to die of flu? None of it made any sense. The boys have gotten it all wrong again. They're always leaving it for me to straighten out their mistakes.*

Stopping outside the house, Harry turned to George. 'How am I going to tell your mother?'

* * *

The funeral was at Evergreen Cemetery, where Harry had attended to bury Nicky thirty years before. Now he was burying his son, something a father should never have to do. Soon he would be back to bury Bessie.

Harry fell into a dark and desolate mood. He had lived a full life and had achieved more than most men, yet he wasn't happy and struggled to recall when last he had been. As his mind drifted, he could hear the voice of Bishop Curley preaching the sacred scriptures. He liked Curley and had often told him he had the build and looks of a good heavyweight and should have chosen the ring rather than the seminary. The bishop's words broke in. 'Our true home is in Heaven, and Jesus Christ, whose return we long for, will come from Heaven to save us.'

Our true home, thought Harry. *Yes, I'm ready to make that journey.*

London had been the hardest of times, but strangely enough, they were the happiest, filled with joy and the warmth of love. Agnes had guessed the truth from the beginning. The way she spoke of love and betrayal during their afternoons on the dunes at Mayport.

He heard Curley begin the Lord's prayer: 'Our Father, who art in Heaven... forgive us our trespasses as we forgive those who trespass against us...'

Harry had always struggled in the confessional, fabricating infractions simply to escape with a few Hail Marys. He wasn't wicked; he knew that. What was he blamed for? For cheating the cruel and greedy? They were the wicked ones, not him. For lying? No. Using words to shape an end for good didn't count as wrong. Was he to be punished for the injustices of the law? It was circumstance, not him, that had turned his good intentions sour. And he couldn't be condemned for lust, envy or laziness; he'd never fallen to any of these. Pride? Yes, maybe pride. He had foolishly allowed his judgement to be clouded by conceit.

Leaving without Eliza had been a mistake. But worse was not returning for her. And then the betrayal. 'Dear Lord, have mercy,' mouthed Harry silently. 'I didn't know... I swear I didn't know.'

Only now, at his son's graveside, did the meaning and truth of the bishop's words strike him. Betrayal, the sin of Judas, was the worst of all sins.

He was ashamed of what he'd done. Shame had gagged

him and been the midwife of all his lies and dissembling, turning all life's happiness to arid dust.

But there was still time to right the wrongs and atone, and there was still time for forgiveness. He would confess all to Rinehart, and he would acknowledge his wife in his will.

* * *

He couldn't remember leaving the cemetery and wondered how he had arrived at St Thomas's Hospital with its high, white ceilings and carbolic aromas. Nurse Ryan was as pretty as ever, and her voice just as lyrical. Doctor MacCormac would soon arrive with Michael to reminisce cheerfully about the old days when they were young and free of doubt.

'Father, can you hear me?'

What's George doing here? thought Harry.

'Father, it's George. Can you hear me?'

Harry replied in a barely audible voice, 'Why aren't you at the hotel?'

'You had a fall at the cemetery. You're in hospital. You're going to be all right.'

'Did Michael bring me?'

'Tom brought you in his car.'

'Is Eliza here?'

'I'm here, Father, your son, George. I'm taking you home to Mother.'

'Mother is at home?'

'Yes, she's waiting for you at the villa.'

'The villa?'

'Your villa here in Jacksonville, Father. Your home.'

'That's not my home. I want to go home, where I belong.'

AFTERWORD

Charles Clark Mason, Harry's second son, died of Spanish Flu on 14 January 1919, aged thirty-three years. Ten months later, on 5 November 1919, Harry, aged seventy-five years, died at Villa Alexandria from pulmonary oedema. His funeral was officiated by the Rev. Milton R. Worsham at the Riverside Parish of the Episcopal Church of the Good Shepherd. Harry and Charles are laid to rest at the family plot at Evergreen Cemetery, Jacksonville – St Mary's Section 1, Block 2, Plot 38.

* * *

After leaving London in 1881, Harry never again saw his first wife, Eliza Elizabeth Price. He bequeathed her two plots of land amounting to 10.9 acres on the Moncrief Shell Road and left $1,675 to be shared equally between his three daughters. To Bessie, he left Villa Alexandria, to his eldest son, George Henry Mason, the Hotel Mason and to his other children, Thomas and Lily, annual allowances.

* * *

Harry was elected to the Jacksonville city council on 15 June 1897, representing the eighth Ward at Ortega, Venetia and Avondale until his death. He was elected to the Florida House of Representatives for Duval County in 1903, serving until 1911, during which he sponsored several pieces of legislation.

***

Bessie Mason (née Bridget Nolan) was born in Ireland, coming to New York with her parents around 1864, aged eleven years. She died of cervical cancer on 25 October 1920, aged sixty-seven years. Bessie was a member of the Church of the Immaculate Conception on East Duval Street, where, after the Great Fire of 1901, she worked tirelessly to raise funds to assist its rebuilding. The church congregation attended her funeral with several hundred members of the Daughters of Isabella, led by Mrs O'Keefe, the grand regent, lining the cortege route. Bessie is laid to rest alongside Harry at Evergreen Cemetery.

***

Ten weeks after his mother's death, George H. Mason and wife Georgia suffered the tragic death of their son, George Henry Mason Jr, aged twelve years. He died from head injuries sustained while playing football at a local children's park. He is buried at the Mason family plot at Evergreen Cemetery, Jacksonville.

***

In June 1922, John Joseph Handley, Bessie's son by her first marriage, died aged forty-four years from alcoholism. He is buried at the Mason family plot at Evergreen Cemetery, Jacksonville.

* * *

On 16 March 1923, George Henry Mason was declared bankrupt. As well as assets inherited from his father, there were considerable debts and outstanding loans, with the Bureau of Internal Revenue claiming payment of $26,000 in death duties. In 1927, George successfully contested the Bureau's assessment, receiving a refund of over fifteen thousand dollars.

* * *

After Harry's death, Judge Henry B. Philips became president and chairman of Harry's South Jacksonville Bank, which had opened on 24 July 1912 on the north-west corner of Hendricks and St Johns Avenue (now Prudential Drive). In 1924, the bank was purchased by the Barnett Bank.

* * *

Villa Alexandria was sold in 1924 to a consortium of investors headed by the attorney, Clement D. Rinehart, who, in 1927, sold it to Telfair Stockton for housing development. Clement Rinehart later wrote that he and his associates lost a quarter of a million dollars on the deal.

***

Hotel Mason was taken into administration in 1924 and sold in 1929 to Robert Kloeppel, who renamed it the Mayflower. It was demolished by controlled explosive charges at 1.15pm on Sunday, 15 January 1978. It is now the site of EverBank Centre on the north-west corner of Bay and Julia Street. The Everett Hotel was demolished in 1959.

***

In 1926, Barron Collier, after whom Florida's Collier County is named, employed George H. Mason as Chief Executive of the Collier Florida Coast Hotel chain, later making him Executive Manager of his Collier Tampa Terrace Hotel at 411 N Florida Street and Lafayette Street, Tampa. Ten years later, George bought significant stock in the Collier Florida Coast Hotel chain, becoming its vice president. George, his wife Georgia and mother-in-law, Lillian Dix Nelson Atwater, lived at the Tampa Terrace Hotel until their respective deaths: Georgia in 1939, aged fifty-six; George in 1947, aged sixty-three and Lillian Atwater in 1951, aged eighty-one. The Tampa Terrace Hotel was demolished in 1964. Both George and his wife Georgia are buried at the Mason family plot, Evergreen Cemetery, Jacksonville.

***

Lillian Dix Atwater's second husband, Capt. Howell B. Atwater, died aged seventy-nine years on 25 May 1921. He is buried at the Veteran's Cemetery, Los Angeles, California.

During the American Civil War, he served as a captain with the First Connecticut Cavalry. His wife, Lillian, is buried alongside him.

* * *

Harry's youngest son, Thomas James Mason, opened one of Jacksonville's first garages. He was declared bankrupt in 1924 and died aged fifty-five years at his Neptune Beach home in June 1944. He is buried at the Mason family plot at Evergreen Cemetery, Jacksonville.

* * *

Lillian (Lily) Beatrice Mason Sperry, Harry's youngest daughter, married Dr John A. Sperry in California in 1913, later moving to Germany and then Norway before settling in San Francisco with their five children. Lillian died aged forty-seven years in October 1938. She was cremated at Cypress Lawn Memorial Park, Colma, San Francisco, California.

* * *

Harry's first wife, Eliza Elizabeth Price (née Cox) died at 5 Angers Road, Totterdown, Bristol, England, aged eighty-four years on 5 January 1932. After enduring poverty throughout her life, she bequeathed £2,330 to her three daughters. Eliza is buried at Arnos Vale Cemetery, Bristol, plot Seddon QQ1075.

Harry's three British daughters, Bertha, Florence and Beatrice, mounted a legal challenge to Harry's will in the Florida courts, claiming the marriage to Bessie Handley was bigamous. Bertha and her brother-in-law, Edward King, travelled several times to Jacksonville between 1923 and 1926 to present their case, which was eventually filed as dormant when they failed to appear at the deliberation hearing in 1926. His daughter, Florence, later claimed that by the time their case was heard, the lawyers had taken whatever was left. The case was eventually closed by Judge Harold R. Clark on 3 March 1972.

* * *

On 20 December 1920, a year after Harry's death, his grandson, Edward (Teddy) Davis, changed his name to John Davis and emigrated to Jacksonville. He married Evelyn Schiffner, the daughter of a Russian émigré, in Bristol, on 10 November 1920. Teddy and Evelyn sailed aboard the SS *Olympic* to New York. Teddy and Evelyn finally settled in Miami, where he worked as a carpenter until his death in 1970, aged seventy-seven years. Both he and Evelyn gained American citizenship.

* * *

James Edwin Theodore Bowden (1857–1930) was a business partner with Harry Mason. Bowden married Laura L'Engle, the niece of Henry Augustus L'Engle, one of Jacksonville's most prominent citizens. Bowden was Mayor of LaVilla in 1887. He was also Mayor of Jacksonville in 1899 and again in 1915. He died aged seventy-three years in 1930. He is buried at Evergreen Cemetery – Section B.

* * *

Admiral James Kelsey Cogswell (1847–1908), an American hero of several military campaigns, including the Spanish-American war, died intestate at the age of sixty-one years. Judge Henry B. Philips appointed Harry Mason to administer Cogswell's estate. During these proceedings, Harry discovered the deeds of the Mitchell House, known as Villa Alexandria, and engineered a Special Master's auction whereby his son, George H. Mason, bought the property for thirty thousand dollars. Admiral James K. Cogswell was laid to rest alongside his sister, Bianca Mitchell (née Cogswell 1846–1882), at Forest Home Cemetery, Milwaukee, Wisconsin – section Lawn Place, Lot 59.

* * *

David Ferguson Mitchell (1876–1942) was the son of Senator John Lendrum Mitchell and grandson of Martha Reed Mitchell, who built Villa Alexandria as her summer retreat. David F. Mitchell lost ownership of the villa to Harry Mason and was shot and injured during a tussle to evict him. Mitchell challenged Harry Mason's ownership of Villa Alexandria in various courts between 1912 and 12 May 1937, when Judge George Couper Gibbs disallowed further litigation, saying "...the petitioners have had their day in court and to continue would not be justified". Villa Alexandria was redeveloped by Telfair Stockton from 1929 to become the present-day town of San Marco.

David F. Mitchell married Kathryn Sutton, stepdaughter of Joseph Parrott. Mitchell died in August 1942, aged sixty-five. His final years were spent in straitened circumstances, resident at the Burbridge Hotel Annex and dependent on the charity of friends. He is buried at Evergreen Cemetery.

* * *

Harry employed the architect Harold Frederick Saxelbye (1881–1964) to design Hotel Mason, which opened on 31 December 1913. Saxelbye was born at Sculcoates, Yorkshire East Riding, England, the younger brother of Frank Norman Saxelbye. Harold began his architectural training aged twelve, progressing to become a member of the Royal Institute of British Architects. He emigrated to New York in 1904 and moved to Jacksonville in 1912, where he gained his first commission from Harry to build the Hotel Mason. After WWI, Harold Saxelbye joined in partnership with William Mulford Marsh and was responsible for over twelve hundred design commissions in Jacksonville, including the Alfred I. DuPont Building on East Flagler Street. Examples of his Mediterranean Revival design can be found in San Marco, many built on the site of Villa Alexandria. More than twenty Marsh & Saxelbye buildings are recorded on the US National Register of Historic Places. Saxelbye lived at 1333 Avondale Avenue, where he died.

Harold Saxelbye's older brother, Frank Saxelbye, was a lieutenant in the East Yorkshire Regiment Fourth Battalion during WWI. He died of his wounds on 11 May 1915 and is buried at Boulogne Eastern Cemetery, Pas-de-Calais, France. Plot II.B.40.

***

Bethia Price, née Smocombe (1822–1901), was Harry's mother. Her first husband, Thomas Price (Harry's father) died from cancer of the nose and throat in 1845, aged thirty-two years. Bethia married again in 1852 to James Harris, a drayman. In 1870, James Harris became Baptist minister at Totterdown Baptist Church, Bristol, where he enjoyed comfortable accommodation at the adjoining tied Highgrove Lodge (now demolished). After Enoch Price (Harry Mason) left for Florida in 1881, Eliza and her three daughters lodged at a house opposite Highgrove Lodge.

***

Nicholas Arend (1847–1898) was proprietor of the European Saloon at 80–82 West Bay Street, Jacksonville, employing Harry as a bartender in May 1881. Nicholas Arend died in February 1898. He is buried at Evergreen Cemetery. One of his pall-bearers was Harry Mason.

***

Colonel James Jacquelin Daniel (1832–1888) served in the Confederate States Army. His wife, Emily L'Engle, was the sister of Henry Augustus L'Engle. Colonel J. J. Daniel was president of the Jacksonville Board of Trade and president of the Citizen's Auxiliary Association, established to fight the 1888 Jacksonville yellow fever epidemic. He died from yellow fever on 3 October 1888 aged fifty-six. The Daniel Memorial Home for Children is named in his memory. He is buried at Evergreen Cemetery, plot Daniel Park.

* * *

Henry Augustus L'Engle (1850–1888) was Florida's state treasurer and president of the State Bank of Florida. A founding member of the Citizen's Auxiliary Association, he died from yellow fever on 14 September 1888, aged thirty-eight years. He is buried at Evergreen Cemetery, plot Daniel Park.

* * *

James Mitchell Fairlie (1845–1888), originally from Scotland, was a pharmacist, drugstore owner, Secretary to the Jacksonville Board of Trade and Correspondence Secretary of the Citizen's Auxiliary Association. Both he and his wife, Margaret, died of yellow fever in October 1888.

* * *

Bion Hall Barnett (1857–1958) was the owner of the Barnett Bank, the most successful of Florida's banks. His wife, Carolina L'Engle, was Henry Augustus L'Engle's niece and was cousin to Laura L'Engle, the wife of James E. T. Bowden. Barnett is buried at Evergreen Cemetery.

Duncan Upshaw Fletcher (1859–1936) graduated in law from Vanderbilt University, Tennessee. He founded the Jacksonville Bar Association and was a Jacksonville city councillor in 1887, mayor of Jacksonville in 1893 and 1901. He founded the First Unitarian Church in 1907 and was US senator from 1909 to 1936, the longest serving of all Florida's senators. He is buried at Evergreen Cemetery.

* * *

Judge Henry Bethune Philips (1857–1940) was lawyer and president of Harry's Bank of South Jacksonville. He graduated in Law from Vanderbilt University, Tennessee and was appointed Judge at the Criminal Court of Duval County. US Highway 1, running through Florida, is named in his honour. He is buried at Oaklawn Cemetery, Jacksonville, Florida.

* * *

Clement Darling Rinehart (1864–1941) was Harry's lawyer, business associate and political colleague. In 1924 he bought, with a consortium of investors, Villa Alexandria. He sold it in 1927 to Telfair Stockton for residential development. Rinehart was president of the Florida Bar Association 1898–99. He died in 1941 aged seventy-seven years and is buried at Evergreen Cemetery.

* * *

Major Cromwell Gibbons (1869–1934), a Duval County court judge and chairman of the Duval Democratic Committee, was elected with Harry Mason to the Florida House of Representatives in 1903, where he was House chairman.

* * *

Napoleon Bonaparte Broward (1857–1910) was a tugboat captain, Duval County sheriff, Democratic member of the Florida House of Representatives in 1900 and the nineteenth governor of Florida in 1905. He is buried at Evergreen Cemetery.

* * *

Stanton Walker (1890–1940) was a Jacksonville lawyer. President of the Florida Bar Association 1929–1930. He unsuccessfully represented David F. Mitchell in a hearing against Harry Mason in the supreme court of Florida on 15 May 1918. Walker served overseas with the Field Artillery, Eightieth Division American Expeditionary Forces in WWI. He is buried at Oaklawn Cemetery, Jacksonville.

* * *

Judge Couper Gibbs (1879–1946) was a judge at the Fourth Circuit Court at Jacksonville and member of the Florida Bar Association. He disallowed any further litigation by David F. Mitchell in his attempt to regain ownership of Villa Alexandria. He is buried at Evergreen Cemetery.

Judge Rhydon Mays Call (1858–1927), Federal Judge appointed by President Woodrow Wilson. He sided with Harry Mason against Florida's Governor Mitchell by proscribing any interference in the staging of the world heavyweight fight between Corbett vs Mitchell. He is buried at St Nicholas Cemetery, Jacksonville.

* * *

Captain Charles Edwins Garner (1853–1915) was director of the Independent Day Steamboat Line, chairman of the Jacksonville Board of Trade and president of the Jacksonville Relief Association (JRA), established by James E. T. Bowden to rebuild Jacksonville after the Great Fire of 1901. He is buried at Evergreen Cemetery.

* * *

John Noble Cummings Stockton (1857–1922) was a business and political colleague of Harry Mason. He was president of the Jacksonville Board of Trade, a councillor on the Jacksonville city council and a member of the Citizen's Auxiliary Association. He was elected to the Florida State House of Representatives in 1896. He is buried at Evergreen Cemetery.

* * *

Telfair Stockton (1860–1932) was the younger brother to John N. C. Stockton, a real estate developer and mortgage banker, a founding member of the Stockton Whatley & Devin Company, the largest real estate and mortgage company in Florida. He developed the district of Avondale and built much of the town of San Marco on the estate of Villa Alexandria. He is buried at Evergreen Cemetery.

* * *

Joseph Robinson Parrott (1859–1913) was attorney to Henry M. Flagler and vice president of the Flagler East Coast Railroad and president of the Flagler East Coast Hotel Company. He married Helen Mercer Bright in 1886, adopting her daughter, Kathryn (Kitty) Sutton, who later married David Ferguson Mitchell.

* * *

James John "Gentleman Jim" Corbett (1866–1933) was a world heavyweight boxing champion, best known for defeating champion John L. Sullivan. Corbett's only defence of his world title was against the English champion Charles Mitchell in a contest promoted by Harry Mason on 25 January 1894 at Moncrief Park, Jacksonville. He is buried at Cypress Hills Cemetery, New York.

* * *

Charles Watson Mitchell (1861–1933) was an English world heavyweight contender. He lost to James Corbett by a knockout in the third round at Moncrief Park, Jacksonville, on 25 January 1894.

Bartholomew "Bat" William Barclay Masterson (1853–1921) was a Wild West gunfighter, buffalo hunter, US marshal and county sheriff, whose friends included Wyatt Earp and President Woodrow Wilson. He was a ringside second for the boxer Charles Mitchell during the Corbett vs Mitchell world heavyweight championship fight at Moncrief Park, Jacksonville, in 1894, later working as a sports journalist for *The New York Morning Telegraph*. He is buried at Woodlawn Cemetery, Bronx, NY. Primrose Section, Lot 185.

* * *

Fire Chief Thomas William Haney (1860–1939) was fire chief during the Jacksonville Great Fire of 1901. He was elected president of the International Association of Fire Engineers. He is buried at Evergreen Cemetery.

* * *

Police Chief William Dawson Vinzant (1852–1930) was appointed Jacksonville's police chief in 1898. He retired in 1913 and was succeeded by Police Chief F. C. Roach, who policed the 1916 disturbances during the Great Migration of African-American labour to the northern states during the tenure of James E.T. Bowden as mayor of Jacksonville.

* * *

Caroline E. Standing was born in Georgia in 1850. She was the nursing matron at St Luke's Hospital, Jacksonville, during the 1888 yellow fever epidemic. She and several of her volunteer nurses contracted yellow fever. Thankfully, all recovered.

* * *

Doctor Broaddus was a member of the American Volunteer Medical Corps, who volunteered to attend the sick during the 1888 Jacksonville yellow fever epidemic.

* * *

Daniel T. Garow (1855–1931) was the elected postmaster general for Jacksonville at the time of the Great Fire of 1901. He later became city auditor. He is buried at Evergreen Cemetery.

* * *

Colonel Charles P. Lovell commanded troops sent to Jacksonville to impose martial law after the Great Fire of 1901. He served in the First Florida Volunteer Infantry during the Spanish-American War and the Florida National Guard until volunteering for service in WWI. He retired as brigadier general in 1920 and was appointed adjutant general for Florida 1921–1923.

* * *

Bishop William John Kenny (1853–1913). In 1884, Kenny became pastor of the Church of the Immaculate Conception at Jacksonville, where he was known to Bessie and Harry Mason. While at Jacksonville, Bishop Kenny led relief efforts during the 1888 yellow fever epidemic and again in 1901 after the Great Fire. He was Bishop of St Augustine 1902–1913.

* * *

Bishop Michael Joseph Curley (1879–1947) presided at the funeral of Bessie Mason at the Church of the Immaculate Conception. He led effective campaigns against the rise in anti-Catholicism, the Ku Klux Klan and segregation. He was a staunch supporter of the American war effort during WWI.

* * *

Judge Joseph Edward Lee (1848–1920) was the first African-American lawyer in Florida, serving in the Florida House of Representatives in 1875 and the state senate in 1881. He was elected municipal judge in 1888. He was dean of Edward Waters College for Freed Slaves and worked alongside Harry Mason as a member of the Jacksonville Relief Association and chairman of the Coloured Relief Association. He is buried at Old Jacksonville City Cemetery.

* * *

Joseph Haywood Blodgett (1858–1934) moved to Jacksonville from Georgia in the 1890s as a railroad labourer. By the time of the 1901 Great Fire, he had established himself as a building contractor with investments in the North Jacksonville Street Railway, Town and Improvement Company, eventually becoming the first African-American millionaire in Jacksonville. He is buried at Evergreen Cemetery.

* * *

Sydney Johnston Catts (1863–1936) was a Baptist minister, insurance salesman, lawyer and politician from Alabama. In 1916, he ran for Democratic nominee for Florida governor. After a controversial recount, he lost to William V. Knott by twenty-three votes. Catts changed allegiances to the Prohibition Party and won the governorship in 1917 on a Prohibition, anti-Catholic, anti-German, white supremacist ticket. In 1920, he ran for the US senate but lost heavily to Duncan U. Fletcher.

* * *

John (Johnny) Wellborn Martin (1884–1958) defeated J.E.T. Bowden in the 1917 election to become mayor of Jacksonville. He served during the early days of Prohibition between 1917 to 1923. In 1924, John W. Martin beat Sidney Catts for the nomination to become Florida's twenty-fourth state governor (1925–1929). He is buried at Evergreen Cemetery.

Richard Dyson (1844–1892) was the owner of warehousing in Manchester and London. On 1 January 1881, he petitioned Registrar William Hazlitt, sitting at the London Court of Bankruptcy, Lincoln's Inns Fields, to have Enoch Thomas Price (Harry Mason) declared bankrupt. Dyson was a resident of Lordship Lane, Dulwich. He died at the age of forty-eight years of a brain haemorrhage.

* * *

William Hazlitt (1811–1893) was registrar presiding in the London Court of Bankruptcy, hearing the case of Enoch Thomas Price on 1 January 1881. Hazlitt is better known as a renowned English author. He died aged eighty-two years in 1893.

* * *

Alfred Edward Rosenthal (1841–unknown) was a solicitor at 32 Holborn Viaduct, London. He represented Enoch Price at the bankruptcy hearing on 1 January 1881. He was resident at 47 Addison Gardens, Hammersmith, London.

* * *

The numerous extended Agombar family, including Hannah, Esther and Rosina, lived at numbers 17, 18, and 19 Harold Street, London. For more than eight years, they were neighbours to Enoch and Eliza Price, who lived at 20 Harold Street (destroyed by enemy bombing during WWII).

* * *

The Herrick Family were from Tiffin and Perrysburg, Ohio. In 1887, they moved to 167 Pine Street, Jacksonville. Between 2 and 27 September 1888, all six family members died from yellow fever.

* * *

Henry Keeley, aged thirty-nine, and his son, William, aged eleven, travelled in 1881 on the same passage as Enoch Thomas Price, aboard the SS *Polynesian* from Liverpool to Quebec, Canada.

* * *

Mason Park was built by the North Jacksonville Street Railway, Town and Improvement Company. What remains of Mason Park today – later renamed Roosevelt Park and now called Simonds-Johnson Park – is near Mason Avenue and Moncrief Road, Jacksonville, Florida.

* * *

Pedro's Revenge, starring Harry Kimball and Laura Lyman, was released in 1913 by Majestic Motion Pictures. It was shot on location in Jacksonville with scenes filmed outside

Harry Mason's Bank of South Jacksonville, where Harry played a cameo role alongside Laura Lyman.

* * *

Harry's nephew, Alfred Stanley Warren (1890–1916), L/Corporal 3193 First/Sixth Battalion Gloucestershire Regiment, was killed in action on 21 July 1916 at the Battle of the Somme. He is remembered at the Great War Thiepval Memorial, France.

ACKNOWLEDGEMENTS

I owe a debt of thanks to those who have helped in the telling of this story, especially the many researchers, genealogists and librarians. Of special mention are Gillian King and John W. Cowart.

With the greatest pleasure, I express my gratitude to my wife, Natasha, for reading and rereading my many drafts and her patience, ideas and scrupulous attention to detail. And to my friend Norman for his unwavering support and encouragement.

This book is printed on paper from sustainable sources managed under the Forest Stewardship Council (FSC) scheme.

It has been printed in the UK to reduce transportation miles and their impact upon the environment.

For every new title that Matador publishes, we plant a tree to offset CO_2, partnering with the More Trees scheme.

For more about how Matador offsets its environmental impact, see www.troubador.co.uk/about/